Bl

Cambridge Libraries, Archives and Information Service

This book is due for return on or before the latest date shown above, but may be renewed up to three times unless it has been requested by another customer.

Books can be renewed -
in person at your local library

Online www.cambridgeshire.gov.uk/library

Cambridgeshire County Council

Please note that charges are made on overdue books.

Copyright © 2014 Rebecca Edney

Cover photo by Rebecca Edney

All rights reserved.

ISBN: 1505866014
ISBN-13: 978-1505866018

DEDICATION

For those who caught errors at the eleventh hour.

CONTENTS

Chapter One   1

Chapter Two   23

Chapter Three   55

Chapter Four   103

Chapter Five   129

Chapter Six   165

Chapter Seven   209

Chapter Eight   249

Chapter Nine   298

CHAPTER ONE

Weyrn ducked a blow aimed at his head. He brought his own sword up to parry, gasping, and slashed at the other elf, aiming to wound. He wouldn't kill if he could avoid it.

He wasn't sure the other elf had the same compunctions.

His sword skidded across armour and he swore, but at that moment the elf dropped with a grunt. Weyrn's wife, Alatani, was standing behind him, her sword raised. She'd hit him with the pommel.

"That the last?" asked Weyrn, crouching to check on that elf and another they'd already wounded.

"Last here," replied Alatani.

Both elves were alive, the conscious one eyeing Weyrn fearfully as he pressed a hand to his bloodied arm.

"Stay and guard these two," said Weyrn.

Alatani nodded. Weyrn dashed back up the path. Their fellow Swordmasters had been following them and he wanted to check if they'd been attacked as well. If not, he'd warn them.

Before he could see them, he heard the crash of blade on blade. He swore, reaching for his own sword again.

Derdhel and Maelli were locked in combat with four other elves. Derdhel was easy to see, towering above three opponents. Maelli was stumbling back, pressing a hand to his forehead. Blood ran from under his fingers.

Weyrn ducked in front of him, parrying a blow.

"Into the woods if you can't fight," he snapped.

At the same moment, the other elf yelled, "Here's another!"

Weyrn punched him, off-handed. He stumbled to his knees and another shove sent him sprawling. He didn't rise.

Weyrn glanced at Maelli. His friend was standing his ground, but still mopping blood out of his eyes.

"A handkerchief!" Maelli said, looking up.

There wasn't time for Weyrn to respond; one elf had stepped away from Derdhel and, at a shout from one of those remaining, chose that moment to attack.

Weyrn dodged a wide blow and grabbed the elf's arm. For a moment they were face to face. The other elf barely looked more than a boy and his eyes were wide, fixed on Weyrn's. Weyrn pulled him over and told him to stay down.

The remaining two had drawn back a little, looking unsure. Weyrn took the moment's respite to toss Maelli his handkerchief.

"We're just looking for some friends of ours who came through here," he said. "We don't mean you any harm. Drop your weapons and back off."

The other two elves were shooting one another worried looks. On the ground, the young one whimpered. The one Weyrn had punched stirred and moaned, raising a hand to his head.

Then one of the standing elves shook his head. "We can't," he said, addressing his friend. It answered Weyrn, though, and he raised his sword again just as the elf who'd spoken darted at him.

Their blades locked hilt-to-hilt. The other elf's sword was shorter and Weyrn would have to get well clear before being able to use his own. Enough space that the elf would stab him.

A flash out of the corner of his eye was Derdhel's knife, deflecting a blow from the other elf. Weyrn grabbed his opponent's wrist and shoved him, but his opponent had planted his feet and didn't move.

Suddenly Maelli dodged round Weyrn and slammed his shoulder into the elf's midsection. He doubled over, gasping, the sword dropping from his fingers, and Maelli put his own sword to his neck.

"I have him," he panted. Weyrn noticed that he'd tied the handkerchief around his brow as a bandage.

He turned to help Derdhel, but at that moment the taller elf threw his opponent over his hip and dropped on one knee beside him, a knife to his throat. "All right," he said, shaking a stray strand of silvery hair out of his eyes.

Weyrn sighed, relaxing for a moment. "Is there any sign of Neithan and Seri?" he asked.

Maelli shook his head. "Nothing. No tracks and they haven't said anything about them."

Weyrn looked around at the four captives, his thoughts also going to the two with Alatani. "Bind their hands," he told Maelli, glancing at the youngest elf as he went to take over guarding Maelli's opponent. The lad was still lying flat, shaking.

As Maelli tied his opponent's hands with his belt, the elf's eyes were locked on Weyrn's face. His breath came quick through his teeth.

"Swordmaster," he said suddenly.

Weyrn blinked, but nodded. "We all are."

"You're supposed to protect us."

Weyrn frowned. "You attacked us. We were defending ourselves."

The elf scowled, but didn't say anything else as Maelli fastened the buckle on the belt.

"Help Derdhel do the same, then join Alatani," said Weyrn. "She's further along the path. Derdhel, bind the third one once you're done there." Meanwhile, he went over to the young elf, who looked torn between trying to flee and remaining frozen.

"D-don't hurt me?" he whispered.

"I'm not going to hurt you." Weyrn crouched beside him. "Have you seen anything of two other elves passing down this road? They're also Swordmasters and have the same badge." He pointed to his sleeve and the patch sewn onto it: a grey beech leaf on a brown diamond.

"Don't tell him anything, Esren!" shouted a voice from behind Weyrn. He heard scuffling and swearing, but didn't look round, sure that Maelli and Derdhel had things under control.

"Have you seen them, Esren?" he asked again.

Esren licked his lips, looking everywhere but at Weyrn. Weyrn kept looking at his face, even as he noticed Maelli hurry past.

"Esren?" he prompted.

"There... there were two elves..." Esren looked past Weyrn at the rest of his group. "They got too close. We didn't realise..." He licked his lips again. After a moment, he tentatively added, "I'm sorry."

"Where are they?" asked Weyrn, hiding his worry as best he could.

Esren opened his mouth, but closed it again as there was a muffled, angry noise from behind Weyrn. This time he did glance round and he saw that the elf Derdhel was standing over was gagged. He nodded and turned back to Esren.

Esren looked torn, still looking past Weyrn.

"We don't have any quarrel with you," said Weyrn. "You're Mixed-blood elves, so, as your friend said, it's our duty to help and protect you."

Esren bit his lip. "But..."

Weyrn waited for a moment to see if he would continue. When the silence had stretched a while, he said, "Have you hurt them?"

"No, of course not. They... they're Swordmasters."

Weyrn nodded, filing away the question of why they had spared two Swordmasters and attacked four. "Where are they?" He asked again.

Esren sighed. "They're... they're back at our camp."

"Will you take me there?"

"But..." Esren looked up, firming his shoulders for a moment. "What happens then? You won't need me any more…"

"If we were only interested in information, we needn't have kept the rest of your party alive," said Derdhel. Weyrn looked round as the other Swordmaster continued. "Your friend here, for example. He's not inclined to tell us anything, so he's no use on that front and if I'd killed him instead of gagging him he couldn't have bitten my fingers." He held up the injured hand, raising an eyebrow at Esren.

Esren gulped and looked pleadingly at Weyrn, who smiled at him.

"We don't mean any of you any harm. Show me where my friends are and you can go."

Esren sighed and nodded. "All right, I'll take you there."

"Is there anyone else back at the camp?" Derdhel asked.

Esren shook his head. "I was, but… when I heard the fight I came running."

"All right," said Weyrn. "Get up, let's go." He glanced at Derdhel. "Don't do anything until we come back. Then you can all be assured that the four of us are safe and sound."

Derdhel nodded.

Weyrn beckoned again to Esren and started into the forest, the young elf tagging awkwardly alongside him. He sighed a little in relief as the cool shade washed over him, a pleasant feeling after the hot summer sun, but then shook his head slightly, refocusing.

They walked in silence until they were a little way away from the rest of the group, then Weyrn asked, "So what's really going on, Esren?"

Esren startled a little and looked at him in surprise. "What?"

"Why did you attack us?"

"We… you got too close to our settlement."

Weyrn sighed. "Why did you imprison the other two, but try to kill us?"

"We… I don't know. I just came running when I heard the battle. We realised who they were when we ambushed them and so didn't kill them because they're Swordmasters, but I don't know what was different."

Weyrn nodded. "So… had they been any other travellers, you would have killed them."

Esren hesitated and that answered Weyrn's question well enough.

"That isn't acceptable," he said coldly.

Esren flinched back a little.

"I'm serious, Esren, I will not tolerate your people just springing on travellers out of the bushes and killing them."

"But -"

"But nothing, and when we get back I'll say as much to your leader."

Esren looked stricken.

"Where are your borders, anyway?" asked Weyrn. "If you have definite borders and can make it clear to travellers where you are, they're less likely to bother you and I'll understand if you drive off those who do."

"I..." Esren fell silent, looking away.

"You don't know?" asked Weyrn, aghast.

Esren kept his eyes on the ground, his shoulders hunched.

"This is ridiculous." Weyrn shook his head, but reminded himself to be fair; Esren was only young and looked like the most junior member of the group. It made sense that he wouldn't be privy to everything. Still, something as simple as the position of the borders he was supposed to be guarding...

"May I ask a question?" asked Esren, his voice very small.

"Of course."

"Why do you support the Irnianam?"

Weyrn's head snapped round as he turned to stare at Esren. "What?"

"The Irnianam..."

"We don't."

"But... you let them come into the valley - "

"Because they were refugees and needed a place to live."

"But now they rule over you and you're supposed to be our leaders, so why do you support them? Especially after what they did to Mixed-bloods in Tishlondi?" Esren's voice rose in pitch and volume for a moment as he spoke, but then he fell silent again, biting his lip.

Weyrn sighed. It wasn't the first time he'd heard that accusation, but it still startled him every time. "It's complicated, but they don't rule over us; we're equals. And my predecessors took steps to make sure they could never abuse the Mixed-bloods of Duamelti the way they did the Piskam in Tishlondi."

"But..." Esren caught himself and looked away, hunching his shoulders.

Weyrn frowned, but looked ahead again as he saw sunlight between the trees up ahead. It looked like they were coming to a clearing and he slowed his step slightly, his hand creeping towards the hilt of his sword. He wanted to trust that Esren was telling the truth and there was nobody else in this camp, but he couldn't.

However, as they stepped out of the trees, there was no sign of movement. Weyrn looked around at a small collection of low wooden huts gathered around a central fire pit and nodded to himself. It looked like it could house the number of elves they had seen and no more.

"Where are my friends?" he asked Esren.

"This way." Esren pointed to one of the huts: a slightly taller, windowless building that looked to Weyrn like a storehouse. Certainly, he couldn't see any sign of a smokehole in the roof, such as the others had.

Esren unbolted the door and led the way inside. As Weyrn had expected, it seemed to be a storeroom. There were baskets piled up between stacks of sacks and chopped logs and it looked like this little community of elves was actually fairly prosperous despite its small size, especially given that it wasn't quite harvest season yet. Weyrn frowned as he walked after Esren. Too prosperous, especially given that they had no farmland as far as he'd been able to see. Where had all this come from?

He was distracted from further questions, though, as he heard a familiar voice whispering from somewhere.

"- there's sure to be a nail. You couldn't build it without -"

Weyrn smiled. Neithan.

"No, I believe you," said another, "But I can't - hsst!" Seri had apparently heard them coming.

One of the corners of the storeroom was walled off, the door bolted from the outside. Weyrn stood back a little as Esren drew the bolt, but grinned as he saw the two elves sitting on the floor inside.

"Weyrn!" cried Neithan, his eyes lighting up. Beside him, Seri sighed a little and smiled.

Weyrn grinned back. He could see that their legs were bound at the ankles and he guessed from the way that their arms were twisted behind them that their wrists were tied. He glanced at Esren. "Untie them."

Esren nodded and darted in.

"Are either of you hurt?" asked Weyrn as Seri leaned forward to let Esren reach his arms.

"No," said Neithan, looking round from frowning at Esren. "Bruises, but no worse than that."

Weyrn smiled, nodding a little.

"Who are you?" Neithan asked Esren.

"This is Esren," said Weyrn. "He's a member of the group that captured you."

Neithan nodded and hitched his shoulders, rubbing at his now-free wrists.

"Can I go now?" asked Esren softly.

"Where are our weapons?" asked Seri.

"I'll go and get them." Esren scurried away.

"It looks like you two should have been able to get free for yourselves," said Weyrn, nodding at the loose ropes now lying on the floor.

Neithan grimaced. "With more time we could have managed," he said. "But we've not been in here long. They spent some time quarrelling over what to do with us - "

"They seemed to have enough respect for the Swordmasters that they didn't want to kill us," said Seri.

Neithan nodded. "Then there was an alarm raised and they bundled us in here."

At that moment Esren arrived back with two swords and a bow. He laid them on the floor and stepped away again, leaving the two Swordmasters to reclaim their own weapons."

"Right," said Weyrn, smiling again at his friends. "Let's get back."

"How did you find us?" asked Neithan as they walked.

Weyrn nodded at Esren. "The same group attacked us as well, but we overpowered them."

"I'm surprised at that," said Seri. Weyrn raised an eyebrow at him and he added, "Not that you defeated them; that they attacked you. As I say, they were horrified when they realised who we were."

Weyrn glanced at Esren, who hunched his shoulders. "We didn't know they were Swordmasters when we set on them," he repeated awkwardly.

"Did you realise before or after you slammed Seri into that tree?" asked Neithan, an edge in his tone.

Weyrn immediately looked at Seri, who raised his hands a little. "I'm fine, really. As Neithan said, it's just bruising."

Esren, meanwhile, was visibly squirming. Seri leaned round Weyrn to look at him. "I tried to explain we hadn't meant to threaten them," he said.

"I didn't do it," said Esren. "I don't know why…"

"I need to speak to your leader when we get back anyway," said Weyrn.

They walked in silence the rest of the way back to the road. Weyrn kept an eye on the two younger Swordmasters, noticing the slight spring in Neithan's step and the way Seri breathed deeply - apparently he was right about the injury not being serious - as he looked around at the trees. He knew relief when he saw it and wondered uncomfortably if those two had expected to be killed at any moment.

And, if these elves were as ruthless as they seemed, they might not be the only ones.

"Esren," he said as they saw the sunlight on the road ahead. "Are you likely to be in danger because you helped us?"

Esren licked his lips, his eyes on the floor. "I'll be all right," he said.

"We can help you."

"No." Esren sighed. "I'll be fine."

The other three Swordmasters had gathered the captured elves together and Derdhel was guarding them while Alatani bandaged Maelli's wound. Alatani and Maelli looked up as Weyrn stepped onto the road and Alatani sighed slightly in relief, grinning as she saw Neithan and Seri.

"All's well?" she asked.

"All's well," said Weyrn, smiling back. "But before we leave… Esren, which is your leader?"

Esren had been hanging back at the treeline, but at the question he pointed out the elf who had previously been fighting Derdhel. Weyrn nodded and went over to crouch beside him.

"Are you the leader?"

The elf shot him a look of deep dislike, but nodded. Weyrn quickly untied the rag that had been used to gag him, but before he could speak, the elf snarled, "You bastard. You're supposed to be helping us, but -"

Weyrn cut him off, teeth gritted. "When we're attacked, we defend ourselves. You've no business saying we shouldn't have fought you. Now what are you doing out here?"

"This is our home."

"Yours and how many others? I've seen the storehouse where you imprisoned my friends; there's more there than a group this size could lay up."

"None of your business. We're defending our home, that's all. Someone has to."

Weyrn sighed slightly, taking a moment to close his eyes and regain his patience. "Defending your home? There's no sign to passers-by that you even live here, until you attack them, and Esren didn't even seem clear on where the borders you're defending are. I can't let that go on, for anyone's sake."

"You can't just drive us out of here as well."

"I'm not driving anyone out of anywhere. You can live here - and wherever else I assume you have settlements - and nobody will stop you, but you can't go on attacking anyone who comes near an unclear border and killing them without warning."

The elf scowled, looking away.

"If you carry on like that, I will come back and I will force you to change your ways."

"Run back to your masters," muttered the elf. "Since they've evidently taught you how to deal with our people." With a sudden movement, he raised his head and spat in Weyrn's face. "Blood-traitor!"

That particular insult was too much. Weyrn's hand flew before he realised what he was doing.

"Weyrn!" cried Seri as the elf shook his head, spitting blood from a cut lip.

Weyrn remembered to lower his hand and take a breath. What he'd just done would have to wait. There was no time to sit and reflect on the fact that he'd just slapped a bound prisoner. So he took another breath and let it out again, then said slowly, "I already gathered from Esren that you think we serve the Valley-elves. We don't. We never have. That's all I have to say on the matter except to ask why it was that you took Neithan and Seri prisoner but tried to kill the rest of us."

The elf looked away. "We still have enough respect and love for what the Swordmasters should be that we didn't want to kill any of you," he said. "But we didn't have a choice. You'd have killed us for imprisoning them."

"Well, I think we can see that's false, for a start."

The elf's lip curled, but he didn't say anything.

"However, you can't carry on attacking innocent travellers. Leave them be unless they threaten you; give some indication of where your borders are; preferably both, but you can't carry on as you are and if I hear any more reports of incidents like this, I will remember you and your settlement. Is that clear?"

The elf nodded, though he still looked furious.

"Right." Weyrn stood up. "We'll be off. Esren, I think it's best if we leave you to untie your companions."

Esren nodded, hugging himself.

Weyrn hesitated, unwilling to leave him behind; he looked frightened and that suggested that he at least thought there was some danger. But he had refused help and they couldn't force him, so Weyrn sighed, shaking his head a little, and beckoned to the others.

As soon as they were out of earshot, Weyrn rubbed his eyes, swearing softly to himself. "I shouldn't have hit him," he muttered. "I know."

"Well, as long as you know," said Neithan dryly.

"He'll be all right," said Derdhel. "You didn't hit him hard."

That didn't make Weyrn feel all that much better and he shook his head again. "Damn it."

"It can't be changed now," said Derdhel.

"I know." Weyrn sighed heavily. "All right. I'll try not to worry about it... Neithan, all was well with that dispute you and Seri went to hear?"

Neithan nodded. "It was pretty straightforward in the end. Yours?"

"All sorted out." Despite his determination not to dwell on recent events, Weyrn's thoughts went back to Esren. He could tell that he wasn't the only one who wasn't entirely happy leaving the lad behind; Maelli was walking beside him with her head down, frowning.

"Does anyone else have a better suggestion for what we should have done with Esren?" Weyrn said at last, turning to look at them.

There was an awkward pause, and then Derdhel shrugged and said, "Kill them." Now the eyes were on him and he shrugged again. "I'm not suggesting it as a serious possibility, but you all know it would have solved problems."

"I don't think we need discuss that one," said Weyrn coldly. While Derdhel was right, murdering other elves was not something he even wanted to consider.

"I don't think it was safe leaving Esren behind," said Alatani.

"I was going to offer to shelter him, but he refused before I could even speak."

Neithan nodded. "We can't force him," he said quietly.

"He knows them better than we do," said Maelli.

"There's no love lost between us and them," said Seri, rubbing his ribs tenderly. "I'd believe that he'd rather be in danger from staying than accept help from us."

Weyrn raised an eyebrow at him. "Are you sure you're not hurt?"

Seri smiled a little. "It's all right," he said.

Neithan nodded. "He's right in saying that they clearly held a grudge, as well. You know I'm all for trying to give a new life to people in danger where they are, but I don't think you could ever talk one of those elves into accepting something from you. They'd not even accept a friendly word from Seri."

Weyrn sighed. "All right," he said. "You two would know best. I don't like it, but…"

"It doesn't sound like it could be helped," said Derdhel.

"Spirits help him," murmured Maelli after a moment's silence.

Weyrn nodded and started walking again. "Everyone keep a sharp eye," he said. "We're not home yet." Still, they stayed together, just watching the woods around them rather than sending out scouts.

As they walked, Alatani reached out to touch Weyrn's hand and he curled his fingers loosely around hers. They still didn't speak to one another, but he shot her a small smile and she smiled back and squeezed his hand.

After a while, Neithan chuckled softly, apparently at nothing.

"What's wrong with you?" asked Weyrn.

"Oh, nothing. I was trying to work out if there was any other way we could have got loose, other than looking for nails."

Seri shook his head a little. "Don't worry about it," he said. "You were right that there was surely a nail end in there somewhere."

Weyrn looked round from the conversation as Alatani's step faltered for a moment. As he turned, she raised a hand to rub her eyes, frowning.

"Are you all right?" he asked.

She nodded and let go of his hand to bring out her water bottle and drink. "Yes, just a moment's light-headedness."

"Well, that should help," he said, watching her drink again. "You'll let me know if it doesn't, won't you?"

She grinned. "What will you do, carry me? I'm as tall as you are." But then she leaned over and kissed him on the cheek. "I'll be fine."

There was a soft "Aww…" from Maelli and Weyrn playfully glowered at him.

"You've been quiet," he said after a moment.

Maelli sighed. "I'm still worried about Esren," he said. "I know why it has to be this way, but…" He shrugged. "Just give me a while to think."

If he'd noticed the kiss he evidently hadn't been that lost in thought, but Weyrn decided not to tease him. Instead, he reached out and gave his shoulder a squeeze. "If you want to talk about it, I'm willing," he said.

"Thanks," said Maelli simply, but didn't speak again. Weyrn nodded and let go of him, instead taking Alatani's hand once more.

***

They arrived home mid-afternoon the next day. Weyrn grinned as they stepped out of the trees onto the clear grassy area that surrounded the Guardhouse: a long single-storey building that had been the home of the Swordmasters for as long as Weyrn could remember. He glanced at the large window into the common room, but he couldn't see any sign of Celes, the most junior Swordmaster.

"Celes!" he called as he stepped through the front door.

There was a pattering of feet from the corridor down to the bedrooms and Celes arrived, rubbing his eyes.

"Oversleep?" Weyrn asked him with a small grin.

Celes smiled back. "A little. I wasn't asleep when you arrived, though."

"Did something happen while we were away?"

"There was a disturbance late last night on the other side of the valley and someone came to fetch me, but it turned out to be nothing."

The other Swordmasters had come in behind Weyrn. Alatani was perched on the arm of a couch. "Actually nothing or just blown out of proportion?" she asked.

"A quarrel blown out of proportion."

"It sounds like you had an easier time than we did," said Maelli, shooting a sidelong glance at Seri and Neithan.

"What happened?"

"We were set on by a group of Mixed-bloods with a grudge against the Irnianam," said Weyrn.

"And us by extension for letting them settle here," said Seri, looking at the floor. Weyrn patted his shoulder.

"Are you still sorry not to have come with us?" asked Maelli, his smile broadening into a grin.

"Leave him be," said Seri.

"Your turn will come," said Derdhel, leaning round Weyrn, his blue-grey eyes sparkling. Seri frowned at him and stepped round Celes to go down to his own room. "I'm going for a walk," he called over his shoulder, already shrugging off his pack. "It's been a while since I visited my family."

Weyrn nodded and looked round at the others again. "All of you can relax. It doesn't sound like there's anything we need to do immediately."

He shot a grin at Alatani and she smiled back, getting up from the couch again.

"I need to put my pack away, then would you care for a game of checkers, Celes?" asked Derdhel.

Celes nodded. "I'll get the board out."

Maelli sighed, sitting down. "Some of us do need to rest."

Celes glared half-heartedly. Weyrn shot Maelli and Derdhel a quelling look, but then followed Alatani down to their bedroom.

Alatani was sitting on the edge of the double bed that they had squeezed into the relatively-small room, pulling things out of her pack. When Weyrn went in, though, she looked up with a smile. "Put this in the cupboard?" she asked, holding out her tinderbox.

Weyrn winced as he heard a thump and a burst of laughter from the common room. Alatani smiled a little and went to their bedroom door to poke her head out and shout, "If one of you breaks something, I'm not clearing it up!"

Weyrn didn't hear the response, but Alatani returned looking satisfied.

"You put them in their place, did you?" he asked, smiling at her.

She nodded and smiled back, then leaned over to kiss his cheek. "I think we've a little time before we need to go and see what they're doing."

Weyrn put an arm around her waist. "We'll have to find some way to entertain ourselves, then," he said, unable to suppress his grin.

She giggled and kissed him again, moving with him as he sat down on the bed.

As he started to pull her down as well, though, she stepped back with a sigh. "Sorry, but... I've been thinking," she said reluctantly, "I'm going to go and talk to someone about those dizzy spells."

Weyrn stared, startled. It took a moment for him to think about what she'd just said, but then he asked, "Dizzy spells... plural?"

She grimaced, nodding. "A couple more this morning." Apparently noticing his expression, she shook her head. "I still don't think it's anything to worry about, but I should talk to someone and make sure."

He nodded. "All right," he said. "You should go down there now, in that case."

"That's what I was thinking." She grimaced again. "Sorry."

"Sorry?" He laughed. "No, if you think you need to talk to a healer, you should go and talk to a healer. Do you want me to walk with you?"

She smiled. "No, it's all right." The smile broadened into a grin. "You stay here." A wink. "Put some sheets on the bed, so it's ready."

He chuckled and they shared a lingering kiss before she left.

Having unpacked and made the bed, Weyrn also left and went out into the common room, which was in a state of only mild disarray. Maelli was lying comfortably on a couch, apparently asleep, though Weyrn could never be entirely sure with Maelli. Celes and Derdhel were playing chequers. Weyrn had been planning to go straight to the window, but those two caught his eye; both of them looked rather tousled and dirty.

"What on earth have you two been doing?" he asked, looking at them.

Derdhel smiled and Celes looked round.

"Playing check-wrestling," said Celes.

Weyrn sighed. He should have known. "Who's winning?"

"I'm winning on chequers," said Celes, "But Derdhel won the first wrestling match."

"First and only," put in Maelli from the couch.

"Where was Alatani going?" asked Derdhel, making a move that prompted Celes to swear.

Weyrn sighed. "She wasn't feeling well, so she went to talk to a healer."

"I assume she's not very ill," said Maelli softly, sitting up.

"She didn't look it," said Derdhel.

"Weyrn?"

Weyrn shook his head. "She didn't seem worried; we just agreed she should talk to someone."

Celes and Maelli both looked unsure, but Derdhel nodded. "I'm sure she'll be fine," he said, "and worrying before we know won't help her if not."

Weyrn sighed and picked up his flute from its shelf, but he wasn't in the mood to play anything; he just sat down on the window seat to watch Celes and Derdhel and await Alatani's return.

***

They stopped playing before she arrived, and Weyrn was grateful; he'd probably have had to pull them apart had they had one more wrestling match. He refused an offer of a game of ordinary chequers with Maelli, to the other elf's clear disappointment.

Fortunately, he didn't have to wait much longer before he glimpsed Alatani through the small panes of the window. He smiled and hurried out to meet her. As he approached, he thought she looked a little flustered, but on seeing him she grinned.

"What did they say?" he asked.

She smiled again, though he thought her smile looked a little worried. "It's nothing to worry about," she said. "I'll explain when we're somewhere a little more private."

After dinner, the couple went back to their room and sat down on the bed together. Alatani had seemed her normal self all evening, which was a comfort, but Weyrn was still curious and worried.

"So...?" he prompted at last, when she didn't say anything.

She grinned hesitantly. "I was trying to think of the best way to put it to minimise the shock, but... I'm pregnant."

Weyrn stared at her for a moment. "That's... wait, what?"

"I'm... pregnant," she said a little more slowly and clearly.

He blinked, looking her up and down, then reached out and put a hand on her belly, half wondering if he'd already be able to feel a tiny foot kicking.

"In there?" he said, "A baby?"

She burst out laughing. "That's what 'pregnant' usually means, Weyrn!"

"But…" He took a deep breath. "Sorry… it is a bit of a shock. Everything's all right, is it? I mean, that fight you were just in…"

"I asked about that. She said that I should avoid getting into any more combats and take it a bit easy, but I should still be able to travel and keep active until I start getting too big."

He nodded. "That's a relief." The words were still filtering through his mind. A baby… he was going to be a father… there was going to be a child in the Guardhouse… "What do you want to do about telling the others?"

"I was going to tell them straight away, but… you… don't seem as happy as I was hoping," she said softly, looking at her hands.

He sighed. "I'm sorry; I'm still getting my head around it. And I'm still worried in case something happens that hurts… him?"

"Him will do until we know."

"Right. I mean… you can take care of yourself."

"Damn right."

"But what if something happens to the baby? Do you want everyone…"

"They're our friends," she said, frowning. "I hope I can trust them and I'd want the support."

"Nonetheless, I do think we should wait a bit before telling them."

She sighed, looking down, her frown deepening. "I suppose," she said. "Has this ever happened? A Swordmaster being pregnant?"

"Well, you know better than any that there's not been a female Swordmaster in living memory." He smiled a little, squeezing her hand. "I don't know, to be honest. The safest thing to do is probably to take you off active duty."

She nodded. "That's what I thought. It makes the risks a little less."

He nodded. "Well, if you're satisfied with that, it's what I'll do. Still, give me a few days to work out if there's anything else. After all, this is something we probably should have planned a little better." He laughed nervously.

"All right. Only a few days, though."

"Thanks." He smiled. The idea was becoming more firmly rooted, and the excitement was starting to build. After a moment, he said softly, his voice a little high, "A baby!"

Alatani grinned and her voice shrilled as she replied, "I know!" and all but leaped into his arms.

***

A few days after their return, Weyrn and Neithan set off again. This time it was a much shorter journey: they were going on a patrol around the border, travelling down the other side of the valley from the Guardhouse. As they left, Weyrn turned back to kiss Alatani, who had accompanied them as far as the turning towards the main city. They lingered over the kiss long enough to make Neithan shift impatiently on his feet behind Weyrn and at that Alatani broke away, laughing.

"I'll see you when you get back," she said. Then she added, in his ear, "And then I'm telling them all, if you won't." She didn't give him a chance to reply, but started off down her road, calling, "Have fun!" over her shoulder.

"Don't do anything stupid!" he called after her.

"I won't if you don't," she said, half turning to smile at them. "Keep him out of trouble, Neithan!"

Neithan grinned. "I will."

Weyrn sighed on a laugh and fell into step beside Neithan.

The two walked in silence for some time, taking in the scenery as they went. They had been friends for years, and didn't need to talk to enjoy one another's company. Neithan seemed to be looking at everything he passed, smiling at occasional ideas as they crossed his mind. At last, Weyrn couldn't stand it any more.

"Whatever are you thinking about?" he asked. "You've been smirking and looking at the clouds for the last half mile."

"I have not," said Neithan in mock outrage. "But since you ask, I was wondering if it would be possible to scrape the stickiness off Silvren spider threads and use it as glue."

Weyrn rolled his eyes. "Silvren spider thread again?"

"Well, my last idea with it worked."

"Only after you'd convinced Taffilelti you were insane."

Neithan drew himself up to his full height, though he was still some inches shorter than Weyrn. "Look me in the eye and tell me it wasn't a good idea. It proved much stronger than rope, and half the threads weren't actually sticky, just as I thought."

"How did you work that out? I know you'd never gone close enough to touch one."

"Simple: the spiders would get stuck. I don't know why no-one else had ever thought of it."

"That's probably because everyone else is concerned with killing the spiders."

Neithan nodded. "I'm sure it could be done, though."

"Well, next time we're in Silvren, you can suggest trying it."

Neithan smiled a little. "I will."

Weyrn patted him on the shoulder and they walked on in silence.

Their journey took them across the valley and through several small settlements where they had friends. As a result, by the time they made it up into the hills it was almost evening. Weyrn was starting to worry again, Alatani's words ringing in his ears. He knew the other Swordmasters had to be told, he just wasn't sure how to go about it or when he should do it. He knew they should have planned the conception of a child, that given their positions they should have made sure that the other Swordmasters were prepared for the changes that would inevitably happen.

When they camped that night he found himself frequently distracted, and the trend continued the next day.

Of course he had to tell them, and why not? It would be wonderful to have a child: a little version of himself or Alatani running around the Guardhouse. But at the same time… it was so long since there had last been a family there. What if something happened to Alatani? What if something happened to him? He could take Alatani off active duty, and would do that within the next few weeks; if something came up, she'd be the one to stay at home until the child was weaned. But could he risk leaving the child to grow up without a father? As he had?

"Weyrn!" Neithan waved a hand in front of his face. "Stars, what's wrong with you?"

Weyrn startled out of his reverie. "Sorry," he said, running a hand through his hair. "Just thinking."

Neithan put his head on one side. "Want to share?"

Weyrn sighed. "I was thinking… about my father."

Neithan blinked. "What brought that on?" he asked softly.

"I don't really know."

"You never told me what happened to him."

Weyrn looked at him out of the corner of his eye. "You know about the Kinslaying of Wrath?"

"I have Mixed-blood friends in Duamelti. Of course I do." Neithan quirked a smile. "I suspect some of them are still waiting for the Valley-elves to provoke a similar rebellion here. Anyway, Thoreni sat me down and told me the whole thing when I was a trainee."

Weyrn grimaced. He suspected that was a job he should have done, as Neithan's mentor, but it was a painful subject.

"Well… my *full* name is Weyrn, son of Terathi."

Neithan's eyes widened. "Terathi? The princes' honour guard?"

"Who vanished *rather suspiciously* at around the time of their murder, yes," said Weyrn resentfully.

"Why did you never *tell* me?"

Weyrn looked sharply at him, and couldn't help the venom in his tone as he asked, "Does it matter?" He'd hoped that Neithan, at least, wouldn't judge him for his father's deeds and he turned his shoulder, quickening his pace.

Neithan grabbed Weyrn's shoulder and stopped him, then stepped forward to face him, folding his arms. "Weyrn, you picked me off the street back in Gildae and brought me here to become a Swordmaster when you could have handed me over to the Watch to have my hand cut off as a thief. Do you *think* it matters?"

Weyrn dropped his gaze. "I didn't think it would," he said. "I'm sorry."

Neithan nodded, relaxing. "I just want to know why you never told me. Did you think you couldn't trust me?"

Weyrn winced. "He's not exactly a well-loved elf. Mother went through Hell on the way here from Tishlondi after the Kinslaying because she was married to him, and for years afterwards. I don't like anyone to know. Many do, of course, or did, but...."

"It can't be as many as all that," said Neithan.

Weyrn blinked, looking at him in surprise.

Neithan shrugged a little. "Nobody's ever told me about it, after all."

Weyrn stared at him. He'd grown up with the constant presence of his father's identity and disgrace and had always assumed that if people didn't mention it to him it was only from good manners.

Neithan shrugged a little. "I don't think it's as bad as all that." He smiled slightly, then, after a moment, said, "I always thought you were born in Duamelti, though."

Weyrn shook his head. "On the road. My father vanished before then."

There was an awkward silence. Weyrn knew that Neithan's own father had abandoned him and his mother and brother; it was how he'd ended up thieving to make ends meet. "I'm sorry," he said. "I shouldn't have –"

"I asked," Neithan interrupted. "Thoughts like this don't just come out of nowhere."

Weyrn sighed. "I don't know," he said.

Neithan looked sceptical, but accepted that with a nod and they started walking again.

"That cloud looks like a ship," said Neithan suddenly, pointing.

Weyrn was glad of the distraction, and he smiled as he looked up. He spotted the cloud in question at once and pointed to another one. "That's a rabbit."

They were now travelling west, down the length of the valley towards its 'trunk': the gap in the hills through which the main river flowed. It was a fairly easy journey and, after that conversation, they were relaxed as they went; they both knew that meeting any actual danger was unlikely, and when they set up camp that night there was no talk of having to set a watch, especially as the only living creatures they had seen apart from themselves were birds and squirrels, apart from a few roe deer fleeing deeper into the valley.

Weyrn lit a fire while Neithan gathered wood, and they made small talk about the day and the people they'd met the day before as they ate their dinner.

"Campfire songs?" suggested Neithan with a grin after swallowing the last of his tea.

"No."

"Thought not." Neithan stretched. "I suppose you plan to start out early tomorrow?"

"Around sunrise, and you'd better be planning to do the same."

"Actually, I considered staying here for the day."

Weyrn ignored that and spread out his bedroll on one side of the campfire. Neithan did the same on the other side and then banked the fire as Weyrn made sure there was nothing around it that might burn.

"Is something wrong, Weyrn?" asked Neithan once they were in their bedrolls. "You still don't seem yourself."

Weyrn sighed. He was still worried about Alatani and the baby, but, since Neithan didn't know, he wasn't quite sure how to put it.

"Weyrn?" prompted Neithan.

Weyrn grimaced. "I'll be all right," he said. "I just have something on my mind."

Neithan shifted, probably rolling over. "Want to share?"

Weyrn sighed. "I'll work it out," he said at last.

Neithan didn't reply to that for a while, but then he said, "It's not like you to keep secrets from me. Not for no reason, anyway, and I still don't believe you started thinking about your father from nothing. Something must be wrong."

"I'll tell you in a while."

"Is it Alatani?"

Weyrn propped himself up on an elbow, facing Neithan. "I'll tell you when I've thought it through," he said firmly.

Neithan frowned. "All right," he said softly, and rolled over so his back was to Weyrn.

***

In the morning, Neithan's feelings were still visibly hurt and Weyrn was deeply regretting his snappishness the night before. They packed up their camp in awkward silence and walked for a while before Weyrn finally took the plunge.

"I'm sorry," he said. "I shouldn't have spoken that way."

Neithan glanced at him and sighed. "It's forgiven," he said, "But I wish you'd tell me what's wrong; something clearly is. As I said, it's not like you to act like this, especially towards me."

Weyrn shook his head a little. "It… is to do with Alatani. We're just not sure how to tell everyone."

Neithan studied him with a small frown. "Has it anything to do with her having to run off to see a healer right after we arrived back?" he asked gently.

Weyrn nodded.

"Everything is all right, isn't it? You'd have told us if there was something seriously wrong."

"Of course. And there's nothing wrong, but... it is a major thing."

They walked in silence a little while longer, Neithan alternating between looking at their surroundings and watching Weyrn, while Weyrn studiously looked ahead.

"Oh, hello!" Neithan suddenly exclaimed, spotting something on the road. Weyrn grinned to himself as his friend hurried on, dropping to his knees beside a small slide. There was a small heap of powdery limestone and a few flint cobbles scattered across the path. Neithan picked up the cobbles and turned them over in his hands as Weyrn looked up the hillside.

"Something's been climbing," he said thoughtfully.

"Nothing large, though." Neithan got up and tugged at a tuft of grass. It came away in his hand, releasing another small slide. "See? This whole thing is unstable. It could have been something as small as a rabbit."

Weyrn nodded. "Don't do that too much. We should organise a party to shore this up; it wouldn't do for it to come down and block this path."

Neithan nodded. "How urgent do you think it is?"

"Not too bad; this isn't used much, but enough. I believe some traders come in this way from the clans."

Neithan sighed. "And some of them would take it as a slight if the path was blocked."

Weyrn nodded. "Still, we don't need to rush back right now."

"Will we be coming back this way?" asked Neithan, weighing the flints in his hands.

"Probably; we should check on this. Why? Are those especially good?"

"Good enough that I'd like to keep them." Neithan laid the flints beside the path. "But not so good that I'd want to carry them. I didn't know there was a source up here."

"Nor did I." Weyrn started to walk again and Neithan hurried up beside him. Weyrn smiled momentarily as he saw that Neithan wasn't carrying any of the flints.

"I wonder what happened to Esren," said Neithan after several minutes.

Weyrn sighed and shook his head. "I don't know."

"Do you suppose we ought to try to find out?"

"I don't think he'd appreciate it; you said yourself they'd not accept anything from one of us."

"I know, but I wonder." Neithan hitched up his pack on his back. "Much as I sometimes wonder what would have become of me had you not brought me here." He shot a small smile at Weyrn.

Weyrn patted him on the shoulder. "I'd have missed a chance of a good friend."

***

They stopped for lunch on a small plateau with a fine view of the valley. A stream ran down one side in a narrow gulley and plunged over and around a harder rock, down a waterfall into a pool below their grassy picnic spot. Near the rock at the edge was the best place to get water without scooping up mud and Neithan looked down at the pool as he was filling the kettle. He stepped back quickly.

"Everything all right?" called Weyrn, who had been building a small campfire.

Neithan came back to sit beside him, putting the full kettle by the fire as he did so. "The edge overhangs, and even though it's not the same stone I don't want to chance it crumbling."

Weyrn grimaced a little. "How far would it be to fall?"

"Not too far, but the water looks rough, not to mention cold."

"It's not meltwater, it can't be too bad."

Neithan shrugged, taking a bite of trail rations. "It looks cold," he said. "And the stream water is none too warm."

"I'll fill the water bottles after lunch," offered Weyrn.

Neithan nodded. "Thanks."

"I didn't think you were scared of heights."

"I'm not; I'm scared of the cliff going out from under me."

They ate quickly, and Neithan put out the fire and replaced the turves they'd cut to make a fireplace while Weyrn went to refill their water bottles as he'd promised. He crouched down beside the stream, wondering if he was imagining the feeling of the ground shifting under him. He glanced over the edge as he was putting the stopper into the second bottle. Looking closely, he could see rocks below the surface and he jumped back. That would not be a safe thing to fall into.

Unfortunately, the sudden movement had been a poor idea.

"Weyrn!" screamed Neithan as the ground cracked by Weyrn's feet. Weyrn hurled himself forwards and grabbed handfuls of grass, sliding until he hung by the edge.

"Neithan! Get me up!" he yelled, scrabbling at the cliff face with his toes to find a foothold.

"Water'll break your fall," said Neithan breathlessly, though by the noise he was rummaging through one of their packs, presumably looking for a rope.

"There are rocks! Get me *up*!"

Their rope dropped into view and he let go of his handhold long enough to grab it. As soon as he put his weight on it, Neithan began to pull and Weyrn was able to scramble over the edge and back onto solid ground.

For a moment he stayed where he was, panting and waiting for his heart to slow down.

"Weyrn?" Neithan shook his shoulder. "Weyrn, what's wrong?"

He couldn't reply; he felt sick.

"Weyrn?"

"All right," he gasped.

Neithan kept his hand on his shoulder as he caught his breath, then asked again, "What's wrong? I've never seen you like this."

Weyrn sighed, closing his eyes. Now that the immediate fear had passed, he knew there'd been no need to panic as much as he had. He sat back on his heels and sighed, then looked round for Neithan again. The other elf offered him a water bottle and he drank, then said to himself, "She's right. This is ridiculous."

Neithan raised an eyebrow.

"The thing is... I've been worried because..." Weyrn sighed, looking for words. "The fact is, I panicked because I don't want to leave my child fatherless."

Neithan's eyes widened and he took a sharp breath. "Your child?"

Weyrn nodded.

"Alatani's pregnant?"

Weyrn nodded again.

"That's what all this is about? Why you're upset and distracted? Why you're suddenly thinking of your father?"

Weyrn sighed. "Sorry," he said, "We should have told you all, but..."

"You really should. How long?"

"We're not sure. She only found out a couple of days ago."

"When were you planning to tell us?"

"When you and I got back."

"Why *didn't* you tell us? It would have been great to all find out right away."

"I..." Weyrn sighed. "I don't know. I suppose I just wanted to think it over before telling everyone and I was worried something might happen and I know this is going to mean big changes..."

Neithan raised an eyebrow. "You're acting as though you've been poisoned. This is something to be *happy* about, you idiot! At least tell me you were more cheerful when she told you?"

Weyrn could feel the colour rising in his face. "I was worried about her!"

"I shouldn't be the sensible one around here where inventions are *not* involved." Neithan sat back on his heels and folded his arms. "We're turning round and going back to the Guardhouse."

Weyrn blinked, startled. "What?"

"You heard me." Neithan got up and held out a hand. "We're going back!" He suddenly grinned. "There needs to be some sort of celebration!"

Weyrn took the hand and got up. "We really should finish our trip..."

Neithan's grin faded. "Is there some reason you don't want to tell everyone?"

"I don't know how everyone'll react. It'll mean her being taken off active duty –"

"Which would happen regardless of when you tell everyone." Neithan put his hands on Weyrn's shoulders. "You're being ridiculous. I'm sure everyone'll be happy for you. Please think for a moment: do you think it will make a blind bit of difference if you delay telling us? Apart from hurting our feelings?"

Weyrn had to admit that he couldn't think of anything, and he sighed. "I'm sorry," he said. "I was just worried."

Neithan nodded. "Just trust me," he said, smiling sadly.

Weyrn hugged him. "I do."

CHAPTER TWO

When they arrived back at the Guardhouse, the others were surprised to see them back so soon. Neithan assured Celes and Derdhel, who had come out to greet them, that nothing was wrong, but refused to tell them what had happened; that was Weyrn's job. Weyrn, meanwhile, had gone to find Alatani.

"Are you sure it's nothing?" asked Derdhel pointedly, looking after Weyrn.

Neithan shook his head. "He'll tell us all in a little while."

It was several minutes before Weyrn and Alatani emerged from their room. Alatani was smiling in a funny way and Weyrn looked rather red in the face. Neithan leaned against the wall by the door, smiling a little as he wondered about the chances that Weyrn might be about to make a run for it. The other Swordmasters gathered around the couple, looking increasingly concerned.

"What's going on?" asked Maelli, breaking the awkward silence.

Alatani and Neithan both looked at Weyrn.

"I... have some news. It's good news and... I'm sorry I've not shared it before now. I'm also sorry if I've been snappy with anyone over the last few days. You see... the thing is..."

"We're having a baby," Alatani interrupted.

There was a moment's shocked silence. Neithan grinned. Then Maelli got up and gave Alatani a hug. Celes' and Derdhel's voices mingled in a confused gabble as they both offered their congratulations, rather briefly in Derdhel's case. Seri added a soft word once Derdhel had finished, but otherwise sat back, looking from Alatani to Weyrn with a distant expression.

Neithan shook his head a little at Weyrn's embarrassed expression as he went over to talk to Alatani and congratulate her properly himself. She looked thrilled at the attention, happily answering their questions and remarks with laughter in her tone.

"I told you," Neithan murmured to Weyrn, moving to stand beside him.

Weyrn smiled a little. "So she's already remarked," he said, nodding towards Alatani. He sighed. "I'm still worried, but you were both right. Getting myself worked up wasn't helping and was just making her unhappy." He smiled. "Not to mention the rest of you."

Neithan nodded a little. "We'll take care of you both," he promised.

"I know." Weyrn grinned.

Neithan gave him a small shove. "And I hope this baby has more sense than his father!"

"I'm sure he will," said Alatani, extricating herself from the crowd and going over to kiss Weyrn on the cheek. He smiled.

"So what does this mean, exactly?" asked Celes, perching on the arm of the couch. "I suppose you won't be coming out on any more trips with us, Alatani?"

She shook her head. "No. From now on, until the baby's old enough to be left with someone else, I'll always be the one left behind." She grinned at Celes. "So you finally get some excitement."

"And what about you, Weyrn?" asked Derdhel.

Neithan grimaced a little at the momentary pained expression that flashed across Weyrn's face. "If something happened to me, Alatani would be able to raise the child," he said, looking over at her as he spoke.

She got up and took his hand. "But hopefully that won't happen," she finished. She kissed him on the cheek. "He'll just have to be careful."

"Would it be better for you to go off duty as well?" asked Seri softly.

Weyrn shook his head. "I'm not depriving us of two," he said.

"I know this is something that'll be worrying you," said Seri. "Seriously, don't you think it would be best?" He glanced around. "You could take over for the time being, couldn't you, Neithan?"

Neithan shook his head. "I'm second, but he's Captain, and we all know it's not like we'd be escorting him. We can all be careful, him included."

Seri was still frowning and Neithan glanced over at Weyrn, who looked still more unhappy.

After a moment, though, Weyrn glanced at Alatani and stepped forward a little. "I understand you're concerned, but I have no intention of sending one of you into danger to protect myself. You have my word on that, and that promise stands for the rest of my time as Captain."

"We didn't..." Maelli's voice trailed off as Weyrn looked at him.

Weyrn smiled. "I understand," he said. "Really, I do. I might wonder in your place, so there's no need to feel guilty. It's true that... I'd rather cut off my own hand than see this child grow up fatherless..." – his voice trembled a little – "but I'm not going to buy that peace of mind with the blood of one of my friends. Alatani is going to leave active duty as of today, but I will not." He smiled. "And nor will I shirk that duty." He laid a hand on his sword hilt. "You have my word."

There was an uncomfortable silence. A couple of times one of the other Swordmasters began to say something, but then stopped. After a while, Neithan realised that he was going to have to break it, as the foremost among Weyrn's subordinates.

"I accept that," he said, stepping forward, "And I trust you." On impulse, though, he added, "But I tell you as your friend that if one of us must make a stand and spill his blood so that the other will live, I want that one to be me. If it comes to it, don't argue."

Weyrn smiled. "Thank you."

Seri sighed. "Weyrn, I'm honestly torn. I would rather not deprive the Swordmasters of another blade, but I think you shouldn't come out with us. While sworn word may strengthen quaking heart, a father's thoughts must always be for his child; I don't protest out of fear for myself, but we must think of all our people. I accept your word, but…" He sighed. "I must ask that you hand command to Neithan when such decisions must be made and that, Neithan, you give us your word that your commands will be impartial."

"The Spirits have given command to Weyrn," protested Maelli, an edge in his voice.

Seri didn't look away from Weyrn. "And they have given him companions to help him."

The joy had gone out of Alatani's face, Neithan noticed, as she stood a little way behind Weyrn, a hand on her belly as she listened to their discussion. He sighed, wishing they could get this over, but he knew that Seri had real concerns, and they had to be addressed.

"If Weyrn gives me command," he said slowly, "I will do everything in my power to remain impartial."

Weyrn nodded. "If possible, I will check my decisions with Neithan."

That seemed to satisfy Seri, for he smiled and got up to go over to Weyrn and offer his hand.

"Forgive me?"

Weyrn smiled and took his hand. "Of course." He looked round at them all. "And you, Celes?"

Celes looked unsure, but he nodded. "I'm happy for you to remain in command."

Weyrn turned to Alatani. "And you?"

She stepped forward and put a hand on his shoulder, almost pulling him towards her so they were eye to eye. "You have responsibilities other than those you owe me. Make me proud."

He sighed, but kissed her in response.

After that it was difficult for anyone to go back to their normal activities, but they did their best. Alatani took Derdhel and Celes out for some archery practice. Seri went with them, but parted from them at the door, saying that he was going for a walk instead. Maelli challenged Weyrn to a game of chequers.

"I'd love to play," said Weyrn with a grin, but as Maelli was setting up the board, Weyrn came over to where Neithan had settled down on the window seat.

"I had no idea it would end that way," Neithan said at once.

Weyrn laughed. "I don't blame you; you were still right, of course." He shook his head.

Neithan smiled. "It'll work out," he said, getting out his penknife and a piece of wood. "I think everyone just needs a bit of time." He looked up again and said seriously, "And that child is not going to be born fatherless. Not while I have blood in my body."

Weyrn nodded. "I appreciate the sentiment. Just… be careful."

Neithan sensed multiple meanings in the warning, but he grinned. "When am I not?"

Weyrn grinned back. "Would you like the list?"

"Later. Maelli's ready for you."

Weyrn squeezed Neithan's shoulder with a grin and went over to play with Maelli. Neithan watched them for a few minutes, then shook his head a little, chuckling at nothing in particular, and went back to carving his piece of wood into a rough wheel.

In the week after the announcement, Alatani's life hadn't changed much. The dizzy spells had gone, for which she was grateful, and there had been no other ill-effects. She knew things would change with time, though. After all, she could no longer go out with the others if they were called, no matter whether they needed her skills. She had to admit that she was worried about the possible results of that. Nonetheless, she knew they could cope; Derdhel was just as good a ranger as her and that was her main skill apart from the sword.

In any case, she wasn't sorry. Unless something truly terrible happened, she would never regret the existence of this baby. Still, while she wasn't too big, she intended to continue practicing and drilling so that she didn't have too far to go to catch up with the others.

As she went through her drills, moving the sword from guard to guard, she did notice that she was tiring more than usual and she paused to stretch, wondering what was wrong. After a moment, she laughed.

"What's funny?" asked a soft voice from behind her.

She looked round and smiled at Seri, who was sitting cross-legged on the grass a little way off.

"I am," she said, still smiling. "I was wondering why I was getting more tired more quickly than before."

He nodded, but didn't smile, looking like he was trying to think what to say.

"I know that's a big reason I'm off duty."

He nodded again.

After a moment, she sighed and went to sit next to him. "You obviously want to say something to me."

He sighed and frowned, but didn't say anything for a long moment. She waited, giving him time to gather his thoughts.

"I'm sorry that I had that discussion with Weyrn immediately," he said at length, "but I trust you understand why I did it."

Come to think of it, she should have been expecting something like that. She wasn't entirely sure how to respond. She'd been crushed that Seri had acted as he had right in front of her as soon as she'd announced her pregnancy. It was the closest she had come to feeling like she needed to apologise.

"What were you trying to achieve?" she asked.

He sighed, but didn't seem sure how to respond.

"Didn't you think you could trust Weyrn to do the right thing?"

"It isn't a question of trusting him."

She started to interrupt, but he continued speaking.

"Not trusting him would imply that I thought he'd deliberately send one of us into danger to save his own hide, and that's not what I think." He frowned. "But that doesn't mean I don't think he'd let it affect his judgement."

Alatani scowled. "Surely, if you trusted him, you'd trust him to watch himself?"

"Not without having it brought to his attention. And, in any case..." He suddenly looked sharply at her. "You both should have discussed it with the rest of us first. Normally I'd consider it none of my business when a couple decided to have a child, but given who you are –"

"I know," said Alatani, stung. "I know. And we... weren't trying to go behind your backs, I know that it's not just a decision for us..." She felt herself starting to blush and looked down, rubbing the back of her neck. "I, uh... we weren't really expecting him."

When she looked up again, Seri was frowning, but he didn't look inclined to argue. Alatani rubbed the back of her neck again, then hastily lowered her hand.

"Anyway," she said, still aware that her face was red with embarrassment, "We have a plan now."

"Yes," said Seri, "But that doesn't make it less irresponsible."

For a moment they glowered at one another, then mutually sighed and looked away. The silence stretched.

Seri spoke first. "I'm sorry. Someone needed to say something. It was never my intent to hurt him or you."

Alatani stared at the grass as she replied, "You made me wonder if you resented our baby."

He shook his head. "I don't." He glanced at her and smiled wanly. "I'm happy for you, truly I am. But… I worry for all of us."

She nodded. "Well… I'd be lying if I said I didn't mind, but I understand."

He nodded, smiling a little, and then hesitantly put his arm around her shoulders. She smiled as she leaned on him.

"Congratulations," he said, his voice low, but sincere.

"Thanks."

Winter rolled round without incident, but Neithan was surprised to wake up one morning and find that snow had fallen overnight. He was apparently the first one awake and he dressed and tiptoed out as quickly and quietly as he could.

The snow was about half a foot deep and he grinned. Perfect for sledging, and he had a snowshoe design he wanted to try. Elves didn't sink very deep in snow, but deep enough to be inconvenient, especially when carrying a pack. He went back to his room and fetched the prototypes, strapping them on in the main room. They were awkward to walk on at first, but he hoped he'd get used to them.

"Neithan?"

He turned to see Celes just entering the main room, rubbing the sleep from his eyes. "Hello, Celes. I'm just going to test my snowshoes."

"Oh." Celes yawned. "Well, good luck."

"Let the others know where I am, will you? And save me some breakfast."

"Of course. How long will you be gone?"

"No more than an hour."

Celes nodded and waved as Neithan turned to leave.

As he'd hoped, he quickly got into the swing of walking in the snowshoes and was able to admire the scenery. Nobody else had walked this path up towards the hills since the snow had fallen, and Neithan's snowshoes only left shallow marks and scuffs, so the fallen snow was almost undisturbed. He smiled, looking up at the trees. Some had snow drifted up against them, or caught in crevices in the bark. The clouds were low and coloured the off-greenish-white colour that promised another snowstorm. He thought he had several hours before that, though.

Without shadows it was hard to tell the time, so he had to guess and deliberately cut it short. He paused, folding his arms. The shoes seemed to work fairly well on the flat; he'd take them for a longer run later in the day, up to the hills. He looked down at them, grinning. He'd run back; that would be quicker and meant he could go a little further and try a small slope. Only a little, though; he was unsure about the time and how far he could run.

The hill wasn't steep, but it was slippery; once one of his feet went out from under him, sending him sprawling on hands and knees, and it took some time for him to get up again.

As he was dusting the snow off his clothes, he frowned, trying to work out what to do. Perhaps he could attach spikes to the soles. He'd try that this afternoon. If the soles were that slippery it might also make it harder to run, so he should head back at once.

"Hello!" called a voice and he turned to look back up the hill. There was an elf-woman hurrying towards him and he carefully started back up the hill to meet her, steadying her with one of his feet braced against a tree as she skidded down the last bit of slope. "Can you help me?" she asked. "I'm trying to reach the Swordmasters."

"You've found one," he said, pushing his cloak back to show his badge. "I'm just about to head back to the Guardhouse. Come with me."

"Thank you," she said. "My village needs help…"

He nodded. "You can tell us all the whole story when we arrive. How long have you been travelling?"

"Only a couple of days, but it wouldn't have taken much less time in good weather."

He nodded. "And what's your name?"

"Jaltan."

"Mine's Neithan the Crafty."

Jaltan nodded and fell into step awkwardly beside him. Even as they walked, Neithan couldn't help noticing that he was able to move faster than her, but he dismissed the idea that it was entirely due to the snowshoes; she was dragging her feet, her shoulders stooped with tiredness, and he slowed down. He considered offering to carry her pick-a-back, but not only was she about his own height and build, but he remembered slipping on the way up and decided it wasn't worth the risk.

When they arrived at the Guardhouse, everyone else was awake and sitting around the fire eating breakfast. Alatani was facing the door and she got up as they entered, looking startled.

"Hello, Neithan. And…"

"This is Jaltan," said Neithan, stepping aside a little.

Jaltan stepped forward. "I come on behalf of my village; the snow has hit us hard and we need help."

There was a slightly startled pause, and then Weyrn got up. "I'm Captain Weyrn," he said, beckoning. "Come and have some breakfast, and tell us what you need."

Jaltan eagerly accepted a bowl of porridge, eating several spoonfuls before she began to speak.

"Many of the buildings are new. We only recently moved there from our old home; our leader had a quarrel with the thane. There weren't many experienced builders with us and though we built well against rain and heat, it was no match for snow."

Neithan had also helped himself to some porridge and perched on the window seat to remove his snowshoes. As Jaltan spoke, he was already imagining how badly-built roofs could collapse under the weight of new-fallen snow.

"We need experienced hands to help us shore up what's left," Jaltan continued, "And shelter for those who have been made homeless."

"How long ago did this happen?" asked Weyrn.

"Two days. I set off the morning after the first snow fell and we realised what was happening."

"Could more damage have happened since then?" That was Alatani.

"How many need shelter?" asked Maelli.

"It has snowed again, so possibly. Most houses were still standing when I left, but we knew many would not last another snowfall. There were seven families left homeless when I left – enough that space could just about be found for them within the village – and if more houses have collapsed…" She trailed off.

"Any injured?" asked Derdhel.

"Not when I left. We were lucky."

"Is there anything else we need to know?" asked Weyrn.

Jaltan frowned, but shook her head. "Not that I can think of. I can guide you back."

Weyrn nodded and looked around. "Neithan," he said, "You're probably best suited to this job, at least to see what's needed."

Neithan grinned. "Will you have tools there, Jaltan?"

She nodded. "Hopefully enough."

"I'll do what I can, then."

Weyrn was still frowning. "Derdhel, you go with him," he said. "And you, Celes."

Celes' face lit up, while Derdhel simply nodded.

"When shall we leave?" asked Neithan, looking from Weyrn to Jaltan.

"When you've eaten and packed," said Weyrn, glancing at Jaltan. "Send word back when you've seen how much worse things are, and I'll see what I can do about getting you more help."

***

They arrived at Jaltan's village late the next day, and judging by her expression things were worse. It was a rather sad-looking collection of houses, several still standing with snow piled on their roofs. A few elves were working on digging out the entrance to a storehouse, which had been buried under a drift. Jaltan called out to them and they started over, looking glad to see her. She led the way down into the little hollow in which the village was built and the three Swordmasters followed, staying a little behind so she could introduce them.

The leader of the little group looked curiously at them for a moment, and then grinned. "Swordmasters?"

Jaltan nodded and turned a little to look at them. Neithan realised that introductions were down to him and gestured to each in turn as he said their names. "Neithan the Crafty, Derdhel the Stoic, and Celes the Gentle."

"I'm Byrick," said the elf. "I'm the leader of this village, and we're glad you could come."

"Jaltan mentioned you had problems with buildings collapsing," said Neithan. Byrick shot a rueful look at his surroundings and Neithan grinned awkwardly. "Why don't you show me the damage and we'll see what we can do."

"First, we should find you somewhere to sleep…" He didn't sound confident about that.

"We brought a tent. If there's somewhere sheltered for us to pitch it, that'll do."

Byrick looked relieved. "I'll show you a good spot; the snow hasn't drifted too much. Once you've pitched the tent, come and find me and I'll show you what happened."

He pointed out a relatively clear area behind one of the standing buildings and left, saying that he was going to carry on working on the storehouse. Jaltan smiled a farewell and also left, presumably to return to her own home.

"It doesn't look like they did a good job on those roofs," said Neithan, nodding at a nearby ruined house as he began unpacking his share of the tent. It looked to him like the roof had simply given way; he could see the splintered ends of beams.

"It's understandable… if they didn't… have anyone… who knew… how to build… well." Celes' words were broken by the force of his blows as he started hammering a peg into the hard ground.

"They should have done, if they were going to set up somewhere new," said Derdhel as he finished clearing away the thin layer of snow.

"Be fair," said Celes, looking up. "They only had the people who were prepared to follow Byrick and start a new settlement. If they had no builders, there was little they could do about it."

"Lend me a hand with this pole, will you, Derdhel?" said Neithan to stave off any further argument.

Once they had the tent pitched, they went in search of Byrick again and found him just finishing clearing the door of the storehouse.

"There," he said, leaning on his shovel and apparently unaware of their presence. One of the other elves opened the door with a slight sigh of relief and Neithan tilted his head to see what was inside. He smiled as the elf went in and returned with an armload of firewood.

"Why shut it away?" asked Celes.

Byrick turned and smiled. "To keep it dry. There are other things in there as well, but we needed the wood most immediately. That spot for your tent suits you?"

Neithan nodded. "We can stay there some time if we have to."

Byrick nodded absently, looking round. "I'm trying to think what to show you first. I don't really know enough about this to know what would be most helpful."

"How about one of the buildings that's still standing, and one that's collapsed? Preferably one where I can see some of the structure," suggested Neithan.

"I'll show you my house," said Byrick, starting to walk. "There are quite a few people in there, but it should be all right."

Indeed, the house hadn't been very large to start with and was apparently now home to three families of elves. Neithan spotted Jaltan leaning against a wall, comforting a grizzling small child.

"I'm not sure there's room for all of us in there," said Celes, drawing back a little.

"We'll look around and try to guess how much work is to be done," said Derdhel, glancing at Neithan for confirmation.

"All right. If I don't see you when we get back, I'll whistle."

They nodded and Neithan followed Byrick into the building.

The light was dim; it only came from a single fire and there was a lot of smoke in the air. Still, once Neithan's eyes had grown accustomed to the light he could see that the ceiling was built with planks laid across beams. There was clearly an attic; the roof above had been peaked, not flat.

"Are they all built this way?" he asked, glancing at Byrick.

Byrick nodded. "Or close enough."

"Close enough?"

"Everyone used different sizes of beam and plank, and different spacing, according to what he thought best and what was available."

Neithan nodded. "How's the outside roof built?"

"There's another like this at the far end" – Byrick patted a stout post by the entrance door – "and they go all the way up to the peak of the roof, then there's a beam running between them and planks leaned on that and nailed. We sealed the gaps with pine pitch."

That seemed sensible and Neithan nodded, following Byrick outside again.

Derdhel and Celes were poking around the remains of one of the ruined houses, and when they saw Neithan and Byrick Celes waved. At the same time, someone called Byrick's name from inside the house and he hesitated.

"You go and deal with that," said Neithan. "We'll wait for you by that house."

Byrick nodded and hurried back inside.

"Look at this," said Derdhel as Neithan came over. "See what's left of the roof? Would it have shed snow?"

Neithan frowned up at the bare roof beam that ran from one end of the house to the other. Judging by its height, the pitch of the roof must have been fairly shallow. "It doesn't look like it." He glanced back at Byrick's roof and then at those of some of the other standing houses. Every one was slightly different, and the steeper ones had, naturally, done a better job of shedding the snow. He sighed. It looked like they'd found at least part of the problem. "This will need to be rebuilt; they'll need new support beams at the ends for a higher roof. Derdhel, you're tallest; will you help me take a closer look at this part of the wall?"

Derdhel let Neithan climb on his back so he could see the connection between wall and roof more closely. It looked like the roof beams were embedded between stones; presumably that was why many of the ruined houses had also lost parts of their walls.

"The top of the wall will need rebuilding, at least," he said, climbing down.

"We're going to need something quicker than that to strengthen the ones still standing," said Celes.

"I know." Neithan frowned.

"And I saw what Jaltan meant about the remaining houses being crowded," Celes continued. "We're going to have to try to find somewhere in Duamelti for some of these people."

"We'll check with Byrick and see if he'll accept that," said Neithan. "Then I think the best thing is for you, Derdhel, to hurry home and see what can be done, then come back."

Derdhel nodded and Celes looked hurt for a moment.

Neithan frowned at him. "What?"

Celes looked away. "Nothing."

"You know perfectly well why I'm not sending you."

Celes sighed. "It still feels like it's just because I'm younger and less experienced and you want to keep an eye on me."

"If it makes you feel better, once this is over you can go and spend a couple of nights camping in the snow with no tent." Neithan smiled to take the sting out of the sarcasm.

Celes scowled at him, but before either he or Derdhel could respond Neithan saw Byrick coming over and went to meet him.

"What do you think?" the other elf asked at once. "I noticed you having a look at that roof." He sighed. "What's left of it."

Neithan shook his head a little. "We can do our best to help you set up shelters, but these houses are going to have to be rebuilt." He explained the problem with the roofs not shedding snow quickly enough, pointing out the difference in slope between the collapsed house and those still standing. "And it looks from the holes in the walls like the ceiling beams were too far apart, so when the roof fell…"

"The ceiling planks snapped." Byrick sighed. After a moment, he said slowly, "I don't want to have to ask you to find places for my people to stay, but I can't ask them to live like this much longer. Do you think it will get worse?"

"The slope of the roofs has helped on the buildings that are still standing, as I said," said Neithan. "We need to try to keep them clear, though. At least then you shouldn't have any more collapses. I'm planning to send Derdhel back, now that we have a better idea of what's happening."

Byrick nodded. "Thank you." Another sigh. "I know we need the help."

"If there are people you need to send away, we should be able to find shelter for them if you let us have the numbers and they can feed themselves," said Neithan.

"Yes, yes they can. If you could find somewhere for the families with young children…"

"We'll do our best," said Celes.

That got a small smile from Byrick and Neithan nodded. "In the meantime, we'll stay long enough to help you get back on your feet."

Another sigh, though Byrick looked more relieved than unhappy. "Thank you. It's already good to know what might have caused these roofs to collapse."

Neithan smiled. "Well, I can try to help with any other problems along those lines. And we'll make a start on rebuilding." Neithan paused a moment, then added, "Though unless there's a disaster I doubt we'll stay more than a few weeks."

Nonetheless, this time Byrick's smile was wholehearted. "That's already more than I'd have asked. Thank you."

Derdhel travelled fast on his own without any of the heavy gear that had weighed him down before – all he carried was a roll of blankets and some food. He knew he'd miss the tent come nightfall, but he could dig himself a snow cave before that and be comfortable enough, especially as he knew there was a warm hearth waiting for him when he arrived home. If he continued to make good time, he'd only need to spend one night camping.

He glanced at the sky as he went, judging the weather by the shape and colour of the clouds. They were low and the curious greenish colour that indicated snow. Seeing that, he broke into a jog, his studded winter boots lending him some grip on the snow.

He'd never minded winter. In his youth it had always been a lean season; he had grown up in a village not unlike the one he was helping now, so he appreciated the fear they felt as the snow fell and the worry that they wouldn't be able to feed themselves and their children until summer. Nonetheless, even as a child he had known that winter passed and spring would soon be here. The thought made him smile, even as he reminded himself that spring and summer would soon go the same way as winter, and snow would begin to fall again. Much could happen in a year.

His smile broadened as he thought of his parents, still living in that same little village. When he, Neithan and Celes had finished this mission, he'd go and visit; it had been a while. Come to think of it, he didn't think he'd been back since harvest time; the days had flown by and he'd barely noticed.

A gust of cold wind made him shiver and draw his cloak around himself a little closer. The cold would pass, but that knowledge could only help him accept it; it didn't make him more comfortable in this moment. As he went, he kept an eye out for likely places to spend the night. If it did start to snow, he'd stop; he'd rather find shelter as the first flakes were falling than in a heavy snowfall.

Nonetheless, he had a duty to get back as fast as possible, and that meant getting as far as he could before the snow even began. He could handle cold and discomfort if it came to it, and anywhere reasonably sheltered would do.

He hitched his shoulders, shivered, and quickened his pace. He'd soon be home.

He was lucky; it didn't snow before night began to fall. He hadn't gone as far as he'd have liked, but far enough to make it worth leaving the village immediately rather than waiting overnight. There were a few conifers with snow built up around their bases and he dug into one drift, hoping to find that it was hollow under the branches.

As he'd hoped, a small natural cave had formed, floored with fallen needles. He crawled in and was able to pull snow back into the hole by which he'd entered – bar a small air hole – and wrap himself in blankets to rest, carefully pulling his gloves back onto his numb hands. He frowned, flexing his fingers, but then shrugged and tucked his hands under his arms, though he kept wiggling the fingers a little. The feeling would soon return.

Even after some time for his body heat to fill it, his little cave wasn't exactly warm. Still, it would do. His hands had thawed and the prickly heat had passed, and he smiled as he slipped his gloves off again for long enough to get a handful of nuts from the bag he'd brought with him. The chill in the air nipped at the just-warmed flesh and he put his gloves on again quickly. Then, after a few mouthfuls of food and a murmured prayer for protection during the night, he pulled a fold of blanket over his head, curled up, and fell asleep.

***

He crossed the border of Duamelti as the sun was setting. He knew he probably should have stopped, but he remained confident that he could make it home, even though darkness had come early due to the low, thick clouds. The air was very clear, still bitter cold despite the fact that the wind had died, and he could see lights beginning to appear in the valley. From here the houses looked like toys that he could reach out and touch, but he shook his head and hastened on down the path. Soon he was surrounded by trees again.

From here, it was about an hour's walk in good weather and with good footing. It would take longer in the dark and snow, but he knew the road well and wasn't afraid. As the night got darker, though, he had to slow his steps. He could roughly pick out where the ground was, but there was no starlight and he didn't want to stumble; to die of cold with a broken leg so close to home would be a shameful end. The thought of how he would be rightfully ridiculed for such a thing made him laugh a little as he carefully placed his feet.

He felt a light touch on his face and paused a moment, taking off his glove so he could hold out his hand. A few more touches on his palm, soft as feathers, told him it was starting to snow again. He frowned, but put his glove back on and kept going.

As he continued to walk the snow got heavier, but he glimpsed a light between the trees and smiled, turning towards it; if he was right in his reckoning, he was nearly home. If not, he had overshot but here was somewhere where he could at least step into the light a while and ask to be set on the right road.

As he got closer, the light grew brighter and he recognised the twinkling panes of the large window in the Guardhouse common room. The door opened and light spilled out around a figure stepping through.

"Hello, Weyrn!" called Derdhel.

"Derdhel?" Weyrn sounded startled. "What the… are you all right?"

Derdhel was clear of the trees now, so he knew the ground was flat and clear until he reached the building. "I'm fine," he said, walking over.

"Go on in," said Weyrn. "I'm just getting some wood."

Derdhel nodded and went in. The other three were already looking at the door and Derdhel smiled as they looked him up and down, checking for anything wrong. He thought fleetingly that he was quite sure Alatani's belly was larger than when he'd left.

"I'm fine," he repeated, going to the fire and starting to take off his outer clothes. "Neithan sent me back with word now that we have a better idea of the situation."

Maelli took the cloak and gloves and went to hang them up. Derdhel held his hands towards the flames with a grateful sigh. Warmth after cold always felt good.

The door opened, letting in a gush of cold air, and Derdhel turned to greet Weyrn.

"How are the others?" the other elf asked as he came over. He put his load of wood down by the fireplace and went to sit by Alatani. "I assume it's nothing too urgent, or you'd have told me."

Derdhel nodded. "I came back to tell you what they need from us." He was distracted for a moment as Maelli returned with a plate of bread and cheese, which he accepted gladly. "They're currently living in a few of the houses still standing. If they follow Neithan's instructions, they should be all right…" He shot a glance at the window. If it continued to come down this fast, he could only hope. "Byrick – their leader – has asked if we could find somewhere for the families with young children over the winter."

"I asked around some people I know," said Seri. "I've had some offers of space for small numbers at a time, provided their hosts don't also have to find food for them."

"They can bring food. It may not be enough in one journey, but they will be able to support themselves."

"How many?" asked Weyrn.

"Six families: one is a mother with one child; the others have both parents and, usually, two children. One has three."

Weyrn looked over at Seri, who was frowning, his eyes closed. After a moment, he said, "I think I'll be able to find places for all of them. I'll speak to my friends again in the morning. And I have a couple of cousins I wasn't able to ask, but they live further up in the hills."

"What else?" Weyrn asked Derdhel, nodding to Seri in acknowledgement as he spoke. "Will you have to stay there any length of time?"

"As long as it takes to at least have finished enough repairs to stave off the weather."

"All right," sighed Weyrn. "Did Neithan send any other word?"

Derdhel shook his head. "I can tell you about the village in more detail, though, and what I saw."

Weyrn nodded. "But do you need to go and rest?"

Derdhel had warmed up and went to sit down. "Being off my feet is a relief," he said with a smile. "I can go longer without sleep, even if I leave tomorrow. Shall I?"

"You should get some rest" – Weyrn settled down himself, his arm around Alatani's waist as she leaned on him – "but tell us about this village before you go to bed."

The morning after they had arrived in the village, Neithan and Celes woke to find their tent half buried. Fortunately, they'd been fairly sheltered by the nearby building or Neithan suspected they would have been buried entirely. He couldn't help worrying as he looked around at the deep drifts that had formed around the houses, blocking several doors. It had even brought down a couple of small trees in the nearby forest. This was weather that could easily kill an unwary elf. He comforted himself with the fact that Derdhel was anything but unwary; he knew how to survive the cold.

Still, Neithan couldn't help a shiver as he turned to look back at the village and decide what they should do next.

It took about an hour to clear the snow from the doorways of the houses with the help of several young elves who had been able to clamber out of windows. Then the two Swordmasters and the youngsters finally sat down to some breakfast in Byrick's house. Being obviously quite young, Celes was soon asked to join a group of boys, and Neithan watched them with a grin as he sat with Byrick.

"Has it been falling in large loads like this?" he asked, keeping his voice down. The house was still full of people and he didn't want anyone to overhear any bad news.

"No, it's normally slow and steady."

"Ah, all right. That's what we've had in Duamelti as well." Neithan frowned, then smiled again as Celes and his new friends went outside to start on the work of clearing the roofs. He'd not reminded anyone that needed to be done, and he was pleased that Celes had remembered.

"If he can keep them busy, it'll be good," said Byrick.

Neithan smiled a little. "I'm sure he will." He glanced at Byrick. "It'll be a couple of days before Derdhel returns, depending on how he handled this new snow. It looks like Celes and his friends will be able to clear the roofs. How many of the boys who were helping clear the doors this morning would be sent to Duamelti if we're able to find places for them?"

"There were three younger than the rest. They will. The others will be able to stay."

"We should make it easier to clear the doors in case of another big snowfall."

"But how? We need to be able to get out to do that."

"If we can build screens to stop the snow drifting so deep against the doors, it'll help."

"Much as this house screens your tent?"

"Yes: a windbreak, basically. If there's time we might also do something similar for the smoke-hole in your roof."

Byrick nodded. "What will you use?"

"Pine branches, probably. I expect you've only a limited supply of wood?"

"Yes. I need to lead a hunting group, but we'll be able to gather more then."

Neithan nodded. "I can come with you; I'll be an extra pair of hands, if nothing else."

Byrick nodded. "Thanks. You can tell us what you need, as well."

After that, Neithan spent some time going round all the houses, deciding which ones were most in need of a windbreak and how large each would have to be. He remembered well how deep some of the drifts had been, and asked one elf if that was the prevailing wind direction.

The elf nodded. "It moves about, but it's usually over there somewhere."

"Has it moved much since the snow started?"

He shook his head. "Always roughly from the same direction, especially when it brings snow."

Neithan nodded, thanked him and went back to his work. It was snow that they really had to worry about; the wind could do what it liked otherwise. He made a mental note to advise Byrick that when the ruined houses were rebuilt the doors should not face in that direction.

He spotted Celes and his little group and smiled as he watched a chunk of snow slide from the roof of the house they were clearing. It almost landed on one unwary boy and Neithan laughed a little at Celes' reproof. He also noted that the children on the roof itself were girls and smiled a little. Presumably, they were lighter, and weight was another thing to bear in mind in case of another heavy fall; they wanted to put as little stress as possible on the roofs, after all.

By noon, the roofs were clear and the hunting party was ready to leave. Neithan had left Celes with instructions to see what tools were available and how much help they would have when they returned. Neithan hoped they could get the windbreaks up before night fell.

***

The trip passed without incident and they returned with a couple of deer and a load of fallen pine branches. Neithan grinned as he saw Celes and his helpers working on digging shallow trenches to hold the windbreaks. Seeing them, Celes came over.

"We're almost ready here," he said breathlessly. "I see you got some branches."

Neithan nodded. "Thanks – having those ready will make it much quicker." The other elves had now removed the deer and Neithan parted from them with a wave to drag the sledge over to the nearest house. "You're doing a good job with those children."

Celes grinned. "They wanted to help."

Neithan nodded. "Well, with them helping, we should be able to set these up before dark."

Neithan's optimism was ill-founded, however; even with help it took some time to get the first screen set up. The branches wouldn't stand up in the trench and it was difficult to pack dirt around them; it was frozen hard. Eventually he used snow instead, stamping it solid. It seemed to work and they piled more snow in a wall behind the branches to plug any gaps.

They had to hurry as the afternoon wore on; clouds were gathering and there would doubtless be more snow. Indeed, the first flakes were beginning to fall as they finished work.

"No more this evening," said Neithan, dusting off his hands. "Thanks for your help, younglings."

The children looked delighted with the praise. One, a boy older than the rest, stepped forward and raised a hand in salute.

"Permission to go home, sir?"

Neithan blinked, but saluted in response. "Gladly granted."

They hurried back to their houses, laughing as they went. Celes and Neithan headed back to their own tent.

"We'll finish those tomorrow," said Neithan, sitting down and rubbing his eyes.

Celes flopped onto his bedroll. "Stars, I'm tired."

"You did a great job today, though."

"Really?" Celes raised his head a little.

Neithan nodded and sighed as he listened to the snowflakes settling on the roof of the tent. "Are you ready to do it again tomorrow?"

Celes fiddled with the clasp of his cloak for a while, then said, "I suppose so." He glanced at Neithan with a grin. "At least we know how to make those screens now; that'll make things faster."

Neithan nodded. "Let's have something to eat and then go to bed. It'll be an early start tomorrow."

***

Derdhel arrived back midway through the morning two days later when Neithan was just finishing fixing a screen around Byrick's smoke hole. He hoped it would hold. If not, they'd have to use guy ropes.

"Hello, Derdhel," he said, climbing down the ladder. "How was your journey?"

Derdhel smiled a little. "Uneventful. I was only snowed into a shelter once."

Neithan blinked. "That's still quite an achievement, given that... how many nights did you spend out?"

"Two," admitted Derdhel.

Neithan nodded. "Well, it's good to see you safe," he said with a grin. "What news from home?"

"Seri asked around some of his friends and apparently he can find space for the six families I told them about."

Neithan sighed in relief. "That is good news. I'll talk to Byrick and let him know. How soon can they set off?"

"Tomorrow, if they're ready; he should have time to make the arrangements. They will need to bring food with them, though, and be able to support themselves."

Neithan nodded. "I'll see about sledges; I imagine they'd not be able to carry much."

Derdhel nodded. "What about shelter? I can sleep in hollows under trees and dug into snowbanks, but they can't."

Neithan frowned. "I don't believe they've anything to make tents," he said slowly. If they had, they'd probably be using them.

"We may be able to find or build shelters as we go – I was travelling fast and sheltering quickly, after all."

"Did you see any likely places?"

Derdhel shook his head. "I didn't look."

"All right." Neithan looked around the village. Eleven adults, twelve young children. At least with a Swordmaster to guide them there'd be as many adults as children, which would help with keeping them safe and warm.

"Would you send me back with them?"

"I was thinking of sending Celes, actually." Though Celes had been doing an excellent job marshalling the older children to help them, he himself wasn't as strong or enduring as Derdhel.

Derdhel nodded. "He won't be as good at finding shelter."

"He's better at that than you give him credit for, as long as it doesn't involve anything heavy..." Neithan looked around again. "To tell truth, that's why I'm sending him: I need your strength here."

Derdhel smiled a little. "Have you told him that?"

"I've told him that I intend him to be the one that takes them back."

Derdhel nodded, looking round. "When do you plan for them to leave?"

"That's up to them, but sooner is probably better, if Seri can organise matters quickly enough."

Derdhel nodded again. "What can I do in the meanwhile?" he asked.

"Go and rest a couple of hours, then come and find me. I need to finish this screen and then talk to Byrick."

"All right." Derdhel smiled a little. "I admit I could do with a rest. Our tent's still where it was?"

Neithan nodded and watched him go, then climbed back up to the roof.

***

Byrick sighed in relief, leaning against a wall outside his house, as Neithan told him that they could find space in Duamelti for all those he wanted to send away.

"You have no idea how glad I am to hear that," he said, rubbing his eyes. "I can't keep them here like this."

Neithan nodded. "We thought as much. Obviously, they'll need to bring supplies and I can help build sledges for that. Otherwise, how soon should we be ready?"

"Do you intend to go with them?"

"I plan to send Celes. Derdhel and I will stay here and help to build shelters."

"Thank you." Byrick rubbed his eyes again. "I'll speak to them, but I imagine they'll agree that the sooner they can be on their way the better."

"I've been wondering... How long have you been living out here?"

"Since spring." Byrick sighed. "We came from further east, away from the hills. There was less snow there, so we weren't prepared for this."

"Wasn't there anyone in your group who had been in this area during the winter? This side of the hills always gets a lot of snow."

Byrick shook his head. "And not many who were experienced in building, either."

"You couldn't persuade any to come?"

Byrick shot him a look. "What did Jaltan tell you on the way here?"

"You left your clan after a quarrel with your thane."

Byrick nodded. "Yes... that is what happened. It was some time building, but eventually I wouldn't bear it any more." He scowled. "We didn't need to be as warlike as he wanted. We had enough land to live on. We didn't need anything else."

Neithan raised an eyebrow. "So you left?"

Byrick nodded. "I should have sent for help sooner, but... I was proud of what we'd built and ashamed when it collapsed and..." He raised his head a little. "We may not be craftsmen, but we're not beggars, either."

Neithan shook his head with a small smile. "Nobody thinks it. Sometimes, everyone needs help."

The first day of Celes' journey with the villagers was a long one and he was grateful when they reached a clear hollow in the on the lee side of a hill where he thought they should be able to build a rough shelter for the night. He paused with a sigh. Alone, he probably could have covered a good distance more before night, but it would take time to build something and everyone needed to stop. Even the adults were tired.

"Is everything all right?" asked a woman who had stepped up beside him.

He smiled wanly at her. "I think this would be a good place to camp."

She sighed in relief and turned to pass this news on to the others as he looked around again. For so many, it would be best to build a single circular shelter with a fire in the middle, but it would take hours to do it properly; such shelters were best suited for long-standing camps, not simple overnight stops. In any case, it would be hard work for tired elves.

That having been said, they needed some kind of windbreak and way of reflecting heat from a fire back into the camp, and it would be best if they stuck together. Some variation on a circular shelter would be the only way.

He looked up, trying to judge what the weather would do that night. There were some clouds, but they were high and thin, suggesting that it would hold fine. At least if they needn't expect any more snow, that would make things easier. Decided, he set about organising the other elves to build the shelter and make it as comfortable as possible.

The adults helped him roughly pile snow around an area just big enough for them all to lie down around a small fire; that, combined with the slight dip in the ground, would serve as a windbreak. The older children, and a few of the younger ones, searched for firewood and brush for beds under the direction of the same woman: Elar. She seemed accustomed to camping in the wild and hurried this way and that, pointing out suitable places to look and good examples of firewood and bedding. Celes had to smile as he watched Elar's small son trying to boss around a girl twice his own size while she carried an armload of brush and patiently ignored him.

As he worked, Celes followed the example of several of the other elves by removing his cloak and tunic. A soft breeze had sprung up, but it did little to cool them and he knew that it would be a bad idea to work up a sweat and end up cold and damp. For a moment, as he shovelled the heavy snow, he wondered if it would have been a good idea to bring proper windbreaks, but he dismissed the thought; they were already carrying a lot of baggage.

At long last, though, they were done and Celes set about setting and lighting a fire. Some of the wood was just dry enough to catch and once it had started he could dry more. Around him, the other adults fussed over and fed their children, then tucked them into bundles of blankets.

"I want a story," one little boy said, his voice ringing high and shrill. A few other children joined in the chorus, despite their tired parents' attempts to hush them and tell them to go to sleep. Celes didn't want to usurp them, but he knew he probably had most energy left, so he turned to the nearest mother who was trying to persuade a fractious child to sleep.

"Shall I tell one?" he asked.

She looked up as her daughter said, "Please? A story I haven't heard before?"

The woman nodded with a sigh. "If you could, Swordmaster Celes."

All eyes went to Celes, who suddenly found his mind empty of all stories. He stalled for a moment by sitting down and making himself comfortable, but the only one he could think of was the origin of the Swordmasters. Surely they'd know at least some version of that story.

Still, it was worth telling and he took a deep breath, remembering how his parents had taught it to him.

"Legend has it that on a starry night many centuries ago, a group of hunters heard starsong out in the woods."

"What's starsong?" one of the children interrupted.

"It's when the stars sing," said another one firmly, then looked back at Celes. "Go on, Swordmaster."

Celes cleared his throat. "Well, he's right. It's a rare thing…" – he got back into the swing of the story – "it is said that the stars only sing when something truly extraordinary is about to happen. The hunters followed the song to a wooden hut among the trees, and as they drew close the song rose to a great climax and then fell away."

It seemed they hadn't heard the story; the children were listening closely now, and even the adults were paying attention.

"Inside the hut, they found a beautiful baby boy, wrapped in a rabbit-skin. He was all alone and there was no sign of his mother and father, though the hunters searched all around. The hut was not a house, for there was no sign that anyone lived there; there was only the cradle and the baby sleeping in it. So, at last, they decided that the baby must be a foundling."

"What's a foundling?" That was a different child, but the same one answered.

"It's a baby that hasn't got any parents."

"That's an orphan," said another one. "It's a baby whose parents didn't want it."

Celes winced as he saw Elar put an arm around her young son, who was listening to the conversation with wide, worried eyes. He didn't know where the boy's father was, but knew the answer had to be one of those options. He hastily said, "It just meant that he hadn't got any parents and they didn't know why."

"So there," said the second child. "Now let him tell the story."

"They took him to their home and raised him, naming him Bladedancer for his nimble movements and his bright eyes, keen as a knife." Celes smiled as he saw a few of the adults shift, recognition suddenly springing in their expressions. "Bladedancer grew swiftly and was well-loved in the settlement from which the hunters came. He was a beautiful child as he had been a beautiful infant, and he delighted in knowledge, in skill and in doing what he could to better the lives of those he met. He learned the customs of his adopted people, to follow his guardians' path as a hunter in the woods and to survive alone as well as to help others live no matter what dangers the wild might bring. He spoke clearly and well and could sway those listening to his words. He learned to heal wounds in the mind and body and to close rifts between the people around him."

A few of the children discussed that among themselves for a moment, but they were quickly hushed by the others and their parents.

"When at last he had grown to manhood, he had risen to lead his settlement. He was loved and respected, and elves came from miles around to meet him and seek his counsel. At length, he began to look for friends to help him."

"It doesn't sound like he needed friends," said one of the older boys.

"Everyone needs friends," his father said reprovingly.

Celes nodded. "He sought among the elves of his own settlement first, and then further afield, seeking other elves who would follow in his footsteps to lead and serve their people as he did. For years he searched, but at last he found a companion who was able to help him. That elf was named Aiona, but in honour of his mentor and leader, he took the title Bladedancer and left his home to follow his new captain."

"So he was called Bladedancer too? How did they know who people were talking to?" asked a small voice from the shadows.

"Don't be silly, it's like the Swordmasters." An older girl pointed to Celes. "He's Swordmaster Celes, not just Swordmaster."

"Exactly," said Celes. "So he called himself Aiona Bladedancer."

Several of them nodded.

It took a moment for Celes to find his place in the story, then he continued, "Over the years, Aiona also found a student, Etsu, and taught him the ways of the Bladedancers. When he was ready, Etsu also took the title Bladedancer and the three companions continued to walk the world from settlement to settlement, serving their people, healing hurts and settling disputes wherever they went, until at last they came to Duamelti."

A few more whispers and mutters, then they looked back at him.

"Bladedancer stood on the border of the valley and looked down into it, seeing the beauty of the forest, the fields and the thousand rivers, and he turned to his companions and told them that they would settle here."

"A t'ousand rivers?" asked Elar's son.

Celes smiled at him, glad that he seemed not to be upset by the allusions to what might have happened to his father. "A thousand rivers." He shifted – one of his feet was going to sleep – then he continued, "So it was that the Bladedancers settled in the valley of Duamelti. They continued to go to the settlements they had visited, and were so loved that many of those elves came to the valley and settled there, becoming one settlement under the rule of the Bladedancers." He sighed. "Such a thriving gathering of elves, living happily under the rule of their three lords, did not go unnoticed. There are dark forces in the world that will always seek to snuff out such prosperity and hope, and now their attention turned to Duamelti." He paused a moment and looked around. He had always found the next part of the story frightening as a child and he noticed that even the younger children were still listening avidly. He wasn't sure how to tone it down for them, though, so he took a deep breath and continued, "Darkness spread like a cloud towards Duamelti, blotting out the sun and the stars as it went. Living things in its path withered and died: plants, animals and elves alike. Those that escaped alive fled to Duamelti and fearfully told the Bladedancers of what they had seen and what had happened in their settlements."

This time it was the adults who reacted, sharing looks of pity for those refugees. At least these elves would have homes to return to.

"Bladedancer knew that the Darkness would soon reach Duamelti and the people he had brought there." Mindful of his audience, Celes hesitated a moment, but decided that the original words of the story would do. "Though his love for the elves outside the valley was great, these were his people and his primary care, and he thought also of the many refugees that had sought safety there; he could not find it in his heart to tell them that, once again, they must flee for their lives." Celes sighed. "He went forth alone to the place where he had first looked upon the valley and watched the dawn break, lighting the trees and the fields and the thousand rivers and gilding them all in gold. He knew that unless he took action, this might be the last dawn that ever graced his beautiful valley, and he asked the morning star for counsel."

"Can the stars talk?" one child asked, the same one as had asked about starsong.

"Maybe they can to Bladedancer," said another one. "Were his parents really the stars?" she asked Celes.

"You're about to find out." Celes realised with sudden worry that he didn't actually know if these elves followed the Spirits. Most Mixed-bloods did, especially outside Duamelti, but it wasn't a certainty. Still, it couldn't be helped now. "The Spirits came to him and whispered that the Darkness had a single great weakness that one alone might seek out, but in the process he himself would certainly die."

There was silence as they processed that. A couple of the younger children huddled closer to their parents.

"Bladedancer thought with sorrow of his friends and the home that he loved, but he knew what he must do and told the Spirits without so much as a tremble in his voice that he would give his life to protect his people."

"Why did he have to do it?" asked one of the older children.

"It was his duty."

"But... why?"

"He had to protect his people; that was his duty as their leader."

The little elf was frowning, but she nodded slowly.

"Then around him, for all that the stars - even the bright morning star - had vanished from the sky, the starsong that had sounded at his birth began to echo. The Sprits told him that he was their child, placed on the earth for just such a moment, and that, indeed, he alone could strike down the

Darkness."

"So they were his parents the whole time?"

"How were the stars singing if they weren't there any more?"

"Well, they were, he just couldn't see them."

"Where did they go?"

Celes cleared his throat, though he wasn't sure how to answer the questions about the stars. Still, at that point silence fell. " 'Then why, my fathers and mothers,' said Bladedancer, 'Why did you not tell me this when you told me that the Darkness could be defeated?'

" 'Of what worth would your sacrifice be then?' they replied. 'It would be no more sacrifice than if we struck you down in this moment. Though you alone can do this, you needed to have the courage to freely pay what it would cost.' "

Around the circle, there was silence. Even the adults who had clearly recognised Bladedancer's name was were listening raptly. Many of the children looked nervous, though many of the youngest ones were starting to look sleepy.

"Bladedancer accepted this and asked them what he must do.

" 'Turn away from the valley and look where all seems barren and cold.'

"Bladedancer looked away, towards the rocky cliff at his back and saw a single crystal, shining in the light of the dawn. He took it and felt its warmth spread through his blood. As he held it, his hand began to glow and the light spread as the warmth had done. He knew that this light could not be overcome."

"Where did it come from?" a little voice asked.

"The Spirits put it there," said Celes.

"Why didn't they just get rid of the Darkness themselves?" It was the same older child. She was frowning as she looked between Celes and the campfire. "Why did Bladedancer have to die? He seems nice…"

"But one of the things that makes him so nice was that he was prepared to die to protect people," Celes explained.

"But wouldn't it be better if he hadn't died?"

"Of course it would. But…" Celes sighed. "Sometimes people do have to die, especially when it comes to fighting to protect people." This was really too much for most of the children there, but he felt it was a question that had to be answered. "We can't always take the easy way, or the more pleasant way."

The girl was still frowning thoughtfully, but at that she nodded.

"What happened then?" asked one of the other children. "Did he go and fight the Darkness?"

Celes nodded, once again taking a moment to find his place. "He returned home long enough to say farewell to Aiona and Etsu and to appoint Aiona as leader in his place. Then he set forth alone."

"Why couldn't they go too?"

"They would have died as well," said Celes. "And it was his task."

"Now hush," that little boy's mother told him, hugging him close. "Let him finish the story."

Celes nodded. "As he crested the hills around Duamelti, he saw the Darkness for the first time, spreading like a canker as it rolled over the land like a black fog, leaving rottenness in its wake. Bladedancer cast one more look at his home and set off down the slope to meet the Darkness, taking the crystal in his hand."

"That must be about where we are!" said one of the children, looking around with sudden fear in her eyes. She huddled close to her mother as she looked at their surroundings, dark beyond the flickering light of the campfire.

"It can't still be here," her father said as her mother soothed her. "Swordmaster Celes is about to tell us what happened to it."

Celes nodded again, smiling at the girl. "Because, you remember, he has the crystal."

She nodded, looking slightly happier.

"Once more the warm light began to spread up his arm. It flowed through his body, growing hotter until his entire body shone and his clothes began to smoulder. He knew he was burning almost before the pain began, but he kept walking." – Celes winced as he heard one of the younger children whimper in sympathy – "His steps burned the grass as he went to meet the Darkness. His clothes flamed and the sword at his side melted, but at last he stepped into the Darkness and held the crystal aloft."

"That must have hurt," whispered one of the older boys, his eyes on the campfire as if he could see Bladedancer burning in its flames.

"For a moment as long as an age the light and dark warred around him, but no shadow can quench a true light and, finally, the Darkness was defeated. It roiled as a cloud before a storm, but advanced no further and, at last, it coiled in on itself and blew away in the wind like a puff of dust." Celes smiled as he heard a few sighs of relief. Apparently that girl had not been the only one worried by the fact that the battle might have taken place close to where they were now sitting. His smile faded, though, as he continued, "But Bladedancer did not live to see it. As the Spirits had warned him, he could not survive; the fire of the crystal had reduced him to ash where he stood."

Subdued silence fell, but Celes cleared his throat awkwardly and shifted again.

"That was all that Aiona and Etsu found when they sought out their beloved leader. With many tears, they gathered up the ashes and scattered them around the borders of Duamelti so that he could always guard the borders of the realm he had founded. Aiona took the title of Bladedancer

Captain and Etsu took a student of his own, and the line has remained unbroken down the centuries. There has always been at least one of their heirs in Duamelti, and there always will be as long as the sun rises and the stars shine overhead." He smiled. "And because Bladedancer will always be there to guard us, we will always be safe."

"The Bladedancers became the Swordmasters," one elf said to the sleepy-looking elfling in her arms. "So you know it's true."

Celes smiled at her, and around at all of them. "So, you see, we keep looking after you." He got up and stretched. "And now it's time to sleep."

This time, there were no more demands for stories. He hoped he hadn't caused any nightmares as he watched parents tucking their children into blankets and lying down beside them, holding them close for warmth and murmuring goodnights. Nobody seemed distressed, though, and he sighed, looking up at the stars for a moment. A clear night meant cold, but no more snow and he nodded to himself and went to bank the fire.

Once that chore was done, he looked around one more time to make sure everyone was settled, then rolled himself in his own blanket and closed his eyes with a sigh. Even if he had to keep some kind of watch and couldn't sleep, he could at least doze and he drifted off with a last, fleeting thought that hopefully the ending of the story had done something to make these children feel safe.

Alatani was starting to worry about the group Derdhel had promised to send back. She'd expected them the day before, and even though she knew they might easily have been delayed leaving and it was a long way to bring a large group of children, she couldn't help some worry. Fortunately, the weather had remained fine since he had left.

But as she sat on the window seat in the Guardhouse's common room, she could see that the clouds were lowering again; it was going to snow.

She sighed and shifted awkwardly. Though she knew she would get bigger before the baby was ready to be born, she already felt huge and ungainly.

Movement outside the window caught her eye and she smiled as she saw Seri crossing the open space in front of the Guardhouse. She got up to open the door and grinned as he knocked the snow off his boots before coming in.

"Still no sign of them?" he asked, going over to the fire.

"Not yet," she said. "Are you worried?"

"If they're not here this time tomorrow, I will be."

"Should we..." Alatani sighed. "Should someone go and look?"

"Not yet."

She nodded. "Well, I'm going for a walk. Want to join me?"

He smiled. "It's cold out there."

"Just bracing." She took her cloak from its peg. "I won't be gone long."

"If Weyrn comes back before you do, I'll let him know."

Alatani nodded and left, making her way up the path towards the hills. She'd keep her promise and not go far, but she wanted to get some exercise. She'd not been able to do much recently – drilling was difficult and she was worried about hurting herself and the baby – and she missed activity. Walking in the snow would be something, at least.

It was certainly effort and she cringed at the thought of how much condition she'd lost. More walking was in order; pregnant or not, no Swordmaster should lose her breath when climbing such a shallow slope. She paused and looked around with a sigh, wondering if she should turn back, though it was humiliating to be this unfit. Then she looked up the slope and saw a group of people just starting down.

She shaded her eyes with a hand – not that it was much help; the snow reflected what sunlight there was – and tried to make out who they were.

One of those in the lead waved a hand and shouted, "Hie! I'm Swordmaster Celes!"

"Celes!" she exclaimed, starting up the hill again. "Good to see you! We…" – she had to catch a breath – "were wondering when you'd arrive."

He hurried down to meet her. "Good to see you again," he said with a tired grin. "Should you be climbing up here?"

"I'm not an invalid. How was your journey?"

He grimaced and lowered his voice a little. "I don't *think* we lost any children."

She blinked. "Well… I'd hope not."

"Do you know where to take everyone?"

"Seri's at the Guardhouse. I can take over guiding everyone there if you want to run ahead."

"Thanks." By now, the rest of the group were catching up and Celes turned to them. "This is Swordmaster Alatani the She-Wolf. She'll guide you to the Guardhouse. I'm going to run ahead to let them know we're here."

As she looked at them, Alatani thought that the members of this group looked even more tired than Celes. "Nearly there," she said with a small smile. "I just walked from the Guardhouse in less than half an hour."

Several of the tired elves did perk up at that news, but they were mostly adults. The children who weren't riding on sleds or in their parents' arms did not look impressed at the idea of more walking, even over a short distance. One little girl had plunked down in the snow at Alatani's feet and was threatening tears.

Alatani sighed and picked her up, setting her back on her feet. "Come on," she said, and took her hand, turning to lead the way.

It seemed much further on the way back than it had on the way out, but they arrived at last. Seri was waiting with a welcoming smile.

"Is everyone all right?" he asked.

"Tired," said one elf with a small smile, "But glad to be here."

"I can understand that. It's not much further now. Celes has gone to speak to the families who will be hosting you. They're all fairly close, so he'll be back soon."

"My toes are froze," whined the girl walking with Alatani.

"If anyone needs to wait inside, they can, but…" Seri grimaced. "There isn't room in there for everyone."

A few children were taken inside, including the little girl, but soon Celes came back. There were a few other elves with him and the group began to break up as the newcomers went with their hosts. Alatani watched as one Duamelti elf went to speak to Seri, looking worried and apologetic, but she had to turn away to help partially unload a sled.

"I hope someone can help me with this," a woman said softly, looking at the large bundle she and Alatani had just taken off the sled.

"I expect so. If not, I'm sure we can find you another sled." Alatani looked back at Seri, who was running a hand worriedly through his hair. The elf he was talking to shrugged helplessly.

Most of the group had left now, and the woman with Alatani was beginning to look really worried.

"What's your name?" Alatani asked her.

"Elar." She fidgeted. "They did know I was coming, didn't they? Me and Lessai?"

"When Derdhel first came back he said there was a lone mother and child with the group."

"That would be me." Elar looked round as Seri called her name. When he caught sight of her, he came over.

"I'm sorry, Elar, but there's been a problem."

She went pale. "Will we have to go back?"

Alatani started to speak, but Seri was already shaking his head. "We'll get something sorted out, but it may take a few days. In the meantime… you only have one child with you?"

"Yes: Lessai. He's inside."

"Good. You can stay in the Guardhouse for the time being." He smiled a little as she sighed in relief. "Alatani, could you show them to a couple of the spare rooms? I need to go and make sure everyone's settling in."

Alatani nodded, relieved. "Come on," she said, picking up Elar's bundle.

"Thanks," Elar said to both of them as she followed.

There was one toddler curled up on the end of a couch, fast asleep, and Alatani nodded to him. "I hope that's Lessai."

Elar smiled. "Yes. Do you mind if he stays there a little longer?"

"I'd hate to wake him; he looks so peaceful." Alatani led the way down the corridor. "The two of you can make yourselves at home while you're here, as long as you don't go into any of the other rooms without permission."

Elar nodded. As Alatani opened the door to an empty room, the other woman asked, "So how long have you still to wait?"

Alatani wasn't sure what she meant by that and looked curiously at her.

"The baby: how long?"

"Oh!" Alatani looked down at herself. "I didn't realise it was quite *that* obvious. A few months yet."

Elar grinned. "I know you've probably been told this, but it is a wonderful thing."

Alatani laughed. "Not in as many words, actually. It's comforting, coming from someone with a young child herself."

Elar nodded. "It's rough sometimes, but well worth it." She looked around at the room and sighed.

"Is it all right?"

"It's perfect." Elar grinned. "Thank you."

"Like I say, make yourself at home. I'll go and keep an eye on Lessai while you get sorted out; he'll be in the next room." Alatani pointed.

Elar blinked. "Lessai will have his own room?" she asked.

Alatani nodded. "Unless you'd prefer him to stay with you, of course."

Elar shook her head a little, as if to clear her thoughts. "We have always shared... I've not lived anywhere where we could have separate bedrooms before now." She forced a small smile. "I know that probably sounds..."

Alatani shook her head, raising a hand. "We have the space, especially as it's only until we can find you somewhere else to stay. It's fine by us if you're comfortable having him sleep separately and he's not likely to be worried by being separated from you."

"It might be nice." This time the smile was a little more genuine.

Alatani smiled back. "If you need anything, come and ask me."

Elar nodded. "I'll come through when I've unpacked. Again, thank you."

It had been some weeks since Neithan had sent Celes back with the families, but as he walked through the village, he thought that he and Derdhel had really done all they could. The extra space in the standing houses had made things much easier for the remaining elves, as had the work they'd all done to reinforce those houses. Neithan had made a proper thatched shelter for the smoke-hole in Byrick's house, also teaching the village elves how to make them. That was a craft that would be useful in rebuilding.

He reached the small stone hut that he and Derdhel had built as a teaching exercise and picked up the broken shovel that he had left leaning against the door. The handle was loose and he hoped to be able to wedge it back into place with the scraps of wood he'd been to fetch.

As he was fiddling with it, leaning against the wall, he saw Byrick walking between two houses a little way off. At once, he lowered the shovel and waved.

"I'm not sure there's much more we can do before spring," he said as the other elf came over.

Byrick nodded. "So you're planning to leave soon?"

"If that's all right."

Byrick nodded again. "I'm grateful for all you've done," he said, smiling. "We should be able to handle things until the snow melts. You and Derdhel have been a great help to us." He looked around with a sigh. "I don't know what we'd have done…"

"I'm glad we were able to help."

"When will you go?" asked Byrick, leaning on the wall beside him.

"Probably the day after tomorrow, unless anything comes up that will delay us." Neithan stretched. "Hopefully the snow will melt before too long."

"Then those that went to Duamelti can come home." Byrick looked absently towards Duamelti, then round at Neithan. "Thank you again for arranging that. It was a great help, and it's good not to have to worry about them, though… we do miss them. It's strange not to have any children around the village."

"They'll be able to come home soon."

As Byrick was about to reply, someone called his name and he looked round. "Excuse me."

Neithan nodded and waved him off, then went back to fiddling with the shovel. Ramming hemp into the socket might actually be better, but it would rot if it got wet, and it would. Best of all would be to hammer it into better shape, but even then the rivets probably needed replacing. Still, a wooden wedge would do for now.

***

They spent what was left of that day, and the next day, finishing a few small jobs around the village. Finally, as night was beginning to fall, Neithan was satisfied

"I think that really is everything," he said to Derdhel as they set about tidying up their own belongings by the light of a tallow lamp in their hut. They didn't have much with them, but he wanted to be ready to leave in the morning, and what they did have had been scattered around as they made themselves comfortable. "Hopefully, someone'll be able to get some use out of this," said Neithan, patting a wall semi-affectionately. He was glad he'd had the idea to build the shelter as a way to demonstrate things like the correct pitch for the roof and the best way to support it. It had held up well and was warmer than their tent, and it felt safer and more solid. He'd been especially grateful for a real roof when they'd had another serious snowfall one night.

"I was glad of it," said Derdhel softly.

Neithan grinned. "Well, if there were any doubt of how miserable living in a tent was, getting a complaint out of you would lay it to rest."

Derdhel smiled a little and went back to strapping up his pack.

"Swordmaster Neithan?" called a voice from outside.

Neithan exchanged a glance with Derdhel and went out to see what was happening.

A young elf was standing there, looking a little nervous. Neithan had encountered him once or twice, but couldn't remember his name. Nonetheless, he smiled as he said, "Hello."

"Byrick would like you and Swordmaster Derdhel to join us in his house tonight," said the elf shyly.

Neithan blinked, a little startled. "Is there room?"

"There is for you."

Neithan wondered for a moment why they hadn't been invited in already, in that case, but didn't ask. "Thank you. We'd be glad to."

The elf nodded and left. Neithan went back into the shelter.

"I suppose you heard that?" he asked Derdhel.

Derdhel nodded, starting to roll up his bedding. "I'd not have minded the cold, but I'll enjoy the warmth." He looked up with a smile.

They made their way over to Byrick's house with their gear, Neithan giving the shelter wall a last pat as he left. When they arrived, they stood blinking a moment in the fire- and lamp-light, but then someone evidently noticed them and there was an enthusiastic cheer around the room, making Neithan smile. Several elves came forward to welcome them, leading them to a place where they could sleep. He could tell, looking around their little clear spot, why they'd not been invited before: this space had obviously only recently been cleared and their surroundings were cramped. It was definitely only big enough for the two of them to sleep. Neithan thanked the people on either side as he and Derdhel laid out their bedrolls.

Byrick arrived as they finished and smiled in greeting.

"I'm sorry I didn't invite you before."

"I can see it took effort to find room," said Neithan. "Thank you."

"I thought we should show you some proper hospitality, since it's your last night with us."

"Well, I've no complaints. You've been very welcoming." Neithan took Byrick's hand. "It's been a pleasure being here. Thanks."

Byrick wrung Neithan's hand with a broad smile. "I have far more to be thankful for. Come and have dinner."

CHAPTER THREE

It was an unexpectedly long, cold winter, with the snow lasting well into the spring. Even the Swordmasters tried to venture out as little as possible, though they still had to take trips around the valley to check on its small settlements of Mixed-bloods and Derdhel once ventured back out to check on Byrick. Alatani had managed to find somewhere for Elar and Lessai to stay, and went to visit her friend fairly regularly while she could still travel easily enough.

On one of the visits, she found Elar on her own, carefully spinning thread by the banked-down fire while Lessai slept nearby. The other woman smiled a greeting and gestured Alatani to a chair on the other side of the fireplace.

"You're definitely starting to show," she said with a small grin.

"It's getting harder to walk long distances." Alatani sighed, feeling ridiculous. "Weyrn's been babying me."

Elar sighed. "Of course he has. He's probably worried about you."

Alatani nodded. "I know, and sometimes it does make things easier, but it does make me feel useless." She frowned at Elar. "And don't you give me the same nonsense the midwife did about being a mother being the most important task in the world."

Elar laughed. "Mothering alone will only feed a little one for so long." She twiddled the spindle between her fingers, then caught it and set it aside for a moment to hand Alatani some cards and wool. "There's a way you can be useful," she said with a smile.

Alatani began carefully dragging the sharp-toothed cards through the wool. "Tell me truly: is it hard? My mother tells me it'll all come naturally, and I am a Swordmaster; having another life depending on me is something I've experienced before. At the same time… A baby can't run away if something goes wrong." The thought made her voice tremble for a moment. She led a dangerous life, after all. Something might easily go wrong.

Elar shook her head. "It's not the same, and for exactly that reason: even if he's hurt, a grown elf can look after himself a little. However, it's not as difficult as it's often made out to be." She sighed a little. "Still, you're lucky that you have someone to look after you while you look after your baby."

Alatani nodded, but she wasn't entirely comfortable with the thought; she knew Elar was referring to Weyrn, who wouldn't be there.

"Is everything all right?"

"Yes... I'm worried, that's all. I'm going to go and stay with my parents after the birth and... I don't actually get on with them very well."

Elar blinked. "I'm sorry to hear that," she said softly. "Why not? Did they not agree with your decision to be a Swordmaster?"

"That's a large part of it. Maybe even the root of it." Alatani sighed. "But to be honest I never understood why my father named me 'Soldier-girl' when he didn't want me to be a warrior."

Elar laughed. "Good question."

"They don't like Weyrn either, and I think they blame him for me deciding to take my oath."

Elar blinked. "It... doesn't seem like staying with them is a very good idea."

"Well, where else can I go?" asked Alatani, a little more sharply than she'd intended. She sighed and looked down. "Sorry, it's just that I don't think it's a good idea either, but they're my only birth family and I can't very well keep a new baby in the Guardhouse."

"Hasn't it ever happened before? You can't be the first..." Elar frowned. "Are you the first female Swordmaster?"

"No, but there was only one before me and she never married."

Elar dropped her gaze for a moment, but then nodded. "Well, Swordmasters must have been fathers before, then. Do their families live in the Guardhouse?"

"Often, yes, especially when it's just a married couple, but the woman does normally leave at least to give birth and wean the baby."

"I suppose it is difficult when they don't sleep through the night." Elar looked over at Lessai with a small sigh. "That is a phase they grow out of, but it seems to take forever."

Alatani winced and Elar smiled.

"You'll do fine. I'm sure you've handled far more frightening things."

"Yes, but that was different."

"Why did you want to be a Swordmaster? It sounds like a lot of danger and responsibility, and especially if your parents were against it..."

Alatani laughed a little. "I wanted to do something great with my life," she said with a small smile. "I suppose I was tired of being my father's little girl."

Elar laughed as well. "I can understand that. Has it been all you expected?"

Alatani nodded. "It's hard sometimes, and it's certainly dangerous" – she had plenty of scars – "but it's a life I love."

"It helps to have the man you love alongside you, I suppose?" asked Elar with a small grin.

"Of course, but… I think I could manage even without him there." Alatani frowned, imagining what things would be like without Weyrn. "Yes… after all, when I went to ask for a place as a trainee, I didn't know him at all except as a name, and he wasn't Captain then either. Even as a trainee I didn't have much to do with him – no more than any trainee would have with another Swordmaster. We both lived in the Guardhouse, we worked and fought together… but we weren't as close as all that until after I was sworn in." She sighed. It was difficult to imagine life without Weyrn now, but she didn't think it would be impossible if something were to happen.

Elar nodded, her expression distant. "I hope you never have to find out," she said, reaching across to pat Alatani's hand.

Alatani smiled, though she knew the possibility was always there. "So do I."

A couple of weeks before the baby was due to be born, a messenger arrived to ask Weyrn to come and see the king. He shot a glance at Alatani, who smiled and waved him off, and as he walked he hoped desperately that it was nothing that would call him away.

At the door, he met Crown Prince Caleb, who looked rather surprised to see him.

"Is something wrong, Captain Weyrn?" the boy asked as Weyrn approached.

"That's what I'm wondering. Your father sent for me."

Caleb looked surprised. "I'm afraid I don't know why," he said in answer to the unspoken question. "I believe he's in his study, though. I'll show you the way."

Weyrn knew the way to Hurion's study, but he didn't say so, simply falling into step beside the young prince.

Hurion was standing by the small fire in his study when Caleb showed Weyrn in. He looked troubled, but smiled as he looked up.

"Thank you, Caleb," he said. "You may stay if you like."

Caleb nodded gravely and stood by the wall, out of the way. Although not even into adolescence, he took his position as crown prince very seriously.

"Thank you for coming, Weyrn," said Hurion, gripping Weyrn's hand.

"I thought it must be important, since you sent for me in this snow."

Hurion nodded. "You know, of course, that Taffilelti sends a few of his men here every spring at about this time?"

Weyrn nodded. "Surely, given the weather…"

Hurion shook his head. "As usual, he sent a pigeon when they set out. They're on their way, but they should have arrived some days ago."

Weyrn's gaze strayed to the window, which showed a fine view of the snow-covered city.

"How likely is it that they got lost?" he asked.

Hurion shrugged a little. "Their leader has been here before and knows the road, but with the snow it's quite possible."

"I take it you want our help in finding them."

"If you could."

Weyrn sighed, looking back out at the snow. "Have your men searched for them?"

"I've already sent scouts along the road, but if someone could alert the mixed-blood tribes to their presence it might help."

Weyrn nodded slowly. Alatani would have their baby soon, but he knew it wouldn't be fair to send the others and stay himself. He could go for a couple of days and then come back if there was nothing, couldn't he?

"I'll see what we can do."

"Thank you," said Hurion fervently. "I owe you a favour."

Weyrn nodded slightly.

"I suppose none of the Mixed-bloods would be likely to harm them…?"

"I doubt it, not without a reason."

Hurion nodded with a small sigh of relief. "That's good. I'll let you go, then. Give my regards to Alatani, won't you?"

Weyrn smiled. "I will. It won't be long now."

"Of course, I wouldn't ask you to miss the birth of your firstborn."

"I intend to be back by then."

Hurion nodded. "If you need anything, let me know."

"Thanks." Weyrn inclined his head a little in farewell. "We'll do what we can."

Hurion bowed his head in response. "I can't ask for more."

Weyrn left again, deep in thought. In weather like this, there was always a chance of getting lost or hurt or overwhelmed by the weather, and it was possible that the Wood-elves had indeed suffered such a fate. Especially if they had left the road… they might have stumbled into anything out in unfamiliar wilderness and that would make it all the harder and more dangerous to find them.

That very danger meant that he couldn't send his own people and stay safe and warm at home himself, especially given that he had played little part in helping Byrick's village. He sighed, watching his breath mist in front of him in the chill air. It couldn't be helped. He was going to have to go.

***

Weyrn chose Derdhel, Celes and Maelli to accompany him, leaving Seri to continue looking after the visiting mixed-bloods and travelling around Duamelti and Neithan to look after Alatani.

"Be back before the baby's born," she said firmly, her hands on his shoulders, as he was checking his pack.

"If I have to hurry back alone, I will be," he said, and tipped his head to kiss her hand. "I promise."

"Good." She squeezed his shoulders gently. "Have you got everything?"

"I believe so." He got up and swung the pack onto his back, then kissed her. She pulled back and grinned.

"Good luck. Find them quickly and come back safely."

He kissed the end of her sharp nose and laid a hand tenderly on her belly. "I will."

The others were waiting in the common room, and they quickly made their farewells and left.

"Do we know the route they took?" asked Maelli as the four Swordmasters climbed up towards the border.

"The main road from Silvren. They should have got within a few days' travel of us before hitting serious snow, so we'll go that far and then start searching off the road. Unfortunately, there aren't many settlements near it, so we can't really ask if anyone's seen them."

"Didn't Hurion send anyone else to search?"

"Yes, and they'll have looked up and down the road, but I'd feel better if we can make a pass along it ourselves. It also means we can find out where they would have hit snow and begin searching from there."

"Would they have headed for a town to seek shelter when they realised the snow was getting bad?" asked Celes.

"They may have done. There are a couple of human towns within striking distance as well as the Mixed-bloods slightly further off, so if we don't find any trace of them we'll ask there if they've been seen."

"I hope they made it there," said Celes, pulling his cloak a little closer around his shoulders. "I'd not like to be caught out in this snow without shelter and they might not have realised how long it would take to find some."

"The settlements aren't that sparse; if they were searching, they surely would have found someone," said Derdhel.

"And even the more violent among the clans wouldn't do them any serious harm if they were lost in the snow," said Maelli.

Weyrn nodded. "That's good to know. I wasn't too afraid of them, but…" He shrugged. There was always a chance in these sorts of things.

They didn't seriously start looking until they were over the border. Had the missing Wood-elves made it that far, one at least would have been able to reach shelter in Duamelti and tell someone what had happened to his companions.

Weyrn couldn't help but feel some hope leaving him as he stood on the crest of the hill and looked out over the forest. The road was a clear path between forbidding black trunks. It was a black-and-white world of snow and shadows and trees. He shivered, thinking of how terrible it would be to be lost out there.

"We'll be able to see at least the remains of a trail if they left the road in the last couple of days," said Derdhel, looking thoughtfully down the slope.

"I doubt it with Hurion's people already searching," said Maelli, absently twisting his long hair back in a ponytail as he spoke. "If there were anything to find, surely they would have found it."

Weyrn was grateful as their voices interrupted his thoughts, but he sighed again as he looked up. The clouds were starting to thicken and he was worried that there would be snow again tonight. Provided they found shelter the Swordmasters would be fine, but he wasn't so sure about the Wood-elves: Gelladar, Othron and Ethiad. Apparently Hurion knew Gelladar and Othron, and Gelladar was probably able to deal with the snow. That was encouraging, at least, but that was as far as the encouragement went.

Celes noticed the direction of his gaze and bit his lip. "It's going to snow again?"

Weyrn nodded. "Let's hurry. We need to get as far as we can before it starts and we need to seek shelter ourselves. Keep an eye out to either side as we go, but walk fast."

As they went, they didn't see any sign that anyone had left the road. Weyrn wasn't very surprised. He expected that if the three Wood-elves had decided to strike out into the forest, they would have done it early, in the hope of finding somewhere to wait out the snow. The fact that there was no sign of them backed up that theory.

He heard a shout from up ahead and looked up to see a Valley-elf coming towards them.

"Captain Weyrn!" He slowed from a jog to a walk as he came up to them. "I'm Ekelid."

"Ah, of the Royal Guard?" Weyrn stepped forward, angling his head to make sure he had identified the other elf's uniform correctly.

"Indeed. Did Lord Hurion ask you to help us?"

"He did. Any news?"

"We haven't seen anything of them. We asked at a human settlement and they said that some of their people had seen three elves heading for Duamelti, but weren't able to say for certain whether and where they'd left the road."

Weyrn nodded. "Were they able to give any hints? Even if we knew they'd gone in one direction or the other it would help."

"Someone said they'd gone west; there would be more shelter in that direction if they were just hoping for somewhere to spend the night out of the snow."

"We'll try out in that direction, then."

Ekelid nodded. "Thanks. We'll go back up and down the road and see if we can meet up with you again."

Weyrn nodded. "Do you have any idea how far they went on the road?"

Ekelid shook his head.

"All right." Weyrn looked round at the other Swordmasters. "We'll start off the road now and see if we can find their trail or ask some of the clans."

Ekelid nodded. "Good luck," he said fervently.

Weyrn nodded. "You too. See you soon."

Ekelid saluted, then turned and left. Weyrn looked back at the others.

"Celes, could you keep an eye out for sheltered spots and good places to look? Maelli, let us know if we're coming close to any clan settlements. Derdhel, you look for any sign of tracks, and I'll do the same."

They nodded and all headed off into the forest.

They searched as long as the daylight lasted, eating lunch as they went. Evening was drawing in when Maelli directed them to a small village of Mixed-bloods. It seemed to be more a collection of houses than an actual village, and they knocked on the door of the first one they came to.

It was answered by a woman who looked curiously at them, her eyes lingering for a moment on Derdhel. Before Weyrn could speak, though, she noticed the badges on their sleeves and tensed a little in surprise.

"Swordmasters?" she asked. "What brings you here?" She stepped out of the doorway and gestured to them to come in.

"Thank you," said Weyrn, inclining his head a little to her as he stepped into the house. "We're looking for three Wood-elves who were on their way to Duamelti and haven't arrived. Have you seen anything of them?"

She closed the door before answering. "I'm afraid not, and I don't think anyone else has. We've not been out much since the snow got very bad."

Weyrn sighed. "Do you know of anyone else who might be able to help?"

She shook her head. "Most of what the others know what I know."

"All right. Thank you, though."

"Come through and sit by the fire," she said.

"Thank you," said Weyrn, glancing at the others, "But we probably ought to continue our search."

"It'll be dark soon," she said. "And you're welcome to stay the night." She looked worried, though, glancing back towards the main room of the house.

"We'd be happy to if you'd not mind having us," said Weyrn, "But…" He glanced back towards the door, his heart going out to those three still out there somewhere.

"You won't be able to go much further," the woman insisted. "And I am happy to have you."

Weyrn glanced around at the others. "What's your name?" he asked her.

"Lyla."

"I'm Captain Weyrn the Linnet. This is Maelli the Faithful, Derdhel the Stoic and Celes the Gentle."

She smiled and bowed her head a little. "I'm pleased to meet you. Will you at least stay and have dinner with me?"

"Thank you," said Weyrn, unwilling to insult her by turning down all hospitality.

Her smile broadened. "Come through when you're ready," she said and went back into the main room.

Weyrn turned to the others. "Do you think we could go much further tonight?"

"I don't like to leave them," said Maelli. "It feels wrong to spend the night in comfort and leave them out there."

"I think Lyla's right, though," said Derdhel. "We'd be turning down her offer only to camp in the snow a little way away."

"And if I were lost so close to here, I'd make for this village," said Celes. "We could see it even from a distance."

"Not so very far," said Maelli, still sounding uncomfortable, "But you do have a point."

"I think if we were likely to find them tonight, they would be close enough to find their way to here," said Derdhel, laying a hand on Maelli's shoulder.

Maelli thought for a moment, then nodded. "I admit we couldn't go much further, and this does place us at a landmark. You're right." He sighed. "It just… doesn't really sit well with me."

Weyrn nodded, understanding. "We'll leave first thing in the morning. It's not snowing or very windy, and the clouds will make it warmer."

After a moment, Maelli nodded. "All right."

Derdhel squeezed his shoulder and they followed Lyla through into the main room of the house.

It was modestly furnished, dominated by a scrubbed table set in front of the fire. There would be room for the four Swordmasters to sleep on the floor, though. Lyla was tending a pot over the fire, but she looked up as they entered.

"Have you decided?" she asked, standing straight.

"We would appreciate spending the night here," said Weyrn.

"You're still welcome to, but..." – she looked uncomfortable – "I'm afraid I can only offer you the floor."

"That's quite all right." Weyrn smiled.

They shared some of their supplies with her, and the four of them sat around the table to eat dinner. There were only two chairs and Weyrn accepted one, insisting that Lyla kept the other. Maelli, Derdhel and Celes sat on upended logs. Maelli said a quick prayer and then they ate almost in silence. Weyrn couldn't help noticing that Maelli kept shooting worried looks towards the door.

"Is it snowing again?" Weyrn asked, not addressing anyone in particular.

"I don't think so," said Celes. "I can go and have a look."

"It didn't look like it would," said Derdhel, glancing up.

"If it didn't, it would make a nice change," said Lyla with a smile.

"And make our search a lot more likely to succeed," said Celes, shooting a sidelong look at Maelli.

Maelli still didn't look entirely happy, but shook his head a little and didn't say anything.

Derdhel shot him a concerned look and said, "We're here now, and they're surely outside striking distance. Nothing to be done."

"I know." Maelli shrugged a little. "Otherwise I'd be more inclined to argue."

"I generally go to bed soon after eating," said Lyla, getting up and starting to clear away the bowls they'd eaten from. "Do you need anything else?"

Weyrn smiled at her. "No, thank you, Lyla."

"All right. I'll see you in the morning, then. Sleep well!"

Weyrn nodded. "Likewise, and thank you again."

"Spirits go with you," said Maelli.

"And with you," she said, then went into a side room and closed the door behind her.

Weyrn looked around at the other three. "We should do the same. We'll set out again as early as we can tomorrow and hopefully have better luck."

"I hope so," said Maelli fervently.

Weyrn didn't really have any comfort for that, and just reached across to pat Maelli's shoulder. "Let's get to bed," he said. "We'll keep searching in the morning."

***

As they'd planned, they set off again first thing in the morning, bidding Lyla farewell. She said that she'd spread word of the search among the other elves living in the little village, and they'd do what they could to keep an eye out. Weyrn thanked her again and led the way back in the direction they'd been following.

As before, Celes looked for likely places the Wood-elves could have sought shelter while Derdhel watched out for any sign of tracks. Weyrn kept an eye on the weather, his gaze continually flicking upwards, looking for any change in the clouds. It hadn't snowed overnight, and he was glad of that; despite their encouraging words to Maelli, he had been worried. Being caught in the snow again might spell the end for the three ambassadors.

Derdhel's sudden cry of "There!" jerked him out of his thoughts and he blinked, swinging round, as Derdhel darted through a gap between two trees. After a moment, he called, "I've found footprints!"

Maelli murmured something as he followed, Weyrn and Celes on his heels.

"Well done," said Weyrn with a sigh of relief as he saw the line of snow between the trees, marked with three sets of footprints.

"It doesn't look as if they were in any trouble," said Derdhel, crouching over the prints. "No limping or dragging, and the path is straight." He pointed on into the forest. "That way."

Weyrn sighed. They had been heading deeper into the forest, away from the settlement and the road. "They really were lost. Can you tell how old the trail is?"

Derdhel poked the edge of a footprint. "It's frozen overnight, so yesterday or early in the night."

Maelli winced, but nodded.

"Come on," said Weyrn, beckoning to them as he set out along the path, though he hung back to let Derdhel get ahead. He doubted that he'd miss any sign that the Wood-elves had left this path, but he didn't want to gamble on it.

"Where in the world where they going?" muttered Maelli as they followed a sudden bend in the track. Judging by the pattern of footprints and scuffs in the snow, there'd been some disagreement.

"*Seriously* lost," Weyrn said again, starting off on the path they'd eventually taken.

It continued to weave about, making false starts and sudden turns but overall going further and further into the trees. At length, they finally found a hopeful sign: a small charred spot against the roots of a fallen tree. The snow that had made its way past the roots had been swept away and it would have made a reasonable shelter.

"I guess this is where they spent the night," said Maelli with an audible sigh of relief.

"And that means that they had a better chance of coming through it all right, since they had fire and shelter from the wind."

"They set off again in the same direction as the road, if I judge correctly," said Celes, who had been looking for more tracks.

"Towards it?"

"No, alongside it."

Weyrn sighed. "At least they're not getting further away from it. Come on, hopefully we can catch up with them before much longer."

"I hope so," muttered Maelli, looking back at the little camp. "They might not find shelter tonight."

After about another hour, they came upon an established path through the forest, covered in snow. The Wood-elves had made their way down it for a while, heading back towards the road, and the Swordmasters followed them gratefully. If they'd made their way back to the road, it was far more likely that they'd be safely found.

After about a mile the tracks of a group of humans crossed the path and the Wood-elves turned to follow it. Weyrn sighed as he changed direction as well.

"At least if they made it back to a human settlement they should be all right," he said.

"I'll believe it when I see it," said Derdhel calmly.

"We've not had much trouble with them recently," said Weyrn, glancing at Maelli for confirmation. "Have the clans?"

Maelli shook his head. "Not that I know of, and Seri hasn't mentioned anything."

Weyrn nodded. "They're probably lucky, then."

He became less confident when the two sets of tracks began to climb a hill and finally reached a bare piece of rocky earth where the snow had slipped. The human tracks vanished and the wood-elves turned back, taking a straighter route back towards the path.

Weyrn had to admit he was tired, and he sat down on an exposed rock to think for a moment. The others settled around him.

"Back to the smaller path?" asked Celes after a moment.

"That's where they were going," agreed Maelli.

"We didn't see their tracks anywhere else there," said Derdhel.

Weyrn shook his head a little. "Let's keep on after their tracks," he said, getting up "At least until night starts to fall. Then we can think again."

As it was beginning to get dark, they finally encountered a human hunting party: possibly the one that had left the tracks.

"Have you seen any trace of three Wood-elves?" Weyrn asked them. "They're late arriving in Duamelti."

The humans looked at one another, and at length one volunteered that he had seen something.

"Just before I came back from my last run, I found some tracks leading away from the road." He gestured towards the smaller path they'd found. "I thought it was odd, but I thought it was just an elven hunting party from the village yonder." He pointed off towards the south. "There were three, though, and they didn't seem to be taking any care, or heading anywhere particular."

Weyrn nodded. "That could be them. Could you give me an idea of their bearing?"

"Straight away from the road back to our village, into the forest. It was only a little way back; you might be able to find them yourselves before dark."

Presumably he was still referring to the small track, not the main road. Weyrn glanced at the group's leader. "Would you be able to spare him to show us where he saw the tracks?"

The man shook his head regretfully. "Sorry, master elf. We have to make it to our waystation before dark. It'll snow again before the morning and we can't delay."

"I won't keep you longer, then," said Weyrn, disappointed. He glanced at the young human. "Could you direct me to exactly where you saw these tracks?"

The human willingly pointed back the way they'd come. "Go back that way until you come to a lightning-struck elm. That was where we met after our runs. My track runs out east and if you follow that, you'll find them."

"Thank you," said Weyrn fervently. Especially if it was going to snow, he wanted to find those elves before night fell. The leader nodded and waved, then the two groups parted.

"Come on," said Weyrn to the others, and they hurried off down the humans' path.

As the young human had promised, they soon came to the lightning-struck elm. There was a mess of trampled snow around its roots, but they eventually managed to identify the path that they were pretty sure was right.

"I don't like it, though," said Derdhel. "There are many paths leading towards the east from here."

"And we're going to have to find a camp ourselves before long," said Celes softly, looking sidelong at Weyrn.

"Cold is passing," said Derdhel with a shrug. "We could rest until the moon rises and then continue to search."

"If it snows, the moon won't rise," said Maelli.

Weyrn nodded. "We'll go down this path first," he said. "If we can find their trail, it'll be something. Then we'll see how much daylight we have left."

"We won't just stop looking for them, will we?" asked Maelli as they started walking.

Weyrn shook his head a little. "We can't track in the dark."

Derdhel pointed up at the gathering clouds. "And he was right about the snow."

"All the more reason to find them quickly." Maelli quickened his pace.

Weyrn matched his speed, looking carefully at the snow as he went.

"Everyone keep watch for tracks. Remember, they may be –"

Celes cried out suddenly and Weyrn spun round. The younger elf was pointing at a faint, scuffed path through the snow, heading deeper into the woods.

"Ah, well done," said Weyrn, relaxing as he spoke.

"They're not heading for any settlement," said Maelli, frowning.

"I doubt they know the land well enough to find them anyway," said Derdhel. "I imagine they're just looking for a natural shelter."

Celes was looking up and down the track. "Would they find it?"

"They might find something similar to last night, if they were lucky."

Weyrn had crouched down to examine the tracks. It looked like three elves, as best he could judge. He was aware that he might be seeing what he wanted rather than what was there.

Still, it was the best sign they'd found since meeting the humans, and he got up to follow the path away from the road.

"Derdhel," he said, "Keep an eye out for any other tracks. I'll follow where these lead, but if it looks like there was anything walking near or towards them, let me know. Celes, Maelli, keep watch."

There was a murmur of agreement as they kept pace with him.

The tracks wavered through the forest, apparently at random. Weyrn's best theory was that the Wood-elves had left even the smaller road to seek shelter – perhaps thinking they could find a settlement across country – and had got turned around and lost.

When darkness began to fall in earnest, there was still no sign of them apart from the wandering tracks. A few times one appeared to have veered away for a while, but he'd always returned to the other two, and they'd continued on together. Weyrn paused and looked around. Maelli looked worried, Derdhel resigned and Celes tired.

"We need to find somewhere to camp," said Weyrn with a sigh.

"But –"

Derdhel cut Maelli off. "You said yourself there'll be no moon tonight, and soon it will start to snow. He's right. We must find shelter, or we'll be in the same pass as them."

Maelli shook his head. "If it snows, we'll lose this trail. How will we find them then? We'll be back where we started."

"When it gets dark, we'll lose the trail," said Weyrn firmly. "I don't like it either, but we need to stop and make camp while there's still some light in the sky. We'll light a campfire, and with any luck it'll act as a signal."

Maelli looked around the forest mournfully. "I feel like we're abandoning them."

"We aren't. Abandoning them would mean turning around and going home. Do you have a better idea?"

Maelli looked around again, first at the forest and then at the other

Swordmasters. Derdhel still looked untroubled by any decision; he was gazing thoughtfully out at the trees. Celes was obviously trying not to shiver.

"You're cold," said Maelli, looking at him.

Celes nodded guiltily. "Now that we've stopped moving."

Maelli was silent a moment longer, then he shook his head and swore. "All right. We'll stop."

Weyrn nodded, reaching over to grip his shoulder. "I'll clear the ground for a fire and pitch the tent. The three of you gather wood." One tent between three – the fourth would keep watch – would be cramped, but that would make it warmer.

Lighting a fire was difficult on the cold, wet ground, and Derdhel eventually had to take over; he was better at it than Weyrn. Even so, it took him several minutes to get the kindling alight. Once flames began to appear, Weyrn stepped away from the campfire and stared out into the swiftly-gathering darkness, searching for any sign of movement against the snow. He couldn't see anything and sighed. Hopefully, Gelladar, Othron and Ethiad had managed to find shelter.

He looked up as a snowflake drifted past his face and sighed again. Snow would make it more difficult to keep the fire burning bright enough to be seen, would hide tracks, and would make it more likely that the Wood-elves would be trapped and die of the cold before morning. Still, it also meant that the Swordmasters couldn't have gone further. The fire would act as a beacon, and for the moment it was all they could really do.

They ate a hasty dinner and drew straws for who would take first watch. It fell to Weyrn. He'd be on watch for three hours, then Maelli would take over. Until then, he just had to keep an eye and ear out and stop the fire burning down.

He went to stand just outside the circle of firelight, staring out into the snowy forest and letting his eyes grow accustomed to the darkness. He couldn't see anything but the occasional flurry of snow, and once the other three had gone to bed he couldn't hear anything either. There was only the low crackling of the fire and the occasional hiss of melting snow. He sighed, wondering if anyone out there could see the fire and would be drawn to it.

The hours went by and there was still no sign of anyone. Weyrn kept the fire fed and burning brightly, still hoping that the lost elves would see it. By the time his watch was over, though, he was starting to give up hope.

He woke Maelli and was just stepping out of the tent doorway to let him out when they both heard something.

They shared a glance, then Weyrn hurried back to the edge of the firelight, looking out in the direction the sound had come from. Naturally, he couldn't see anything, but when he listened he heard it again.

This time, he was sure: it was a call for help.

"Hello!" he shouted. "Maelli, get a torch."

As soon as Maelli had a branch from the fire, they set off into the forest, heading towards the source of the voice.

It wasn't far before the flickering light fell on a dark form sprawled in the snow. His heart in his mouth, Weyrn dropped to his knees and gently rolled the limp figure onto his back. It was immediately clear that this was a young Wood-elf. His skin was chill to the touch and his lips and ears were blue-tinted with cold. When Weyrn gently patted his cheek and called out to him, there was no reaction.

"Bring the torch closer," said Weyrn, shrugging off his cloak. The cold bit through his clothes, but this elf needed it more and they'd soon be back at the camp. Weyrn gently wrapped the warm cloak around him, biting his lip as he once again felt the dreadful chill of his skin. But as Weyrn started to lift him, planning to carry him across his shoulders, the elf finally stirred, whimpering.

"Too hot..." he slurred, pulling at the cloak. "'m too hot."

Weyrn blinked. "You're frozen half to death," he said softly. "Come on, we'll get you back to camp and warm you up."

The elf stirred again. "But..." He tried to push Weyrn's hand away.

"It's all right." Weyrn picked him up. Like all Wood-elves, he was stocky but relatively short, which made him easier to lift. "You're cold. That's why everything else feels hot."

The elf started to reply, then apparently fainted again.

"I'll go and see if I can tell where he came from," said Maelli. "You can make it back without the torch."

"Yes. Come back in a couple of minutes, though."

Maelli nodded and left.

The elf revived again as Weyrn laid him down near the fire. "No... you'll burn me!" he gasped, twitching away from the flames.

"It's all right, you're not close enough to be burned." Weyrn opened the cloak a little to let in the warmth.

The elf sighed, relaxing as if about to fall asleep, but then he murmured, "My friends...?"

Weyrn leaned a little closer. "Yes?"

"Odnon fainted..." He stirred a little, moaning faintly. "Gelladar... stayed with him. You have... to find them."

"Your name's Ethiad?"

Ethiad nodded.

"All right. We came out to look for the three of you. Do you know where you left them?"

Ethiad shook his head. "I walked so far..."

Weyrn stroked his hair. "We'll find them. You stay here and rest." He looked round as someone stepped up behind him and smiled a greeting at

Maelli. "Any luck?"

"He wavered quite a lot, but we can follow the tracks. I'll go wake Celes and Derdhel."

"Right." Weyrn gently shook Ethiad's shoulder. "You can rest, but you can't sleep, I'm afraid. We need to get you warm first."

"I'm already warm... 'm just so sleepy."

"You're not warm; you're freezing." Weyrn moved him a little closer to the fire. Apparently he didn't feel as hot as he had done; he didn't complain.

Maelli returned with Celes and an armload of blankets. Weyrn nodded a greeting and began carefully wrapping the blankets around Ethiad. "Celes, I need you to stay here and look after Ethiad. When he's warm, he can sleep, but not before."

Celes nodded, rubbing the sleep out of his eyes, and crouched down beside Ethiad as Weyrn got up and Derdhel arrived, carrying a lantern. Weyrn put his cloak back on and took the lantern, then he, Derdhel and Maelli headed out into the forest.

Ethiad's tracks were easy to see, even though the still-falling snow was beginning to dull their edges. He'd walked straight towards their fire for a short distance, but before that had been following a confused, wavering path between the trees. It was difficult to predict where the trail would go and the three Swordmasters had to walk slowly, bent over the tracks by the light of their single lantern.

"Do we know how far he went?" asked Derdhel. "If it's much further, we may lose the trail before we find them."

"He said a long way, but in his state..." Weyrn shrugged.

The snow was beginning to let up, but all the same the trail was almost covered over. They came upon two places where Ethiad had fallen into snowdrifts and scrambled out of them, leaving obvious holes. At least that meant they were still on the right trail.

"We'll lose it soon," said Derdhel softly.

Weyrn paused and looked around.

"We're not going back, are we?" asked Maelli.

"No, there's a little left yet." Still, Weyrn held the lantern above his head and looked about for any sign of a sheltered spot where Ethiad's companions might have decided to hide. There was nothing obvious. Weyrn took a deep breath and shouted, "Hello!" at the top of his voice. The sound fell dead in the snow. "Gelladar! Can you hear me?"

Still nothing. Weyrn sighed, remembering the state that Ethiad had been in. Sitting still, Gelladar might have succumbed even faster, and Othron had already been unconscious when Ethiad had left them.

As Weyrn set off again, he reflected that at least they couldn't have gone far from the end of Ethiad's trail.

At last, thought, they reached a point where they could no longer make out any tracks. They had been shallow to start with, and the fresh snow had covered them.

"We may be able to guess his path." Maelli was wandering around at the edge of the lantern's light, his red-blond hair clearly visible though his cloak made the rest of his body look formless. Weyrn reflected uneasily that they might easily mistake a huddled elf for the shadow of a bush or rock.

"We don't want to get lost ourselves," said Derdhel.

"We can't just leave them out here to die."

"There's a good chance they're already dead, and we shouldn't join them."

"We're supposed to help them, not leave them to their fate!"

"Hush, both of you. Let me listen." Weyrn held the lantern up again and shouted, "Gelladar!" He paused, then again, "Gelladar! If you can hear me, answer!" Again, there was a long period of silence. Weyrn shot a worried look at the other two, then decided to try once more. "Gelladar!"

This time, he thought he heard something: a faint sound that might have been a voice.

"That way," said Maelli, pointing and leading the way.

They pushed between the trees and Weyrn stopped to shout again. "Where are you?"

"Help us!" This time the cry was clear enough to identify, but Weyrn couldn't quite place it.

"Can either of you tell where they might be?" he asked Maelli and Derdhel.

Maelli closed his eyes to listen more closely, but Derdhel was looking around, frowning.

"They must be fairly well in the open for the sound to carry, so probably just in a dell somewhere," he said. "Let's get out of the trees. Keep shouting."

Now he led the way, Weyrn a little way behind him with the lantern while Maelli followed. Weyrn could hear Gelladar – he presumed – calling out from time to time, and kept shouting back to reassure the other elf that he hadn't been abandoned.

"There!" said Maelli suddenly, grabbing Weyrn's shoulder and pointing. "There's a hollow in the hill. Where those bushes are."

Weyrn nodded and headed for the bushes. On the other side, there was indeed a small dell, like a scoop taken out of the hillside. He could see a shapeless lump below him. A pale blotch on top of it was a face, looking up.

"Hello?" Gelladar called weakly.

"All right," said Weyrn, waving. "We see you. Just give us a moment to get down there."

Maelli was already on the way down, picking his way through the snow.

Weyrn followed, and by the time he and Derdhel got there Maelli was already crouching beside the two Wood-elves and talking softly to them.

Gelladar was still shivering, which was a good sign. Othron, however, barely even seemed to be breathing. Gelladar had wrapped blankets and cloaks around the two of them, but though that extra warmth might have kept them alive, it wasn't much.

"Is it t-too late?" asked Gelladar as Weyrn wrapped an extra blanket around Othron.

"We'll do what we can," said Maelli.

"Did Ethiad reach you?"

"Yes."

Gelladar sighed in relief and coughed. "He ran off before I c-could stop him."

"The last member of our group is looking after him back at the camp."

"Thank you."

"Do you think you can walk?" asked Maelli. "I'll help you."

"What about Othron?" Gelladar's voice was beginning to slur, but he shook his head hard to rouse himself

"Derdhel, you take the lantern; you're tallest." Weyrn handed it over and bent to pick up Othron. "I'll carry him as far as I can. Then, Maelli, you take over."

Maelli nodded as he helped Gelladar to get up. The Wood-elf was weak and had to lean heavily on Maelli, still shaking.

"Are you hurt?" asked Maelli, shifting to support him a little better.

Gelladar shook his head. "Cold and hungry." He paused, wracked by shudders for a moment. "That's all."

"We'll be back at our camp soon. There's a fire and food there."

Othron was a dead weight across Weyrn's shoulders, but he thought he'd be able to carry him most of the way back. They'd have to hurry, though, and he started walking without another word.

Celes was only vaguely sure of what he was doing as he tried to warm Ethiad. He knew he had to keep him conscious – if he fell asleep he might never wake – but it was difficult to do. At least Ethiad had stopped complaining that he was too hot; now he was shivering bitterly and moaning in pain as the blood seeped back into his frostbitten ears. Celes had to stop him rubbing them, in between warming a cycle of blankets to wrap around him.

"You'll make it worse," he said softly. "You just have to wait for them to thaw."

Ethiad startled a little, then tucked his hands back inside the blanket. "Why d-does it hurt?"

"It's like pins and needles – the blood's flowing back after it's been cut off for a while."

Ethiad nodded and gasped. "It'll stop?"

"Yes, once you've warmed up."

"You keep... saying that."

Celes went over with a fresh blanket and replaced the outer layer wrapped around Ethiad. "Do you feel any better?"

"C-Colder..." Ethiad sighed, his eyes sliding shut.

Celes shook his shoulder. "You have to stay awake."

"How long?"

"Until you've stopped shivering."

Ethiad laughed softly, but nodded. Celes went back over to the fire to warm the blanket he'd just removed.

"Do you think they f-found them?"

"I don't know. They're following your tracks, though, so I expect so."

Ethiad nodded. "I just wanted to find someone t-to help."

Celes smiled at him. "And you did."

"I wandered... all over the... place." Ethiad's eyelids were drooping and Celes gently shook his shoulder.

"They'll find them, don't worry."

Another nod, then Ethiad's eyes finally fell closed.

"How are your ears?"

Ethiad groaned. "I'd almost forgotten them."

"Have they stopped hurting?"

"It's better, but..." He opened his eyes and raised a hand to touch the point of one ear. "No."

"Don't rub it."

"I know." He huddled back down in the blankets. He was shivering a little less, and when Celes took the now-warm blanket back over he paused to feel Ethiad's temperature.

"You're warming up now," he said, switching over the blankets again. "You'll be able to move into the tent and sleep soon."

Ethiad nodded. "I'm getting hungry again, too."

"When the others get back, we can see about making some soup."

"That would be good." Ethiad smiled.

Celes was just about to suggest moving Ethiad into the tent when he saw the lantern approaching slowly between the trees.

"Weyrn?" he called.

"Yes, it's us! Come and lend a hand."

Celes glanced at Ethiad, who was looking up hopefully. "I'll be back in a moment," he said and headed towards the lantern.

As he approached, he could see that Derdhel was holding the lantern, while Maelli was carrying what looked like a long bundle over his shoulders and Weyrn was supporting an exhausted-looking Wood-elf.

"Help Maelli," said Weyrn quickly.

"I can make it a little further…"

"You've already come further than me. The two of you can chair-carry him."

Celes nodded and helped Maelli lower the unconscious elf into his arms. Fortunately, they were much the same height.

"Is he all right?" the other elf asked hoarsely.

Maelli and Celes picked the elf up again between them and Derdhel slid a hand under the blankets to check his pulse.

"He's alive," he said softly.

"Let's get him back." Weyrn glanced round. "Nearly there, Gelladar. You'll be fine."

Gelladar nodded, leaning a little more on Weyrn, then the little group started back towards the camp.

Ethiad had sat up, hugging the blankets around himself, and his eyes lit up as he saw them.

"You found them!"

Weyrn nodded, helping Gelladar to sit down by Ethiad. The two friends embraced as Celes and Maelli took Othron over to the tent.

"He'll need to be warmed slowly," said Maelli, pulling away the damp blankets and replacing them with dry ones. "Go and get these dry."

"Is he going to be all right?"

Maelli glanced out of the door at the other two Wood-elves, and lowered his voice. "I don't know."

Celes hesitated. Maelli's tone suggested that he had doubts.

"Go and dry those!"

"Right." Celes hurried back out. Weyrn had put the blanket he'd been warming around Gelladar's shoulders and the Wood-elf was sitting by the fire, nursing frostnipped ears and fingers.

"How's Othron?" he asked as soon as he saw Celes.

"Maelli says he needs to be warmed very carefully," said Celes as he arranged the blankets by the fire. "He's given him some dry blankets."

Gelladar looked sceptically at him and put an arm around Ethiad's shoulders. Weyrn got up and went to talk to Maelli, leaving Derdhel to continue making some broth.

After a long moment, Ethiad asked, "Is he dead?"

"No." At least Celes could say that with complete confidence.

"Dying?" asked Gelladar.

Derdhel glanced up from his work. "We're doing what we can," he said calmly. "If he does die, it's clearly his time and there's nothing any of us could do."

Gelladar narrowed his eyes, but Derdhel went back to his work with no indication that he knew he was being glared at.

The next morning, Weyrn sent Derdhel to seek out the members of the Royal Guard who were camped nearby. The tent was cramped and he sent Maelli and Celes to find some more firewood. He stayed with the three Wood-elves.

Gelladar and Ethiad were quiet, sitting huddled together and only occasionally murmuring to each other or Weyrn. Othron hadn't regained consciousness, though he was still breathing and seemed to have warmed up well enough. Weyrn wasn't sure what to do, and it was becoming difficult to hide that fact from Gelladar and Ethiad.

"You can tell us," said Gelladar, breaking the silence. "Is he going to survive?"

Weyrn glanced at him. "I think so. He's warmer now, but I'd feel better if he showed any sign of waking."

Gelladar glanced towards the door of the tent. "About Derdhel…"

"I'm sorry about that, and I've had a word with him. He… doesn't always realise that other people don't think the way he does."

Gelladar nodded. "Apology accepted," he said, though he still sounded unhappy.

"He will do his best to get help, though, won't he?" asked Ethiad.

"Yes. He'll do everything in his power." Weyrn looked round as he thought he heard Othron stir, but the Wood-elf was still lying in the same position as before.

Gelladar reached out to touch his brow and sighed. "At least he feels like he's alive."

Weyrn nodded.

Maelli and Celes returned after some time and Weyrn went to help with the fire while Maelli took over looking after Othron.

"How long do you think it'll take Derdhel to get back?" asked Celes.

"I'm not sure." Weyrn stood up and looked around, his breath misting in the cold air. "He's got to find them, and we left them two days ago, so it might be that long or longer, depending on how far they went and in which direction. I just hope Othron wakes soon."

"Would he then be able to walk?"

"I think we should keep them here for the time being, where it's sheltered, at least until we're sure."

Celes shot a look at the sky. "What if it snows again? We've only got one tent and we can't all be in there at once."

"Well, finding the Royal Guard will help with that." Weyrn looked around again. "We'll see how things go, but I shouldn't think we'll be moving today." He sighed heavily.

"What's wrong?"

Weyrn grimaced. "I'm… worried about getting back in time, nothing more." He glanced at Celes. "Have we any more of that soup from last night?"

"I think so." Celes fetched the pot from the edge of their camp and looked inside. "Yes, enough for all of us." He glanced back at the tent. "Including Othron, if he wakes up."

"He will," said Weyrn with more conviction than he really felt. "It'll just take time." He crouched down by the fire to warm his hands. "I imagine he's exhausted. Gelladar said he was on the point of collapse for some time."

Celes poked at the soup. "He doesn't look to me like he's asleep, that's all."

"He's still breathing." Weyrn looked back at the fire. "There's hope."

Once the soup was warmed through, Celes spooned it into bowls, saving some for Othron. Weyrn stayed by the fire while Celes took their share to those in the tent.

A couple of hours passed and the three Swordmasters took turns looking after Othron. It was Celes' turn when Gelladar came out to sit with Weyrn by the fire.

"How is he?" asked Weyrn, looking up at the Wood-elf with a smile.

"I'm not sure." Gelladar reached out to warm his hands by the fire.

"And you? Have your ears stopped hurting?"

"Yes, I think they're thawed now." Gelladar glanced back towards the tent. "Ethiad's are better too. They've blistered, but it should be all right. I've seen frostbite before and his wasn't too serious." He sighed. "He and I were very lucky."

"Othron might be too."

Gelladar hadn't missed the 'might', but he didn't acknowledge it except with a glance. "You're Swordmaster Captain, aren't you? I've seen you when I've visited in the past."

Weyrn nodded. "H- Lord Hurion asked me to help search for you when you didn't arrive when expected."

"Thank you." Gelladar looked up as Maelli arrived; he'd been looking around for any sign of Derdhel.

"Anything?" asked Weyrn.

Maelli shook his head. "And it's getting late. I hope he's all right."

Gelladar nodded agreement and pressed his now-warm hands to his cheeks.

"You should go back into the tent if you're cold," said Weyrn.

Gelladar shook his head. "I need some fresh air." He looked around. "Do you think it'll snow again tonight?"

"Possibly," said Weyrn. "If so, we'll all have to stay inside, but that'll make it warmer."

Gelladar shuddered a little. "Are we likely to be buried?"

"If so, the three of us can dig it out." Weyrn smiled. "Don't worry."

Gelladar didn't look entirely happy, but he nodded and went back to warming his hands. After a moment, he said, "What will happen if Derdhel isn't back soon?"

"Well... it'll depend. We can stay here a few more days, then we'd probably make shift to carry Othron if he hasn't recovered, and we'll go back without Derdhel. Either way, you needn't worry. We'll get you back safely." Nonetheless, Weyrn couldn't stop his gaze straying towards Duamelti. He looked back round, hoping Gelladar hadn't noticed.

The Wood-elf was frowning. "You're worried, though."

Weyrn shook his head. "I have personal reasons for wanting to get back quickly, though I'll not hurry you if that's not what's best."

At that moment, there was a startled cry from the tent. Weyrn recognised Celes and got up as Maelli hurried over to the tent. He met Celes on his way out.

"Othron's awake," said Celes, grinning.

At that, Gelladar scrambled up from his seat by the fire and the two Swordmasters made way for him to duck into the tent, Weyrn following him.

Othron looked dazed, but at least he was conscious and able to recognise Gelladar.

"What happened?" he asked hoarsely.

"Ethiad ran for help and Captain Weyrn and a group of Swordmasters found us," said Gelladar, taking Othron's hand. "How do you feel?"

"Tired..." Othron closed his eyes again with a sigh, but then looked up. "Ethiad...?"

Ethiad moved a little. "Here I am."

"Good." Finally, Othron looked round at Weyrn. "Ah, Captain Weyrn."

"It's good to see you awake."

"Thanks to you."

Weyrn smiled. "I'm glad we found the three of you in time. I've sent one of my people to meet up with members of the Duamelti Royal Guard who are also searching for you. With their help it'll be easier to get you back to Duamelti." He glanced around at them. "Gelladar, Ethiad, I'm sure you could walk back with us, but I'd rather not put you at risk again."

"And I couldn't walk," Othron finished with a wan grin. "I don't think any of us will take offence."

Weyrn smiled. "I didn't think you would, but I thought it might be best to explain." He looked round as Celes poked his head into the tent. He was holding the final bowl of soup and Weyrn took it with thanks. "Do you think you can sit up?" he asked Othron. "There's some hot soup here."

Othron licked his lips. "I'll at least make the effort."

He needed help from Gelladar, but once he was sitting up he was able to take the soup and eat. When he was sure of that, Weyrn excused himself, giving the three Wood-elves a moment of privacy.

Maelli was waiting just outside while Celes looked after the fire. Weyrn nodded at them. "I think he'll be fine," he said. "We just have to make sure he stays warm."

Maelli sighed in relief, looking down and running his fingers through his hair. "We can do that."

Now that the fire was no longer needed for a signal, Weyrn and Celes set about collecting branches to build a screen that would reflect heat back towards the tent.

By the time they'd found an armload each of roughly-suitable branches it was starting to get dark. Fortunately, Maelli had not let the fire burn down and they were able to use it to find their way back to the camp: something that would have been easy enough in daylight but was far more difficult in the gathering dusk.

"I hope Derdhel's all right," said Celes, looking at the sky again with a shiver. The clouds that had been waiting all day looked very threatening in the twilight.

"He'll have found somewhere to camp by now," said Weyrn, also looking up. "And that's if he's not already safely with the Royal Guard and able to join their camp." He smiled a little. "He's sensible and knows how to travel in the snow. He'll be all right."

Maelli was making tea and Celes and Weyrn accepted a cup each. Weyrn also took some to Gelladar, who was the only one still awake.

"You should get some rest too," said Weyrn, noting that Gelladar's eyelids were almost visibly drooping.

"I'd prefer to keep an eye on Othron."

"Would you like one of us to sit in here with you?"

Gelladar sighed, cradling the cup in his hands. "Perhaps. I admit I would appreciate sleep."

"I'll ask Celes to wait with you."

"Thank you." Gelladar smiled. "Perhaps we can talk more later."

Weyrn was a little surprised – it seemed an obvious statement – but nodded.

"Celes!" he called as he emerged from the tent. "Would you stay with them and keep an eye on Othron?"

Celes nodded and ducked in, taking his tea with him.

***

It was dark by the time Weyrn and Maelli had finished the screen and they sat down side-by-side by the fire to catch their breaths. It already felt warmer in the space in front of the tent.

Celes stuck his head out and smiled as he saw them.

"How are they?" Weyrn called softly.

Celes emerged. "All right," he said. "They're asleep."

"I'll go and sit with them," said Maelli, getting up. Celes came over to take his place by the fire.

"How soon do you think we'll be able to get home?" he asked.

Weyrn shrugged. "I hope soon." He glanced back towards Duamelti. Apart from anything else, he knew full well it was starting to get close to the baby's time. He wished in passing that he'd stayed behind, but he knew he'd not have wanted to stay behind in warmth and safety and send someone else in his place. "We'll have to wait for the Royal Guard to reach us. Othron may be able to walk soon – he's the one I'm most worried about – but I don't want to push him and a larger group will mean more help should something go wrong."

"Why did he sleep so long?"

Weyrn shook his head. "Honestly, that's something you'll have to ask a healer. I just know that it happens sometimes."

Celes nodded. "How much do Swordmasters talk to Wood-elves?"

"Probably not as much as we should." Weyrn sighed. "To be honest… Tishlondi caused a rift between us."

Celes hugged his knees to his chest. "I always thought Silvren and the Tishlondi Mixed-bloods were on good terms."

"Up until they abandoned us to the Irnianam," said Weyrn bitterly. He glanced sideways at Celes' expression and smiled. "Is that look because I said 'us'?"

"Actually, it's because you said 'Irnianam'. I thought you liked Hurion and the Valley-elves."

"They've changed since coming here. They aren't the same race any more." Weyrn sighed. "Nonetheless, I have to admit I still… don't entirely trust them. None of my predecessors really did, and…" He shook his head. Now was not the time to think of Ninian, his first trainee, who had died when denied a healer by a Valley-elven regent. "I have my reasons. But they're better than the Irnianam." He ran a hand absently though his long hair. It was only a little way past his shoulders, but even that would have been too long in Tishlondi. "But Silvren had been our ally and left us to our fate."

"I asked because Gelladar wanted to talk to you at greater length, as well as to Hurion," said Celes softly.

Weyrn remembered that Gelladar had mentioned that, and looked round. "That's interesting," he mused. "It would be good to patch it up, I admit. It… has been some time."

"You can't hold onto it forever," said Celes earnestly.

Weyrn smiled at him. "You're a child of Duamelti as I never was," he said, reaching over to pat Celes on the shoulder.

"Your son will be, though."

"I suppose so." Weyrn looked back into the fire, smiling at the thought. His child would be a Duamelti elf: a Duamelti Mixed-blood. He would be at home here as Weyrn never truly had been, rather than an incomer. That was something he'd always wanted for himself, and at least he could give it to his child.

The next morning, Gelladar was pleased to find that Othron was recovering well; he was able to sit up without help and eat the food that Celes brought them.

"How do you feel, Othron?" Ethiad asked: a question he'd asked several times.

Othron sighed. "Well enough," he said tolerantly. He glanced over at Gelladar. "I didn't expect to see the Swordmasters here."

Gelladar shook his head. Whenever he and Othron had visited in the past, they and the Swordmasters had kept their distance, using Hurion almost as an intermediary. This might be an opportunity to change that, since Weyrn had taken the step of agreeing to come and help them.

A sudden desire to reassure himself made him reach out and touch Othron's hand. The older elf seemed to understand; he smiled a little.

"I'm all right," he said softly.

"I know, I just... it was close."

Ethiad shifted uncomfortably and Othron's smile widened to a grin. "You were right, though: we probably shouldn't have left the road."

"Or we should have started looking for other elves as *soon* as we realised we couldn't handle the snow," said Ethiad.

Gelladar shook his head. "I still think we did the right thing by staying away. We don't know what we might have found."

"I know what we nearly did find," said Ethiad dryly.

"Either way," said Othron, "We're here." He glanced at Gelladar. "Have you an idea about what we should do next?"

"I think we've been given an opportunity." Gelladar glanced at Ethiad. "How much do you know about the Swordmasters?"

Ethiad shook his head a little. "They're a powerful Mixed-blood group that isn't under the jurisdiction of the king of Duamelti."

Othron nodded. "But more so: they're entirely separate. Duamelti is more like two realms than one."

"And Silvren only has a relationship with one," said Ethiad. "Why?"

Gelladar shook his head. "An old bitterness from a long time before you were born, when we were at war with the Irnianam in Tishlondi."

Ethiad nodded. "Before the Mixed-bloods killed them all," he said, glancing towards the door.

"Careful what you say to the Swordmasters about that," said Othron, raising a hand. "Gelladar's right: there's a lot of bitterness on the matter."

He glanced at Gelladar. "It may be time for us to take a step, though."

Gelladar nodded. That had been his thought, and it seemed the right time; they had the opportunity to talk to the Swordmasters on neutral ground, after all. Personally, he believed that stories of the massacre in Tishlondi had been greatly exaggerated. Certainly, Ethiad was wrong about the Mixed-bloods having killed all the Irnianam; Irnianin blood flowed in King Hurion's veins, after all.

They looked up as there was movement at the door of the tent, and Maelli poked his head in, smiling.

"Everything all right?" he asked.

Gelladar automatically glanced around at the others before he smiled and replied, "Doing well, thank you."

"Mind if I come in?"

Gelladar shook his head and Maelli ducked into the tent, sitting down near the entrance.

"We're sorry about the delay," he said, glancing back towards the outside.

"It's mostly my fault," said Othron. "I'm sure without an invalid to worry about we could all have long been on our way."

Maelli grinned a little, but shook his head. "We'd probably have stayed a little longer in any case, just to be sure." He glanced around at them and his voice dropped a little in tone. "The last thing we want is having to stop again once we've started."

Gelladar nodded. There was no point in giving up a settled camping place when they had one.

"Where's Captain Weyrn?" he asked. "I'd like a word with him."

"He went to find some more firewood," said Maelli. "I can let you know when he returns, if you like."

"I'd appreciate it."

Maelli nodded. "How are your ears?" he asked Ethiad.

Ethiad twitched, but managed to stop himself touching the frostbite. "Painful, but well enough," he said softly.

"The Royal Guard will have a healer with them who can check the damage."

Ethiad nodded gratefully.

After an awkward pause, Maelli said, "I've been wondering: why didn't you stay on the road? It would have made it much easier to find you."

Gelladar was not someone inclined to hide his own mistakes – his kingdom's, maybe, but never his own – and he laughed a little. "I thought it would be a good idea to seek shelter among the trees."

Maelli smiled slightly, but then said, "You went a long way. We were following your trail for a while."

Gelladar shook his head. "After that first night we tried to get back to the road, but couldn't find our way. All we could do was search for help or shelter."

"Until I couldn't go any further," Othron put in softly.

Gelladar patted him on the shoulder. "Perhaps we should have sought help from the Mixed-bloods," he said carefully, not wanting to voice their doubts on how helpful they would have been.

Maelli nodded. "We considered that you might have done and had asked around a little."

Gelladar nodded. "They might have seen something of us, at least."

"Exactly." Maelli glanced out of the tent. "Ah. Weyrn's back. Shall I go and tell him you want to talk to him?"

"If you would," said Gelladar. "I'll be out in a moment."

Maelli nodded, smiled at the other two and ducked out of the tent again.

Gelladar glanced at Othron, who nodded. "I think you know what you're doing," he said.

Gelladar certainly hoped so. "If I need help, I'll ask for you, Ethiad, so be ready."

Ethiad nodded, touching his ear absently. "Good luck!"

Gelladar left the tent and went over to where Weyrn and Maelli were standing by the fire. Weyrn saw him coming and waved. He smiled back.

"Maelli tells me you three are doing well," said Weyrn as Gelladar walked up.

"We are indeed. Thank you again."

"He also said you wanted to talk to me. Care to sit?" Weyrn gestured to a log beside the fire as Maelli left.

Gelladar sat down and automatically reached out to warm his hands. Weyrn sat next to him, waiting in silence for him to speak first. He paused to gather his thoughts.

"We've not spoken at any length before," he said slowly.

Weyrn shook his head. After a moment, he smiled, a long scar on his cheek twisting strangely. "You and I, or Silvren and the Swordmasters?"

"Well, you and I have never spoken before," said Gelladar lightly. "I was referring to Silvren and the Swordmasters."

Weyrn shook his head again. "Barely at all since I became a Swordmaster."

"There are Mixed-bloods living near Silvren, but I've never had much contact even with them."

"Nor have I, actually. We sometimes go there, but I myself have only been once or twice, and I never went into Silvren itself."

Gelladar nodded. "I'm not even sure I'd describe it as antagonism."

"More indifference," agreed Weyrn. "Wary, perhaps, but still just indifference."

At least it seemed that they were on the same page. "I'd like to change that," said Gelladar.

Weyrn looked at him in silence for a moment, then nodded. "I'd like that too," he said thoughtfully. He smiled. "And I appreciate your approaching me about it now."

"Rather than in Duamelti?" Gelladar guessed.

Weyrn nodded.

"You're an independent group. It's fitting that I should come to you separately from Lord Hurion."

Weyrn grinned, but then sobered again. "Would Lord Taffilelti agree to this? Surely you're only empowered to speak to Lord Hurion."

Gelladar was pretty much certain that Taffilelti would approve, and nodded. "I think he'll agree."

"There's... been bad blood in the past," said Weyrn carefully, after a pause.

Gelladar thought carefully about what to say to that. He was sure Weyrn was referring to Tishlondi, but he didn't want to assume it. "Between Swordmasters and Silvren, or between Silvren and... other Mixed-bloods?"

Weyrn smiled a little, humourlessly. "Tishlondi."

"That was a long time ago."

"There are Piskam – Mixed-blood elves from Tishlondi – in Duamelti still."

"They fled after we made peace with the Irnianam?"

"And after the Kinslaying itself," said Weyrn, looking away. He took a deep breath and looked back at Gelladar. "That alliance... would you be prepared to discuss it in more detail?"

Gelladar didn't think he knew enough about it. It was before he'd even been born and he'd had no special instruction. "I would be prepared to listen to stories, but I can't talk about our side of the matter."

Weyrn nodded. "It would be good to be able to discuss it."

"I understand that, especially as it's caused a rift between us for so long."

"Given that, I'm especially glad you acknowledge that the Swordmasters are not under the command of the Ir-" Weyrn almost visibly caught himself. "The Valley-elves."

Gelladar frowned. "The Irnianam? Surely they were defeated."

"Some survived," said Weyrn with a shrug. "And given our history with them, it's a sore spot."

"That does answer one question, though," said Gelladar, remembering Ethiad's words about the massacre. "Many in Silvren believe the Mixed-bloods killed all the Irnianam."

Weyrn blinked. "We did not!" he snapped.

"I thought it unlikely," said Gelladar, doing his best to soothe him.

Weyrn nodded a little. "Many did die, but many made it to Duamelti and settled there."

"Ah… and became the Valley-elves? I thought they were of the same roots."

"The very same." Weyrn shook his head. "If we're going to discuss it, though, I can find people who were there."

That did seem more helpful than just trading rumours, and Gelladar nodded. "That might be best."

"I'll try to organise something while you're in Duamelti."

"I'd appreciate it." Gelladar absently rubbed at a dry spot on his hand, where the cold had got to him, and said, "I will have to discuss this with my king, but for my part I would be pleased to forge a link with you."

Weyrn smiled. "I will talk about it with my friends, but I can say that I'm pleased to have the opportunity." He held out a hand. Gelladar clasped it with a sigh of relief. That had gone far better than he'd dared to expect.

After another day had passed, Weyrn was starting to get worried about Derdhel. He walked around the edge of their camp and looked hard into the snowy woods, hoping to see some sign that the other Swordmaster was on his way back with the Royal Guards. Perhaps he hadn't been gone for an unreasonable length of time, but Weyrn was worried nonetheless.

"Something's wrong," said Gelladar softly, stepping up beside him.

Weyrn glanced at him and sighed, nodding. "I was hoping Derdhel would be back by now."

Gelladar also looked out into the woods. "How much longer can we stay here?"

"Another couple of days. Then we'll have to move." Weyrn wasn't happy with the idea of keeping the three Wood-elves out too much longer and they were fast running out of supplies. In any case, although he didn't think there were any threats to them nearby, he didn't want to take the risk for too much longer.

"If it snows again…"

"We'll dig the tent out." Weyrn smiled sideways at him. "Don't worry. We'll keep looking after you."

"Thank you." Gelladar smiled, his shoulders relaxing a little.

"How's Othron?"

"Doing well. I think he could travel again."

"If we do move on before help gets here, we'll take it carefully and not rush you."

"I appreciate that." Gelladar looked back at the forest. "I'm still recovering, just as the others are." He sighed. "We should have planned more carefully."

Weyrn patted him on the shoulder. "It worked out," he said, smiling. "You made it far enough that we found you."

Gelladar smiled a little, but then asked, "When did you meet the Guard?"

"Soon after we left Duamelti."

"Then surely it would take a couple of days for Derdhel to find them again? And then the same again to get back here?" Gelladar smiled again, tilting his head a little as he looked sidelong at Weyrn. "I think there's a deadline pressing you."

Weyrn laughed a little, running a hand through his hair. "You're probably right about the first, and I admit the second. Still, I know Derdhel, and he'll have been heading straight back to the road rather than taking a wandering path."

Gelladar nodded. "Do you mind if I ask what the deadline is?"

"My wife's pregnant, and they said the baby would come around this time. We probably have another week or two, but these things are never sure…"

"I know. Congratulations, though." Gelladar patted Weyrn on the shoulder. "And… thank you again for coming for us at such a time."

Weyrn smiled back at him. "I wasn't going to leave you to freeze."

Gelladar nodded and looked around, about to say something else. Then he frowned, leaning forward. "Do you see that?"

Weyrn looked round and saw movement between the trees. He narrowed his eyes to focus better, then laughed as he recognised the form of an elf, making his way towards the camp. He'd not spotted him at first because his dark clothes and face and silvery hair blended with his surroundings. Now that he did see him, it was clearly Derdhel.

"There's Derdhel, at last." Weyrn waved at him.

Gelladar nodded. "And he'll have others with him?"

"I'm going to go and meet him. Wait here."

Gelladar nodded again and stepped back as Weyrn set out.

Indeed, it was Derdhel. He looked tired, but smiled as Weyrn came up to him.

"They're coming along behind me," he said. "Sorry I was delayed. It took some time to find them."

Weyrn nodded. "I was starting to get worried, but you made fair time and it's good to see you."

Soon, the little clearing contained several more tents. There were only a dozen Royal Guard members, but it seemed like more after Weyrn had spent a few days with a small group.

The Guards' healer was finally able to inspect Ethiad's frostbite and make sure Othron really was recovering properly. Fortunately, it seemed that he was. The healer did, however, say that Ethiad was going to be scarred.

When he heard that, Ethiad sighed deeply and rubbed his ears. Weyrn touched his hand and he pulled it away.

"I suppose I shouldn't be surprised," he said sullenly. "It hurt badly enough that I should have suspected it."

Weyrn nodded. "We'll help you keep it from getting worse, at least."

Ethiad raised an eyebrow at him. "As long as I don't rub them?"

Weyrn grinned and patted him on the shoulder. "You're learning."

"I'd hope so." Ethiad's hand twitched and he forced himself to lower it. "They're setting up camp. Aren't we heading on to Duamelti?"

Weyrn shook his head. "We have to stay another night; we'd not get far before dark and since there's a camp established here, we might as well use it." He fought the urge to look back towards Duamelti.

"Will it snow again?"

"Not tonight, I don't think."

"If it does tomorrow…"

"We'll take care of you." Weyrn patted him on the shoulder again and left the tent.

"How soon can we move on?" he asked the healer when he saw her.

She looked up from the salve she was making and frowned thoughtfully. "Probably tomorrow. We'll need to take it a bit more slowly than we did on the way out, but they're strong enough."

"Good. I was thinking they'd be able to travel soon." Weyrn looked towards Duamelti. "We'll set off tomorrow, then."

She nodded. "I think they could have moved a few days ago had it been strictly necessary. They were exhausted and had been hungry, but they've recovered well from that."

"All right. Tomorrow, then."

Again, she nodded and went back to her work.

Weyrn went to the edge of the camp nearest to Duamelti and looked into the forest. He was starting to worry about being back in time, but if they weren't delayed it would be all right. He smiled at the thought and went back to join the others.

"You think we can make it?" asked Maelli.

"We'll leave tomorrow, so I expect so, if we aren't delayed."

"If we are, I can take over. We have enough company to help, so don't make yourself late. There's no need."

Weyrn smiled. "I appreciate that. Thank you."

***

They set out the next morning in a group. Weyrn and Derdhel led the way while Maelli and Celes brought up the rear. The Royal Guard had taken over the job of minding the three ambassadors.

Weyrn couldn't help noticing that they were moving slowly. Perhaps it was the larger group, or the thicker snow, but it seemed to take forever to cover a distance he and the other Swordmasters had taken minutes to walk.

Derdhel noticed the way he kept looking over his shoulder and smiled a little. "We're going too slowly for you?"

"I know we can't rush, but…"

"It'll be all right. You'll get back."

"Well, I'd rather that be *before* Alatani has the baby. I want to be there."

Derdhel shrugged a little. Weyrn huffed a breath through his teeth.

"You have *got* to stop that."

"Stop what?"

"Being indifferent to other people."

Derdhel's eyes widened in shock and confusion. "But –"

"I know you look at things like life and death and time differently, but you *must* realise that we don't all think like you do!" Weyrn kept his voice down with an effort.

Derdhel was still staring at him. "Is this about what I said about Othron…?"

"Among other things."

"But it's true: had he died, it was meant to be and there was nothing we could do."

Weyrn ran a hand through his hair. "Perhaps, but it was a callous thing to say to his friends. You should have just left it at the fact that we were doing all we could."

Derdhel frowned. "And not prepare them for what might happen?"

"I'm sure they were perfectly aware that he might die. Afraid of it, in fact." Weyrn raised a hand to forestall Derdhel's objection. "And, for most of us, it is something to be feared."

Derdhel sighed and looked away, shaking his head a little. "Well, I'm sorry," he said softly.

Weyrn fought the urge to roll his eyes. He didn't think he'd managed to get Derdhel to understand it this time either. "And although I know that if I miss my child's birth he'll still be there when I arrive, I want to be there."

Derdhel just nodded.

"Look at it this way: Alatani will be happier if I'm there. It'll make her feel better and probably make it easier."

Derdhel did smile at that. "That makes more sense than most explanations you try on me."

Weyrn laughed a little. "Well, I'm glad about that, at least."

They walked on in silence apart from occasional comments on the road and the weather until lunchtime. Then, as they were eating, Weyrn noticed that the clouds were starting to lower again.

"I think it's going to snow this afternoon," he said, his heart sinking.

Several other elves looked up. From where he was sitting, Weyrn noticed Ethiad drawing his cloak closer around himself while Othron looked genuinely scared. Ekelid studied the cloud for a moment, then nodded. "We'll wait until it's over," he said, then glanced at Weyrn. "Do you agree?"

Weyrn sighed. "It might be best. We've time to get tents up, anyway."

As they were pitching tents, Maelli came over to Weyrn.

"You go on," he said. "We're already moving slowly and this will delay us further."

Weyrn glanced towards Duamelti. "You're sure?"

"Yes. Go on. I'll make your excuses."

Weyrn shook his head at that and went over to Ekelid.

"Captain Ekelid?"

"Yes?" He looked up from the patch of ground he was clearing for a tent.

"I have to head on alone. I'm leaving Maelli in charge in my place."

Ekelid frowned. "Why? Shouldn't you at least wait until the snow's passed?"

Weyrn just shook his head. "It can't wait."

"Well…" Ekelid looked up at the clouds. "Are you sure you'll be all right?"

"Yes."

"All right, then." Ekelid sighed. "Good luck."

Weyrn smiled, grasped Ekelid's hand, and went to gather his pack.

"You're going?" asked Celes, hurrying up.

"Yes. I can make some progress even if it's snowing."

"I hope she's all right."

"I'm sure she will be." Weyrn smiled. "Where's Derdhel?"

"He went to gather wood." Celes looked round. "I don't know how he plans to light a fire in the snow, but perhaps when we're getting ready to set off again…"

Weyrn nodded. "Let him know I'm gone, would you?"

"I will."

Maelli was talking to Gelladar, and Weyrn went over to say goodbye to him as well.

"I'm going to continue on my own," he said. He couldn't help smiling as he added, "That deadline is still pressing me."

Gelladar nodded. "Congratulations again, and good luck. I'll see you when we get to Duamelti."

Weyrn nodded. "Goodbye for the present," he said, and grasped Gelladar's hand. Then, at last, he turned and hurried into the forest.

Alone, he could travel faster than with a group, and he made good time for a while, picking his way between trees and drifts. His feet sank a little way into the snow, but not enough to seriously slow him.

Nonetheless, it was tiring work, and his heart sank as the first few flakes of snow began to fall. He was going to have to find somewhere to camp.

He frowned a little as he paused and looked around. Perhaps, if the snow didn't get too heavy, he could keep going. It was a risk, but he wanted to get home as early as he could. He could find shelter in a hurry if it got much worse or he needed to stop and rest. It wasn't as though he was having to look after someone else as well now; he could afford to take more risks.

He decided to keep going until it began to get dark, and plunged on.

As he went, the snow was growing heavier in the air and thicker on the ground and he had to pause again after only a short amount of time. The soft, fluffy new snow collecting around his feet was far harder to walk on than the more packed snow underneath it and he didn't think he was going to be able to walk much further before he was worn out and had to rest.

He sighed. He wanted to hurry on, but he knew that he would be much more vulnerable to the cold if he exhausted himself. He'd keep going, but stop at the next promising piece of shelter and wait out the storm.

He had to laugh at himself. He'd probably gained a couple of miles on the rest of the group. Perhaps it would have been better had he stayed with them. There was no time to regret it now, though, and he started walking again. He was still more manoeuvrable, not having a tent, so he could start off again as soon as the snow thinned. It would be hours before night fell.

He pulled his hood a little closer around his face and huddled into it to keep the snow from blowing down his neck. Every now and then there was a gust of wind and he had to clutch the loose cloth around himself to get any benefit from it, but when it did break the wind it was fairly warm. His own exertion helped there. Still, he looked about as he walked for somewhere to shelter.

As time passed and nothing suitable caught his eye, he was starting to get worried. The snow was still deepening and it was getting harder to walk as the wind continued to strengthen. He needed to rest.

He stopped and turned his back to the wind to catch his breath. Looking around, the forest looked like a wilderness of flying snow, but then something caught his eye. He shaded his eyes and squinted, trying to make out its shape. It looked like a low building, half buried already. It was worth a look; if nothing else, he might shelter beside it.

He picked his way over, careful not to slip and fall into any drifts. As he got closer, the building became clearer and he smiled. It looked like a hunting blind, built from stone and roofed with branches. It would certainly do as a place to rest for a few hours.

He looked in and was a little startled to see a small campfire already burning in the middle of the room. A human was bending over it, though now he was looking at Weyrn with an equally startled expression.

"Mind if I join you?" asked Weyrn. "I just need somewhere to wait out the worst of the storm."

"It's still getting worse?" asked the human, beckoning him in.

"The wind's picking up. I'm hoping it'll blow itself out in a couple of hours."

The human nodded, stretching. "I'm glad I knew about this place. I came straight here as soon as it started." He stretched again and offered Weyrn a hand. "My name's Merthas."

Weyrn took it. "Weyrn."

"Pleasure to meet you." Merthas poked at the fire as Weyrn set down his pack and sat down. "So, what brings you out here?"

"I'm on my way home to Duamelti," said Weyrn, absently stretching his hands towards the fire.

"Horrible weather to travel in," said Merthas, nodding towards the doorway.

"That it is, but I'm trying to get back quickly." Weyrn smiled. "My wife's going to have our baby soon."

Merthas grinned. "That is a good reason. Congratulations."

Weyrn smiled. "Thanks. How about you?"

Merthas patted a bundle in the corner of the shelter. "This was supposed to be a three-hour trip to check our fish traps."

Weyrn grimaced in sympathy. "At least it looks like it wasn't entirely fruitless."

"There is that." Merthas looked back at the door. "I hope this doesn't last much longer, though. It's cold enough that the fish'll keep, but my daughter will be worrying."

"Have you far to go?"

"Far enough in snow. It's probably a mile and it'll drift past my knees." Merthas made a frustrated noise. "At least it shouldn't be too hard to find my way."

"That's good. It's bad weather to be lost in." Weyrn hitched his cloak a little closer around his shoulders and leaned back against his pack.

"You look tired."

"It's been a long week."

Merthas grinned. "You'd best get used to it, with a new baby on the way. Unless little elves are better-behaved?"

"They wake in the night and need to be fussed over, if that's what you mean?" said Weyrn uncertainly.

"That sort of thing, yes. Will your wife take charge of that?"

"I'll help, of course, but I've heard mothers often find it easier than fathers to comfort their babies."

"Don't try that on your wife."

Weyrn smiled. "I've no intention of it."

That made Merthas laugh. "Ah, my Grete was a terror to me after Maidre was born. I wish you all the luck in the world, and advise you to humour your wife." He smiled. "Whatever she might have to say about you."

Weyrn forced another smile, though he was beginning to get rather nervous. "Thank you."

***

As Weyrn had predicted, the storm only lasted a couple of hours and the two men were able to leave their shelter. Their routes lay together for about half a mile and Weyrn hung back to keep Merthas company, despite his hurry. The human plodded gamely through the snow, throwing the occasional jibe at the fact that Weyrn barely sunk into it a few inches, even after offering to help carry the fish.

At last, though, they parted ways with good wishes. Weyrn wished Merthas luck in getting home – fortunately, it wasn't much further – and headed for Duamelti, half turning to wave. Merthas waved back and started off up the snow-covered road.

Weyrn knew he'd not make it back to Duamelti that day. He was taking a straighter route than they'd used on the way out, but it was still a long way and the storm had delayed him. He had about another hour before he would have to look for somewhere to stay the night.

He sighed. Maybe he should have stayed back at the hunting blind.

He dismissed that thought, though. An hour was an hour, and he could cover a couple more miles.

He picked his way between the drifts, keeping as straight as he could towards the tops of the hills. The ground was gradually sloping up now, and he had to be careful not to slip. Still, he was glad to see the uphill slope. It meant he was getting closer.

He came upon a relatively clear path through the trees and decided this was as good a time as any to turn towards the road that led through the pass. Something had tramped through the snow here before the last fall and it wasn't too deep. He walked quickly along the snow-covered trail, glancing to the right every now and then to make sure he wasn't getting further from the border.

He was almost at the road by the time it started to really get dark. The clouds were clearing and it was also getting colder, the air nipping bitterly at his exposed skin. He paused, looking around, and rubbed his hands absently up and down his arms. He'd stop at the next sheltered place. He had a good idea of his own strength, but he didn't want to take too many risks; he didn't know what he might meet tomorrow.

He found shelter in the lee of a large fallen tree: just enough to lie down in. He wrapped himself in cloak and blanket and resolved to make the best of it, taking some food from his pack.

Even after he'd eaten, he couldn't sleep; he kept shivering. No matter how hard he tried to warm himself up, he could feel the warmth leeching out into the chill ground and air.

At last, he got up, rubbing his arms, and set out again.

He was shivering bitterly, but knew he'd warm up faster walking than lying down. There was one good thing about the relatively clear night: there was a moon, and there was enough space between the trees for the light to filter down. The snow made everything brighter and he hitched his cloak a little closer around his shoulders, determined. He was going to get home as fast as he could.

He was near exhaustion after a couple more hours' walking, and he paused on his feet, his eyelids drooping. The road was getting steeper and he needed to get some sleep. Keeping warm was wearing him out.

Still, he'd not forgotten how cold it had been behind that tree. He gritted his teeth, shook his head and carried on.

At last, he crested the hill. Duamelti was a beautiful sight, spread out before his feet under its blanket of snow, dark and quiet; it was well past the middle of the night and there were no lights in the city or any of the little settlements scattered around the valley. Weyrn sat down on a rock with a sigh, his breath misting before his eyes. He felt his eyelids droop again, but shook his head. Considering how far he'd come, it was hardly any distance to the Guardhouse. He'd sleep when he got there.

He still had a little food with him and ate it; he was almost home and didn't need to save it any more, and he knew he needed it. Then he got up with a sigh and started off down the hill.

The snow was already lighter on this side, as they'd noticed on the way out. It was slippery, though, and he had to walk slowly. Even so, he was too sleepy to watch himself properly and slipped twice, landing hard. Both times, he stumbled up, cursing, and carried on.

He was almost home; the slope was flattening out and he quickened his pace, thinking of the warmth of the Guardhouse. There were only a couple more hours left before people would be starting to wake. He hoped he'd not startle anyone by arriving so early in the morning…

He'd picked up his pace still more without thinking about it and wasn't looking where he put his feet. Suddenly, one foot landed on an icy patch under the fresh snow and he slipped. As he tried to catch himself, a bolt of pain shot up his other leg. He landed hard in the snow and lay still a moment, gasping.

"Damn," he muttered. His ankle was throbbing and he wondered how badly it was injured. "Damn, damn, *damn*." On the final word he punched the snow.

He wasn't going to get back as soon as he'd thought, it seemed. He pushed himself up, leaning on a tree, and looked down at his ankle. There was nothing visibly wrong and he put weight on that foot gingerly. It hurt, but he was sure he could hobble on it. He shook his head. There was little choice, really. After all, it was cold out here, he was tired, and it would be hours before anyone came by.

He sighed, winced in anticipated pain, and started to walk again.

Fortunately, he'd been right: the ankle was just about weight-bearing. It sent lightning up his leg every time he put his foot down and he moved as fast as he could to get the weight back onto his good foot, but he could limp.

He cursed with every step, berating himself for not watching his feet. Hobbling was very tiring, and doing so on no sleep was even worse. Still, it wasn't far now before he'd be home. He'd have to stick to the road until he was almost there, then he could cut a corner through the trees. Then he could rest the injured ankle in front of a fire and get some sleep in the warmth. He still didn't regret his decision to leave the shelter of that fallen tree. He was convinced he would have frozen there.

He limped on for two hours. By that time, he was starting to wonder if his good leg was going to fall off; the extra work he was heaping on it had made it ache terribly. He turned off the road once he was on the flat and started through the trees towards the Guardhouse. Under the trees, the snow was actually thinner, though it was much darker there and he had to be careful. Once he knocked against a tree and it deposited its whole load of snow onto him. After that, he learned to avoid the trunks.

At last he pushed aside a snowy pine branch – having shaken it clear first – and found himself looking across the clear space to the Guardhouse. There was a tramped path to the door already, clearly visible in the growing light, and he smiled. It seemed someone was up.

Hope and gratitude that he'd made it home carried him across the clear space, and he let himself in as quietly as he could.

"Weyrn?" asked a startled voice. Seri was sitting by the fire, nursing a cup of tea.

"Good morning," said Weyrn, smiling at him. He hoped the smile came out properly and wasn't as grimace-like as it felt.

"What…" Seri scrambled up, looking Weyrn up and down with a shocked expression. "What happened? Where are the others?"

"They had to stop and camp when we were hit by a snowstorm yesterday, around noon. I pressed on alone because I wanted to make sure I was back in good time." Weyrn looked around. The Guardhouse was remarkably quiet, even given how early in the morning it was. "Speaking of which, where is everyone?"

"What have you done to your leg?" Seri asked at the same time, moving over to help Weyrn stand without leaning on the doorframe.

"I slipped on some ice. I've twisted my ankle." Weyrn leaned on Seri's shoulder and started to limp over to a couch. "But where is everyone? Not up yet?"

Seri looked around, then took a deep breath and said, "They're at the healing house."

Weyrn felt a sudden shock go through him. All his tiredness vanished in an instant. "What?"

Seri stepped away. "You should have something to eat before you go anywhere."

"Seri!" protested Weyrn.

Seri grimaced. "The baby started early this morning."

Weyrn scrambled to his feet, catching himself on the arm of the couch as he almost fell.

Seri raised his hands. "Stay there! You can't walk down there on that leg. It'll be hours yet."

"I thought it was supposed to be *days* yet!"

"When we took her down there, they said we were very early and she still had a long time to go." Seri pushed Weyrn back onto the couch. "Stay here, rest, eat some breakfast. A friend of mine has a pony and sled I can borrow; that's how we got her down there. I'll go and get it, and take you down."

Weyrn started to protest. He didn't want to sit here and wait, but Seri cut him off.

"I'll not let you walk all the way to the city," he said firmly. "Not with a twisted ankle. Stay there." He passed Weyrn a plate with some bread and honey. "Promise me you'll not do anything stupid."

Weyrn sighed, but he had to admit that even now his ankle was throbbing mercilessly. "All right. I promise. But hurry!"

***

It seemed to take Seri forever to come back with the cart. Weyrn finished his breakfast and sat on the edge of the couch, twitching with nerves. He wanted to get up and pace, but on the one occasion he tried his ankle felt like it was in a vice.

"Come on," he muttered, tapping his fingers on his knees. "Damn it, Seri, did you stop for tea or something?"

At last, he saw Seri arrive on the clear space outside. At once, he got up, gritting his teeth against the pain in his ankle, and hobbled to the door.

Seri looked round and sighed. "Sit on the sled," he said, pointing. "We can only go so fast on this snow, but it'll be fine."

Weyrn sat down and pulled his cloak around himself, feeling slightly ridiculous. Seri smiled and clicked at the horse to urge it forward.

Weyrn was glad that the road down into the city was empty. Even when they got there, there was nobody around. They were probably all still in bed, or eating breakfast inside before going out to face the snow. Weyrn hugged the cloak around himself a little more closely. Sitting still, he got cold much more quickly than he had walking.

The pony was moving so slowly that Weyrn toyed with the idea of insisting on walking. Surely even on his injured ankle he could be faster. He quelled the urge, though; he knew that wasn't true and would just lead to a time-wasting argument with Seri.

Still, he heaved a sigh of relief as they finally arrived at the healing house.

He scrambled off the sled with Seri's help and limped to the door. One of the healers' assistants came out to greet them.

"Captain Weyrn?" she asked, looking startled. "I thought you were away."

"I hurried back," he said, pausing with his bad foot off the ground. "Am I too late…?"

"No, she's got a little while to go yet. The midwife is with her."

Weyrn sighed in relief and leaned more heavily on Seri as the panic drained out of him. "Good. Thanks."

"I told you," said Seri, smiling a little. "Come on, let's get you inside."

The assistant looked at his foot. "Are you injured?"

"I slipped on some ice."

"We'll have a look at it while you wait," she said, making way so they could get through the doorway.

They took Weyrn down several corridors to one of the private rooms. The assistant knocked on the door and Neithan answered.

"Hello, Weyrn," he said, smiling. "She'll be pleased to hear you're back in time."

"So will I," said Weyrn, accepting help to go in and sit down on the bench in the anteroom.

"What have you done to yourself?"

"Twisted my ankle, I think."

"I'll go and tell her you're here," said the assistant, and she slipped into the inner room.

"I'll go and take that pony back." Seri smiled a little. "And I'll keep an eye on the Guardhouse."

"Thanks," said Weyrn fervently. "Sorry I gave you a hard time when I arrived."

Seri nodded. "You're worried. I understand. How far behind are the others?"

"They were moving slowly – it might be a few days yet."

"All right. I'll keep an eye out anyway."

Weyrn nodded and Seri left.

The assistant came back out of the inner room, smiling a little. "She says you took long enough, but she takes it from the fact that you're back that things went well."

Weyrn nodded again. "She's all right?"

"Doing well. We'll let you know how things are going."

"Thanks."

"All right. Let's have a look at your ankle?"

Weyrn sighed a little. He still felt jittery, but there was nothing he could do now. He was there, and she knew he was there, and now he just had to wait.

Neithan put a hand on his shoulder, making him jump.

"Are you going to let her see what you've done to your ankle?" he asked with a grin.

Weyrn shook his head. "Yes, sorry." He started to unlace his boot carefully. Every time his ankle shifted it hurt, but he gritted his teeth and finished with the laces. He gripped the edge of the bench, trying not to yelp, as the assistant eased the boot off his foot, and let out a sigh once it was done.

"Can you describe the pain?" she asked.

He was about to reply when he heard a yell from the inner room. He startled to his feet and almost fell, but Neithan caught him.

"She's fine," said the assistant, getting up. "She'll be all right."

Weyrn sighed, relaxing a little. "You're sure?"

"Yes, I've sat in on births before."

Weyrn let Neithan help him sit back down.

He couldn't really concentrate on what anyone was saying to him; his mind kept weaving between exhaustion from the long journey without sleep and quickened excitement with energy that couldn't go anywhere. He kept shifting on the bench, much to the increasing annoyance of the assistant trying to strap up his twisted ankle.

"Weyrn," said Neithan sharply. Weyrn startled and Neithan grinned a little. "Are you listening?"

Weyrn shook his head, flinching as he heard Alatani cry out again.

"Are you sure she's all right?"

The assistant went back in to check and was back in a minute or two. "She's doing fine."

Weyrn winced as Alatani screamed several curse words. "That doesn't sound fine," he said, his voice a little higher-pitched than he'd have liked.

"Really, she'll be all right. This is perfectly normal." The assistant glanced over her shoulder. "Though I've never heard anyone swear *quite* that much."

"I have," said Weyrn, "When they're in a *lot* of pain!"

Neithan put his hand on Weyrn's shoulder again. "They explained this to me when it looked like I was going to be the only one here: having a baby does hurt, and that doesn't mean anything's going wrong."

"Can I go and talk to her?"

"No," said the assistant. "You can't go in until she's done."

Weyrn was convinced he heard a note of accusation in her voice. "I'd have got back earlier if I could..."

"I'm not denying that, sir, but the fact remains that you can't go in."

Weyrn buried his face in his hands, feeling suddenly very tired. Hearing Alatani scream again made him whimper in sympathy.

It seemed to go on forever. No matter what he heard, or what he said, the assistant kept telling him everything was fine. Neithan put an arm around his shoulders and kept him sitting on the bench, adding his own reassurances, though he sounded rather more worried than the assistant did.

Suddenly, though, Weyrn heard something new. It took a moment for his weary senses to recognise it: the sound of a baby crying.

He gasped, looking up. The assistant had gone to check what was happening. He looked over at Neithan, who smiled. "That sounds hopeful," he said.

Weyrn nodded wordlessly.

Neithan gave him a hug. "We told you she'd be fine."

"Yes... I know, just..."

Inside, the baby had stopped crying. The assistant came back out and Weyrn got up. At once, Neithan moved to help.

"Everything's all right?"

The assistant smiled. "They're both just fine. Congratulations."

"Can I go and see her now?"

"I'll just find you a crutch. Unless Swordmaster Neithan...?"

"I can limp," said Weyrn.

Neithan shook his head a little and Weyrn was about to protest when he told the assistant, "I think it would be best if it were just them first."

Weyrn smiled at him. "Thanks." He looked back at the assistant. "Seriously, I can limp that far. I walked miles on this ankle."

She raised an eyebrow, but then sighed and stepped out of the way. "Go on, then."

Putting his foot down was agony, but Weyrn ignored it as he went in.

The midwife was doing something off to the side, but he ignored her in favour of the woman sitting up in the bed. Alatani looked tousled, sweaty and even more exhausted and drained than Weyrn felt, but she looked up with a wan smile.

"Welcome home."

Weyrn smiled back as he went over. "How are you?"

"I think one is enough for now," she said, looking down at the bundle in her arms.

He kissed her hair. "I'm sorry I cut it so fine."

"Don't worry. At least you're here now."

Finally, Weyrn's full attention went to the baby. All he could see was a very red little face with a button nose and a fuzz of fair hair, the same yellow-blond shade as Weyrn's own.

"Do you want to hold him?" asked Alatani.

Weyrn nodded and carefully took him, careful to support his head as she instructed. Suddenly, as he felt this solid weight in his arms, the idea of having a child seemed much more real. He wasn't sure he was ready for this; it felt like many times more responsibility than he'd ever faced before.

It wasn't just tiredness or pain that made his knees suddenly go weak. He sat down on the bed before he fell down.

"Have you given any thought to a name?" he asked Alatani.

She nodded. "Seregei."

He looked up in some surprise; Seregei was the northern form of Terathi.

"Do you think that's a good idea?" he asked carefully.

She nodded and reached out to touch his face with one hand, laying the other on the baby's head. "Either you and he have nothing to fear from being Terathi's descendants, or – and I prefer to believe this – he died a hero. After all, that's what you are."

Weyrn smiled a little, looking down at the baby again. "I…"

"Of course, if it makes you that uncomfortable…"

Weyrn shook his head a little, still looking at the baby. His son.

His mother had had a terrible time because of who his father was. He'd come to the Swordmasters in the first place because he didn't think anyone else would have anything to do with them. He was still wary of letting anyone know his ancestry. Was this really a good idea?

But it wasn't as if he was directly naming the child after his father. Would it be so obvious to anyone who didn't already have the connection in his mind? Neithan hadn't even known about it and he couldn't be the only one. To those who would harass the child, it would probably be enough that he was *Weyrn's* son.

The words made his heart skip a beat. His son.

He gently stroked the soft hair with the tip of one finger.

"Hello, Seregei," he whispered, and saw Alatani grin out of the corner of his eye.

Seregei opened impossibly-huge blue eyes and stared at Weyrn. He looked almost indignant at having been woken.

"Say hello to your daddy, Seregei," giggled Alatani, leaning forward a little to rest her head on Weyrn's shoulder, putting her arm around him.

Seregei yawned and closed his eyes again.

Weyrn turned to look at Alatani and kissed her hair again. "I'll teach him the flute," he whispered. "Maybe he'll be better at it than Neithan."

"I hope so," she said, hugging him.

Again, he kissed her. "I love you."

She smiled. "I love you too."

Gelladar breathed a sigh of relief as they finally crested the final hill and looked down into Duamelti. Though he'd been to the valley several times, he thought this was the best it had ever looked. He could see Lord Hurion's palace from this vantage point and smiled; It would be good to have a really warm place to sleep and a proper roof over his head.

He glanced round at the rest of the group. Ethiad and Othron were flagging a little, but overall had held up well. He was especially glad that Othron seemed to have recovered so thoroughly. Apparently he'd need more time to rest when they arrived, but then would be back to normal.

"How long do you think it will take to get to the palace?" he asked one of the Royal Guard who was walking with him.

"Still a few hours yet, sir, but we'll be there by nightfall."

Gelladar nodded, wondering absently if Weyrn had made it safely.

They went on down into the valley, walking carefully on the thick snow. It was almost undisturbed; Gelladar doubted that anyone would leave the valley if they didn't have to. Presumably it would be easier when they were closer to the city. He sighed a little, hitching his cloak up around his shoulders. After this experience, he was very tired of snow and grateful that they would stay long enough for it to thaw.

"Do you want us to walk with you into the city?" asked Maelli suddenly.

Gelladar looked round and saw that Derdhel and Celes had paused by a well-used side trail.

"This is the path to the Swordmaster Guardhouse," Maelli explained.

Gelladar thought it would probably be politic for them all to arrive together, especially if there was to be a new friendship between Silvren and the Swordmasters, so with a glance at Othron and Ethiad he replied, "I would appreciate it if you at least would accompany us, Maelli."

Maelli smiled a little and nodded, then spoke softly to Celes and started up the road towards Gelladar. Celes darted off up the path.

"I've sent him to carry news of our return. Derdhel and I will join you."

Gelladar nodded. "We'll be glad of your company."

Everything was silent around them as they walked, apart from the soft crunch of their feet on the snow. There had been some traffic on this road, Gelladar noticed, presumably going back and forth to the Guardhouse. He looked up and around at the bare, black skeletons of the trees, edged in white where the snow had blown against them, and felt a moment's homesickness. In Silvren, the pines and yews never shed their leaves. It was warmer there, too, he thought as he took a breath. It seemed to cut at his throat and he could almost feel it drying his already-chapped lips. He couldn't help a shiver and pulled his cloak closer around his shoulders.

There was no-one else about. Just the three Wood-elves, two Swordmasters and the elves of the Royal Guard. None of the Duamelti elves seemed to have any trouble with the cold. It had been a long winter, and, if this lingering snow was anything to go by, a harsh one. Presumably they were used to it.

They came to the top of a low ridge at the edge of the trees and Gelladar smiled as he saw the city of Duamelti spread out in front of him, clustered around a bend in the great river. Every river in the valley joined that one, above or below the city, and there were many. It looked strange: a black ribbon against the snow. He wondered if it had ever frozen.

As they stepped clear of the trees, a sudden wind made him wince and pull up his hood.

"Master Gelladar?" asked one of the Guardsmen.

"I'm all right. The wind came as a shock." He looked around for Othron and Ethiad. Othron looked paler than he had, but he smiled wanly as Gelladar looked at him. Ethiad was fidgeting with his own hood.

"We'll be there soon," Gelladar assured them.

"That we will," said the Guard captain with a grin, leading the way again.

Gelladar had been here once in summer and these fields had been full of growing crops. Now they were bare apart from the snow. He could see trails in other fields and churned, dirty snow around their gates; presumably they held livestock. High up on the hills, he knew there were sheep. Lower, by the river, would be cows, but he guessed that in this weather they would be safely shut away in their barns to eat summer's hay. The thought made him smile as he looked forward to his own warm place to rest. Every building of any size and many of the smaller ones down in the city had little threads of smoke rising from their chimneys, suggesting warm fires and hot food. He could see more plumes of smoke against the cloudy sky, telling of other homes and villages out in the forest. He wondered fleetingly how many of those were home to Mixed-bloods under Weyrn's rule and how many to the Irnianam that he now knew lived here.

The wind made him wince again as it whipped up ice crystals from the snow at their feet.

"Will it snow again tonight, do you think?" he asked.

"It's difficult to tell, sir, but it might."

"I'm glad we'll be inside for it," said Ethiad, a shiver in his voice.

"Warmth always comes after cold," said Derdhel. Gelladar noticed with a twinge of resentment that he'd not even put his hood up.

"I'll still be glad to see it," said Ethiad.

Maelli huffed out a breath and it misted in front of him. "It has been a long winter. Come on."

Gelladar was only too glad to keep walking. Fortunately the road, under the trodden snow, was smooth. He'd been worried that it would have hidden ruts and potholes, but it seemed to be well maintained. Perhaps the cold meant that it had frozen solid before it could be churned into a mire.

There were an increasing number of tracks as they came closer to the city and the snow was becoming packed hard. That alone made their footing treacherous; it was like walking on ice. Even Derdhel and two members of the guard almost fell.

"Try the edge," said Maelli, leading the way to the side of the road. "It'll be easier once we get to the city; they've cleared the roads." Fortunately, the verge wasn't as trodden and they were able to walk quickly.

Gelladar had rarely been so glad to walk through a gateway as he was to enter the city of Duamelti. As Maelli had promised, once they had passed that border, the roads were clear. The snow was piled up to the sides with tracks to individual buildings beaten through the drifts. There were more elves here, mostly Valley-elves, but though some paused to look at the newcomers, most of them hurried by. Gelladar could understand that; the wind was still picking up, bitterly cold as it whistled between the buildings. At least it wasn't far now; the palace was right on the bend of the river and fairly near the edge of the city when they approached from this direction. He raised his head and smiled as they walked on, grouped together instinctively to shelter one another.

They were still in a tight group when they arrived, but in the sheltered courtyard they began to move apart again. Gelladar sighed in relief as they stepped through the main door into the entrance hall. He felt the warmth wash over him and sighed again, closing his eyes for a moment.

He opened them again, though, as he heard Ethiad step up beside him. Othron was close behind.

"It's good to be here," said Othron softly, smiling as he pulled his hood back.

Ethiad nodded, his hand twitchily going to one of his ears. Gelladar touched his shoulder and he quickly lowered the hand again.

The sound of footsteps made Gelladar look up and he smiled as he saw Lord Hurion walking into the entrance hall. He was smiling broadly as he approached and the three ambassadors bowed.

"Lord Hurion," said Gelladar. "It's a pleasure to see you again."

"The pleasure is mine, Master Gelladar," said Hurion, grasping Gelladar's hand. "I'm glad to see the three of you safe."

"Thanks to the Swordmasters," said Gelladar, turning to gesture to Maelli and Derdhel, who were standing back a little.

Hurion nodded to them. "Weyrn got back a few days ago," he said. "I had some news that you were on your way, but that doesn't make me any less glad to see it true."

"How's Alatani?" asked Maelli.

"Doing well. Weyrn arrived just in time."

"I'm glad to hear that," said Gelladar.

Hurion nodded. "I'm sure you're tired. I've ordered the usual Wood-elven rooms prepared. Feel free to rest for the remainder of the day."

Gelladar thought longingly of a real bed and nodded. "Thank you, Lord Hurion." He looked at the two Swordmasters again. "And thank you. We owe you our lives."

Maelli smiled and bowed his head slightly. "I'm glad we could help. If you'll excuse us…?"

Hurion dismissed them with a wave, but Maelli didn't leave at once.

"I'll speak to Weyrn about the things you discussed and we'll see you again," he said to Gelladar and grinned.

Gelladar nodded. "I'll see you soon."

The three Wood-elves were shown to their rooms and Gelladar went into his with a grateful sigh. He was exhausted and put down his pack with another long sigh. Perhaps he should have accepted the offer of someone else carrying it, but he'd grown attached to it. It seemed forever since they'd lost their horses, and for all that time that pack had been all he'd had. He patted it fondly and flopped backwards onto the bed. He wasn't sure he could be bothered to undress; he felt like sleeping as he was.

Still, he knew he'd feel better when he woke if he didn't sleep in his clothes and started to unlace his tunic while still lying on the bed.

Hopefully the others were settling down well. It had been a long trip and Gelladar knew that once he was less tired some of the things that had happened would snap into greater focus.

He rubbed his eyes. The foggy memories of some of the more frightening moments were there, but he ignored them. The worst hadn't happened. They were alive, and… he smiled. Put simply, they had made some new friends.

CHAPTER FOUR

For Weyrn, the first two weeks after he returned had passed in a blur. Alatani and Seregei seemed to take up every waking moment, even though she was staying at her parents' house for the time being. The others were understanding, but he thought he'd caught a worried look in Seri's eye from time to time. He hoped it was only worry and not resentment; he'd thought it was tilting towards anger when he'd said that he was going to visit Alatani again this morning before anything else.

He had managed to organise a meeting between Othron and some Duamelti elves to discuss the matter of Tishlondi. He wished that all three ambassadors had been able to attend, but Gelladar and Ethiad had other appointments. Still, one spoke for all, so there would be no problem with that. He was grateful that Gelladar had been interested in getting closer to the truth; as the Valley-elves grew in power, the Mixed-bloods might need the extra recognition that friendship with the Wood-elves would give them.

As he walked, he rubbed his eyes, letting out a weary sigh. It was a long road from Alatani's parents' house to the hall in Duamelti where he'd arranged the meeting and he only had about half an hour to make the journey. He was glad of the walk, though; after the visit he needed to clear his head. He took a deep breath of the frosty air and smiled, feeling the muscles of his neck and shoulders beginning to relax a little. He couldn't understand how such a tiny creature could make so much *noise*.

He chided himself; at least he had had a full night's sleep, which was more than poor Alatani had. She didn't look like she'd slept properly in a week and, though Weyrn did what he could to help with Seregei and give Alatani a few moments' peace, it wasn't easy.

He wondered if he would be able to do more if he could stay overnight with her. At least then when Seregei cried in the night he would be able to try to do something... but he shook his head and rubbed his eyes again. He and she had both suggested it several times, but her father was adamant: Weyrn was not allowed to stay the night in his house.

Again, he shook his head and paused a moment to look around, relying on the freezing air to wake him a little. His breath misted before his eyes as he sighed, then he started walking again, turning his mind firmly to the upcoming meeting. It was almost the only official thing he'd managed to do since Seregei's birth, and he wanted to make it worthwhile. He also couldn't help the feeling that he needed to prove that trying to be a good husband and father was not causing him to neglect his role as Captain.

He sighed and rubbed his eyes, mentally running through the names of the elves he had invited to meet Othron. Hopefully, everyone would be able to attend. There were two Piskin refugees from Tishlondi – Derakil and Tashe – and an Irniani named Sakin. Derakil and Sakin were considerably older than Weyrn and had actually taken part in the Kinslaying, while Tashe had been a child at the time. That meant his memory would be rather spotty, but Weyrn hadn't found it easy to find Piskam who were prepared to discuss Tishlondi.

Three was a good number, though, especially as he'd been able to find one elf from each race who'd actually been involved.

To his embarrassment, when he arrived at the meeting hall, Othron was already there. He got up as Weyrn entered.

"Weyrn, it's good to see you again," he said.

"Likewise." Weyrn grasped Othron's hand. At least he would be here to introduce Othron to the Duamelti elves.

"Your wife and son are still doing well?"

"Very well, thank you. And I'm glad to see you've recovered."

Othron smiled. "Thank you. When do the others arrive?"

"Soon, I hope. I organised a meeting place close to you, though that meant the rest of us had to travel."

"I appreciate that."

"It seemed fairest; you're least familiar with the roads."

Othron nodded. "And I'd prefer not to have to travel in the snow again, so soon after last time..." He shuddered a little.

Weyrn nodded. "That's certainly understandable."

"I know I'd not be so far from civilisation, but I can't deny some fear."

Weyrn nodded again. He was about to say something else when the door opened with a gust of cold wind. He looked round and smiled a welcome at Sakin.

"I hope I'm not late," the Valley-elf said as he closed the door behind him.

"Not at all," said Weyrn. "Sakin, this is Ambassador Othron." He glanced at Othron. "Sakin is one of the Irnianam who escaped Tishlondi alive."

Sakin bowed. Othron inclined his head a little in response and chuckled softly, but then he shook his head slightly and sighed.

"Is something wrong?" asked Weyrn.

"No, sorry. I was just making a mental note to tell Ethiad something."

Weyrn glanced back at Sakin, who was just fiddling awkwardly with the ends of his long hair. It didn't seem that he was going to learn any more about that, though, so he shook his head and took off his cloak.

"We're also expecting two Piskam," he said as he hung it up, then he turned to see Sakin's expression. He was aware that there could be trouble from putting the three of them in the same room and asking them to discuss such a difficult memory. Sakin, however, just nodded and Weyrn breathed a small sigh of relief. "Do you have to go anywhere, Sakin? If we need to cut things off, it would be best to know now."

"No... sir. My wife expects me back before too late this afternoon, but not apart from that."

Weyrn nodded. "I hope we won't be here all day."

"So do I." Othron had sat back down. "I appreciate your coming to talk to me, though."

As Sakin was also hanging up his cloak, the door opened again. Tashe came in first with Derakil close behind him. Weyrn started to greet them, but then Derakil and Sakin saw one another.

Weyrn sighed as both elves immediately tensed. Derakil pulled his long braid free from his collar so it was clearly visible. Sakin's upper lip curled. Tashe stepped aside, shifting from foot to foot.

"Sakin, Derakil," said Weyrn firmly. The two startled a little and stepped away from one another as Weyrn put himself between them. "I know we're here to talk about a very sensitive subject, but fighting one another won't make those events not have happened."

Derakil looked down. "I'm sorry, sir."

Sakin just nodded and turned back to the cloak hooks.

Once the two Piskam were inside and had hung up their cloaks, Weyrn introduced them to Othron. They didn't look entirely comfortable with him; Derakil greeted him politely and bowed his head, but his tone was cold. Tashe just smiled fleetingly. Weyrn sighed and gestured the three of them to some chairs near where he and Othron were sitting.

"Ambassador Othron and his companions have expressed an interest in forming a friendship between Silvren and the Mixed-bloods," he told them, "especially the Duamelti Mixed-bloods. However, I explained that Tishlondi was still a sour memory. We thought it would be useful to hear from some of those who remember what it was like to live under Irnianin rule."

Derakil shot another look at Sakin, who studiously ignored him.

Tashe leaned forward in his seat, resting his elbows on his knees.

"Captain Weyrn?"

"Yes, Tashe?"

Tashe looked down, tucking his hair behind his ears. "I was only a child at the time…"

"I know. I do think you have something to contribute, though." Even if it was just his presence.

Tashe smiled. "Thank you, sir."

Weyrn nodded and glanced at Othron, who said, "Thank you all for coming to speak to me, especially in such difficult weather; I appreciate it cannot have been an easy journey. As Captain Weyrn says, I'm interested in hearing about life in Tishlondi, especially during the war between my own people and the Irnianam. I gather that our actions during that time have led to a rift between the Wood-elves and the Mixed-bloods in general and the Piskam in particular."

Derakil sighed and glanced at Weyrn, who nodded.

"Things were already bad for us, sir," he told Othron. "No disrespect, but…"

"None assumed. I want to know."

Derakil smiled for a moment, but then the smile faded and he sighed, running a hand over his hair. "They treated us as little more than slaves. We couldn't even hold schools for our children."

Tashe nodded and jumped in before Sakin could speak. "I remember my mother wouldn't let me play with many of my friends at a time; she said it would get us in trouble."

"We were at war," protested Sakin. "The Mixed-bloods of Tishlondi were kin of our enemy – present company excepted – what else were we to do?"

"You could have treated us *better*," snapped Derakil.

"We were right to keep you under control as best we could; how many of your people attempted to betray us?"

"Fewer than had reason. If you wanted friendship, you shouldn't have treated us like your enemies!"

Weyrn cleared his throat and Derakil stopped there, shifting back in his chair. Nonetheless, he and Sakin continued to glower at one another.

"So the Irnianam treated the Piskam more harshly after the war began?" asked Othron softly.

"Yes," said Sakin and Derakil together.

Sakin continued, "I'm sure you can understand why. As it happened, you and they didn't join forces" – Derakil made a noise in his throat and Sakin ignored him – "but we had no way of knowing that at the time. We had every reason to expect –"

"As did we," said Derakil softly. He looked plaintively at Othron. "With respect, Ambassador, why *didn't* you help us?"

Othron sighed. "I was only young myself and certainly wasn't high up in the court, so I cannot answer that. I'm sorry."

Derakil sighed. "We hoped that you would."

Sakin nodded. "You see? We had every reason to expect it, and so we did what we could to keep them from aiding you; you were our enemies at the time and they were your kin and there were thousands of them living among us."

"But we were people of Tishlondi just as you were!" protested Derakil. "Had you not so abused us –"

Othron raised a hand. "Excuse me," he said. The two arguing elves fell silent. "Thank you. To add my own 'if only': what would have happened had Silvren intervened in the treatment of the Tishlondi Mixed-bloods?" He glanced at Derakil. "Would it have ended your troubles, or" – he turned to Sakin – "caused the Irnianam to act more harshly?"

There was a long silence. Not even Weyrn could surely answer that. His instinct was that had Silvren put pressure on the Irnianam to be kinder to their subjects, rather than worrying only about their own quarrel, things might have been easier. However, he had to admit that it was just as likely that the Irnianam would simply have turned on the Piskam.

After a while, Tashe spoke. "I was only a child at the time, so I don't really remember what things were like, but it sounds like we really can't know. I will say, though" – he glanced at Sakin – "when Piskam were trusted, we showed ourselves trustworthy."

Sakin looked hard at him. "Didn't the king have a Piski as honour guard for one of his sons?"

Weyrn gritted his teeth. That had been his father.

"And look where that got them!" Sakin continued, his fists clenched. "When Terathi should have been protecting Prince Kusin, he murdered him!"

"That's never been proved," said Weyrn, more harshly than he'd intended. Everyone looked at him again as he took a deep breath and continued, "We don't know what happened to anyone in that group. It could easily have been the other way around, so I don't think we should start making accusations."

"The other way around?" Sakin's voice rang shrill. "You think *Prince Kusin* might have murdered *Terathi?*"

Weyrn didn't, but he said, "There's nothing to show either way, so we're not going to discuss it; it can only end in hurt feelings."

"In any case," muttered Derakil, "Terathi isn't exactly the best example of a Piski, blood-traitor that he was."

Weyrn winced and took a moment to steady his voice before saying, "We need to return to the point. I think Tashe's right: there really is no way of knowing what would have happened."

"I would like to ask about the Kinslaying, though," said Othron. "The tale in Silvren is that the Piskam killed all the Irnianam: men, women and children, even infants in their cradles." He nodded at Sakin. "I can see that isn't true, but I would like to know what really happened over those days."

Sakin looked away, going pale. Derakil swallowed hard. Tashe hugged himself.

Othron sighed. "If it's too much to ask for the story, I understand."

"No, sorry, sir, it's just…" Derakil swallowed again. "I think we all lost family and friends during the battle and the journey here."

Othron nodded. "I'm sorry to ask you to relive it, but please tell me what you can."

Derakil nodded. "It… started with a gathering of our people: mostly women and children. We've already said that the Irnianam wouldn't allow many of us to come together." He swallowed again and Tashe reached over to touch his arm.

"They were being threatening and disorderly," said Sakin. "The king sent some of the guard to disband them."

"Threatening and disorderly?" echoed Derakil. "This was a peaceful gathering and the Irnianam set upon them from horseback with swords!"

"Because they threw stones at the guard when told to disperse!"

"Calm down, both of you!" said Weyrn, and they fell silent again, glaring at one another.

"I only know what I've been told," said Tashe, "And that was by my family, but I can try to carry on the story. At least I wasn't there."

Weyrn nodded at him. "Thank you, Tashe."

Tashe nodded back and squeezed his hands together in his lap, looking at the floor for a moment. Then he said, "It wasn't an especially large group and the Irnianam killed several of them. Those that escaped ran home, of course, and their families went out to see what was happening. Word spread fast. I remember my father telling my mother to keep me inside. We… we were sure that this meant we were all going to be killed." He hugged himself again.

Sakin had been listening wide-eyed, but at that he shook his head, leaning back in his seat. "We would never have gone out killing innocent children," he said.

"That's what we were afraid of, though," said Derakil.

"Is that why you then began killing *us* in the streets?"

"We did *not* –"

Weyrn interrupted again. "Let Tashe tell the story."

"We did fight," said Tashe. "It wasn't a massacre, though; we didn't have any weapons. We just didn't want to die."

"The killing started at some point, though," said Sakin.

"I don't know when." Tashe shrugged, looking from Weyrn to Othron.

"There were swords already drawn," said Derakil.

"And reason to use them now, even if you think there wasn't before," said Sakin.

Weyrn sighed. "And then it just got worse from there."

"They killed all of us they could catch," said Sakin, his voice trembling. "It didn't matter they didn't have weapons, they'd use stones off the street if they had to. It…" He took a shuddering breath.

"Well, what of what the Irnianam were doing?" asked Derakil hotly. "When you were cutting down anyone with short hair –"

"While you would stone or club anyone whose hair was long! I know two elves who cut theirs to save their lives!"

"Stop that!" snapped Weyrn. He knew the significance of hair length: the Irnianam had been the only ones permitted to wear their hair long while the Piskim had to crop theirs short.

Again, both elves fell silent, but they were glowering at one another.

Othron nodded. "I think I understand," he said. "We needn't go any further into what actually happened at the time or who struck the first blow. What happened after that? I assume you three were not the only ones to escape?"

"Oh, no, of course not," said Derakil as Weyrn and Sakin shook their heads. "There were far more Irnianam than Piskam leaving, but…"

"Well, that was because you'd driven us out. What's the point if you don't stay to enjoy the spoils?"

"You say that as if it weren't our *home*."

"It was our home too!" Sakin's voice rang shrill and he started forward in his seat. "I was born and raised there the same as you! Why should you have had the right to stay there in peace and not me?"

"We've lived there since elves *first walked the earth*. It was given to our fathers by Valcae's grace, not to you. That land was *ours*. *You* were the ones that came in and imposed your rule on us!"

Weyrn got up. "Stop it, both of you!"

Sakin had already been halfway out of his seat and at that he sprang up. "I will *not* be accused of usurping my own *home*!"

Weyrn turned to face him and looked him straight in the eye. "Sit down, Sakin. This is in the past and temper will solve nothing."

Sakin scowled, though Weyrn could see tears in his eyes. "They could return. I can't. If I went back I'd be killed, but it was my home. It was all I'd ever known and then…" His breath caught. "And now he tries to tell me that I somehow deserved this…" He buried his face in his hands.

There was an awkward silence, broken only by the sound of a couple more stifled sobs from Sakin.

Weyrn sighed and looked over his shoulder at Derakil, who looked caught between guilt and anger. Then he looked at Othron, who also looked deeply uncomfortable.

"Derakil, Tashe, please continue the story. We'll be back in a moment."

"I'm all right," said Sakin. His voice sounded muffled behind his hands. "I'll not have them only tell their side."

"You'll have a chance to set things straight. Come on." Weyrn glanced at Othron again. "Please excuse us."

"Of course."

The hall's porch was cold, especially as they'd left their cloaks inside, but at least it was peaceful out here, and some fresh air might help as Sakin calmed down. There was a bench by the wall and Weyrn brushed the snow off it and told Sakin to sit.

"I'm sorry," he said softly as he obeyed. He was still visibly trying not to cry. "I just couldn't stand it any more."

Weyrn nodded. "I understand."

"You don't, though. You're a Piski too, aren't you?"

"Yes, by blood. I wasn't born there, after all."

"Still." Sakin wiped his eyes again. "I... I loved it there. I still dream of the sea sometimes..."

Weyrn nodded. "But you've made a new life here in Duamelti. All your people have."

"That doesn't make it better." Sakin sniffed. "And Derakil can talk all he likes about how his people were there longer, but it wasn't their home any more than it was ours."

Weyrn did reluctantly agree with him there, though he still thought that the Piskam had been quite justified in their rebellion. He also didn't feel entirely guilty for letting Derakil and Tashe tell Othron about how the fleeing Irnianam had treated the Piskam in their midst. Not given that his mother had been among them. He didn't say anything, though.

After a few minutes, Sakin took a deep breath and shook his head, rubbing his eyes. "I'm all right," he said softly. "Thanks."

"Do you want to go back in?"

"Yes, I think I'm ready now."

Weyrn nodded and got up. He was glad to go back; the warmth washed over him as soon as he was through the door. Nonetheless, he didn't regret forcing Sakin to take that break.

Othron, Derakil and Tashe were still sitting where Weyrn had left them. Tashe and Othron were leaning forward and talking quietly while Derakil sat upright, rubbing his eyes. They didn't seem to have noticed Weyrn and Sakin coming back in.

As they approached, though, Othron looked round and straightened up, smiling a welcome.

"Do you feel better now?" he asked Sakin, who just nodded as he sat down.

"Yes, sir." He glanced at Derakil and Tashe. Derakil ignored him and Tashe looked away, biting his lip.

"What have we missed?" asked Weyrn.

"Tashe was just telling me about the journey here, and that some Piskam were even among the refugees."

Weyrn nodded.

Sakin just sighed. "Half-breeds, most of them," he said, glancing at Derakil, who nodded.

"And some who'd worked with the Irnianam and were afraid their own people might take revenge."

"That can't have made for easy company," said Othron.

Tashe hugged himself. "Not at all."

"In our defence, they had just slaughtered many of our people and driven us from our home," said Sakin bitterly. "It's only natural that we had little love for them."

Othron nodded and glanced at Derakil and Tashe, but neither of them said anything. Weyrn was a little startled at that – he might have had something to say in their place – but he didn't break in.

When the silence had stretched a while, he shook his head and shifted in his seat. The movement drew their attention to him.

"Unless anyone has any more to say or ask…" He looked around at them. Othron looked thoughtful, Sakin and Derakil fraught and Tashe weary. None of them spoke. Weyrn continued, "I think that's enough for now. Thank you all for coming; I truly appreciate it, especially as reliving these events has obviously been harrowing."

Sakin sighed, looking away. "That's it, then?" he asked.

Weyrn nodded. "You can go when you're ready."

Sakin forced a smile and went to get his cloak. After a moment, Tashe got up and beckoned to Derakil.

Derakil sighed. "Thanks for asking us to come, Captain," he said with a weary smile.

Weyrn nodded. "I know it was a lot to ask."

"Nonetheless, it was good to have a chance to tell our side." Derakil got up. "And thank you for listening, Ambassador,"

Othron inclined his head a little. "Thank you for telling the story."

Once they'd left, Weyrn also got up and stretched. The movement seemed to wake Othron from a reverie, for he startled a little.

"Was that helpful?" asked Weyrn.

"I have a lot to discuss with the others, but I think it was." Othron smiled slightly. "Thank you for organising it." He brushed his braid back behind his shoulder. "I am a little curious, though – stop me if I'm prying – but why didn't you speak for the Piskam?"

Weyrn blinked. "Pardon?"

"Derakil told me that you are a Piski yourself."

Weyrn looked away. "Well, I wasn't even born at the time of the Kinslaying. My mother was among the refugees, though." He shrugged, hoping it looked careless. "I thought it would be better for me to be as impartial as possible, in any case."

Othron nodded. "I understand that." He sighed and closed his eyes for a moment. "I should return to the palace and speak to Gelladar and Ethiad."

"Do you need a guide?"

"No, I can find my way well enough." Othron smiled. "Give my regards to the other Swordmasters."

"I will."

It had taken a long time for Alatani to get Seregei to sleep, and once she'd finally laid him in his cradle, she flopped down on her bed, wondering if it would be a bad idea to fall asleep right then and there. Weyrn helped when he was visiting, but she was exhausted nonetheless and starting to wonder if she was just a bad mother. Seregei seemed to spend so much time *crying*. Was he unhappy? Too cold? Did she not entertain him enough or let him nurse often enough? *What?* Surely, in the month since he'd been born, she should have been able to work out how to care for him properly.

It didn't help that her mother had told her a dozen times that she hadn't been nearly such a troublesome baby. Occasional friction aside, she loved her parents and knew they'd raised her well, so what was she doing wrong that her own son was so fretful?

"Alatani?"

She opened her eyes to see her mother at the door and smiled as she sat up. "Shh…"

Her mother smiled. "Yes, I saw he was asleep," she whispered, nodding to the cradle.

Alatani nodded, rubbing her eyes. They felt gritty with tiredness. "Mother, would you mind if Weyrn spent the night from time to time?" She'd probably still wake when Seregei cried, but if there was someone else there to sit with him…

Her mother frowned a little as she came to sit beside Alatani. "You know your father doesn't much like him."

Alatani supposed she should have expected that; they had received the same answer every other time they had asked. "I think having him about would make things easier." She sighed. "At least there'd be someone else to share the work."

"Work?" her mother smiled teasingly. "Caring for your beautiful little baby?"

Alatani felt tears well up in her eyes and it was all she could do not to wail herself. "Mother, that's not fair!"

Her mother chuckled and hugged her as she wept softly. "All right. I do know what you mean, especially as your little one is so restless."

"I don't know what I'm doing wrong…"

"It's always hard at first."

Alatani sniffed and rubbed her eyes. "I didn't think it would be this hard," she mumbled. "I just want to get it right." She gestured towards the cradle. "If I do something wrong raising him…"

"Children are resilient and their mothers usually know what to do," said her mother, hugging her again. "I don't think you're likely to do anything too terrible."

"Then why does he always cry?"

"Perhaps he's just fractious. After all, just because you were a well-behaved little girl doesn't mean that Weyrn was."

"I wish you wouldn't keep saying that."

"Well, it has to come from somewhere."

"You could at least not say it to his *face*."

Her mother just patted her on the head. "You get some sleep. It's always worth sleeping when the baby does, especially when you have people to take care of you." She kissed Alatani on the cheek. "You know we're proud of you, but I'm glad you came back here to lay in. A house full of warriors is no place to raise a child."

Alatani sighed. "And at least he's not keeping all of them up too." She couldn't help a smile. "Though I'm sorry if he wakes you and Father."

"Occasionally, but not every time. A mother always hears her own baby's voice more clearly than anyone else." Another kiss. "You get some sleep."

Alatani sighed again and nodded. Her mother slipped out and she curled up on her bed and pulled a blanket over herself without even undressing. After all, she had no idea how long it would be before Seregei woke again.

She woke to the sound of him crying and scrambled groggily out of bed. It took a moment for her to get her bearings – her head was spinning and she still felt half-asleep – but then she went over to the cradle and gathered him up with a sigh.

Once she was holding him, though, he calmed down fairly quickly. It seemed that he hadn't actually wanted anything more than to be held. Alatani sat down with a sigh, rocking him gently.

"Still coping?" asked a voice from the door.

Alatani looked up, startled, but smiled a greeting as she saw Elar.

"Yes," she said with a sigh. "Come on in."

Elar came and sat beside Alatani on the bed. "You look like he's giving you a rough time."

Alatani made a noise halfway between a chuckle and a sob. "You could say that." She glanced at Elar. "What was Lessai like? My mother seems to think Seregei's unusually fractious and I'm worried I'm doing something wrong."

Elar ran a hand over her hair distractedly. "You know that mortals say they go grey when stressed?"

Alatani hadn't known that, but she nodded.

"Well, elf though I am, I think Lessai gave me a grey hair or two. Some babies are just louder than others."

Alatani sighed with relief. "So it's normal?"

"Yes, don't worry. Of course, if you really can't stop him crying it might be a good idea to speak to a healer, but for the most part I think you're fine." She smiled. "I know that doesn't make it easier."

"It's a great comfort, actually." Alatani leaned her forehead on her hand. She still felt like she didn't know whether to laugh or cry. Seregei, evidently feeling smothered, began to whimper again and she sat upright. "I... didn't expect it to be like this."

Elar nodded. "I don't think it's ever like anyone expects. I've spoken to women who have many children and they say that every child is different."

"And I get frustrated with him sometimes and I'm worried that makes me a bad mother."

"I can't begin to tell you how many times I cursed Lessai's father, though I love Lessai with all my heart." Elar sighed. "Especially when he woke me in the night and I had work to do the next morning."

"But you never cursed Lessai?"

"Maybe once or twice..."

Alatani nodded. Though she wouldn't say she'd ever cursed Seregei, there were times... she shook her head, feeling ashamed.

"Seriously, though: it's never going to be simple and clean. It's hard work and I think any mother who says at the time that she knows exactly what she's doing is a liar." Elar put an arm around Alatani's shoulders. "The three of you will be just fine: you and Weyrn and little Seregei here."

Alatani leaned her head on her friend's shoulder. "You have no idea how glad I am to hear that."

"I'm glad I can help, then."

"Do you mind if I fall asleep on you?"

Elar laughed. "That's fine. Shall I hold Seregei?"

Alatani lowered him so that he was lying in her lap, though still supported by her arms. "He should be all right. I'm sure he'll wake me if he's not."

"I'll keep an eye on him."

"Thanks."

Weyrn always had the uncomfortable feeling that Alatani's parents didn't much like him. It wasn't that they were rude or even especially cold to him, but he never got the impression that there was any more than social ritual to the welcome he received when he visited them. It was only one step above the greeting he would have expected from strangers simply because of his rank.

Still, when her mother answered the door, he smiled and asked after her health and that of her husband as if he hadn't noticed the slight frown that crossed her face as she saw him.

"We're both well, thank you, Weyrn." She smiled a little. "Alatani and Seregei are through in her room."

"How are they?"

"Doing well. Seregei's sleeping a little more."

Weyrn sighed in relief. It had been a month now, after all. "Thank you for letting her stay here."

"She is our daughter, after all. Alatani!" she called. "Weyrn's here!"

Weyrn wondered if this was how other men felt when they were courting, but he shook the thought away as he made a show of wiping the mud off his boots. Then he went through to look for Alatani.

She greeted him at the door of her room and he embraced her eagerly, pulling back a moment to kiss her.

"How are you?" he asked, as they went into the room and she shut the door.

"Tired," she admitted. "But managing."

He kissed her cheek. "I've missed you. It's strange, living alone at the Guardhouse."

She nodded. "I'd like to come back, but..." She looked down at Seregei, who was sleeping peacefully in his cradle.

"I gather he sleeps more now."

"Yes, but not through the night." She sat down, rubbing her eyes. "It wouldn't be fair on the others."

He nodded, putting his arm around her. "I'm sorry I've not been able to do more."

"It's not your fault; it's the only real problem with staying with my parents."

He nodded. "I'm sure they'd not mind –"

"The other Swordmasters? Maybe not, but I would."

He'd guessed she'd refuse and sighed. He knew she was right, after all. Nobody would argue, but it really wouldn't be fair. He shook his head a little. "Come back to visit for a while, then. Just today. We'll all be glad to see you."

She smiled, tucking her hair behind her ear. "Would it be too cold to bring Seregei?"

"I'd expect not, if you wrap him up warmly."

She grinned, moving to look down into the cradle. "I think he'd like to meet his uncles."

Weyrn laughed and reached into the cradle to stroke Seregei's head, as gently as he could. The baby didn't stir. "He'll wake if you pick him up, I assume."

"I think so."

"Let's let him sleep for a little longer, then." He kissed her hair.

She nodded, tilting her head against his. Together, they sat back down on the bed, and he put an arm around her while she rested her head on his shoulder.

"I've missed you too," she said softly. "It's... hard. I never know what to do and Mother just always tells me how I was so much better-behaved and —"

Weyrn interrupted. "You're not blaming yourself for the fact that he keeps crying, are you?"

"Elar says that all babies are different, but..." She sighed and shook her head.

"I'm sure you're a very good mother," he said awkwardly, unsure what to say to comfort her, especially as he didn't know anything about mothering.

She sighed. "Thanks."

"Why don't you take a nap while we wait for Seregei to wake up."

She nodded against his shoulder. "All right."

She curled up on the bed and he laid a blanket over her, then sat beside her and stroked her hair and shoulder as she fell asleep.

He did genuinely miss her. It seemed forever since they'd last been together, sleeping in each other's arms in peace. Not that he would ever dream of resenting the reason, of course... he smiled tenderly as he looked over to the cradle where Seregei also slept. He would be glad to have them both to live with him in the Guardhouse, to share in the massive disturbance that had come over their lives.

He couldn't ask the others to do the same, though. He lent down and kissed the corner of Alatani's mouth, smiling as she smiled in her sleep, then went over to look down into the cradle.

Seregei stirred a little and Weyrn looked back towards Alatani, his heart in his mouth. If Seregei woke he'd wake Alatani and she'd only just fallen asleep... hopefully he'd be able to calm the baby before he really began to cry.

Seregei stirred again, opening and closing his fists, and whimpered softly. At once, Weyrn scooped him up as gently as possible and rocked him as Alatani had taught him. To his relief, Seregei quietened.

He was already much heavier than when he'd been born, Weyrn noticed as he sat back down. He looked more like babies he'd seen before as well:

less red in the face. It helped that he hadn't just been crying. Weyrn shifted his grip to gently touch Seregei's cheek and smiled as the baby turned towards his finger and tried to bite it. He didn't have teeth yet, of course, and Weyrn just chuckled softly, rocking Seregei again until he'd gone back to sleep.

By the time Seregei really did wake, Weyrn's arms were aching terribly. It had been some time, though, and he was glad; that meant Alatani had had a decent nap. Seregei opened his eyes and peered blearily up at Weyrn for a moment, looking unsure what to do next. Weyrn reached over and shook Alatani's shoulder, and that apparently set Seregei off. If Weyrn shaking her hadn't woken Alatani, the long, loud wail did.

Alatani startled awake with a curse and Weyrn winced. When she was fully awake, though, she took Seregei from him with a sigh to let him nurse.

"He didn't wake up when you picked him up?" she asked, leaning on Weyrn.

"No. He looked like he would – that's why I did it – but then he quietened down."

She frowned, though the look was interrupted with a yawn. "How... how come he quietened down for you? He never does for me."

"I just rocked him like you showed me to. He was only about half awake."

She nodded, but when he tilted his head to look at her he saw that she was biting her lip and looked halfway between crying and being angry.

"Alatani?"

"I just don't understand what I'm doing wrong," she said, looking down at Seregei. He seemed oblivious and just continued to nurse, one small hand tangling in the fabric of her shirt.

"Doing wrong?" Weyrn echoed.

"Mother never had this much trouble with me, I don't believe Elar had this much trouble with Lessai and even you find it easier to handle Seregei than I do..." She sniffed. "The problem *must* be me."

Weyrn shook his head. "You're tired and you're not thinking straight. I'm sure there've been plenty of times when you've calmed him down and I never could."

She sniffed again and tried to wipe her eyes on her shoulder. He pulled out a handkerchief and wiped them for her.

"Honestly, I'm sure you're doing fine."

She just sighed and didn't say anything more.

***

It seemed a very long way to the Guardhouse with Seregei bundled up and slung on his back, but Weyrn was looking forward to it. Even though Alatani and Seregei weren't moving back in just yet, it would be good for everyone to see them. Alatani spent the whole journey hovering at his shoulder, keeping an eye on Seregei who, fortunately, didn't make a peep the whole way.

It was a relief to get into the warm Guardhouse; though the snow was beginning to melt now, it was still cold outside. Nobody was in the common room, but Weyrn waited for Alatani to get Seregei off his back before he called out a hello.

"Weyrn!" said a muffled voice from down the corridor. Weyrn smiled as he recognised Celes.

Alatani shifted Seregei slightly in her arms as Celes came into the room. It clearly took him a moment to take in the tableau, but then he grinned broadly and came over to greet them.

"It's good to see you," he said, giving Alatani a careful hug. "How are you?"

She sighed. "Tired," she said with a slight laugh.

He nodded. "Are you coming back?"

"Not yet." She looked down at Seregei. "He doesn't sleep through the night yet. It wouldn't be fair on you."

In Alatani's arms, Seregei stirred slightly. Weyrn couldn't help flinching and Alatani glared at him. Seregei didn't cry, though. He just opened his eyes and looked around vaguely.

Celes looked down at him with a grin. "Can I hold him?" he asked.

Alatani looked a little worried, but nodded. "Be careful. You'll need to support his head."

Celes nodded. However, as soon as he had Seregei, the baby started whimpering and Celes nervously handed him back. Alatani started to rock him.

"Where are the others?" asked Weyrn. "Has Derdhel come back from checking the grain stores?"

"No, not yet, and Seri is visiting the village elves. Neithan had an idea and I believe he went to find a smithy."

"And Maelli?"

"Here I am." Maelli walked in, grinning. "Sorry, I was in the middle of oiling my boots and had to clean off. It's good to see you, Alatani."

"And you," she said, looking up from Seregei, who had quietened again. "We're just here to visit."

"How much longer are you planning to stay away?" asked Maelli.

"Another couple of months, maybe," she said with a deep sigh.

Weyrn thought of another couple of months with Alatani living with her parents and couldn't help a wince. Fortunately, she didn't seem to notice, though Maelli caught his eye and smiled.

Celes was frowning, tilting his head to look at Seregei.

"I'm sure we could manage," he said slowly.

"I'd not ask it of you. Seriously, he wakes me up every night." Alatani went to sit down on one of the couches. "He'd do the same here and it wouldn't be fair."

"You don't have to ask," said Maelli with a smile. He crouched down beside her and stroked Seregei's knuckles with a finger. The baby looked up at him, pouting.

"You know perfectly well what I mean," said Alatani. "I can't come back until he's sleeping properly."

Seregei had now grabbed Maelli's finger and Maelli was distracted by gently pulling at it, so Celes said, "Surely there would be something we could do to bring you a bit closer. It feels strange to never see you."

She sighed and was about to reply when the door opened and Seri arrived. He glanced over towards them as he went to hang up his cloak, then paused mid-step and smiled. "You look well, Alatani," he said warmly.

She smiled back, glancing up from where Maelli was still playing with Seregei. "Thanks. I feel exhausted, though."

He winced. "I suppose that's why you've stayed away."

She nodded and was about to reply when Weyrn interrupted, having noticed that Seregei was starting to look upset again.

"Maelli, you should stop pulling him around, I don't think he likes it."

Alatani looked down too, distracted, as Maelli froze.

Weyrn went over to Seri as the other elf hung up his cloak.

"How is everyone? Celes told me you were visiting the village elves."

"Doing well. Now that the weather's finally warming, I think those that want to will be able to start going back."

"Those that want to? I don't think you mentioned any wanting to stay."

"There are a few families that have actually settled down here. I can let you have the names. Of course, they know they'll have to start making their own lives as soon as they can."

"Indeed." Weyrn glanced back at Alatani as she giggled softly. She did sound tired and he sighed, wondering what he could do to help. Still, he dragged his attention back to the business at hand. "Are there likely to be any problems with them staying?"

"They've been making an effort to settle in and there aren't many of them. With some support from us, they should be fine."

Weyrn nodded. "That's good. How much do we already know? You said you had some names?"

"Yes, at least those that are considering it. I understand Elar is serious, but the others are still wondering."

"I got the impression she was happy here." Weyrn glanced round again. Alatani had given Seregei to Celes again and he seemed to be doing well this time, though she hovered over his shoulder protectively. "Actually, she's been doing a lot to encourage Alatani, so I'd be delighted if she could stay. Where is she living at the moment?"

"With a family a few miles from Alatani's parents' settlement. She won't be able to stay there much longer, though."

"She'd have to find somewhere to live alone in any case."

"Yes." Seri frowned. "Do you think we could help her there?"

Weyrn hoped so. "That's a thought, actually: if we could find somewhere where she and Alatani could stay together, that could help both of them."

"Is she not happy staying with her parents, or are you not happy having to visit her there?" asked Seri dryly. "Or both?"

Weyrn looked sidelong at him and didn't reply.

"You do look tired, Alatani," said Maelli. Weyrn glanced round, glad of the interruption. Maelli continued, "Would you like us to watch Seregei while you take a break?"

Weyrn immediately looked at Alatani. She needed some time to rest and it would be good to spend time with her away from Seregei and her parents, even if all they did was to go for a walk.

"I really don't think I should leave him," Alatani was saying slowly. "What if something happens?"

"We'll be able to find you, especially if you let us know where you're going and even more so if you only go as far as your room for a nap," said Celes, grinning. He sobered as he added, "You look like you need it."

She shook her head. "I'm fine, I'm fine."

Weyrn went over and shooed Maelli out of the way so he could sit down beside her and put an arm around her shoulders. "You need a rest, Alatani," he said softly. "How about a trial run? You go get some sleep and we'll look after Seregei."

To his surprise, tears started to well in her eyes. "D-do you think you can all do a better job with him than me?"

Weyrn blinked. "That's not what I'm saying."

"Then what? Why insist on taking him away?"

"No-one's suggesting taking him away. You're not thinking straight and –" Weyrn cut himself off. That last comment had been a mistake. "I mean you're tired and –"

Her brows drew down further, though the lingering tears took the sting out of her glare. "I am trying *so hard* to be a good mother," she said, her voice midway between a snarl and a whine. "I don't need to be told by you *or* my mother that I'm not *thinking straight*!"

At that moment, she burst into tears.

At once, the others withdrew a little, apart from Celes, who was still holding Seregei. The baby was also growing distressed as he heard his mother's raised voice.

"Rock him and try to calm him down," said Weyrn quickly, looking from Celes to Alatani, who was now curled up and sobbing into her folded arms. "Come on, Alatani, let's get you somewhere quiet." Weyrn started to get up as Celes shifted away, awkwardly rocking Seregei.

"Where's Seregei?" Alatani's voice was muffled, but distinct.

"Celes is still holding him, come on, he'll be fine."

"No, where is he?" She raised her head and looked for Celes. "I need to keep an eye on him or something might happen."

"What could possibly happen? You'll only be in the next room and these three are here to look after him."

"But…"

Weyrn leaned down to look Alatani in the eye and she looked away. Seri took a step forward, looking worried, and Weyrn quickly waved him away. Unfortunately, at that moment Seregei started to cry.

"I'm sorry," said Celes, hurrying over with him. "I rocked him, but…"

"Give him to me," said Alatani wearily, wiping away her tears. "I expect he needs changing."

Judging by the smell, she was right. She took him into their bedroom and, with a glance at the others, Weyrn followed her and sat down on the bed to watch as she quickly changed Seregei's nappy.

"I'll need somewhere to put this," she said, holding up the soiled one. "Just to take it home in…"

"I'll deal with it and bring it back to you," said Weyrn, taking it. He tried not to wrinkle his nose.

"Thanks," she said with a sigh, picking Seregei up again. Now that he was clean, he seemed happier.

After a long pause, she said, "I'm sorry I lost my temper."

Weyrn shook his head. "I'm sorry I upset you. I mean it, though: you're very tired and you know that nobody makes their best decisions when tired."

"I know that," she said, looking away. "But I barely know what to do and Mother keeps saying that a baby's mother will *always* know what to do so – and I know they're all good people and very clever and can deal with most situations – but how could they cope with him?" She looked as if she was about to start crying again as she looked down at Seregei.

Weyrn shook his head. "As you say, they're all good people and not stupid by any means, and surely nothing so terrible could happen over a couple of hours while you get some proper sleep."

She bit her lip. "I feel like… I shouldn't leave him with anyone. Not even my friends."

"Why?"

"I don't know! I'm just scared something'll happen and I should have been there to stop it."

Weyrn sighed, resisting the urge to run his hand through his hair. If she realised he was getting exasperated, it would just upset her all the more.

"Alatani," he began, but then sighed. He wasn't sure how to persuade her. At last, he said slowly, "I can't stand seeing you like this. You're obviously driving yourself into the ground. I want to help, but the only thing I can see to do is to find you some way of getting some *rest*."

"But I can't just foist my baby off on someone else!"

"Who said anything about foisting? They're your friends, I'm your husband and his father, and we want to help you look after him and look after yourself." He took her hand. "Please *listen* to me. You're a Swordmaster, love, you know that you can't help anyone when you're so in need of help yourself."

She looked away, shaking her head. "I... this is different. He needs me, and I'm his mother. I can't..."

"Alatani," – Weyrn tilted his head to look at her – "remember that I'm his father. He's my responsibility too."

She bit her lip, still looking tearful, but didn't answer.

"Even if you don't quite trust the others with him –"

"It's not a question of trust," she snapped, but then shook her head. "Sorry. But seriously, I do know I can trust them not to hurt him or anything like that, but..."

Weyrn smiled. "Well, how about me? I'll look after him. Just a couple of hours."

"I'm not sure I could sleep."

"Well, try it." If he could only persuade her to let someone else take over caring for Seregei, he might have any hope of seeing her, and of her truly smiling again...

She sighed heavily, looking down at Seregei. "All right," she said at last, and slowly handed him to Weyrn. "Careful to support his head."

"I've held him before," he said, and leaned over to kiss her cheek. "I'll not take him further than the common room, you needn't worry about that."

She nodded. "Come and get me if he needs anything."

"Only if it's something I can't handle. You get some sleep."

"Don't let me sleep too long!"

"If he needs you, I'll come and fetch you." He kissed her again. "I promise. Until then, I'm letting you sleep."

She frowned, but nodded. "All right. I'll do my best."

He kissed her again, then got up and left, carefully cradling Seregei as he went.

Gelladar accepted the glass of mead that Hurion handed him and smiled his thanks, though internally he winced; he had never liked mead, no matter how many times he had been to Duamelti. "Thank you for seeing me at such short notice."

"Not at all." Hurion sat down opposite him, on the other side of the fireplace. "I was hoping to speak to you anyway, and this afternoon was convenient."

Gelladar nodded. As a matter of fact, he had been expecting to have a couple of days to finish the trade agreements that he and Ethiad had been working on, but the drafts were good enough for approval, at least. "What do you wish to talk to me about?" he asked.

Hurion took a sip of his own mead and Gelladar thought he saw a fleeting smile as the king glanced at the untouched drink in Gelladar's hand. It vanished, though, as Hurion said, "I gather you've been seeking out meetings with the Swordmasters and other Mixed-bloods in the valley."

Gelladar paused a moment to find the best response. He had never had the impression that Hurion would mind, but perhaps that attitude had changed now that friendship between Silvren and the Swordmasters had become a real possibility. "Yes, my lord," he said. "Do you object?" He would be in a delicate position if so; he was still the ambassador to the king of Duamelti, not the Swordmasters, and he had to put that duty first. He didn't want to cause offence to either Hurion or Weyrn.

Hurion also paused before answering. "I have no strong objection," he said. "After all, you have the good of your kingdom to think of, not mine."

"Nonetheless, I am your guest and came here in friendship with you," said Gelladar. To emphasise his point, he took a mouthful of mead and tried not to grimace. He always expected it to taste like honey, but this was much more like over-sweet wine.

Hurion smiled. "I appreciate that, but I do mean it: if I had any strong objections to your befriending the Swordmasters, I might have hesitated to ask for their help in finding you. But your lives are worth far more than any advantage I might have gained."

Gelladar wasn't sure what to make of that; he didn't think it came to a compliment.

Hurion continued, "That having been said, while I don't object as such… I do have questions about it."

Gelladar nodded, sitting forward a little.

"What exactly will this new relationship consist of? A friendship such as I and Lord Taffilelti share?"

Gelladar paused a moment. "I cannot say as yet. I would have to consult Lord Taffilelti; this is, after all, a spontaneous initiative on my part."

"But one he would approve of?"

"I believe so."

Hurion frowned a little, taking another drink. "And is it only with the Swordmasters, or other groups?"

"I was given to understand that the Swordmasters rule the Mixed-bloods." That was a point – the Mixed-bloods were very numerous and

Hurion might feel that such an alliance would be a threat to his own influence.

"In name, at least." Hurion swirled his drink in his glass. "We have had problems with other groups." He looked sidelong at Gelladar for a moment. "There are Mixed-bloods on the Silvren border, aren't there?"

"To the north, yes, my lord."

"Do they recognise the Swordmasters?"

"As far as I'm aware."

Hurion nodded a little, though he was still frowning slightly.

"My lord, may I ask a question?" Gelladar asked carefully.

Hurion smiled a little and nodded again. "Of course."

"Even if you have no objection to a friendship between Silvren and the Swordmasters… you clearly don't desire it. Why not?"

Hurion frowned and for a moment Gelladar thought he had gone too far. Then the Valley-elven king sighed and looked out of the window. Snow was falling in windswept flurries and the view was white and shadowless.

After a moment's silence, Hurion said, "The details aren't really your concern or Taffilelti's."

"Of course, my lord."

"I do wonder, though, why now and not before. Weyrn isn't stupid and he's never hesitated to be civil towards me, but he's never extended the same had to Taffilelti. Do you mind if I ask why not?"

"Ancient history, my lord," said Gelladar with a small smile and drank some more mead.

Hurion raised an eyebrow. "How ancient? I understand Othron met with Weyrn and some of the Tishlondi natives a couple of weeks ago."

Gelladar nodded. "Yes, they wished to discuss the end of the Irnianin rule in Tishlondi."

Hurion's expression twitched, but he hid it with another sip of mead. "I see."

For a moment there was silence. Gelladar wanted to speak, but he knew better than to interrupt the king's thoughts or change the subject. He had to wait until Hurion decided the subject was closed. He did wonder, though, if the Piskam were the only ones who held grudges.

"I assume it goes without saying that I do expect you to continue to prioritise Duamelti's relationship with Silvren over that of the Mixed-bloods."

Gelladar bowed his head. "Of course, my lord."

Again, silence fell. Gelladar had time to wonder whether it would be a good idea to recommend to Taffilelti that the Swordmasters and Hurion receive separate embassies.

Abruptly, Hurion sat up a little straighter in his chair and sighed, setting his drink aside. "I don't think either of us have any more to say on this, do we?" he said, looking directly at Gelladar.

Gelladar smiled, though he wondered what to make of the sudden change in demeanour. "Of course, I'll be more free to discuss the matter once I have approval from my king."

"Of course," said Hurion. "Now... you wished to speak to me as well."

Gelladar sighed faintly in relief as he reached into his bag for the draft trade agreements. At least this was something that was less likely to be contentious.

The day before they were to leave, Weyrn went to the city to see the ambassadors one last time. Gelladar had specifically invited him to come and speak to them in his own quarters. Spring was now well underway and the snow had melted, so it was a pleasant walk down to the city, if wet. Weyrn guessed that Hurion would lend the three Wood-elves horses, and possibly guides.

When he arrived, Gelladar was already waiting, working on a document. He put it away, though, as soon as Weyrn walked in.

"Weyrn, it's good to see you," he said with a smile, standing up and offering a hand.

Weyrn took it. "And you, Gelladar. Thanks for inviting me."

"Your wife and son are doing well?"

"They are indeed. I hope you'll be able to meet them properly next time you visit."

Gelladar nodded. "I look forward to that. I do intend to come back in person next year, and hope to continue our friendship." He gestured to the couch and went to sit down at his desk again, turning the chair slightly to face Weyrn.

Weyrn spoke as he sat down. "I hope so. In fact, I've been wondering about sending one of our people back with you."

Gelladar nodded. "I would be happy to have him," he said slowly.

"But...?" prompted Weyrn.

Gelladar smiled. "I should speak to Lord Taffilelti. I'm confident he'll approve of what we've done, but nonetheless I should speak to him before I take any further steps."

Weyrn nodded. Though he didn't much like the reminder that there wasn't really a friendship between Silvren and the Swordmasters, he knew it was true. "We can discuss that later, then."

Gelladar smiled. "I'll be glad to see it happen."

There was a knock on the door and, at Gelladar's invitation, Othron came in. He inclined his head to Weyrn with a smile.

"It's good to see you again, Captain."

"And you."

"Weyrn and I were just discussing future plans," said Gelladar as

Othron took his place on the couch beside Weyrn.

Othron nodded. "I'm not sure I'll be returning next year," he said sadly.

Weyrn glanced at him in surprise. "Why not? Because of the journey?"

Another nod. "I know that the weather this year was unusual, but... I don't think I could face that again." He shook his head with another small smile, eyes downcast. "I think it would be tempting fate, since I came so close to death this time. If you come to visit, though, I would be glad to welcome you."

Weyrn nodded. "It won't be this year, though. Depending on Lord Taffilelti" – he nodded to Gelladar – "maybe next year."

At that moment, Ethiad arrived with an apology for his lateness. He had been discussing a trade agreement with one of Hurion's clerks and had lost track of time. They summarised the conversation so far for him as he sat down beside Othron.

"Will you come back, Ethiad?" asked Weyrn.

Ethiad touched one ear absently. The frostbite had healed, but he still bore noticeable scars. "I... need to think. Not if it's snowing" – he smiled wanly – "though I've enjoyed my time here and I know it's a poor show to stop coming after only a single visit."

Weyrn glanced at Othron and Gelladar, the two veterans. They didn't give any sign of what they thought.

"How long will it be before you know what Lord Taffilelti thinks, Gelladar?" he asked.

"Not long after we arrive home, I expect. I intend to ask him immediately. Should we write and let you know?"

Weyrn frowned a moment. "If there is a messenger coming to Duamelti, I think that would be useful."

"We can make arrangements, then," said Othron decisively.

Weyrn smiled. "I'm glad we've got this far."

"I appreciate your help," said Gelladar. "We'll certainly be able to set some minds at rest." He glanced at Othron, who smiled.

"About Tishlondi?" asked Weyrn.

Othron nodded. "I told them everything I learned from the meeting you set up for me."

"I asked a few people as well," said Ethiad. "Though no Mixed-bloods."

Weyrn nodded. "You'll have heard a... biased point of view."

"I know, but I've only really interacted with Valley-elves while I was here."

"Well, hopefully that will soon change."

Gelladar smiled. "I'll do everything in my power to make sure of it, if only from gratitude to you and yours; you've been very good hosts and we all owe you our lives."

Weyrn smiled and inclined his head. "I'm glad we could help you," he said. After a moment, he added, "With the politics and the snow."

Gelladar had to admit he was glad to be on his way home again. Though still cold, it was a fine spring morning and he felt secure in the knowledge that they would make it safely back to Silvren.

Weyrn and his wife, Swordmaster Alatani, had come to see them off. She had their baby slung on her back and was currently laughing as Ethiad pulled faces at it. Othron was standing near Gelladar, stroking his horse's nose, and when he sensed Gelladar looking at him he glanced over and smiled, nodding at the trio.

Gelladar chuckled, but before he could speak, Lord Hurion arrived with his own family. Gelladar handed his horse's reins back to a groom and went to meet them, Othron falling in beside him. After a moment, they were joined by Ethiad.

Hurion smiled at them and bowed his head slightly in greeting. They bowed in response as Queen Melannen and the prince curtseyed and bowed to them. Gelladar noticed that the queen had some difficulty; she was heavily pregnant with her second child.

Fortunately, once the ice had been broken, the prince took his mother over to a bench to sit down while Hurion addressed the three ambassadors and the two Swordmasters.

"Another year comes and goes," he said with a smile, "But it appears our t- three realms are getting closer."

Gelladar couldn't help glancing at Weyrn as Hurion stuttered over the number. The Swordmaster was smiling broadly.

"I hope you have a pleasant journey and Lord Taffileti is happy with the discussions we've had. I've a letter here for him that I'd like you to take back." A clerk stepped forward and handed Othron a scroll with Hurion's seal on it.

Othron took it with a nod. "We'll give it to him as soon as we arrive."

"Thank you. I trust at least one of you will return next year?"

"I will," said Gelladar. "It's no reflection on your hospitality, Lord Hurion. You have been a most gracious host and we thank you."

Hurion didn't smile as he said, "One of the things I mention in my letter is the possibility that we will start sending ambassadors to Silvren, every other year, perhaps."

Gelladar bowed his head. "I'm sure Lord Taffileti will give it full consideration."

Hurion did smile a little at that and he nodded. "I won't keep you from your journey any longer. I'm sure you wish to make it as far as possible before night begins to fall."

Gelladar bowed, as did Othron and Ethiad. "Indeed we do, Lord Hurion. Thank you again for lending us guides and horses."

Beside Gelladar, Ethiad shot a sorrowful look at his mount. Gelladar sighed lightly. Ethiad had been extremely attached to the horse he had lost on the way here. Still, neither of them said anything and it was little more than a glance.

Hurion didn't seem to have missed it, but he didn't react except to pause before he spoke. "I hope they serve you well and you have better luck on your return journey. Though" – he glanced at Weyrn and smiled – "some would say you had good luck coming here."

Weyrn raised an eyebrow. "Ethiad was strong enough to reach us in time and my people are good trackers," he said dryly.

Hurion nodded. "Luck nonetheless," he said. "Well… unless Captain Weyrn has anything more to add, I'll let you go on your way."

Weyrn nodded and turned to Gelladar. "As I say, it was good to meet all of you. I hope that we can form more of a friendship between Silvren and the Mixed-bloods and Lord Taffilelti approves of it. If nothing else, I hope we can cultivate a personal friendship."

Gelladar smiled. "I would be happy to call you my friend, Captain Weyrn." He glanced at Othron and Ethiad, who nodded.

"I'll certainly not forget what you've done," said Othron with a weary smile.

Ethiad was about to rub one of his ears, but Weyrn narrowed his eyes and the Wood-elf lowered his hand quickly and said, "Nor will I, and I appreciate your calling me strong." He smiled wanly. "I didn't especially feel it, and I never did actually make it into your camp."

"It was a long path and a rough one, but you got close enough. Hopefully we'll see one another again soon. Let me know what Lord Taffilelti says and I'll send one of my own people to visit."

Gelladar nodded. "I look forward to it."

Weyrn grinned and stepped back. "Safe travels!"

"Thank you." Gelladar nodded to Alatani, who bowed her head in response. "Congratulations again, Swordmaster Alatani."

She smiled. "Thank you."

The three Wood-elves said their farewells, mounted their horses and left, following the guide and guards that Hurion had sent with them. Gelladar turned in the saddle to wave and Weyrn and Alatani waved back. Hurion also raised a hand, though slightly uncomfortably. Then they were around the corner and out of sight.

CHAPTER FIVE

Neithan was enjoying lying on the floor of the Guardhouse common room and playing with Seregei. He'd grown quickly over the past year and was now old enough to stand and crawl about, which meant he was also old enough to be a troublemaker. The Swordmasters had to watch him almost constantly since, as well as getting into places he shouldn't be, he liked to explore the world by putting things into his mouth.

Neithan confiscated one of Seregei's toys just as the baby was about to start chewing on it.

"No," he said firmly. "We do not chew on sheep."

Seregei frowned. "Mine," he said, pointing at it.

"Don't chew it," said Neithan, handing it back. "I spent a lot of time carving it for you."

Seregei just smiled at him and went back to pushing the wooden sheep around the floor aimlessly.

Neithan propped his chin on one hand as he watched. Seregei didn't seem to mind that his companion wasn't really taking part in the game, whatever it was. He was quite absorbed in moving the toys around.

Neithan was glad he'd thought to carve those. Though Weyrn and Alatani had found and made all sorts of toys for Seregei, he was always looking for something new and, in a house full of warriors, there was always a chance that whatever he found would be sharp. Neithan had once turned his back for only a moment and then looked round to see one of his carving knives halfway to Seregei's mouth, despite having been left safely on a table.

He still hadn't told Alatani about that. Though she had relaxed considerably as Seregei grew – and as she spent time away from her mother – she would have been furious. Understandably so, he had to admit.

Seregei had evidently tired of pushing his sheep around and started bashing it against the ground, laughing at the noise it made. Neithan hastily tried to make him stop; Derdhel had been out all night and was probably trying to sleep in his room.

Neithan heard footsteps coming down the corridor behind him and winced as he rolled over to look. He relaxed and grinned as he saw Weyrn.

"Da!" said Seregei happily, abandoning his toys to crawl towards his father.

"Hello, Pestling," said Weyrn picking Seregei up and swinging him around. "Have you been behaving?"

"When he's not trying to eat his toys or tunnel through the floor with them, yes." Neithan linked his hands behind his head and looked up at the ceiling. As Seregei laughed shrilly, he added, "Derdhel's probably asleep."

"I know. Hush, Seregei!"

Neithan looked up again as Weyrn bounced Seregei up and down and shushed him.

"Thanks for watching him." Weyrn set Seregei down again. "Just a moment, Seregei; Daddy needs to talk to Uncle Neithan."

"Up!" Seregei tugged at Weyrn's trouser leg. "Up!"

"In a moment."

"What's happening?" asked Neithan, sitting up.

"Up!"

"Would you mind – in a moment, Seregei! – going on another trip around the border?"

Neithan tilted his head to the side. "Any reason?"

"I've, uh… not done it for a while."

"Up!" Seregei shouted again.

Neithan laughed. "All right. Now?"

"At some point today, and you'll want to be back before dark." Weyrn smiled and finally scooped Seregei up to balance him on his hip. The baby giggled and reached for a handful of Weyrn's hair.

"Now, then." Neithan scrambled up.

"Sorry to ask you to do it, but…"

"No, that's fine. I could do with the walk." Neithan patted Seregei's head. "You look after your Da for me while I'm gone."

"Neeth!" said Seregei happily.

"Good enough."

***

The recent rain had dried up in the warm sun and Neithan enjoyed the walk up into the hills. He wondered for a moment if he should actually follow the border or stick to the roads and he eventually decided on the border. There were several places where the roads didn't go up to the hilltops that marked the edge of the valley and those were probably the places that would need the most care.

As he walked, he looked about for any sign of disturbance in the undergrowth on either side. In some places a hedge would push up close to the path or a tree would overhang so that he had to duck. Fortunately, he'd thought to bring a hatchet and was able to clear the path a little as he went. Every time, he crouched to inspect the branches he'd cut, looking for anything useful. Hazel was good for carving and he took some time to cut it into manageable lengths and tie it to his backpack, alongside some of the more bendable twigs. He wasn't sure what he'd use them for, but they were bound to come in handy and he smiled to himself as he shouldered the bag and walked on.

At length, though, he had to leave the path and then things became much more difficult. He was going along a ridge at the top of a hill now; although the trees had thinned out, the ground was rocky and he had to scramble between broken stones, some taller than he was.

After about an hour, he stopped to rest, perched on a rock. The view from this vantage point was spectacular, but the sun was hot and even on the hilltop there wasn't much of a breeze. He puffed and fanned himself, shrugging off his bag to take out his water bottle. He also unfastened his cloak. It was only light, but it was still too much for this weather and he wondered why he'd worn it. He resolved to break the habit.

He took a long drink of water and looked around again. it would be some distance before he could get back under the shade of the trees and he wondered again if he should just follow roads around rather than sticking to the hilltops. He suspected that the climb down into the next pass would not be an easy one, though if he remembered correctly there were at least some deer-paths.

Something to keep the sun off would be a good start.

His gaze fell on the withies he'd tied to his bag and he smiled. There weren't enough for any sort of wickerwork sunshade, but if he could make a frame and stretch his cloak over it... he untied them and set to work, looking up and around from time to time to take advantage of his view of the surrounding area.

It took about half an hour, but he couldn't help admiring the result. Once he got back into the trees the wicker frame would be unwieldy especially with the long carrying-handle he'd added so he could hold it over his head – but then he'd no longer need it. He finished tying his cloak over it and carefully picked it up, balancing the carrying-handle on his shoulder. It cast a pool of shade over his head and body down to the waist and he grinned as he walked on. Perhaps it looked clumsy, but it would do its job.

Scrambling over the rocks with it was difficult, though, and his smile soon faded. He really needed some way of attaching the sunshade to his shoulder so that he didn't have to hold it in place, but just as he was starting to wonder about a harness – perhaps he could make use of his backpack –

he heard a noise. It sounded like a voice shouting and he paused to listen, lowering the sunshade.

When it came again he realised it was from outside the border. The tone was low and a little rougher than the elven voices he was used to, and he recognised it at once from his youth: that was a human. It wasn't common for humans to come close to Duamelti – many of them feared the elves – but it happened from time to time.

Curious, Neithan removed his cloak from the sunshade and set down the frame, then started down into the forest, navigating by rough guess towards the nearest road.

Fortunately, he heard raised voices again before he'd gone far: several humans arguing over something. He hit a stream and followed it gratefully; its banks were fairly clear, but it was swelling as he went and he frowned. He thought he knew this stream and there was a ford a little further along. Perhaps that was the trouble the humans were having.

He had to move away from the stream as he got closer; the water was still rising, but he glimpsed movement between the trees. He slowed down and squinted to see what it was.

He could see a small group gathered around a cart on the road up ahead, on the other side of the ford. It looked like they were trying to test the depth of the ford, presumably intending to cross, and Neithan made his way over. If nothing else, he would check that all was well.

An hour or so after Weyrn had sent Neithan on his scouting trip, a message arrived from one of the settlements within Duamelti. Alatani answered the door and listened as the elf explained the problem.

"Over the last couple of weeks, sheep have been going missing. We thought they were getting lost at first, but then someone said they'd seen Irnianam in the fields and wondered if they'd been stolen, and then someone else found what looked like wolf prints."

Alatani frowned. "There aren't any packs in Duamelti as far as I know," she said slowly. "I suppose one might have moved in recently, though."

"I didn't see the tracks, and I still think, if something is taking them, it's other elves. Would you come and have a look, and, if it is elves, help us deal with it?"

Alatani nodded. She'd at least be best suited to see if it was wolves, and she'd not be going far; the messenger had said that his settlement was just on the other side of the valley.

"I'll ask Captain Weyrn," she said. "But I'd certainly be prepared to help."

"Where are you going?" asked Weyrn as he entered the room. Alatani explained the problem and Weyrn nodded. "I'm fine with that," he said with a smile. "I can look after things here."

Alatani grinned. "I'll be back before too late." She kissed him on the cheek, just beside his scar, and then hurried to join the messenger.

It was a pleasant day and Alatani couldn't help enjoying the walk across the valley. She had to admit that it was nice to get some time away, and she was looking forward to going to look at tracks. It seemed forever since she'd last been able to use her ranger training.

She wondered whether to hope that there were wolves in the valley. On the one hand, they were potentially dangerous to the people who lived there and their livestock. On the other, she liked wolves and she knew there were precautions the villagers could take to stop them doing too much damage.

"I think it would be best to have a look at the places people saw tracks, and possibly saw Irnianam, before actually talking to anyone," she said as they went. "I'd like to form my own opinions."

He nodded. "I'll take you there, then go back to the village to let them know you've come."

"Is the village clear to see from the fields?"

"Yes."

"All right. I'll go straight there when I've finished."

He nodded with a small smile. "Thank you for doing this. I know it must be difficult to spend time away from your child."

"His father can take care of him for a few hours," said Alatani, hiding a flash of unease at the thought. Though she liked to think she was much more relaxed about being parted from Seregei than she had been when he was an infant, it did still make her uncomfortable. "I'm still a Swordmaster as well as a mother."

He nodded and they walked on in silence, passing through the forest until eventually the trees gave way to fields and heather. Alatani looked around and took a deep breath of the clean, fresh air, listening to the sound of bees buzzing in the heather and the soft bleating of sheep.

"Near here is where we saw the Irnianam," said the messenger. "And the wolf prints were around the edge of the forest over there." He pointed.

"Thanks," said Alatani. "I'll go and take a look."

He smiled a little. "The village is just down that path and across the stream. I'll let them know you're here."

Alatani nodded and turned her attention to the ground.

The short, springy grass would not easily take tracks and she frowned as she walked back and forth. It didn't help that elves were light-footed and as she drew close to the forest there was still nothing to see.

Once she was under the trees, though, her heart skipped a beat as she saw some pawprints. They were indistinct, but she crouched down for a closer look. Four toes, all a fair distance from a roughly triangular pad. She laid her hand on the ground next to it to check the size and nodded slightly. The whole thing was about the size of her palm. This was a wolf's pawprint.

It was too large for any but the largest dog, after all, and the toes were narrow and all close together. She couldn't help the grin that spread across her face. Wolves in Duamelti! The grin turned into a giggle before she could stop it and she quickly put a hand over her mouth, looking around to make sure nobody had heard that. After all, these wolves had potentially been picking off sheep.

She stood up and looked around, sniffing the air. If wolves had taken a sheep, they'd not have cleared up after themselves. She couldn't smell anything decaying and there were no carrion fowl in sight, so it didn't look likely that there was a carcass anywhere nearby. In any case, she couldn't imagine that the farmers and shepherds would have missed something so obvious.

She made her way through the forest for another couple of hours, walking back and forth and looking for any prints from elves or animals. She saw a few more wolf prints, and also some that looked like they were from dogs, but no sign of elves. Nor was there anything to suggest carcasses. She sighed, wondering why the wolves wouldn't have attacked the sheep, since it did seem like they came here fairly often.

She crouched down to look at some more tracks. Admittedly, they looked recent. Without more, she couldn't tell if there were multiple wolves, but perhaps they had passed through only once? She made a mental note to ask about the wolf sighting when she returned to the village.

Then she went back out into the field and looked around. The sun had moved, but other than that nothing seemed to have changed. The bees still buzzed, the sheep were still wandering around her. She looked back towards the forest and couldn't help a smile. There might be wolves in Duamelti…

Weyrn was playing pat-a-cake with Seregei on one of the couches in the common room when he heard a soft laugh from the door. He looked up and grinned as he recognised Elar and Lessai. Elar was still smiling, though Lessai looked rather mutinous.

"Hello," said Weyrn, getting up. Seregei grabbed his hand and he pulled him up to stand on the couch. "It's been a while since we've seen you two."

"We were coming this way and thought we'd drop in. Is Alatani out?" asked Elar.

"I'm afraid so. You're welcome to stay, though."

"Perhaps for a while." Elar came in and sat when Weyrn gestured to a chair.

"Lessi!" said Seregei with a broad grin. "Play!"

Weyrn picked him up and set him on the floor. Lessai didn't look impressed at the idea of playing with Seregei.

"Ma… I'm not a baby," he whined.

Elar frowned at him. "Play with Seregei, Lessai. You're a guest here, so be polite."

Lessai pouted, but sat down on the floor with a huff.

Weyrn turned back to Elar. "How have things been with you?" he asked. "I don't believe we've spoken for a couple of months now."

She smiled. "Getting along. Thank you for finding me that apprenticeship; it has been a huge help."

Weyrn smiled. "I'm glad of that. I know that having a trade can settle you in a new place, even apart from being able to support yourself."

Elar nodded, looking back at the two children. Lessai had taken out a piece of string and was weaving it into patterns between his fingers while Seregei stared at him, fascinated. As they watched, though, Seregei grabbed for the string and Lessai had to jerk it away, prompting Seregei to start whimpering as he kept trying to get hold of it. Weyrn quickly got up to separate them.

"Seregei, that's Lessai's toy. It's not nice to snatch."

"Wan' it!" protested Seregei, the first tears spilling over.

"You can't just take other people's things. How would you like it if he went to your room and took away one of your toys?"

Seregei sniffled, putting his hands over his ears.

"Seregei," said Weyrn a little sharply. "You listen to me. What don't we do?"

"Snash," muttered Seregei.

"Good. Now play nicely or you'll have to sit on the couch."

Seregei's lip wobbled, but he nodded and Weyrn kissed him on the forehead, then went back to sit with Elar. She smiled at him.

Just as she was about to speak, though, they heard voices approaching the door. Weyrn smiled as he recognised Celes and Eleri, the healer who had attached himself to them over the past few months.

The two came in, laughing at something Celes had just said, and Celes smiled a greeting at Elar and Weyrn. Eleri hung back slightly until Weyrn waved him in with a warning to mind the children on the floor.

"Of course," said Eleri and nodded to Lessai and Seregei.

"'Leri!" exclaimed Seregei, crawling over to greet Eleri. "Up!" He reached out to be picked up. Eleri picked him up and handed him to Celes, who swung him round, making him shriek with joy.

"How are things down in the city?" asked Weyrn, getting up to let Lessai go over to Elar.

"Pretty much as normal," said Eleri after a glance at Celes. "My superior says that I may be able to start spending less time in the healing house and more with you if you think it's necessary, though."

Weyrn frowned a little. "I appreciate it, but it's probably best for you to stay based down there for the time being, since things seem to be quiet."

He absent-mindedly licked his fingertip and rubbed it behind his left ear to ward off bad luck. Eleri did the same.

"All right. I'll be ready if you call, though."

"I'll earmark a room for you, in case you do have to spend nights here." Weyrn grinned. "Thanks for joining us."

Eleri smiled back. "It's an honour."

Neithan got a little closer to the humans before he turned towards the road himself; it was probably best to approach them that way rather than appearing out of the trees. He smiled wryly as he reflected that it was lucky he was on his own; relatively short and slight, he wasn't too alarming a figure.

It seemed that they didn't see him coming even then, though. They'd pulled a couple of planks off the cart and were apparently trying to push them across the river to form a makeshift bridge.

"Hie!" he called, waving.

A couple looked round, startled. "What do you want?" one shouted.

"I was going to ask if you needed any help."

They looked awkwardly around at one another for a moment before the same one carefully asked, "In return for what?"

Neithan blinked. "Nothing. Where are you going?"

They looked at one another again.

"I can see you're trying to cross the river, but were you trying to reach my people in Duamelti? If so, there's a shorter road into the valley."

"No, uh… actually we were trying to go around the elven valley. It's just on the other side of these hills, isn't it?"

Neithan nodded. "I just came from there."

"Well, we're trying to ford the stream, but it's far deeper than it should be this close to its source." He shot Neithan a suspicious look as if the elves were somehow responsible.

"There's been rain recently," Neithan explained. "I came down this stream from the hills and it's high the whole way. You'll probably not be able to cross here."

The human huffed irritably. "Is there another crossing point within a sensible distance?"

"You could go back the way you came until you come to the place where the road forks, take the other fork and there's a bridge about ten miles along that road."

"That'll add another couple of days to our journey! Is there no way we can just bridge the ford?" He pointed to the planks. "We've been trying, but…"

"I don't think those will take the weight of your horses, apart from anything else," said Neithan slowly. "You could brace them with stones, perhaps. Then they wouldn't flex as much." There was a row of broad stepping stones crossing the river, running beside the ford, though they were awash. "Lay the planks across the stepping stones and they might bear the weight of the cart. Will your horses go through the deep water without it?"

"Yes, I expect so, but then how are we to bring the cart across without the horses?"

Neithan looked around. "Have you got any long ropes?"

"To attach to the horses and drag it across that way?"

"Yes. Or if we could make a pulley system of some kind..." Neithan looked around again, but the human made another huffing noise.

"All right, elf, we'll play it your way."

"It's either that or you add those couple of extra days, or find a way to bring a cart through that ford," said Neithan dryly.

The human sighed and turned to his companions. They whispered for a while, then a couple of them started unhitching the horses while the spokesman stepped forward again. Neithan folded his arms and waited while that human and another one inspected the edge of the stream.

"All right," the spokesman said, loud enough for Neithan to hear him. "It shouldn't be too slippery. Let's go."

Two humans mounted the horses and rode them across the ford. The water came up to the horses' bellies and Neithan could see when he tilted his head that they had been right to hesitate; it would have flooded the cart entirely.

The humans looked awkwardly at him as they rode up to him and conversed for a moment in a language he couldn't understand. He hesitated. Perhaps these two didn't speak Elven. There were an increasing number of humans who didn't, and the human languages were far different from one another...

When he asked, it was confirmed: they didn't understand Elven or the only human language he know: that of the city where he had grown up.

He sighed and gestured to them to stay where they were; he'd have to keep talking to the same translator.

The villagers were less pleased with the news of wolves than Alatani had been. She had expected that, but it was a slight disappointment nonetheless.

"Given that I couldn't find any carcasses, I think I can safely say that the wolves aren't what's been taking your sheep, at any rate," she said firmly. "They don't clear up after themselves. You'd have found bones and seen carrion-birds before now."

"But what if they come down towards the village?" asked one elf worriedly. "I have children, I'll not risk them if there are wolves about."

"It's not likely that they will come down. They tend to be scared of people. Let them be and they'll let you be."

"But even if they're not taking the sheep now, who's to say they won't start if we don't drive them off?"

That was a fair question and Alatani paused a moment before answering. "Do you have dogs who could stand guard?" she asked.

There were a few nods. "Against sheep-thieves and - in lambing time - foxes."

"How large are they?" It was something she needed to ask in any case, just to make sure that those hadn't been dog tracks in the forest.

They took her to see their dogs: large, shaggy creatures that looked half wolf themselves. She smiled, patting one. It looked up at her with the wide, panting smile of dogs everywhere and wagged its tail. "If they're brave dogs, I imagine they could keep wolves away from the sheep as well."

The elf she was talking to still didn't look happy. "I don't trust them," he said slowly. "The wolves, I mean."

"Then trust me. I've met wolves many times before. If you don't give them reason to come near the village - don't feed them, for example - and don't interfere with them, your dogs should be able to keep them from the sheep. As I say, if they were going to go after them I don't doubt they would have done so already. If they do, you'll know, and you can tell me. I'll do what I can to deal with them. In the meantime, I think we need to worry more about the possibility that the thieves are Irnianam."

The elf nodded, though she noticed the wary look he shot towards the hills. "All right," he said slowly. "Will you speak to them for us?"

"I'll walk around the nearby settlements. I should do that anyway, to warn them of the possible arrival of wolves."

"I thought they would be no danger?"

"Provided they're not interfered with or given any reason to approach the villages." Alatani smiled. "As I say, don't feed them: be careful how you dispose of any carcasses, for example."

He nodded. "I'll spread the word around. I'd feel happier if they were gone, but…"

"I won't help with that. Not unless they do cause unprovoked harm."

"All right."

"But I will talk to the other villages and see what can be done about finding your sheep."

He looked happier about that, at least, and nodded again. "Thank you."

The stepping stones were not quite wide enough to form a secure base for the cart. Neithan reflected that he should have tried to measure them somehow before suggesting them, but it wasn't worth worrying about that now. He frowned, absent-mindedly rubbing one of the small scars on his forearm. He knew that there was no real need to worry about this, but he'd accepted the challenge now and he had no intention of walking away until he'd tried to solve the problem.

"All right," he said slowly, looking around. "What's in there?"

The human raised an eyebrow. "Why?"

Neithan resisted the urge to roll his eyes. "How heavy is it?"

"Do you think that if we empty out the cart, it'll float?" the human asked sceptically.

That hadn't been something Neithan had thought of, and he shook his head. "If we had something to float it on, that would be a good idea, but I was actually thinking more that we could make it light enough to be less likely to break the planks if we lay them across the stepping stones."

"Then how are we to get our goods across?"

Neithan looked around. The stream wasn't that wide and it might be possible to make something like a giant pot-tripod if he had a long enough branch and could fit it into the fork of a tree. The same thing that made it easier to move pots on and off a campfire might make it possible to move bundles across the stream.

Alternately... "How heavy are the goods?" he asked again. "Could the horses go back and forth with them?"

"They're not pack horses. We trained them to pull and sometimes to be ridden."

"But could a man ride them carrying a bundle?"

The human considered a moment and nodded. "Some things."

"Well, there's an idea for a start. How heavy is the cart when it's not loaded?"

"I suppose it could be light enough. We can draw it by hand when it's empty."

"Well, that seems a good place to start, then."

The human still looked suspicious and consulted with his companions for a moment. Neithan folded his arms to wait, still looking around at the surrounding forest for anything that might help get the heavier things across. He wondered idly if they were just being awkward about the possibility of carrying bundles on horseback, but dismissed the idea. It was in their interest to find a way across, after all.

He couldn't see a branch that would do to carry anything across like a pot-tripod. It would have to be very long and strong with it, after all, and he wondered whether that idea was at all practical. After all, if he didn't have one of the things he needed for the plan, he would have to find either a way to get it or a new plan.

Still, the human spokesman called for the two riders to come back and the other members of the group started unloading the cart. Neithan went to inspect the stepping stones to make sure they were stable.

What did he have? The horses, the planks, the stones, the trees, a length of rope and some helpers, most of whom he couldn't talk to. How could he use that to get the cart and its contents across?

Well, the lighter things were settled. The men could pick their way across the stones and the horses had already shown they could get through the ford. They had a plan for the cart… could the heavier things be floated on a raft of some sort once they had finished with the planks?

The humans had unloaded the cart and the horses were coming back with their first load. Neithan offered to help the two riders with it – using gestures – but though he was sure they'd understood they just shook their heads and one stayed with the bundles while the other rode back. Neithan was about to call across to the spokesman, but the human also saw the problem and sent someone over to guard the goods while the rider went back. Neithan fought the urge to roll his eyes. Apparently they thought he would start going through their belongings right in front of them.

Once again, he ruefully asked himself why he was helping these people, but then he smiled a little. It was a challenge. That was all there was to it.

Alatani had been in the nearest Valley-elven village for a couple of hours now and was finding them all very unhelpful. She hadn't seriously suspected anyone there of being a sheep thief before she arrived, but after the third time an elf became completely unco-operative the moment she asked to see his sheep and compare their marks to the one she had been given, she did have to wonder.

"Look, this is actually suspicious now," she said to the village's leader. "Let me inspect the sheep for marks and I'll be on my way without further questions."

He folded his arms. "I'll do no such thing without authority from the king's court," he said. "You have no right to come in here and call us thieves."

"I'm not calling you any such thing. Stray sheep doesn't make anyone a thief. *You're* the one putting that name on yourself, but I *will* start using it if you don't let me look!"

The Valley-elf shot her a look of deep dislike. "I don't answer to the Swordmasters," he said curtly. "Come back with a messenger of the king."

Alatani frowned, but she couldn't very well barge into their sheep folds without permission of any kind. She'd have to go and find someone to help her.

"Very well," she said, equally curtly. "I'll see you soon." Then she turned and left. She'd have to talk to Weyrn first; he was Captain, after all. She'd go straight there.

***

When she arrived, it was to find Elar and Weyrn sitting out on the bench outside the Guardhouse. Seregei and Lessai were playing on the grass. Or, rather, Lessai was trying to build a tower of blocks while Seregei occasionally decided that he wanted one of the blocks.

"Seregei!" chided Alatani as Seregei made a grab for the bottom block in the tower.

They all looked up and Weyrn smiled a welcome as Seregei scrambled up and stumbled towards her.

"Ma!" he cried, reaching out to be picked up.

"What do we not do?" she asked firmly.

He pouted. "Snash."

She smiled and picked him up, kissing him on the nose. He giggled. "Has he been good?" she asked Weyrn.

He also got up and came over to kiss her cheek. "He has, actually."

"There's no need to sound quite so surprised." She grinned at Elar. "It's good to see you. It seems like it's been forever."

"It does. That's why I decided to come and visit." Elar got up, brushing off her skirt.

"How were things at the village?" asked Weyrn.

"I need to talk to you about a couple of things."

Weyrn nodded, but then glanced at Elar. "Urgently? Because I can look after the children if you two want to talk for a while."

"It can wait an hour," said Alatani thoughtfully. "I did have a confrontation with a Valley-elven village. I was asking about the sheep and they said they wouldn't help unless I had Hurion's authority."

"I'll see what I can do," said Weyrn.

"Thanks." Alatani set Seregei down again. "You go play. I'm going to talk to Lessai's ma for a while."

Seregei smiled up at her, then scrambled off towards Lessai.

"I'll keep an eye on them," said Weyrn.

"I'll be back soon," said Alatani. "And I'll tell you what's happening."

"Thanks. I will need to know some details before I speak to someone at court."

"I could go."

"It would probably help to have my authority behind the request."

"All right." Alatani smiled and squeezed his hand. Then she turned to Elar. "Shall we walk and talk?"

"That suits me," said Elar. "Be good, Lessai."

He looked up. "You'll be back soon?"

"I will." She patted his head and came over to join Alatani. Together, they set off down the path towards the archery butts; that seemed the best way of getting a circular walk.

"Is anyone practicing today?" asked Elar, gesturing along the path as they went.

"Celes and Derdhel might be." Alatani cocked her head to listen for the sound of arrows hitting targets. She couldn't hear anything, though. "Seri went to visit friends, but those two went this way with their bows. Derdhel doesn't like these butts, though."

"Sometimes I wonder about learning to shoot." Elar looked down at her hands.

"Why? It's a useful skill, but not one I'd expect you to need."

"Mostly because it's useful. I often feel worried that if we did have to leave I'd not be able to feed myself and Lessai. At least if I had any ability to hunt…"

"Is it likely?" asked Alatani, her step faltering for a moment.

"Well, I wouldn't say likely, but…" Elar shrugged. "I can't help worrying. I never feel quite like I fit in here."

"Why?"

"Well… everyone else around me has lived there for centuries. They all know one another and spend time together, and I'm not… one of them."

Alatani frowned. "I didn't know you were having problems like that."

Elar smiled. "I'm probably being a bit over-dramatic. It's really not so much of a problem. It just worries me sometimes."

"Anything that makes you wonder about the possibility of being forced to leave is a problem."

Elar nodded. "It's just a moment's paranoia. I don't think we'd be forced to leave, but… I'm not sure we fit in."

Alatani bit her lip, but nodded. "How are things apart from that?"

"Actually going well. The weaver I'm apprenticed to is very kind to me."

"Good. I hoped she would be when we found her."

"I'm learning a lot from her, especially about finer weaving, and she pays me very well considering that I'm only an apprentice."

Alatani smiled again. "Good. And you don't get the feeling that she resents the fact that you're an incomer?"

"No, actually. I was worried, but I'm probably closely related to Duamelti mixed-bloods, after all… I just hope Lessai doesn't have trouble."

"I shouldn't think so." Alatani sighed. "There are incomers who have lived here all their lives without trouble except when there's some other reason for people to take exception to them." She sighed again, but then shook her head. "There's no reason for you and Lessai to have that problem."

Weyrn had tucked Seregei in for a nap and was sitting on the couch in the common room, trying to think of a story to tell Lessai, when Elar and Alatani returned. Elar saw at once that Lessai was tired and bored and promised to take him home so he could nap.

"They were well-behaved?" asked Alatani, going to sit beside Weyrn as Elar and Lessai left.

He nuzzled her hair, inhaling the smell. They didn't often get a chance to curl up next to one another on the couch, but he forced himself to draw away with a sigh. "Yes, they were. But... you had some news for me?"

She nodded, also moving away a little. "First, I think there's a sheep-thief out there, and I suspect a nearby Irnianin village."

"The one you had trouble with, I assume?"

"Yes, and that's why I'm suspicious. All I wanted was to see their sheep and I even said it could just be that the ones I was looking for had strayed, but..." She shrugged, looking irritated.

"All right. I'll go and let someone know and get authority." Weyrn sighed, tilting his head back against the back of the couch. He didn't like the fact that he had to ask, but he knew it couldn't really be helped. There was too much separation between the Pure-bloods and Mixed-bloods and this wasn't the first time one group had refused to listen to the representatives of the other. "Was there anything else that I should know about?"

She suddenly grinned, leaning her head against his shoulder. "I think there's a wolf pack in the area."

"That... doesn't seem like something to be so happy about."

She poked him in the ribs. "You know I like wolves."

"And you know I don't like potential –"

"Oh, don't you start." She twisted to sit upright and look at him. "They won't bother the villagers if let alone and given no reason to go into the village. They've not taken any sheep so far and I looked at the sheepdogs; I think they'll be enough of a guard to make sure it doesn't happen in future."

He sighed. He still wasn't happy about this, but she knew wolves better than he did. She'd been a ranger and scout even before she came to the Swordmasters, after all.

She apparently saw his expression change; she leaned against him again. He once more smelt her hair, losing himself for a moment in the warmth of her presence. There had been so few peaceful moments recently...

With a regretful wince, he raised his head again and did his best to turn his thoughts back to his duties. He still needed to find help to confront these Valley-elves and, regretfully, it really would be best coming from him. "Are you all right to hold the fort while I go down to the city?" he asked.

Alatani also stirred and nodded. "Yes, I'll wait for the others. See you soon, though?"

He kissed her hair. "See you soon."

***

It didn't take long for him to walk down to the city and he immediately went to find one of Hurion's clerks; this wasn't important enough to take to anyone higher up. He explained the problem to the elf he found, who looked uncertain what to do.

"Are you sure the Swordmasters alone can't handle it?" he asked awkwardly. "It sounds like it's a problem with Mixed-bloods more than Valley-elves."

"The loss of the sheep may be, but the ones refusing to help us are Valley-elves and won't speak to us about it."

The clerk tapped the end of his pen against his chin. "I don't think anyone from the court would be able to accompany you today," he said.

Weyrn was pretty sure that wasn't true. "It need only be a short visit."

"Nonetheless, we're all very busy."

Weyrn fought the urge to roll his eyes. He was happy to be accommodating and diplomatic, but he was sure this elf was being deliberately obstructive. "Listen, I'm trying to settle this amicably. You know perfectly well that some of the clans even within Duamelti take livestock theft *extremely seriously*. They've called my people in to help and I don't want trouble any more than you do, but I will keep pushing this until I either get the help I need or come to the conclusion that you want us to take this into our own hands."

"I hope you're not accusing those Valley-elves of –"

"At the moment I don't have a lot of choice. It looks a lot like someone there has a guilty conscience and good reason not to let us see the marks on his sheep. Whether he's just being obstructive or whether we'd find that not all those sheep had the same marks, I don't know, but it doesn't exactly look good, does it?"

"Is everything all right here?" said a voice from behind Weyrn. He turned and smiled tensely at Master Aklamarth, a minor Valley-elven judge he vaguely knew. Aklamarth nodded a greeting. "Captain Weyrn. It isn't often we see you here."

Weyrn gestured to the clerk, who looked considerably more comfortable now that someone more senior had arrived. "I was hoping for help with a dispute between Mixed-bloods and Valley-elves."

"A dispute?"

Again, Weyrn explained about the sheep and Alatani's unsuccessful journey to the Valley-elven village. "He says that nobody can be spared to accompany me."

Aklamarth sighed, eyes upturned for a moment. "Certainly not for any length of time," he said, looking at Weyrn again. "How far is it?"

"Not far. Across the river and up the hills to the edge of the trees."

"I see. Well, I have a few things that I need to handle here, but in an hour or so I could be spared for a little while."

Weyrn nodded. "I appreciate it."

"Will you return in an hour? I'll meet you here."

"Very well." Weyrn nodded to the clerk, bowed his head a little more to Aklamarth and turned to go.

It had taken some time for the humans to get all the lighter things across. They refused any help from Neithan apart from advice, but they had slowly begun to move the cart, rolling it carefully from plank to plank balanced on the stepping stones. Neithan couldn't help a grin as he saw that the plan was working. The planks bent, but not enough to break; they were on wide enough supports. Neithan turned his thoughts back to moving the heavier things. There were six planks. Perhaps that was enough to make a raft, if there was any way to make it float.

"How bad would it be if any of that were to get wet?" he asked the spokesman, pointing to the things still piled on the far bank.

The man looked towards the pile. "Bad," he said after a brief hesitation.

A raft probably wouldn't work, then. Neithan huffed out a breath and looked around again. That also ruled out any ideas such as dragging the bundles on the planks as if they were sled runners. It looked as if some sort of pot-tripod might be the only way, unless… He looked up at the branches over the stream. Might they be strong enough to hold a weight?

He looked down as the cart finally reached dry land. The spokesman nodded to him and looked worriedly over at the man he had left guarding the last of their goods.

"How heavy are they?" Neithan asked again, pointing. "Would the rope carry them if it were tied to one of those branches?"

The human looked up, also guessing at the strength of the branches. "I… suppose it might. What have you in mind?"

"Toss a rope over one of the nearer branches, hoist up each bundle at a time and swing it over."

The human looked sceptical, but nodded. Neithan had to wonder how heavy the things in the bundles actually were, but decided that they'd be able to get the heft of them as they swung and the humans would know what was in them. He doubted they'd let him handle anything.

He was right. He stood and watched as they tied a stone to the end of the rope and tossed it over a tree branch that he indicated, then held his breath as two of them tied the first bundle to the other end and lifted it, ready to swing it across. It did look heavy and he hoped the branch would hold.

It creaked ominously as the first bundle swung across the river, but two men on Neithan's side caught it and lowered it to the ground. Neithan let out the breath in a sigh. So far, so good.

The second and third bundles also went across easily, but, just as he was starting to feel satisfied with himself, the fourth arrived and the man catching it slipped. It started to swing back. Neithan dashed forward to grab it before it could go – he wouldn't risk it hitting the men still on the far side – but one of those with him shoved him aside, pushing him over, and let it go.

Neithan got up, brushing himself off and staring at the spokesman. "Excuse me?" he said softly, nodding towards the man who had pushed him.

The spokesman looked uncomfortable and said something quickly to the man, who responded immediately.

"He apologises."

"Well… good. But what was that in aid of?" Neithan fell silent as they made another attempt to get the troublesome bundle across. This time it was caught and lowered to the ground without any trouble. "I was trying to stop it swinging back."

"Yes, but…"

"I've gone out of my way to help you, why are you so suspicious of me? Anyone would think you had something to hide."

The spokesman blinked and looked around for a moment. The two other men, ignoring the conversation, caught another bundle. There was only one left.

"Where exactly are you going, anyway?" asked Neithan.

"Just… around the valley. I don't really think you need to know any more, since that means we'll not be troubling the elves."

"I'm a Swordmaster. That means I'm not only concerned with the elves in Duamelti."

The human frowned. "What does that mean?"

"It means that I want to make sure you're not planning to harm or harass any of the elves living outside the valley."

"Oh, no, of course not. We're just heading for a settlement of humans on the other side of the valley. We're not going to attack anyone who doesn't attack us."

Neithan nodded. "That's all I needed to know. We are keeping an eye out, though, so don't be too surprised if you see other elves with this badge." He tapped the Swordmaster emblem on his sleeve: a grey leaf on a brown diamond. The human nodded.

"We'll bear that in mind. And we do appreciate your help today." Behind him, the last bundle swung across.

Neithan nodded. "I'm glad I could help. Just…" He rubbed his bruised shoulder pointedly and the man smiled.

"I'm sorry about that." He glanced round. The two men who had been swinging the bundles across had joined them and they were packing the cart up again.

Neithan nodded. "Well, good luck with the rest of your travels."

"And you with yours," said the man with a small smile, though he still didn't look quite comfortable. One of the others shouted something, nodding towards Neithan. The spokesman winced.

"What did he say?" asked Neithan.

"Oh... nothing."

Neithan narrowed his eyes and the spokesman sighed. "All right, he was wondering – and I admit we all are – what you're expecting in return."

"For helping?"

"Yes."

"Well, I would like to know what you're doing, but..."

The man looked around, then said, "That really is all we're doing: just going to this settlement. We have things to trade."

Neithan nodded. "That's a fair reason." He shrugged. "I suppose chance meeting can't be trusted."

The man looked relieved and shook his head. "I'm glad you understand. And, really, thank you."

Neithan nodded. "Good luck," he said, and turned to go. He'd head a little further back up the road, then go back through the trees and continue his circuit of the valley from where he'd left off.

Weyrn and Aklamarth walked in silence up into the hills. Every time Weyrn glanced over at the Valley-elf, he was walking steadily with his eyes fixed on some point in the distance, his hands folded behind his back. He never looked at Weyrn.

"It's a nice day," he said at last.

The sudden speech had actually startled Weyrn, but he nodded. "It is. Enjoying the walk?"

"There are worse ways to spend an afternoon," said Aklamarth with a small smile.

"Well, thanks for coming, anyway."

Aklamarth glanced at him. "It is an important thing to help with," he said seriously. "Perhaps someone less senior would have done just as well, but then you do things that are far below your dignity all the time, don't you?"

Weyrn frowned. "What do you mean by that?"

"Well, I'm told that the Captain of the Swordmasters is equal in dignity to the king. What *are* you doing investigating sheep theft?"

"Well, actually it was Alatani investigating it, but we knew I had a better chance of promptly getting help in the city. After all, it's not as if there was an immediate reaction when *I* asked."

"My question stands, nonetheless."

"Well... it may not be important to the overall affairs of the valley, but it's important to that village."

"And I don't suggest that you ignore the need, but do *you* really need to be the one to deal with it?"

"They asked for our help and there was no reason for them not to have it. If there were something more important and more urgent, we would have to find someone else to help them, but that wasn't the case."

Aklamarth sighed. "You don't find that it reduces your power and dignity to be always running after every stray thing?"

"Same to you," said Weyrn with a small smile, gesturing along the path in front of them.

"*I* am here at the request of the Swordmaster Captain," said Aklamarth lightly, shooting Weyrn a small smile in response.

Weyrn did have to laugh at that. "And that means it's not below your dignity to go chasing sheep-thieves?"

"Indeed not." Aklamarth looked up the path again. Weyrn sensed that the conversation was over and looked ahead himself.

***

The village leader who came to meet them upon their arrival in the village seemed to know that things were more serious now.

"Swordmaster Alatani was here earlier today," Weyrn told him. "She wanted to see some sheep that may have strayed from a nearby village and she said you told her that she couldn't see them until she had authority from the King's Court."

Aklamarth stepped forward. "I am Aklamarth, judge of the lower courts, here to grant Captain Weyrn what further authority he needs."

The elf looked between them for a moment, several times looking as if he were about to speak and thinking better of it. At last, he sighed and hung his head.

"Come this way," he said softly.

Weyrn smiled at Aklamarth and they followed the elf through the village to the fields beyond. Alatani had given Weyrn a sketch of the mark he was looking for and he glanced at it as he went. Aklamarth glanced over at it as well and Weyrn tilted it for him to see better, but he just nodded and looked ahead.

"These are mine," said the elf, gesturing to a dozen sheep grazing nearby. He put noticeable emphasis on the word 'mine' and Weyrn raised an eyebrow at him before climbing over the fence. Aklamarth didn't follow.

The sheep milled about as Weyrn approached and he considered asking the shepherd to help him corner them so he could inspect them, but then he spotted a familiar mark on one woolly shoulder.

"Hah," he muttered and dived for that sheep, grabbing her by handfuls of wool to lead her back over to the fence, where he had left his slate. The elf still standing with Aklamarth was looking increasingly nervous.

"What's your mark?" Weyrn asked him.

The elf looked from Weyrn to Aklamarth, hesitating. Weyrn frowned. If he tried to claim that this was his mark, that was outright theft. Some clans demanded hanging for livestock theft: a penalty Weyrn had never liked, especially when the livestock could be returned."

The elf sighed, his shoulders drooping "That's not it. I found those sheep straying and nobody ever claimed them."

Aklamarth nodded, also moving back a little. Weyrn frowned at him for a moment, then said, "You didn't try to find their actual owner?"

The elf blinked. "No. Why should I?" A little more confident, he squared his shoulders. "If they can't keep good enough track of their own sheep, that's not my concern."

"But if you find sheep that you know aren't yours and make no attempt to find their owner, then you've stolen them."

The elf turned to Aklamarth, who shook his head. "That's not our law, Captain," he said. "If livestock are found straying, the one who finds them holds them for their owner for three days and if nobody has come to search for them before then they become his."

Weyrn's frown deepened. "Aklamarth, can I have a word in private?"

"Of course."

Weyrn climbed back over the fence and he and Aklamarth walked a little way off. As soon as they were out of hearing, Weyrn said, "He stole those sheep from a Mixed-blood farmer and you plan to let him keep them?"

Aklamarth visibly bristled. "He didn't steal them - they strayed and he found them; it's a fair claim, if nobody ever came looking for them."

"He knew they weren't his and he kept them anyway."

"If your people can't keep proper track of their livestock…" Aklamarth shrugged a little.

Weyrn frowned. "Regardless, they belong to a Mixed-blood farmer, so what has happened here is theft."

"He's not a Mixed-blood," said Aklamarth, also frowning. "Why should your laws apply over ours?"

"Because those are the victim's laws."

"They're much harsher than ours and it's hardly reasonable to hold someone accountable under laws not their own in their own home. If he were travelling in another kingdom it would be different, of course."

Weyrn took a moment before replying to marshal the words correctly, then he said slowly, "You are aware that there are two systems of law in this valley just as between here and Silvren."

"I am."

"So why shouldn't he be held accountable under our laws?"

"Because in this valley our laws are just as valid. Those are the ones by which he lives, regardless of the laws of the original owner of those sheep, and it's not fair to apply any others."

Weyrn frowned. "Well, what would your laws call for?"

"How long has it been? More than three days?"

Weyrn sighed a little. "Yes."

"Then I say he should be permitted to keep them." Aklamarth spread his hands. "It's harsh on the original owner, but he should have made proper enquiries. What would your law dictate?"

Weyrn shook his head a little. "It depends a lot on the clan, but –"

"Well, then," Aklamarth interrupted, "If this were between two clans, whose law would you apply?"

Weyrn took a moment to think about that. He'd not fully apply the harshest one, that was certainly true, but if one law said a crime had been committed and the other said it hadn't… "I'd find a compromise," he said. "Some middle road."

"But here that would still leave him guilty of theft, wouldn't it?"

"Yes."

Aklamarth paced up and down. "That isn't right," he said firmly.

"It's also not right that the actual owner of the sheep should be left with nothing."

Aklamarth looked as if he was about to protest, but then he nodded. "I take it these things are flexible among your people," he said.

Weyrn nodded.

Aklamarth paused, then said, "I don't want him to be held guilty of a crime that doesn't exist under our law," he said firmly. "Nonetheless, if you can find a compromise, I'll accept it."

Weyrn nodded. "I'll go and find out what they're expecting. But I think he should at least return the sheep."

"I'll speak to him."

***

It wasn't far across country and Weyrn soon arrived at the Mixed-blood village, where he met with a warm welcome.

"Any news?" the elf who had met him asked.

Weyrn smiled. "We've found the sheep."

The elf sighed in relief. "Where? What happened?"

Weyrn winced a little. "Where's your village elder? I need to discuss it with him."

"Were they stolen by Irnianam?"

"Found and not returned." Weyrn sighed. "I need to discuss it with your elder."

The elf nodded. "This way."

When they got there and Weyrn explained, the village elder listened to the problem with an increasing frown.

"I don't understand," he said at last. "You're our ruler and you're responsible for enforcing our laws. Why should you listen to this Valley-elven judge?"

Weyrn sighed a little. "Because I would go to your defence if he were trying to impose an unfair law on you."

The elder nodded slowly. "That's true, you would," he said with a small sigh. "Well, our laws dictate that the thief should return the sheep and also be fined twice their value from his own flock."

Weyrn nodded. That wasn't as harsh as many punishments for livestock theft, but he didn't think Aklamarth would agree to it and he had to admit that if their positions were reversed then he wouldn't have accepted it either. "Would you accept a return of the sheep?"

The elder sat back a moment, scowling. "Captain… if our laws aren't to apply to them, then they'll target us all the more."

"They wanted there to be no crime and for him to be allowed to keep the sheep without quarrel," said Weyrn. "I do intend to put the name of thief on him."

"I appreciate that." The elder sighed again. "I… I will accept that, but I would like some form of assurance that this won't happen again."

Weyrn nodded. "I'll see what I can do." At least he'd make sure that Aklamarth now knew of the Mixed-blood laws and would take word back to his own court.

***

When he returned to the Valley-elven settlement, he found Aklamarth in the middle of settling some other small dispute, but as soon as the Valley-elf had finished he came over to Weyrn.

"What did you decide?" he asked.

"Their law requires that the sheep should be returned plus twice their number as a fine."

Aklamarth's eyes widened. "No," he said flatly.

Weyrn raised a hand. "I explained the situation and they are prepared to compromise on the understanding that it should be noised around that finding and keeping is still theft."

Aklamarth frowned, but nodded a little. "I'll make that clear at court. But I will not agree to such a thing as him being fined twice as many sheep when he hasn't done anything wrong."

Weyrn shook his head a little. "I do understand that, and I think they do as well, but something has to be done." Weyrn sighed. "Spread it about that finding and keeping livestock is considered theft, even if you want to add a caveat in this case, but I want those sheep returned."

Aklamarth sighed a little, but nodded. "I'll do that, and see to it that you can drive them back with you."

Weyrn sighed, relieved. "Thank you."

It took Neithan two days to make his circuit of the valley, and he was glad to once more be on the road leading down from the hills to the Guardhouse. Since he'd cleared it on the way up it was far easier to pass and he smiled a little as he saw the places where he'd cut the undergrowth back.

At last, with a sigh of relief, he turned the corner onto the path that led to the Guardhouse. As he walked, he could hear laughter drifting between the trees, along with the clashing of wooden swords. He sighed, grinning, then called a greeting as he paused at the edge of the clear grass around the Guardhouse.

Alatani and Celes were the ones practicing and they stepped apart when they saw Neithan. Celes was still smiling and Alatani wiped her brow with the back of her hand, puffing slightly.

"Out of practice?" Neithan asked her with a grin.

She nodded. "Still getting back into it." She gestured at Celes with her free hand. "And he's getting better."

"Thank you." Celes went to lay his sword on the bench by the door. "How was your trip, Neithan?"

"Mostly uneventful."

"Mostly?" asked Alatani. She nodded thanks as Celes passed her a handkerchief.

"I met some humans just outside the border. Do you know where Weyrn is? I should mention it to him."

"He's off in the city. He took Seregei with him for the day." Alatani smiled, but her eyes strayed towards the city.

"They'll be fine," said Celes gently.

"I know," said Alatani, a little impatiently.

"Who else is around?"

"Seri went to visit friends on the other side of the valley. Derdhel's around here somewhere, but I couldn't say where."

"And Maelli?"

"Here." Maelli stepped out of the doorway, smiling. "You must be tired, not to have seen me."

Neithan laughed. He wasn't especially tired, he just hadn't been looking at the doorway. Still, he nodded.

"I can go to find Weyrn if it's urgent," said Maelli.

"Not especially." Neithan went to sit on the bench, carefully pushing Celes' sword to the side. "It can wait."

***

Weyrn arrived back a few hours later, giving Neithan time for some food and rest. When Weyrn arrived, he waved a greeting and grinned in response to Seregei's attempt to call his name, but didn't say anything until Weyrn had returned Seregei to his mother and come over.

"How was it? Alatani said you'd asked for me as soon as you arrived. Is something wrong?"

"I met a group of humans outside the border. There are a lot of swollen streams, but they're not causing any trouble except at the particular ford where I met them." Neithan described the stream and ford that he meant.

"But they weren't coming into the valley? Where were they going?"

"That was the strange thing: they were very unwilling to tell me. Even when I pressed them, they wouldn't say exactly where their new settlement was."

Weyrn huffed out a breath. "I don't much like the sound of that."

"Nor do I. They assured me they'd not trouble any elven settlements, but…" Neithan shrugged. "I also couldn't make out what was in that cart. They wouldn't let me help to handle anything – in fact, they pushed me away when I tried."

"They must have been hiding something." Weyrn sighed. "I've not heard anything about trouble with humans recently, but it might be worth sending someone to take a look around that area. Derdhel, perhaps. He's good at keeping himself hidden."

"Less good at giving an account of himself if he meets someone," said Neithan with a smile. "I'm afraid that's all I know, though."

"I'll send Derdhel and Maelli, I think. Then I'll see what they say and decide what to do next."

When Derdhel and Maelli returned, they reported that there was indeed a scattering of humans appearing throughout the forest, but for the most part they seemed to be disorganised, limited to small family groups. As the humans that Neithan had met had said, they didn't seem inclined to trouble any elves and Weyrn was content with that.

Hurion, however, didn't seem quite so sure. He had sent Weyrn a message asking to speak to him about the humans in the area. Weyrn sighed, but went to see him.

When he arrived, Hurion got up from his desk to greet him with a small smile.

"It's good to see you again, Weyrn. It seems we hardly speak to each other."

Weyrn nodded. "Indeed, it's been some time since you last asked for a meeting with me." He chose his words carefully to make it clear that it had been a request, not an order.

"Perhaps I should do so more often?"

Weyrn paused before answering. They rubbed shoulders frequently, but he could never shake the feeling that Hurion only spoke to him when he wanted something. Good had come of Hurion's request that they rescue the Wood-elves – not that Weyrn begrudged them his help – but it wouldn't do for it to become a habit.

The silence had stretched uncomfortably long and Hurion coughed. "Please sit," he said, gesturing to a chair by his desk. Weyrn nodded and sat.

"You wanted to speak to me about humans?" he said, leaning back.

"Yes." Hurion also returned to his seat, leaning forward with his elbows on the desk. "I know they're not in the valley yet and so technically not my concern, but I'd like to know what to expect before they *become* my concern. What are your thoughts?"

"Neithan met some travelling by. Apparently they seemed a little uncomfortable about Duamelti and were quick to assure him that they weren't going over the border, but they refused to give him any details of what they were doing."

"I don't like it," said Hurion.

"They've kept to themselves, according to Derdhel and Maelli."

"They've spoken to them?"

"What happens outside the border may not be in your purview, but it is in mine. As soon as Neithan came back with that news, I sent out scouts."

Hurion frowned, glancing away. "Well… I suppose that's your business. I would have liked to know, though."

"It is my business," said Weyrn softly. "And if they'd come back with anything concerning, I would have told you about it."

"I appreciate that. And, of course, I didn't mean to suggest that you should have sought my approval."

Weyrn nodded. "Well, I can assure you that we are keeping an eye on them."

"Good. That's a relief." Hurion leaned back in his chair. "Do you know what's bringing them here?"

Weyrn shook his head. "Just expanding to greener pastures, I think. They really weren't willing to talk to Neithan or any of the elves Derdhel and Maelli met, let alone to Derdhel and Maelli themselves. But they're scattered and don't seem to be organised."

"That's good. I worry sometimes."

"I don't think there's anything to worry about at the moment."

***

Another year passed without incident, though Gelladar returned that spring with two ambassadors Weyrn hadn't seen before. They were friendly enough and informed him that Ethiad might return the next time, though Othron intended to remain safely at home from now on, if he could. Weyrn arranged to send Maelli and Celes back to Silvren in late summer.

Now, though, it was only late spring: a fine, warm day. The ground was dry, though the grass was still thick and green. Weyrn took a deep breath and let it out again in a laugh. It was a good day for practicing and he wondered whether to go and get his wooden waster and drill.

Then he had another idea. Seregei and Lessai were playing together in the common room, watched over by Elar while Alatani was investigating a report that her wolves were causing trouble, but soon Elar and Lessai would have to return home and they would have to find another way to entertain Seregei. Perhaps today was a good day for his first lesson with a sword.

With that thought, he went to find Neithan. He'd need a second pair of eyes and hands.

He found his friend down by one of the streams near the Guardhouse, fiddling with what looked like a fishing rod. As Weyrn approached, though, he looked up with a smile.

"What are you working on?" asked Weyrn, nodding at the fishing rod.

"A reel to hold extra line. It'll mean we can put a hook further across a river." Neithan lowered it. "What's happening? I assume you were looking for me."

"I can't just be looking to speak to my friend?" teased Weyrn, sitting down on the riverbank. He sobered as he thought about it more. "Neithan, do you think I've been neglectful?"

Neithan looked at his fishing rod for a moment, then set it down. "Well... I think you've kept your word. You've not sent us into danger or used us to shield yourself, but I also think we're all lucky that the last few years have been peaceful and you've never needed to make the choice."

Weyrn sighed, the words hitting deep. "But given the circumstances, what do you think?"

Neithan spun the reel with his finger and blew a stray strand of ash-blond hair back from his cheek. "I'd not say you've been neglectful, but I do think that you're suffering from the number of hours in the day. You have Seregei to care for, and you have your duties as Captain, and..." He shrugged.

Weyrn sighed, reading the meaning in the shrug. "I am sorry. It's especially wrong of me to let it reach the point where I would only be coming to speak to you because I want something."

Neithan smiled. "I was joking, but I accept the apology."

"I'm glad, especially as... I actually *did* want your help with something."

Neithan chuckled. "What is it?"

"I'd like to give Seregei his first lesson with the sword."

"Good luck," said Neithan fervently. After a moment, he added, "You, um... don't think he's a little young? He's only two."

Weyrn shook his head. "It's nothing especially strenuous. I expect he'll think of it as a game."

"Nonetheless... I'm not sure Celes is ready for a trainee either." Neithan smiled, but his tone was serious.

Weyrn looked sharply at him. "The sword is a good skill to have. It'll make him strong and nimble and help his balance and co-ordination."

"He's two years old," said Neithan gently. "I'll help with a first lesson or two, just playing with a practice sword, but I think he's too young for serious training." His voice dropped and he looked away.

Weyrn tilted his head to look Neithan in the eye. His friend forced a smile.

"It's nothing, I'll be fine."

"I know you were young when you had to be an adult, but I'm not considering pushing him to anything he's not ready for. It's not the same."

Neithan laughed a little. "I know, but still." He stretched. "I meant it. I'll play with you and your son and a wooden sword. But I don't think you should formally train him."

Weyrn nodded. "Point taken. I won't. And… I'll also try to pay a little more attention to the rest of you." He smiled, knowing it looked forced.

Neithan took the thought for the deed, though, and smiled back. "Come on, then. Let's go and find him."

***

Once Elar and Lessai had left, Weyrn went down to the armoury in the city with Neithan and Seregei. It took some time to get there; it seemed everyone wanted to stop Weyrn and talk to him. Most of them wanted especially to play with Seregei, who was delighted with the attention. At last, though, they walked into the cool stone armoury. Weyrn put Seregei down and kept firm hold of his hand as the little boy looked around, wide-eyed, at the racks of weapons on all sides. On the left, there were bows of many different strengths, all unstrung and stored in buckskin cases. On the right were the swords.

Weyrn looked down at Seregei. His eyes were wide as he looked at the shining hilts of the swords and daggers.

"Down here!" called Neithan. Weyrn tugged gently on Seregei's hand and started off down one of the aisles between the racks. Seregei lagged along behind, tugging on Weyrn's hand.

"Da, want that one!" he cried suddenly, stopping in his tracks. Weyrn looked down to see Seregei reaching for one hilt just out of his reach. He laughed.

"It's too big for you, little one," he said.

Seregei pouted and reached again.

"Come on," said Weyrn, pulling on his hand again. "Uncle Neithan's looking for one for you."

"That one," said Seregei firmly. "Mine."

Weyrn shook his head. "Come on, your sword is down here. You can't have that one, it's too big for you."

Seregei dragged along behind him, whining softly. "My sword," he said, pointing back.

Neithan had found the wasters. Seeing Weyrn and Seregei coming, he held one out. It looked like it was actually a practice dagger, but it might do for someone Seregei's size.

"Let me see?" said Weyrn, reaching for it. "You hold on to Seregei."

Neithan took Seregei's hand, keeping hold of him as he tried to pull back the way they'd come. Weyrn took the dagger and felt the point.

"No, it's too sharp."

"What?" Neithan took it back. "This wouldn't cut butter!"

"Feel the point. It's too sharp."

Neithan touched the point of the dagger to his finger and scowled as Weyrn began his own search. "All right," he said thoughtfully and put it back.

As Weyrn continued to search, he suddenly noticed that Neithan was peering under the rack.

"Neithan? What are you…" Then he realised Seregei was no longer by his feet. "*Neithan!*" He almost threw down the sword he was holding as he looked around. "Seregei! Seregei, where are you?"

There was a sudden crash and clatter from further down the aisle. Weyrn's heart leaped into his mouth as he dashed towards it.

The sight he saw as he rounded the corner made him feel almost giddy with relief. Seregei was sitting in the middle of a mess of scattered weapons, but he himself was unhurt. He was holding the sword he'd pointed out before and grinning proudly.

Weyrn sighed in relief as Seregei scrambled up, still gripping the hilt.

"Mine!" he proclaimed.

Weyrn shook his head. He could see the whole sword now and it would have been comically large even for him. "Seregei, it's too big for you."

"No. I'm big. I'm grown up." Seregei pouted at him. "Is mine."

"How about this one?" asked Neithan, coming up beside Weyrn. He was holding out a small wooden sword that he had presumably grabbed at random. Fortunately, it looked blunt enough.

Seregei looked at the wooden sword, but shook his head. "This's mine."

"This one's for you," said Weyrn, pointing to the wooden sword. Seregei shook his head.

"I'm big! I can have mine!" As if to prove his point, he spun round, dragging the sword off the ground by sheer momentum.

Unfortunately, Neithan had just been reaching for it and the blade caught him across the hand.

Neithan swore, dropping the wooden sword and raising his bleeding hand to his mouth. He glared at Seregei, who started to cry, still holding the sword.

"Neithan, are you all right?" asked Weyrn, even as he went to Seregei's side. The little boy was wailing in earnest now, but he still wouldn't let go of his chosen sword.

"'m fine," said Neithan, still licking his wound.

"Let me see it."

Neithan held out his hand awkwardly, trying to shield it from Seregei's sight. The cut was long, but looked shallow, and Weyrn sighed in relief, turning his attention back to carefully cuddling Seregei.

"You should go to the healers, though, just in case."

"No, it'll be fine."

Weyrn looked up with a raised eyebrow and Neithan shrugged self-consciously.

"I don't especially want to tell them I got it from a two-year-old."

Weyrn chuckled, looking down at Seregei and taking out a handkerchief to dry the child's eyes. "Ask Eleri. He won't judge."

Neithan nodded.

"Sorry, Uncle Neeth," said Seregei softly, sniffling a little.

"That's all right." Neithan dropped on one knee. "Come and give me a hug to make it better."

Seregei ran over and threw his arms around Neithan's neck. Neithan hugged him back, careful not to get blood on his shirt, and shot Weyrn a significant look over his head. It took Weyrn a moment to realise what he was getting at, but then he quickly gathered up the dropped swords and put them away, with Seregei's favourite on a high shelf. Hopefully he'd not be so interested in the others.

"There we go. All better." Neithan sat back and smiled at Seregei. "Come on, let's go home."

Seregei looked for the metal sword that he'd dropped and frowned as he saw it was gone. He looked suspiciously at Weyrn, who proffered the hated wooden sword.

"Here. This one's yours."

***

Weyrn had found a wooden dagger for himself – it seemed unfair to use a weapon longer than Seregei was tall – and was trying to teach him some basic blocks while Neithan watched. Every time Weyrn glanced over at his friend, he saw a look of mingled disapproval and amusement. Apparently this was too close to teaching rather than playing.

Seregei, meanwhile, was growing increasingly frustrated. Eventually, he threw down his sword and plumped down beside it.

"Are you tired?" asked Weyrn, though he could guess the actual problem.

Sure enough, Seregei kicked the wooden sword. "Want bigger. Want mine."

Weyrn sighed. "Seregei, you're not big enough to use a real sword yet. You'll hurt someone."

"Will not," said Seregei, closing his eyes and turning his back to Neithan.

Weyrn went over and picked Seregei up, but the boy deliberately made himself a dead weight and flopped to the ground again as soon as Weyrn let go of him.

"Seregei, you have to learn with a wooden sword first." Weyrn caught himself wishing Alatani was there. He didn't know what to do and there were tears starting to appear in Seregei's eyes again. His face was getting redder and redder and Weyrn tensed in readiness for the scream.

Then Neithan broke in. "Seregei, you don't want a big sword."

"I do, I do, I *do*!" Seregei's voice rang shrill and he threw himself on his face, thumping the ground with one fist.

"No, you don't." Neithan came over, winking at Weyrn. "You know why? Because a warrior must be tickled in proportion to the size of his sword!" He scooped Seregei up and immediately started tickling his ribs. Seregei shrieked and giggled, flailing at him, and Weyrn couldn't help laughing too as he sat down, relaxing at last.

"Still want a big sword?" asked Neithan, grinning.

"No!" giggled Seregei, rolling away and scrambling up, wooden sword in hand. "This's my sword!"

Weyrn smiled and started to scramble up, picking up his own wooden dagger. Then he glanced at his wooden sword, leaning against the wall of the Guardhouse. "We've been at this for some time, Seregei. Are you tired?"

Seregei looked thoughtful, though he was still grinning. Weyrn picked up the sword, then turned as Seregei spoke.

"Da... *you* have a big sword."

"No, no, *no*!" Weyrn turned to run, but Neithan was fast enough to catch him.

Alatani returned from her visit to the villages in a foul temper. She had had to spend some time convincing a worried group of elves that trying to trap the wolves and move them somewhere else, such as outside the valley, would most likely result in someone being killed.

As she turned onto the path towards the Guardhouse, though, she heard a yell and a burst of laughter, three voices mingled together. She smiled as she heard Seregei's high-pitched voice ringing above the deeper tones of Weyrn and Neithan.

Then her smile broadened into a grin as she rounded the corner and saw them on the green space in front of the Guardhouse. Neithan was pinning Weyrn's arms and shoulders while Seregei sat on his stomach, tickling him. Their practice swords and a pair of daggers were scattered on the grass.

Alatani paused a moment at the edge of the clearing, leaning against a tree to watch. Neithan and Seregei made a truly merciless pair, she reflected as they finally let Weyrn up. For his part, he grabbed his waster and waved it at Neithan, shouting threats as the younger elf doubled over laughing. Alatani did her best to smother her own laugh, unwilling to interrupt the scene. Seregei was waving one of the wooden daggers triumphantly and Alatani sobered a little as she looked at him. She wondered if that was how this had started. Surely Weyrn knew better than to hand little Seregei a weapon...

The boy looked very happy with his new 'toy', though, and she couldn't help another fond smile. Maybe they had another Swordmaster here, many decades in the future, once she and Weyrn were dead.

"Ma!" he shouted, spotting her. He dropped his dagger and scrambled over to her, tripping and picking himself up once or twice, and she went to meet him.

"What have you been doing while I was away, little one?" she asked, and kissed him on the cheek. He smelled of fresh air and dirt and she smiled.

"Da and Uncle Neeth are teachin' me swords," he said, pointing back to where he'd dropped his dagger. "I wanted a big sword, but Neeth said I had to get tickled. So then we tickled Da."

Alatani wasn't entirely sure she saw the logic behind that, but she nodded and picked him up, going over to where Weyrn and Neithan were dusting themselves off.

"I hear you were teaching him to use a sword?" she asked, absently bouncing him on her hip. He was getting heavy to do that, but she was still strong enough.

Weyrn nodded. "I thought it would be a good thing for him to at least start learning."

She looked down at Seregei with a frown. He smiled at her. "I got a sword."

Weyrn picked up Seregei's dagger and handed it to her for inspection: a miniature sword with flat, sanded-off edges and a round point. She sighed in relief. "All right. That's probably safe enough." She put Seregei down and he reached up for his sword, but she shook her head. "Just a moment, Seregei. I need to talk to your Daddy."

He pouted. "Sword," he said, pointing. "Is mine."

"He wanted a full-sized metal one," said Weyrn.

"Yes, he's been eyeing yours for some time." Alatani sighed. She knew there'd been several close calls.

"Mine!" yelled Seregei, reaching for the sword again. Alatani carefully tested its edge and point again, weighing it in her hand. Not too heavy and, indeed, completely blunt.

"All right," she said slowly, and passed it down to Seregei. He laughed and ran off, waving it around and cutting the air.

"You should have checked with me," said Alatani bluntly.

Seeing where this was going, Neithan took a few steps back, presumably to give them some privacy. Weyrn folded his arms.

"There's no reason not to try to teach him."

"What if he's hurt?"

"I don't think that's likely. You checked the sword yourself." He reached out to pat her shoulder. "You don't need to worry. I've been taking care of him."

She sighed. She knew she could trust him, but that didn't make her any less worried. "I know, it's just... I don't like it. He's only young and isn't as dextrous as he will be when he grows up." Perhaps when he was a little older she'd worry less about him.

Weyrn hugged her and she rested her cheek against his shoulder, holding him close.

The moment was broken as Seregei came running back over. "Ma! Swordfight with me!"

Seregei quickly took to carrying the little sword with him and he had carefully tucked it into his belt when it was time to attend the Midsummer feast at Hurion's palace. Weyrn looked down at him with a proud smile as they walked. He remembered that it had taken some time for him to get used to walking with a sword and he was glad Seregei was taking to it so well. He avoided Neithan's eye; he knew his friend still didn't approve.

When they arrived at the feast, Weyrn bade the others farewell and went to take his seat at the high table. They were really invited as a gesture, but he was glad of the recognition that he was supposed to be Hurion's equal. The other Swordmasters also had reasonably honoured seats at the top end of one of the main tables.

As Weyrn took his seat, he nodded a greeting to Takari, Hurion's chief advisor. The Valley-elf hesitated a moment, but then nodded in response before returning to his conversation. Weyrn sat back and looked around, feeling uneasy. He and the other Swordmasters were the only Mixed-bloods present.

Seregei wasn't the only child in the hall; young Prince Kerin was there too, sitting on his father's other side. Weyrn couldn't see him from his seat, but knew he was there: a quiet, well-behaved little boy only a month or so younger than Seregei.

As soon as the first course had been served, laid out on common platters at intervals on every table, Hurion stood up. Silence fell as he looked around the hall.

"Tonight we once again gather to celebrate midsummer's day. I welcome you *all* to my home and bid you drink and be merry as long as the night lasts." He looked around again with a smile. "And now, without further ado, let the feast begin!"

Weyrn nodded down the table at him and he smiled in response, then turned away to speak to Caleb. Weyrn, for his part, glanced down at the other Swordmasters again, mentally judging when it would be time to leave.

He preferred the Mixed-blood celebrations, but it would have been an insult not to have come and, what was more, it might encourage Hurion to ignore him in future.

He became aware of eyes on him as he reached for a piece of bread, and he glanced round to see Takari looking hard at him.

"Is something wrong, Takari?" he asked after a moment, when the Valley-elf showed no sign of looking away.

"That's Master Takari, Weyrn" said Takari softly.

Weyrn frowned. He'd had this argument once or twice, and had thought they'd come to an agreement. "In that case, it's Captain Weyrn."

Takari sniffed, going back to his food.

"You didn't answer my question, Master Takari. Is something wrong?"

"No, it's nothing. My lord knows what he's doing, I'm sure."

The only question in Weyrn's mind was whether that was even subtle enough to bear the name 'sarcasm'. He put his bread down very deliberately.

"Doing about what?"

"Some of the guests he's invited tonight."

"Like who?" Weyrn asked very deliberately.

Takari paused a moment, looking at him, before gesturing carelessly around the hall. "There are some here who I don't think should be seated in places of honour with the king."

Weyrn paused a moment. He knew perfectly well that Takari was talking about him. The only question was whether to make a fuss in the middle of the feast, in front of everyone.

"If you disagree with Lord Hurion about who he invites to sit with him," he said slowly, "you should take that up with him and not sit staring at me." He glanced past Takari at Hurion, who was deep in conversation with his wife and seemed not to have noticed the building confrontation. As Weyrn went back to his dinner, though, ignoring Takari, he saw that the Swordmasters were watching him carefully as they ate. Even Seregei squirmed uncomfortably in his chair, though that could have been simply because he didn't like the formal setting.

"I was rather hoping you'd have the manners to leave," said Takari softly.

Weyrn stiffened and looked round again, his grip tightening on the knife he was holding. "What?"

Takari's lip curled. "I believe you heard me, whelp."

Weyrn glanced past Takari again, but if Hurion knew what was happening, he ignored it.

"Watch your manners, Takari," he said softly.

"I'm not the one giving himself airs by sitting with his betters."

"You are the one insulting a fellow guest, though." Weyrn leaned in a little closer. "Whether you like it or not, I am Swordmaster Captain. I am *High Thane* of the Mixed-blood elves and that means you should treat me with respect. Is that clear?"

"Captain?" said a rather nervous voice behind him. Weyrn looked round. A Valley-elf about his own age pointed at his right hand. He looked down as he realised that he was gripping his knife so tightly that his knuckles showed white through the skin. He slowly let go and laid it down.

Takari looked over Weyrn's shoulder at the other elf and nodded. "Thank you. Someone who named his son after Terathi can't be trusted with a knife in his hand."

That was the final straw. Weyrn slammed his hand down on the table and sprang up. Silence fell up and down the table. Out of the corner of his eye, he saw Neithan also stand.

Hurion looked round and got up as well. "Captain Weyrn?"

Weyrn scowled at him over Takari's head. "Lord Hurion, I did not come here to be insulted by members of your council. I suggest you teach them better manners. For now, though, I and my people are leaving."

Hurion shot Takari a savage look, but then looked back at Weyrn. Most of the hall was staring now.

"Captain, I apologise. Please sit down and continue your meal."

"No." Weyrn picked up his cup. "I will drink a toast, though. It's a Mixed-blood tradition at festivals." He raised it to the room. "To Bladedancer!"

"To Bladedancer!" echoed the other Swordmasters, though they were the only ones in the room who spoke. Then Weyrn drained his cup, marched around the table and started for the door. He heard the others falling in behind him, walking by rank with Neithan on his right and Seri on his left, Maelli and Alatani behind them and Derdhel and Celes bringing up the rear. Weyrn led the way up the aisle between the tables, not looking round as he went. He knew everyone was staring and kept his head up, retreating with all the dignity he could muster.

At last, the heavy main door slammed behind them and they set off down the road into the forest, grouping together a little more now that there was more space.

"What did he *say*?" asked Neithan after a long silence.

Weyrn sighed, finally relaxing a little. "That we had no right to be there and, specifically, that I had no right to be at the high table. Then he added that someone who would name his son after Terathi couldn't be trusted with a blade."

Neithan drew a hissing breath through his teeth and looked over at Alatani. Weyrn followed his gaze. Alatani was carrying Seregei, who was staring at him in confusion, chewing absently on a lump of cheese. Pieces dropped unheeded from his small fist.

Celes stepped forward and put a hand on Alatani's shoulder as she bent her head to nuzzle Seregei's hair. Weyrn enveloped the two in a hug, making Seregei wriggle and squeak in protest against his chest.

"I admire your nerve in mentioning Bladedancer's name after that," said Seri dryly. "I wonder how many of them even know who he was."

Derdhel stepped back a little to look around. "It's still a fine night," he said. "What shall we do now?"

"Go and find a celebration where we'll be welcome," suggested Maelli.

"That was my thought," said Weyrn. "I imagine there'll be plenty tonight."

They set off again, Weyrn still with an arm around Alatani's shoulders. Seregei was still gnawing on his cheese, looking up at Weyrn with wide eyes.

"Da," he said at last. "Why'd we go?"

Weyrn sighed and patted him on the head. "Because someone there was being very rude. You'll understand better when you're older."

It didn't take long for Seri to find some friends who were having their own celebration, singing and playing instruments around a bonfire. They welcomed the Swordmasters with delight and Weyrn sat down gratefully by the fire.

"Did you bring your flute?" asked Neithan, sitting beside him.

Weyrn laughed before he answered, watching Seregei's expression as one elf began roasting an apple on the fire. "I didn't, I'm afraid. I wasn't expecting to want it."

"Well, you will." Neithan started to get up, but Derdhel stopped him.

"Stay and enjoy the fire. I'll go. It's a nice night for a walk and it will still be here when I return." With that, he turned on his heel and walked away.

Celes sat down on Weyrn's other side and shrugged. "If I were feeling malicious, I'd say that he's going to go have words with Takari."

Weyrn scowled. "Let's not talk about him any more tonight." He accepted a mug of cider with a grin and a nod, then raised it. "To Bladedancer!"

This time, the answer was an enthusiastic roar. "To Bladedancer!"

CHAPTER SIX

Weyrn was sitting outside the Guardhouse, playing his flute in the sun, when he heard a voice call his name and smiled a welcome at Eleri. The healer waved and came over to join him on the bench outside the Guardhouse.

"I always forget what a nice place this is to sit," he commented as he sat down.

Weyrn grinned and stretched his legs out, wriggling his toes in the grass. "Why do you think I decided to live here?"

Eleri laughed, also sitting back. "Listen, about –"

"Eleri!" cried a high-pitched voice and Weyrn's grin broadened as Seregei came running out of the Guardhouse. Six years old now, his dexterity and intelligence had outstripped his size.

Eleri got up to greet up, picking him up and spinning round with him.

"You're starting to get heavy," he said, putting him down.

"He's not grown that much." Weyrn also got up and patted Seregei on the head. The little elf looked up and stuck out his tongue. "Manners," chided Weyrn, tapping him on the head with a fingertip. "Where's your mother?" He knew she'd gone on a patrol to the far end of the valley, but he asked anyway.

"Gone out." Seregei pointed. "She said she'd be back t'morrow."

"Good. Why don't you run and play?"

"Derdhel showed me a bird's nest today," said Seregei. "There were three baby birds in it. They went like this!" He tilted his head back and opened his mouth as wide as he could.

Weyrn glanced at Eleri, who was hiding a smile.

"Yes, they do that so their mother can feed them."

"Derdhel said the mother bird throws up and the baby birds eat it." Seregei made a face.

"Yes, that's disgusting." Weyrn smiled and picked him up to give him a hug. "I need to talk to Eleri. Do you mind?"

Seregei shook his head. "I'm going to build a den."

Weyrn grinned and kissed him on the cheek, then set him down and watched him run off into the woods.

"He'll be fine," he muttered and turned back to Eleri, whose smile had faded a little.

"Do you worry?"

"Sometimes." Weyrn sighed and shook his head a little. "I know there's little that can happen to him so close to the Guardhouse, but that doesn't stop me worrying."

Eleri nodded and went to sit down.

"What were you saying?" asked Weyrn, going to join him.

Eleri frowned for a moment, then nodded. "I remember: I was going to say that there's actually quite a lot of concern in the city. This feud between you and Hurion has gone on for four years now. That's a long time."

Weyrn frowned. "I'd not go as far as 'feud'."

"I would," said Eleri seriously, "and I'm not the only one."

Weyrn's frown deepened. "How much of a problem is it?"

"There... have been worse, but it has people worried. It's... not been long enough."

Weyrn looked sidelong at him. "Since Ninian died?" he asked, keeping his voice steady. The death of his first trainee still haunted him, but he could talk about it now; he accepted that the healer that had come to help had done all he could.

Eleri was nodding. "I know it's not something you like to discuss."

"I know what you mean, though." Weyrn leaned back against the wall. "You think it's starting to be that serious again?"

Eleri frowned. "I wouldn't say quite that serious. There hasn't been a real split, after all, and at least it's only over an insult and not a death. Think about it, though. I'd hate to see it go too far."

"Do you... remember those days?"

"I'm younger than you, but not that young." Eleri sighed. "I was an apprentice at the time."

Weyrn glanced at him. "Did you know Healer Santhi at all?"

Eleri winced. "Only by name. And... several people in the healing house did want to help, but —"

"Eleri, you don't think I blame you, do you?"

"Well... not really, but that doesn't mean that we didn't blame ourselves." Eleri hitched his shoulders. "I was only an apprentice. There was nothing I could have done, but there was always a question. In any case, it was an alarming experience and I'd rather not see that sort of quarrel again."

Weyrn swallowed the question that immediately came to mind. He knew that if there were to be a similar event, Eleri would stand with them. And he would be better protected than poor Santhi had been.

"I'll do what I can to avoid that," he said at last.

"See that you do," said Eleri firmly. "Takari is a fool. It's not worth tearing the valley apart over him."

"All I want is an apology. Preferably from him, but Hurion would do."

"You didn't need to respond in kind."

"Respond in kind?" Weyrn twisted to look at Eleri straight on. "I *do* think he let it go as long as he did deliberately."

Eleri shook his head slightly. "I doubt it. He's not that stupid." He sighed. "Listen, Weyrn, every time you or one of the others goes into the city everyone holds their breath."

Weyrn blinked. "Really? I know meetings with members of the court are tense, but…"

"But nothing," said Eleri firmly. "You need to do something about this." He looked away and leaned back against the wall, apparently considering the subject closed. "Where are the others? I know about Alatani, but apart from her?"

Weyrn explained that Seri was visiting friends, Neithan was still testing his fishing reel – apparently it was almost perfect after only four years' tinkering – and Derdhel had taken Celes off towards some of the rockier hills to practice climbing. Maelli had escaped going with them because Weyrn had sent him to look into a dispute about a Valley-elven judge trying to count the Mixed-bloods living in a village. Given the current situation, he'd thought it would be a bad idea to go himself.

Eleri winced when he heard about Derdhel and Celes. "I'd better wait until those two get back. Derdhel never knows when to stop. What is it he always says about pain?"

" 'Pain is fleeting' or 'Pain is weakness leaving the body'?"

"I don't think I've ever heard him say that second one." Eleri looked up just as Weyrn also heard someone approaching, pushing their way down the path that led to the road. He didn't recognise the step, so it probably wasn't a Swordmaster, and he got up to greet the visitor.

A young Mixed-blood came hesitantly out onto the clear space around the Guardhouse. He looked around a moment, but then saw Weyrn and Eleri and bowed his head in greeting. Weyrn stepped forward.

"Good afternoon. What's your name?"

"Eteline, sir."

"What brings you here, Eteline?"

"Well, there's a messenger come looking for you. He says he's from one of the clans outside the valley."

"Looking for us? Why did you come instead of him?"

"He was worn out and didn't know the way. We thought it would be faster for one of us to come and get you, and would give him a chance to rest."

Weyrn nodded. "Is it far? And do you know anything about his message?"

"My settlement isn't so far, but he didn't say much, just that it's about a quarrel between his clan and some of their neighbours."

Weyrn nodded and looked around for Seregei. He shouldn't really leave the Guardhouse entirely unoccupied, especially with Seregei running around, but there wasn't really a choice; he couldn't be sure when anyone would be back.

"I can babysit," said Eleri. "Especially as I'm staying in any case."

"Thanks," said Weyrn. "I doubt he's gone far, but maybe go and look for him if neither he nor I is back in an hour?" He looked at Eteline again. "Which settlement is it?"

"At the foot of the mountain," said Eteline, pointing to a particular peak on the edge of the valley, not far off.

"I know it." Weyrn asked Eleri, "If anyone comes looking for me and can't wait, tell them where I've gone?"

Eleri nodded and, with a wave, Weyrn followed Eteline.

***

In fact, it took about half an hour to reach the settlement: a collection of only about ten houses grouped around a well. Weyrn spotted the messenger immediately; most of the inhabitants of the village were gathered around a tired-looking elf sitting perched on the edge of the well. When he saw Weyrn, he got up and the group around him parted a little.

"Swordmaster," said the messenger with a small bow. "My name is Surian. I come from a clan that calls itself Stone's Breath. For some years, we've had a feud with a neighbouring clan, but it recently became more violent. I was sent to ask for help."

Weyrn nodded. "Sit down, Surian. I understand you had a long journey."

Surian gratefully sat back down on the edge of the well. "Yes, sir. Some days, and I came as quickly as I could."

Weyrn nodded and looked around at the crowd. "Do you mind giving us some space?" he asked dryly, softening the words with a smile. They unwillingly dispersed, though he could still see a few, mostly children, peering around the corners of buildings and doorways.

"I'm Captain Weyrn. Why don't you tell me more about this feud, and I'll see what we can do to help."

Surian smiled. "Thank you." He sighed, looking down. "It's been some years, as I said, but the most recent quarrel is over a river crossing. They charge us tolls to cross there, but" – his voice rang indignantly as he looked up – "we helped to build the ford in the first place."

"And this has been going on for years? If your respective thanes couldn't decide the matter between themselves, why didn't you come to us before?"

Surian shifted uncomfortably. "It just got worse."

Weyrn nodded. "So what's happened?"

"We... think they've kidnapped our thane."

Weyrn blinked, startled. "What?"

"We think they've kidnapped our thane," Surian said again. "He was to go and meet them. The agreement was that he and their thane would meet at the ford and discuss it. They'd go alone in order to avoid a fight breaking out, and..."

Weyrn winced. "I suppose he kept that promise and they didn't."

"That's what we think, Captain, though it's difficult to read the tracks. There are many people who go through that ford; it's the only way to the Naith from this direction."

"The Naith?"

"You don't know it?" Surian looked a little surprised, but got down from the wall and crouched to draw in the dust. Weyrn crouched beside him as he drew two lines to form a triangle with a line from the point, then a circle a little way off. "That's Duamelti," he said, pointing to the circle. "These are rivers" – he pointed to the lines – "and this is the Naith." He pointed to the inside of the triangle, then glanced hopefully at Weyrn.

Weyrn frowned. "I think I know it," he said slowly. "I'll have to look at a map when I return to the Guardhouse. Go on, though. Where's the ford?"

"Here." Surian drew two lines across one of the rivers. "This is our territory" – he outlined an area on the Naith, next to the ford – "and this is theirs." Another area on the other side of the ford.

Weyrn nodded and watched as Surian drew a line to show the road across the ford and towards Duamelti. "How did you get here, if that's the only way out? Pay the toll?"

"No." Surian smiled a little. "I swam the river. An elf on foot can do that if he knows how, especially at this time of year, but horses and carts can't, or if you're carrying much baggage."

"Why haven't you built another ford?"

Surian raised his head, jutting his chin. "We already built one, which we have every right to use." Then he looked away with a sigh. "Anyway, the river's deep, and where it isn't deep it's rocky. There aren't many places where we could build a ford wide enough."

Weyrn nodded. "But to return to your thane... do you think they'd harm him?"

"I... don't think so, but..." Surian sighed. "I wish we could handle it for ourselves, but it's gone too far for that now."

"I agree."

Surian smiled tiredly. "Will you help us?"

"I'll speak to the other Swordmasters, but I expect we'll at least be able to do something. Can you stay here? If not, we can put you up in the Guardhouse."

"Thank you. I've been offered a bed here, though." Surian sat back on his heels with a sigh. "Everyone's been very welcoming."

Weyrn nodded with a small smile. "We'll probably have to come by here when we go, so we could even pick you up on the way. However, we may have more questions. Could you come to the Guardhouse tomorrow? Then we'll be better able to make arrangements."

"I will, Captain. Thank you."

When Neithan arrived home, carrying several fish and very pleased with himself, he was surprised to find Eleri sitting on the bench outside the Guardhouse, cleaning up Seregei's scratched knees. More than that, he was surprised that Weyrn wasn't there.

"Uncle Neithan!" cried Seregei, jumping up and coming running over. Neithan ruffled his hair.

"Don't jostle me, I've got fish."

"Is that for dinner?" Seregei stepped back a little to look at Neithan's basket. "Can I see?" He tried to peek under the cover. Neithan moved it away.

"Why don't you go and put this somewhere cool? In the cellar, perhaps." Even there they wouldn't last long in summer warmth, but it was better than nothing.

Seregei's eyes lit up; he wasn't allowed into the cellar very often.

"Come back at once," said Neithan, handing over the basket. "And be careful. I'm trusting you with this."

Seregei nodded gravely and trotted off, hoisting the basket over his shoulder.

"Where is everyone?" asked Neithan.

Eleri smiled a little, looking at the sky, then started counting on his fingers. "Derdhel and Celes have gone climbing; Alatani's on patrol; Seri's visiting friends; Maelli's dealing with a dispute and Weyrn went to see about a messenger who just arrived from one of the clans."

"From one of the clans? What about?"

"We don't know. Someone else came to fetch Weyrn and he could only say that it was about a clan quarrel."

Neithan frowned. "That could mean anything."

Eleri nodded. "Weyrn left me here to watch the Guardhouse, not to mention Seregei."

"All right. I hope you don't mind being on babysitting duties?" Neithan smiled.

"I'm Swordmaster healer," said Eleri dryly. "It's what I volunteered to do. I was planning to stay in any case; I should be here when Derdhel and Celes get back."

"Just those two?"

"I trust Derdhel not to do anything that will actually result in falling from a cliff, but no further than that."

"Uncle Derdhel doesn't fall off cliffs," said Seregei as he came back out of the Guardhouse.

"You shouldn't listen to other people's conversations," said Neithan.

Seregei pouted. "When's Daddy get home?" he asked Eleri.

"Probably soon. Why? Do you want to show him what you did to your knees?"

Seregei looked down at himself; evidently he'd forgotten the scrapes where he'd tripped and fallen. They were still quite obvious, despite the care Eleri had taken cleaning them. Then he shook his head. "I want to show him my den."

"Well, he's doing something important at the moment. He'll be back soon."

Seregei folded his arms and looked at the floor, scuffing his feet back and forth. Neithan sighed and crouched down to his level. "You know your parents do a very important job, Seregei."

Seregei nodded, still pouting.

"What do they do?"

"Kill monsters," muttered Seregei.

"And other things too, but yes." Neithan ruffled his hair. "I'll tell you what: why don't you show *me* your den."

Seregei looked a little more cheerful at that and nodded. Neithan stood up, checked that Eleri didn't mind continuing to look after the Guardhouse, and followed Seregei into the forest.

***

It was another couple of hours before Weyrn returned. Seregei had got tired of waiting and was curled up fast asleep at one end of the couch. Neithan had just decided to start cooking some of the fish when he heard footsteps approaching the door.

"Hello, Neithan," said Weyrn. His voice dropped in volume as he saw Seregei.

Neithan waved. "What news?"

"We'll wait until everyone else is here."

Derdhel and Celes arrived first. As Eleri had suspected, they each had several bruises, but fortunately there were no serious injuries. Seri was next, looking cheerful and relaxed. Finally, Alatani came in, stamping her feet slightly and scowling. She wouldn't say what was wrong, though, just accepted a plate of bread and fish and sat down beside Weyrn, letting Seregei snuggle up to her as he ate his dinner.

"Where's Maelli?" asked Weyrn.

"I haven't heard anything from him," said Seri.

"No, I suppose not." Weyrn sighed. "I don't know how long he'll be… we'll just have to start. I'd like to at least have some thoughts."

"So," said Neithan, leaning back on his chair. "What news?"

"News?" asked Alatani.

Weyrn quickly explained about the messenger and the trouble his clan was having with their neighbours.

"Do we know anything about this ford?" asked Alatani, glancing at Seri, who shook his head.

"I know a lot about the clans close to the valley, and I do know about the Naith – it's a real place and he's right that it's difficult to get to it – but I don't know these clans and I've not been there for some time."

Weyrn nodded. "Still, you're probably most knowledgeable about the area, at least."

"You'd like me to go and see what's happening?"

"It sounds urgent," said Celes.

Weyrn nodded. "Surian couldn't say what was likely happening to their thane. He didn't think his life was at risk, but he was clearly worried."

"We might need numbers if it is dangerous," said Alatani. "And if it's difficult to find tracks…"

"We may need you there too," Weyrn agreed. He sighed, tilting his head back.

"So Seri and Alatani?" Neithan asked. "If there's likely to be trouble sorting out this quarrel, should you go too, Weyrn?"

Seregei twisted to look up at his parents, wide-eyed. "You're both going?" he asked in a small voice.

Alatani put her arm around him, but he wriggled away and ran off down the corridor.

"I'll go," she said, scrambling up to dart after him.

Weyrn also half got up, watching them. Neithan watched him carefully for a moment, then looked around at the others. Celes looked uncomfortable. Derdhel was sitting back, but frowning slightly.

Finally, Neithan's eyes landed on Seri, who was leaning forward, frowning deeply at Weyrn.

"Seri?" Neithan asked after a moment.

Weyrn also looked round and met Seri's eye. For a moment they stared at one another.

"I haven't forgotten, Seri," said Weyrn quietly, once the silence had stretched uncomfortably long. "If both Alatani and I should go, I'm not going to turn my back on that."

Seri looked away, scowling. "I know," he said, though he didn't sound all that convinced. "But... I know it's difficult."

"I said I'd balance everything, and I intend to."

Seri looked for a moment as if he was going to argue with that, but Celes made a shushing motion, glancing at Weyrn, and he subsided. "I'm sure you're doing your best," he said softly.

Neithan, however, couldn't help remembering Weyrn's fear of leaving Seregei fatherless. It was easy to imagine that that fear would have an influence even if Weyrn wasn't aware of it.

Still, Weyrn hitched his shoulders and said, "I do think you're right, Neithan. I should go. This needs to be sorted out quickly."

Seri nodded, sitting back. "So you, Alatani and me?"

"Derdhel's a good ranger," said Celes uncertainly, glancing back down the corridor. The sound of Seregei's voice raised in a wail drifted from the direction of his room.

"He should get used to his parents being away," said Derdhel.

Weyrn looked sharply at him. "While we're on the subject, Derdhel, you've been quiet. Do you know much about the Naith?"

Derdhel shook his head. "Not especially. I can learn, though, if I'm needed there."

Weyrn sighed. "There's a lot we don't really know. Perhaps we should speak to Surian again – all of us together."

"I've clearly missed something," said Maelli, walking in.

Again, Weyrn explained the situation, adding that he'd chosen himself, Alatani and Seri to go.

Maelli also glanced down the corridor as they heard Alatani scolding Seregei. "Someone's... taking it well."

"Why don't I stay to babysit?" asked Neithan. "He likes me, and it might soften the blow a little while not holding Weyrn or Alatani back."

Weyrn frowned. "It's an idea."

"From what I've heard, I'm not sure we'll need you especially," said Maelli, perching on the arm of a couch. "But what about me, Derdhel and Celes? Should we come?"

"Three may not be enough in terms of numbers," said Seri. "Perhaps us and Derdhel?" he asked Weyrn. "Then that's two who can track, as well."

"And it leaves three at home," said Weyrn slowly. "One of whom is my second." He smiled at Neithan. "I'm also thinking that things are difficult here. Eleri said that the city is tense."

"It is," said Maelli. "Tempers are running short on both sides. I think it would be a bad idea for all the Swordmasters to leave the valley."

"That dispute..."

"It was a misunderstanding." Maelli sighed, shaking his head a little. "As

I say, tempers are running high."

"But we do need enough to help settle this." Weyrn frowned for a moment, then nodded. "I, Alatani, Seri and Derdhel will go, then, and if necessary we can send one back or send for more help."

They nodded. Neithan looked worriedly down the corridor, wondering how Seregei would react when told that both his parents were indeed going to leave him for a while.

As they were preparing to set out, Seri came over to Weyrn.

"Can I have a word?" he asked softly.

Weyrn nodded and followed him outside. He suspected it was something to do with Seregei.

Sure enough, Seri said, "I know I've been blunt about this ever since you announced that Alatani was pregnant, and I'm sorry if I've upset either of you."

Weyrn nodded. "Apology accepted, though I do wish you'd lay off a bit."

"But don't you see? I can't just lay off, because it's important." Seri folded his arms.

Weyrn frowned at him. "What do you mean? Do you really think we're neglecting our duties?"

"I know it's a difficult balance and it worries me. This mission, for example: would you have sent another in your place or agreed to leave Alatani behind in order to placate Seregei a couple of days ago if nobody had said anything? Even though your authority and her skills might be needed?"

The accusation stung and Weyrn had to take a moment to calm himself. At length, he said, "I don't think I would deliberately go against what was obviously right. We were discussing the best plan, not making definite decisions."

"Until Seregei complained that he would be left alone." Seri raised his head a little. "You know how I feel on it."

"Sometimes –" Weyrn cut himself off.

"Sometimes what?" Seri asked softly.

Weyrn shook his head, trying to think of another way to end the sentence. He'd been about to say that he sometimes suspected Seri would rather Seregei had never lived.

"Do you think I'm forgetting my place? I do know you're my Captain, but –"

That was not at all what Weyrn wanted Seri to think. "No. You know I don't say things like that. Without criticism, I'd make a lot more mistakes, I know that."

Seri was still tense, his head up. "But sometimes I think that you don't even realise you're making mistakes."

"Well, I'm sure you won't hesitate to tell me." The words came out a little more sarcastically than Weyrn had intended them.

Seri paused a moment, then said, "I won't."

Weyrn sighed, looking away. "All right," he said, making an effort to modulate his voice. "All right, this is just getting worse and worse. Seri, I'm sorry if I've not made a good enough balance. I have been trying, but even you've noticed that it's not easy."

Seri nodded. "Apology accepted," he said dryly. "And yes, I know it's hard, but I also know that…" He sighed.

"I swore I wouldn't let Seregei interfere with my duties, and I still intend to keep that."

"I know. You've said." This time the smile was more genuine. "It just worries me."

Weyrn nodded. "You can tell me if you're worried, you know. You don't need to wait until you're seriously upset about something."

Seri smiled and looked down. "All right. You know I don't like speaking against you…"

"Really?" Weyrn asked, now intentionally sarcastic.

Seri glared at him. "Yes," he said curtly. "You're my Captain. The Spirits have given you command and I should respect that, in particular when it comes to your relationship with your own son."

Weyrn sighed. "Still, I do have responsibilities to you and the others, and our people, so I do appreciate being told if you think I'm not balancing them properly."

Seri smiled. "I'll do my best."

"Thanks." Weyrn laid a hand on Seri's shoulder and squeezed it gently. Seri returned the gesture and they turned to go back inside.

A few hours after the others had left, Neithan went in search of Seregei. The little elf was sitting on his bed, his knees drawn up to his chin, a horn book abandoned beside him.

"Seregei?" said Neithan.

Seregei glared at him and buried his face in his knees, saying something muffled.

Neithan guessed that he was in no mood to continue his lessons. "Come and sit on the roof with me," he said.

Seregei's head shot up. "The roof?" he echoed.

Neithan nodded, holding out a hand. At once, Seregei scrambled off the bed and darted over. Neithan couldn't help a small smile. Alatani would probably have his hide if she found out; she didn't think Seregei would be safe up there, but Neithan had no intention of letting him fall.

"I'm going to hold onto you, so don't wriggle. If you fall off the roof, you'll hurt yourself."

Seregei nodded, still smiling. He followed Neithan up the stairs to the attic and looked around at the large, empty room with wide eyes. Neithan smiled. "If the Guardhouse is ever attacked, we can put archers up here," he said.

Seregei nodded. "I can use a bow," he said, looking around. "Could I come and fight?"

"Not yet. Your bow doesn't shoot very far, does it?"

Seregei sighed. "No. I'm good with it, though."

Neithan didn't think that was true, but it was difficult to tell with a toy bow. He had to admit that he knew Seregei's stance was good, but he'd never seen him hit a target.

Still, he just patted Seregei on the head and led the way over to one of the hatches. "This is where archers would shoot from," he said, pushing it open. "And, see? There's a flat space were we can sit. Careful!"

Seregei slowly climbed out onto the flat bit of roof and sat perched there, perfectly still. Neithan sat beside him, an arm around his waist to make sure he didn't fall.

The view from here was better than from ground level. They couldn't see over the tallest trees, but they could see further and anyone coming along the path towards the Guardhouse would be clearly visible. Neithan pointed that out to Seregei.

"And one day you'll learn how to spot movements in the bushes that mean someone's coming through the trees, as well."

Seregei stared wide-eyed at the bushes around the edge of the grassy clearing, as if imagining some unseen villains hiding there.

"The Guardhouse is designed to be defensible, at least until help gets here."

"But aren't we the best fighters?" asked Seregei. "Why do we need anyone to come and help?"

"Sometimes if there are lots of people against us, we still need help. You can't fight on your own; that's why it's good for there to be lots of Swordmasters. This trip your parents are on, for example. Where would they be if there were only one Swordmaster?"

Seregei frowned, starting to curl up again. Neithan's grip on him tightened, worried that he would slip.

"Why d'they always leave me behind?" he asked in a small voice. "They never want to do anything with me."

Neithan glanced at him. "You're too young to have gone with them on this trip."

Seregei scowled.

"You won't be too young forever."

"They *always* leave me, though. And it's always to do something more important." Seregei's voice tilted towards a whine. "It's not fair! And that's all anyone ever says: it's something *important*."

"Well, it is. Do you know what they're doing this time?"

Seregei shook his head.

"They're going to help someone in trouble. That's one of the important things Swordmasters do. You remember that time we talked about monsters?"

Seregei smiled. "Mummy scared away the one under my bed."

"Yes, she did. That's one of the most important things we do." It was the easiest way to put it. No need to tell Seregei yet that most monsters didn't look like what he was probably imagining.

"I want to kill monsters," he said softly.

"You see? It's important. It's not all we do, though."

Seregei pouted.

"We also help people who need it. Like this elf your parents have gone to look for. Someone lied to him so he went to talk to them all on his own about an argument, and now they've locked him up. You wouldn't like that, would you?"

Seregei shook his head. "So Mummy and Daddy have gone to fight people so they'll let him out?"

"Yes."

Seregei rested his chin on his knees and leaned on Neithan. "Is that always what they're doing?"

"Not always, but we help people in other ways too. That's really our job: to be guardians and rulers of the Mixed-bloods."

Seregei made a face. "What's that mean?"

"It means we look after them."

Seregei nodded. "By hunting monsters?" he asked hopefully, raising his head.

Neithan laughed. "Sometimes."

"Could I hunt monsters one day?"

Neithan hugged him. "Perhaps. But you have a lot of things to learn first."

At dawn the morning after they had arrived at the Naith, Weyrn and Alatani bade farewell to Seri, who was staying behind at their camp in case anything happened, and headed towards the little cluster of houses nestled in the hills up ahead. Derdhel had crossed the river the night before with Surian to join the Stone's Breath clan.

They could see a few columns of smoke rising in the still-cool air as the elves of the clan also started their day and Alatani commented, "It all looks normal."

Weyrn nodded. "I don't see why it wouldn't."

"Are you looking forward to having to pull rank?" she asked, looking at him with a sly smile.

He sighed. "Not especially, but that's what I'll be doing, so it can't be helped."

"You sound a little like Derdhel."

He couldn't help a small smile at that and put an arm around her shoulders briefly. "With any luck, I won't need to say much."

"Well, if it was going to be easy we'd not need to be here."

He nodded at that and let go of her again; they were getting close to the settlement and that wasn't the first impression he wanted to give.

They were near enough now to see the place properly, though fortunately nobody seemed to have spotted them yet. Weyrn looked it over with a small frown. Like most villages out here, it was just a collection of low houses, mostly built of stone or wattle-and-daub. That made sense; they would be the handiest building materials. He counted fifteen buildings of any size, with several more that were obviously storage or animal pens. He fleetingly wondered where the captured thane was being held. From here, he couldn't tell if any of the buildings would be a likely prison.

They didn't have to go too much further before an elf came running out to meet them. Weyrn paused when he saw him coming and took a moment to look him up and down. He didn't seem to be armed, which boded well. As he ran up, Weyrn stepped forward to greet him.

"Good morning. I am Swordmaster Captain Weyrn the Linnet. This is Swordmaster Alatani She-wolf. We've come to speak to your thane."

The elf outright stared at them for several seconds, the wind entirely taken from his sails. At length, though, he caught himself and bowed. "It's, uh… it's an honour, Captain. We weren't expecting you."

"No, I didn't send word ahead."

"May I ask, uh… to what we owe this, um… visit?"

"I'd rather discuss that with your thane. Will you take us to him?"

The messenger nodded. "Come with me," he said, and turned to lead the way. Weyrn shot a small smile at Alatani and followed.

It took a little while for them to get there, but the thane, Lefet, looked as if he'd been hurried out of bed: his clothes were disordered and there was an obvious tangle in his hair. Nonetheless, he greeted Weyrn and Alatani politely and bowed his head as Weyrn introduced himself and her.

"What brings you here?" Lefet asked as he gestured them each to a chair in the room that served as his hall.

Weyrn sat down, but leaned forward, looking Lefet directly in the eye. "We received word from your neighbours that there was trouble. We came to see what was happening."

"Trouble?" Lefet asked.

"The neighbours in question are the Stone's Breath clan."

"Oh, I see..." Lefet looked around distractedly. "Well... we didn't want to trouble you with it, but if you've already heard their side I'd best put mine..."

"First," said Weyrn, "The messenger said that you'd imprisoned their thane."

"Yes." Lefet drew himself up. "I went to meet him in good faith, but he'd brought a greater escort than we agreed. I don't think it was that unreasonable for us to imprison him once we'd captured him; I don't doubt that he'd have killed me if our positions had been reversed. Of course, when Stone's Breath agrees to shoulder their responsibilities, I'll release him unharmed."

"How is he currently imprisoned? I want to speak to him." Weyrn didn't think it would be wise to tell Lefet what he'd been told about the battle until he'd at least spoken to the captive thane, and preferably not until they'd done something to find out for themselves.

"We're not mistreating him, if that's what you think."

"Then there shouldn't be a problem with me going to see him," said Weyrn flatly, still looking Lefet straight in the eye.

The other elf blinked first and looked away. "Very well, then," he said with a sigh and gestured to the elf that had brought the two Swordmasters in. "Take them to see the prisoner."

The Stone's Breath thane was being kept in a small, low building that Weyrn suspected had been intended as a pigsty. At least, judging by the smell, it wasn't currently in use.

"Wait out here and watch my back," he told Alatani as the messenger unbolted the door. Then he ducked through the door.

He had to keep his head down and shift to the side to avoid blocking all the light, but he could see an elf lying by the back wall, his eyes screwed shut against the sudden sunshine.

"Who's there?" he asked, his voice steady though he still hadn't opened his eyes.

Weyrn crouched down beside him "Swordmaster Captain Weyrn. And you?"

"Thane Petir of Stone's Breath. Are you here to get me out?"

Weyrn nodded. "One of your people came and told us what had happened. We're trying to sort it out. How are they treating you?" In the dim light it was difficult to tell if Petir was hurt. All Weyrn could tell was that his hands were bound behind his back and his legs were curled up behind him.

Petir sighed. "I can't feel my arms any more." He raised his head, squinting at Weyrn. "The door's locked. Do they need to keep me chained up like this?"

"Let me see?" Weyrn helped Petir to move slightly so that he could see the bonds holding his arms behind his back. His wrists were trapped in a single iron ring connected to a chain that was wrapped around his ankles. "I doubt it." He called over his shoulder, "Alatani!"

She stuck her head through the door and he asked her to find out who had the keys to Petir's chains.

"We need to find out what exactly happened before I can demand that they let you out of here entirely, but that should make you a little more comfortable, at least."

"Thanks. But…" Petir looked up again. "What's complicated about it? I went to discuss the fact that they won't let us use our own ford and they kidnapped me!"

"That's what your messenger said, but Thane Lefet is telling a different story."

Petir looked up at Weyrn with a mixture of disbelief and pleading. "Do you believe him?"

Weyrn smiled. "We'll get you untied and then you can tell the tale from the beginning. They haven't hurt you, I hope?"

"I took a few blows when they captured me, but nothing serious."

Weyrn looked up as the light from the door was blocked. It was Alatani, holding out a rough iron key. "They didn't want to give it to me, but I insisted," she said with a small smile.

Weyrn took it with thanks. It unlocked the padlock holding the chain around Petir's ankles, and when he looked closely he saw that the shackle around his wrists just had a simple catch. Unwound, looked like an animal hobble of some kind. He set it aside with a shrug and helped Petir to sit up and rub some life back into his arms.

"Alatani, keep watching the door," said Weyrn, glancing at her. He couldn't shake the feeling that someone might shut and bolt it behind him and, while he was confident he could break it down if he had to, he didn't want to find out. As she left, he smiled at Petir. "What's your side of the story?"

Petir smiled, rubbing his wrists absently. "What do you already know?"

"I'd prefer to hear it from you."

After a moment, Petir nodded. "All right. Well, did our messenger tell you about the ford? These Cats' Eyes helped us to build it, but we put in most of the work. We agreed that both clans could use it freely, but they recently started to charge a toll."

Weyrn nodded.

"We can leave the Naith without using the ford, but it's hard, so they were trapping us unless we paid," Petir continued resentfully.

"That's when you came to speak to them?"

"Yes. We agreed that Lefet and I would meet one-to-one and talk, to see if we could agree anything. I came alone and he brought guards." He scowled at the memory. "They dragged me back here and I've been locked in this pigsty ever since."

"Have they told you what they want of you? What would get them to release you?"

"They want me to agree that we'll pay their tolls." His eyes flashed. "I'll do no such thing; we have every right to use that ford."

Weyrn nodded. "All right. I'll go and speak to Lefet and see what I can do."

Petir nodded, looking wistfully around at the walls. "Do you think you could persuade them to let me out of here?"

"I'll do what I can. Certainly, at the moment I don't think they have reason to hold you. They claim they're doing it because you broke faith and brought armed men to the meeting, but –"

"I did no such thing," Petir interrupted hotly.

Weyrn nodded. "Exactly."

"They're holding me to extort an agreement. By their own logic it should be Lefet locked in here!"

Weyrn couldn't help a small smile, but he just nodded. "I will speak to him again and get you out of here, or at least find a situation where you're both subjected to the same thing until we know what happened."

Petir still looked unhappy, but he bowed his head with a sigh. "Very well. I'll be patient." He rubbed his wrists again. "If nothing else, thank you for untying me," he said fervently.

Weyrn nodded. "Have you had food?"

"Yes."

That was something. "I'll be back soon. You'll have to stay here for now, but I'll get you out."

Petir smiled and gripped Weyrn's hand. "Thank you."

Derdhel had spent the night comfortably with the acting thane, who had been delighted to learn of his arrival. First thing in the morning, he accompanied a party of Stone's Breath elves down to the ford.

"You can see their guards on the other side," the acting thane told him, pointing. Derdhel could see a stone shelter built against the hillside on the other side of the river. An elf peered out of it at them. "We'll be all right as long as we don't set foot in the water."

"Where did the fight happen?" asked Derdhel. "When the thane was captured?"

"On the other side. Had it been this side, he might have been better able to escape them." The elf gestured to the rocky landscape. "He knows this land well and it's easy to evade pursuit."

"Then we'll have to cross," said Derdhel. "In any case, I should see what's happening with the other Swordmasters."

They looked at one another, but then the acting thane smiled. "I'm with you, Swordmaster Derdhel. Let's go."

Derdhel nodded and started into the water, smiling as he felt the gravel of the ford crunch under his feet and watching for any reaction from the guards. He heard the other elf splash into the water behind him.

They hadn't long to wait before several elves came forward to block the far end of the ford. Derdhel didn't stop, ploughing his way through the knee-deep water as if he were wading in a Duamelti stream.

When he and his companion arrived on the far bank, the elf blocking their path stepped forward, his eyes darting from one to the other as if he were unsure which to speak to.

"I am Swordmaster Derdhel the Stoic," said Derdhel, drawing the elf's eyes to him. "I want to look at the ground on this side of the river, where the thane of the Stone's Breath clan was captured."

The elf's back stiffened and he raised his head a little, but his tone betrayed his uncertainty as he said, "Whatever your name, sir, you must still pay a toll to pass the ford."

Derdhel looked him in the eye until he looked away. "I shall do no such thing. Not until my Captain has told me that the feud is decided and he approves the toll."

The elf hesitated, shooting a glance over Derdhel's shoulder. "What about him?" he asked. "He's no Swordmaster."

"No, but he's with me. Now, let me see these tracks." Derdhel half turned to the acting thane, who quickly smothered a smug smile. "Do you know where the meeting took place?"

"I can't just let you through," the guard said. "It's my thane's orders…"

"Go back to your settlement and speak to Captain Weyrn, then," said Derdhel. "We'll wait; time is of no concern."

The guard looked nervously at the other two elves who were with him, but then nodded. "Wait here," he said, and fled.

Derdhel folded his arms and turned his gaze on the elves who had remained behind. They looked very nervous and hung back, looking everywhere but at Derdhel.

"What if they still say we can't come any further?" asked the acting thane.

"I'll find a way."

Lefet was clearly upset, but Weyrn pretended not to see the thane's set jaw. "You had no right to hold him like that."

"He set on us when we came in good faith to meet with him. It was only through luck that I'm not his prisoner, or worse!"

"He says the same of you. Frankly, I think I would be within my rights to imprison you both, if that's the customary punishment for coming to a negotiation in bad faith, until I knew what had actually happened here."

Lefet hesitated, looking around. "You wouldn't..." he said uncertainly.

"I'd not treat you harshly, but I do wonder if it would be worthwhile."

Lefet sighed, looking away. "All right, all right," he muttered. "He can go freely about the settlement."

"He can go freely home," said Weyrn. "I and my people will keep an eye on him and on discussions between the two of you. We'll make sure all's fair and safe."

Lefet sighed, looking martyred, but then he nodded and glanced at an elf who stood nearby. "Go and bring him."

Weyrn smiled and unfolded his arms. "Thank you."

Before the elf arrived back with Petir, a different guard came running in, panting. He shot Weyrn an uncertain look that lengthened into a stare when he saw the badge on his left sleeve.

Lefet cleared his throat and the guard startled. "Sorry, sir. I... there's an elf at the ford. Two elves. The leader claims to be a Swordmaster and is demanding to be allowed across without paying the toll: him and his companion. He said his Captain was here..." He looked at Weyrn again, who smiled.

"That would be Derdhel the Stoic."

Lefet sighed. "Let him pass," he said. "And his companion, as long as they're together."

The guard nodded, bowed to Weyrn and left again. Lefet looked at Weyrn with a raised eyebrow. "You sent Swordmasters to them too?"

Weyrn nodded. "They were the ones who told us what was happening, after all."

Lefet sighed. "Well, I'm honoured that you personally came to us," he said, and smiled.

"Would you have let him cross the ford?" asked a voice from the doorway and Weyrn turned to see Petir led in by the elf who had gone to fetch him. The elf was holding his arm, not tightly enough to prevent a serious escape attempt, but enough to act as a reminder that he was a prisoner.

Lefet looked pained for a moment, but then said, "Release him." Addressing Petir, he added, "Captain Weyrn has insisted that I let you go free, despite... everything."

Petir's lip curled mid-smile at the last part, but he stepped away from the guard who had brought him and bowed to Weyrn. "Thank you," he said fervently.

Weyrn smiled. "Now," he said, "Let's all sit down and hear the story while Derdhel looks at the tracks."

At a gesture from Lefet, chairs were brought for Weyrn and Petir and the room emptied apart from the three of them.

"Now," said Weyrn. "You first, Lefet. Tell me about the toll."

Petir shot Lefet a poisonous look, which the other elf ignored.

"Well... as you've no doubt heard, Captain, our two clans built the ford to the Naith together. Stone's Breath has a wealth of Shining-stone on the Naith, but poor farmland, so we could trade."

"Shining-stone?" asked Weyrn.

Lefet tapped one arm of his chair. The ends of the arms were made of granite – the crystals in the stone glittered – and Weyrn nodded.

"Well," Lefet continued, "we built the ford and agreed that we would share the cost and trouble of maintaining it. Stone's Breath has never done anything for it, so we started charging the toll."

Weyrn turned to Petir. He didn't even have to speak; the other thane was already talking. "What work have you ever had to do?" he demanded. "We built the ford to last even when carts were driven across it and even when there were floods. You've never told us you weren't satisfied with its state and I've never had word that you were working on it. How can you now say we never did anything to help?" He scowled, folding his arms. "The one time you and I have actually managed to work together. I thought it might be the beginning of peace, but..." He shrugged bitterly.

Lefet stared at him. "After everything, you thought that was all it would take? I wanted to trade with you, not be friends with you!"

"Why?" asked Weyrn. "Why can you never be friends?"

For a moment they stared at one another, then Lefet hissed, "He murdered my brother."

Weyrn's eyes instantly went to Petir, who didn't look especially startled by the accusation. He just sat back in his chair and folded his arms, his gaze locked on Lefet's face.

"Petir?" Weyrn asked at last.

"It wasn't my fault," said Petir quietly. "We went exploring further up the river into the mountains. Fog came down, we got separated and I found him dead." He looked at the floor with a sigh. "Never did find out what happened."

Lefet growled and Weyrn held up a hand. "An accident?" he asked. "Fog in the mountains is dangerous, after all."

"I doubt it was a *rock* that cut his throat," snapped Lefet. Then he seemed to catch himself. "Sorry, Captain. I don't mean to be rude."

Weyrn shook his head. "It's an upsetting subject. I understand."

Petir's arms were still folded and he was still looking at the floor. "No, it wasn't an accident. I know that, but I wasn't the one who killed him."

"Then who?" demanded Lefet.

Petir's head went up and his voice rang suddenly loud as he said, "He was my friend! What possible reason would I have to kill him?"

Lefet sprang up, but Weyrn also got to his feet.

"Sit down, Lefet," he said, as gently as he could. "I know this is difficult, but we need to get to the bottom of it. Petir, what happened?"

"Just that." Petir shook his head again, looking blankly at the floor. "I saw him lying there and when I touched him he was cold. I rolled him over, saw the wound and ran for help and…"

"How long ago was this?" asked Weyrn.

"Five years," they both said together.

Weyrn winced. That was a very short time to recover from the loss of a brother or friend. "And you've been enemies since then."

"Of course," said Lefet softly. Petir just nodded.

"Lefet, why do you think it was Petir?" asked Weyrn, holding up a hand to indicate to Petir that he should be quiet.

"Who else could it be?" asked Lefet bitterly. "He was there and had a knife." Weyrn continued to look expectant, his hand still raised to Petir, but Lefet just shrugged. "No-one else lives out there."

"But travel? Could he have been set on by bandits of some sort?"

"Nothing had been taken."

"We even found his rope later," said Petir.

"Not bandits, then," mused Weyrn. "Are there any nomads up there?"

Lefet shrugged. "Who knows? They don't stay long enough for us to notice them."

"A few come through sometimes: humans and elves," said Petir. "They keep to themselves mostly. I know there is one group that is very wary of strangers. They're related to us from a long time ago, but –"

"Oh, so that's how you did it?" Lefet started forward in his chair. "Got these kinsmen of yours to kill him and kept your hands clean?"

Petir's voice rose to a shout. *"Why would I do that?"*

"Did you see anyone else that day?" Weyrn cut in.

Petir shook his head, eyes still locked on Lefet, breathing hard.

Lefet stared back. "Captain," he said suddenly, "If he did murder my brother… What will you do?"

"I think it's difficult to make that decision now," said Weyrn. "I'm not sure we'll ever know who did it."

"But if it was him, I want him hanged. You have authority to do that."

Weyrn stared. It took a moment for him to marshal a response; he didn't want to agree, but he knew that was something Lefet had the right to demand, if hanging was the penalty for murder. On the other hand, he didn't think he should make that promise, especially since he suspected the demand was based on politics rather than justice.

He did believe Petir was telling the truth, though. And if that was the case, it wouldn't be a problem.

"Petir, can I have a word in private?" he asked.

Petir nodded, looking confused. Lefet frowned, but said, "There's an anteroom through that door," and pointed.

Weyrn led the way and Petir followed, still looking mystified. As soon as the door was closed, though, he said, "I'm telling the truth. I don't know what happened to him…" He sighed. "I thought I could finally put it behind me." His voice caught a little, but he closed his eyes and collected himself.

"I want to make sure," said Weyrn. "I do believe you, but I also think that Lefet has a right to your neck if you're lying, and if you lie to me right now, I will be the one to tie the noose, is that clear?"

Petir's eyes widened, but he nodded. "It is."

Weyrn drew his sword and held it out flat. "Lay your hands on the blade and swear to tell me the truth."

Petir obeyed. "I swear on my honour and my life, by the rocks and the trees and the river, under the eyes of the Spirits, that what I say is true: I did not murder Lendë, Lefet's brother."

'Murder' was too specific a word. "Did you kill him or do him any harm?"

"I did not." Petir kept his eyes on Weyrn's. "It happened just as I said, I swear: we parted in the fog and he was alive. Then I found him dead. I didn't see him in between."

Weyrn nodded, lowering the sword. "Thank you. I believe you. But I meant what I said: if I've found out you've lied…"

"If I lied, I'll tie the noose myself."

Weyrn smiled despite himself and patted Petir on the shoulder, then went back into the main room.

Lefet had been talking to a couple of guards, but he looked round as he heard the door open and dismissed them with a wave.

"Everything all right, Captain?"

"Perfectly. I'm actually convinced of Petir's innocence, but I'll agree that if I'm presented with undeniable evidence that he did murder your brother I will hang him."

Lefet smiled. "Thank you. That's a weight off my mind."

"The same goes for anyone else," said Weyrn seriously, watching him.

He just nodded. "I don't think you need worry about that, but…" He shrugged, going back to his chair.

Weyrn returned to his own seat. "But if I'm shown no reason to believe he's not innocent, I hope you'll accept that conclusion," he said, making to effort to keep the edge out of his voice. "We finish this business over the ford, and then the feud is over. I'm not expecting you two to be dear friends, but I hope you can at least not be sworn enemies." He looked over at Petir. "That goes for both of you."

"I don't want this to continue," said Petir.

Lefet sighed. "If… if he can prove that he didn't kill Lendë… then yes,

I'll at least try not to be his enemy."

That wasn't what Weyrn had been hoping for, but it was better than nothing and at least now they could perhaps turn to other things. "Thank you."

"But I will never be his friend."

Neithan looked from one to the next of the three elflings staring up at him. "You want me to do what?"

"Lessai and me are gonna be Swordmasters," said Seregei, "And you've captured Kerin and we have to rescue him."

Neithan looked down at little Kerin, who looked at him with wide eyes. "Are you all right with that, Kerin?"

Kerin nodded. "I want to play."

"Well... all right, then." Neithan bit his thumbnail, thinking what to do and aware of the three pairs of eyes looking up at him. "You come with me, Kerin, and you two give us five minutes before you come and look for him."

They nodded and Kerin took his hand to walk with him into the Guardhouse.

"It won't hurt, will it?" he asked softly as soon as they were out of earshot of the other boys.

Neithan stared at him. "Of course I'm not going to hurt you."

Kerin nodded, looking happier, but then his small smile faded as he said, "I listened to a ballad in the great hall a few days ago. I couldn't sleep and went down to listen... you won't tell?"

Neithan shook his head as he let them into one of the empty rooms in the Guardhouse. "What ballad was it?"

"It was about the elf who hid out in the woods and had a black sword and then he was caught by evil people and they killed almost all his friends and..." Tears were starting to well in Kerin's eyes.

"All right, calm down, Kerin," Neithan said softly, taking the boy's hands. "I'm not going to do anything like that to you." The elf in the ballad had been rescued by his one surviving companion, but had been tortured first. Neithan couldn't remember how much detail the ballad had of what he had suffered.

Kerin smiled wanly.

"I can go and tell the others you don't want to play any more."

Kerin shook his head. "I don't want them to think I'm a mouse."

"All right, then. Why don't you sit in here and I'll go stand outside and pretend to be guarding you."

Kerin nodded and climbed up onto a chair at the back of the room to sit and swing his legs. Neithan grinned at him and left.

Outside, he wondered if there was time to fetch his waster so he could actually put up a fight in defence of his 'prisoner', but decided against it. It would be no fun for anyone if he wasn't even there when Seregei and Lessai arrived for the rescue.

He did, however, have time to wonder whether this was really a suitable game for them to be playing. He was glad that they were trying out the task of rescuing a captive, and he knew that his talk with Seregei probably had something to do with it, but things like this were no game.

He shook his head. They were children. There was time for them to learn.

At that moment, he saw a movement down the end of the corridor and grinned to himself. Seregei was peering around the corner and Neithan decided to ignore him, to all appearances staring at the opposite wall.

Seregei, however, evidently didn't think it was necessary to hide his presence for long; he came dashing down the corridor with a yell, waving his wooden sword over his head, Lessai hot on his heels.

Neithan was genuinely startled for a moment, then he let out a shout and picked Seregei up, leaving Lessai free to chop at his legs while Seregei flailed at him.

After a couple of blows he fell carefully, keeping hold of Seregei, who was still yelling and wriggling. Once he was on the floor they set about him in earnest with their little swords.

"All right!" he yelled, waving his hands. "All right, I'm dead!"

They did stop hitting him then and he sat up to see Lessai opening the door for Seregei to dash through. After a moment they emerged again with Kerin, looking very pleased with themselves. Neithan smiled at them, brushing himself off.

"Did we hurt you?" asked Seregei, the smile fading from his face.

"No, not really," said Neithan. He'd have a bruise on his shin from one of Lessai's blows, but he could live with that.

"Can we play again?" Seregei hopped from one foot to the other, his grin back. "That was fun!"

Neithan laughed a little awkwardly. "Why don't you play so that you take turns being rescued? And I could make it a bit harder."

They considered that, then, after a moment's discussion between themselves, they chose Lessai as the next captive. Neithan noticed that Kerin looked considerably more comfortable with that.

The game went through a few more rounds before they got bored. Neithan made slightly more attempt to guard his 'prisoner' each time, but he never really made it difficult for them.

"You said Mummy and Daddy were rescuing someone," said Seregei. "Would it be easy like this?"

Neithan raised his eyebrows. "Probably not, even for them, and they're bigger than you."

"We're big, strong warriors!" crowed Lessai, waving his sword.

Kerin, however, just kept looking at Neithan with wide eyes and Neithan guessed that he was remembering the Ballad of the Black Sword.

"I'll tell you what," said Neithan quickly, "Sometimes brave warriors have to be very quiet when they rescue people. Why don't you try it that way?"

They looked at him, then at each other, then nodded.

"All right. Two of you run along, and I'll guard the third."

***

That evening, the children had finally worn themselves out and Lessai and Kerin had returned to their parents while Seregei went to bed early. Neithan was slumped on the couch in the common room, wondering why he had agreed to help teach Seregei to use a sword. The boy already had a strong swing.

"Tired?" asked Celes. Neithan felt the couch shift as he sat down.

"You must be too," he said, not opening his eyes. He had enlisted Celes' help after about an hour.

"You were the one fighting them. I just had to let them 'rescue' me." Celes shifted and Neithan opened one eye to look at him.

"Do you think they got it all out of their systems?"

"I think Kerin had had enough, anyway." Celes stretched. "Still, it's good to see them interested in such things."

"Yes…"

"You're not sure?"

Neithan opened the other eye and pushed himself a little more upright. "Well… I keep wondering if we should try to make it clearer that it's not a game, and it's not as easy as we were making it for them. But then I think that they're just children."

Celes twisted to face Neithan. "Then why do you even think you ought to tell them?" He smiled. "Did they hurt your pride?"

Neithan scowled, dismissing the idea as best he could. It didn't help that Celes was now openly laughing.

"Honestly, Neithan, you said it yourself: they're children. When you and Weyrn set out to teach Seregei to use a sword, you didn't tell him all about the pain of a wound, did you?" His smile was dying now and he sighed as he added, "Or how it feels to strike with a weapon that will draw blood?"

Neithan shook his head. "To be honest… I thought we started teaching him to fight too early. I know he loves it and I'll admit that Weyrn's done a good job of keeping it at the level of a game. I just… I worry that that's all it will ever be to him and then one day he'll have to find out the hard way just how hard such things can be."

"I doubt anyone here plans to raise Seregei thinking that the life of a Swordmaster is just a game. I certainly don't." Celes put a hand on

Neithan's shoulder and smiled as Neithan looked up and met his eye. "But I do think your instinct is right: wait until he's older. Then he'll be ready and will be able to understand."

Two days after the Swordmasters had arrived at the Naith, Weyrn finally brought Petir back. They got a warm welcome when they arrived back at his house: a stone building much like the others in the little village, save that it had carvings around the door. Weyrn could tell by the way so many elves seemed to want to get close to and speak to him that he was not the only one who had suspected he'd be killed and he stepped away with Derdhel to give them some privacy.

"What did you find?" he asked softly.

Derdhel shook his head a little. "Time has passed, so there would always be some uncertainty, but as best I can tell Surian told the truth: Petir went alone and was met by a greater force."

Weyrn nodded. "Thanks. I wonder if Lefet planned treachery from the start." He thought uncomfortably of Alatani and Seri for a moment and wondered if it had been wise to leave them in Lefet's power, but the thane didn't strike him as stupid. It wasn't likely he'd imprison or harm the two Swordmasters when their whereabouts were well known, and he had treated them with respect so far. He shook his head to banish the thought, then stepped forward as Petir turned and beckoned.

"This is Captain Weyrn of the Swordmasters," he said to the elves around him. "He was the one who persuaded Thane Lefet to free me unharmed."

Weyrn bowed his head in greeting, watching those around him. They all bowed in response, many of them keeping their eyes on the ground even after they had straightened up.

"Come in," said Petir. "I would be honoured if you would stay with me."

"Thank you, I accept," said Weyrn, following him into the building.

Once they were inside, he was startled to see someone already waiting in Petir's audience hall. It was the tall elf Derdhel had fought during the battle with Esren's settlement. Weyrn frowned and glanced at Derdhel as the elf stood up to greet them. He could tell that the elf had recognised them too; he frowned, shifting his balance onto his back foot.

Petir seemed not to have noticed any tension. He just turned enquiringly to the elf who had acted as thane in his absence.

"He came the day before yesterday," the acting thane explained. "He says he wishes to speak to you about developments to the east of here and call on our kinship."

"If this is private clan business, Derdhel and I can leave," said Weyrn.

Petir looked a little relieved that Weyrn had offered. "Thank you. I will seek you out once I've dealt with this." He gestured to one of the other elves. "Please show the Swordmasters to somewhere they can stay."

Weyrn inclined his head and left with Derdhel, following their guide.

They were given a pair of small rooms next to one another, each with a bed and a small table and lamp. As soon as Weyrn had put down his pack and hung up his cloak, he went through to the other room.

Derdhel had kicked off his boots and was lying on the bed, staring up at the ceiling. As Weyrn walked in, he glanced at him and smiled a greeting, but didn't get up.

Weyrn went and leaned on the wall beside him. "What do you think of the situation?"

Derdhel sighed. "If they're determined to dislike one another, they will."

"Petir seems inclined to let the quarrel go."

"Not so for Lefet, though."

"Don't you think he can be persuaded?"

"People can be as stubborn as mountains, especially when they're unable to recover from a death." Derdhel sighed again. "I could try to persuade the river not to flow so quickly against the rocks."

"There's no need for sarcasm," said Weyrn, glaring at him. He just smiled back and closed his eyes. Weyrn shook his head. "Why did I bring you?" he said, mock-irritably.

"I read those tracks as if they were words," said Derdhel simply, without opening his eyes.

Weyrn couldn't help a chuckle.

"Who do you think that elf was?"

"Seri told me just before we left the Cats' Eyes that he'd met someone from Esren's group while he was waiting for us."

Derdhel smiled again. "I *thought* I recognised him." His fingers flexed and he opened his eyes. "What do you think brings him here? They seemed against any contact with other elves. I know they could change their minds, but..."

"It is a fair question," said Weyrn, also looking at the ceiling for a moment. "But Petir mentioned that they're related to some of the nomadic clans, so it could be that one is among them."

"Do you think it matters?"

"It might." Weyrn looked down at Derdhel. "Don't you?"

"I don't know." Derdhel sighed. "I can't see it having but so much bearing on this quarrel unless we can prove that it was them that killed Lefet's brother, but I can't see much chance of that and, as I said before, if they want to quarrel, they will."

"Aren't you curious?"

"If we find out, we'll find out."

"Not without asking. Petir might tell us if he thinks it'll help..."

"And I don't doubt that he'll know." Derdhel smiled and Weyrn couldn't help smiling back.

"All right. You win this time."

Derdhel closed his eyes, still smiling, and shifted a little. "Aren't you going to sit?"

"You're occupying the whole bed."

Derdhel shifted his legs over and Weyrn sat down.

"It's odd to see you so relaxed."

"We have to wait for something to happen, so I may as well be comfortable."

Weyrn laughed a little. "Fair enough."

***

Petir seemed preoccupied when Weyrn and Derdhel met him later that evening. They ate dinner together at a table in a corner of the receiving hall, screened off with curtains.

"Is everything all right?" Weyrn asked Petir, looking at him carefully across the table.

"Oh… yes. I'm sorry, there's just… a lot to catch up on."

"I understand, and hopefully we'll be able to find a solution to this quarrel over the ford soon."

Petir frowned. "Yes… of course, you'll understand if I don't want to speak to him again alone?"

"Of course. We wouldn't ask you to."

"Thank you. I know you'd not let me get into the same situation again, but…" He sighed. "It was all a bit of a shock."

Weyrn nodded. "Are there any other conflicts we ought to be aware of between you two?"

"Not that I know of. Though I thought he'd forgiven me for being there when Lendë died."

"Well, if it's just the toll…" Weyrn frowned. "I'm sure we can think of something."

"I'm not sure he ever will forgive," said Derdhel. "He's not accepted it, after all."

"Accepted what?" asked Petir.

"That anger at you will not bring his brother back." Derdhel shrugged. "That nothing will."

Petir sighed. "I know that."

Weyrn shot Derdhel a quelling look, but the other Swordmaster apparently ignored him, just going back to his meal. After a moment, he said, "Why has he started charging a toll if the reason he gave is a lie?" He glanced at Weyrn. "You told me the whole story, didn't you?"

"Of course," said Weyrn, and looked back at Petir, who was frowning thoughtfully at the table.

"I don't mean to sound bitter," he said after a moment. "But... I can't help wondering if he does mean to just strangle us. It's hard to trade with such a hold on our only way off the Naith."

"What's to the east?" asked Weyrn. "Is there no way out there? I assume not normally, but in the circumstances?"

"The ground's too rocky for carts and we've never managed to build a road. We originally settled here because it was difficult to reach; we wanted to stay away from other clans, but then it was only a few families and we could farm all we needed. There are more now and we need that contact with the outside world."

"Does Lefet know that?"

"Yes. We'd discussed it in the past."

"What did you tell him?"

"I don't really remember. Mostly about the importance of the barges. That was what we used before the ford. We could go back, but... it would be hard. Our numbers have increased since then."

It was difficult to say whether Lefet was acting maliciously, in that case. Weyrn didn't especially want to think it, but in the circumstances he had little choice. "Well, we'll see what we can sort out. If he has other reasons, though, that may make it harder to find an agreement."

Petir sighed, but nodded. "I don't want to leave myself and I'd not force others to go, but... we can't stay here if we can't use that ford."

"I understand, but unless Lefet mentions another reason to Alatani and Seri, I think we should work on the one he gave."

"He's never told us of any need for repairs," said Petir resentfully. "And I asked around a little – none of my people have seen such repairs being made."

Weyrn nodded. "Well, if he's lying then we can still act as if we believe him. Then he'll have to either continue his lie or come up with another one and admit the first."

Petir looked a little happier about that. "You'll speak to him tomorrow?"

"We'll at least contact the other two Swordmasters. With luck, we can have this sorted out over the next couple of days." He thought of the possibility of being on the way home soon and smiled.

Petir also looked hopeful. "If that's possible... there's a human settlement nearby that we were hoping to trade with."

"A human settlement?" echoed Weyrn, speaking over Derdhel's comment that the humans would presumably stay some time.

Petir nodded. "That was what the visitor who came today wanted to tell me: they feel threatened." He sighed. "They feel threatened by everything."

Derdhel snorted and Weyrn glared at him.

"Why do they feel these humans are a threat?"

"They're encroaching on lands where the clan is accustomed to live." Petir shrugged. "They're not as settled as us, so someone starting to build and farm in their wide area is more threatening than it would be to us."

Weyrn nodded. "Well, we'll do our best to get it done quickly. Trust me on that."

Petir smiled. "Thank you."

Alatani was glad to see Weyrn again the next morning, but she knew it wouldn't be appropriate to hug him in front of everyone. She just took his hand for a moment and smiled. "How was your night?" she asked.

"I think we're getting close."

The other two had drawn away a little to give the couple some privacy, but Weyrn let go of Alatani's hand with a sigh and beckoned the three of them into a small side room.

"What did we miss last night?" he asked with a smile as he sat beside Alatani on a bench on one side of the room.

She waited until the other two were comfortable: Seri sat on her other side – she wondered whether he was consciously acting as chaperon – and Derdhel leaned against the opposite wall.

"Lefet told us that they did all the work on the ford, but most of the time he kept chewing over his claim that Petir murdered his brother."

Weyrn winced. "He swore to me that he never harmed that elf."

"Lefet's convinced."

"He's not going to be dissuaded easily," said Derdhel with a small shrug.

Weyrn shook his head. "Not unless we can find out what really happened."

Seri looked at him sidelong. "It's a cold trail and I never heard anything about the death, let alone who might have murdered him."

Alatani couldn't think of any way they could solve this themselves, not after so long, especially with no idea of where to even start asking. After all, apart from Petir it seemed that the only person to see Lendë after the fog came down was his murderer.

"It pains me to say this," said Seri, "But surely they don't actually need to be on good terms. They just have to tolerate one another."

"And refrain from sabotaging one another's settlements," said Weyrn.

"That's what this is?" asked Alatani, startled.

"Petir thinks so, and I admit it doesn't look good."

"They won't move," said Derdhel. "No matter how hard they believe this life can become if they stay on the Naith, they won't leave."

"Of course not," said Seri. "This is their home, just as Duamelti is ours."

Derdhel shrugged. "If life were unbearable there, I could leave, were it not for my bonds to you."

Seri narrowed his eyes at Derdhel and Alatani elbowed him.

"I think Derdhel might be right about Lefet being unwilling to let it go," said Weyrn.

"I could go and speak to him," said Alatani, though she knew her doubt probably showed in her voice. Lefet had very little to lose by continuing things as they were, after all.

"Perhaps I should," said Seri. "I did think he and I got on better last night."

Alatani couldn't help a smile. She suspected that Lefet had also guessed her doubts.

Weyrn looked from one to the other, then he nodded at Seri. "See what you can do."

Seri nodded and left.

"Shall I speak to Petir?" asked Derdhel.

"I will," said Weyrn.

Derdhel frowned slightly, but nodded and watched as Weyrn also left. Alatani sighed and settled back on the bench, gesturing to Derdhel to sit beside her. He shook his head.

"What's wrong?" she asked.

"I don't understand why Weyrn doesn't trust me."

That made her stare at him. "Doesn't trust you? What...?"

"Every time I turn around, he's looking at me with suspicion." He sighed and shook his head. "It shouldn't bother me, but... it does. I've not been able to set it aside."

"I don't think it's that he doesn't trust you," said Alatani carefully. "But... this *is* a delicate situation and a word out of place could make a huge difference. He's probably worried about you saying something... tactless."

Derdhel opened his mouth to respond, but then hesitated. "I... admit I've done that in the past. But is he so unwilling to believe I could have learned better?" Finally, he sat down beside her.

Alatani shook her head. "This isn't the place to test it, that's all." She patted him on the shoulder. "Listen, just think before you speak, would you? Remember how upset Gelladar was about what you said about Othron."

"I do remember, but it was true." He sighed. "It's not something to be feared and I don't understand..."

"Nobody wants to be pulled away from the things and people they love."

"But it's to go to a better place and, given the cruelty of the living world, there's every chance their loved ones will join them soon."

Alatani sighed. "But in the meantime... look what Lendë's death has done to Lefet and Petir."

"Because they cannot accept that he's gone. An elf's life has a season just as anything else does. You don't go into fits of anguish when summer turns to winter, do you?"

"But you've always said yourself that winter will turn back into summer. That's not how things go with death."

He smiled. "You're a warrior. We both are. One day, we'll both be in the land of the dead. That's the return of summer."

Alatani shook her head. "You can think that all you want, but I'll never be content with the idea of leaving Weyrn and Seregei behind, even if I could be reconciled to losing the rest of you."

"Then I suppose that's a point of difference between us." He smiled a little. "Don't worry about me; I'll set this aside, given time."

Alatani started to reply, but then sighed; she didn't have a response for that.

Seri had got nowhere with Lefet and eventually had to go and fetch Weyrn in the hope that a higher-ranking Swordmaster might have better luck. When he returned to the room where the four of them had met, Weyrn was already there.

"Back already?" he asked.

Seri shook his head. "He won't listen to me. I thought I'd see if you could try."

Weyrn winced. "Not at all?"

"Nothing. He keeps insisting that he won't ally with Petir in any way. Although he wouldn't say what it was he'd done to the ford."

"Petir said last night that he didn't think he'd done anything," said Weyrn. He stepped away from the bench where he'd been sitting with Alatani. "Will you come back with me, or stay here?"

"I'll come," said Seri. He smiled a little at Alatani and Derdhel – only Alatani smiled back – and then turned to follow Weyrn. As they walked down the corridor, he said, "I assume Petir took the suggestion better?"

"He's only too happy to try and form a relationship despite the accusation of murder. In fact, it was what he thought building the ford was." Weyrn sighed. "It's just Lefet that's being stubborn."

Lefet was still sitting in his chair in the receiving room, but he got up when he saw Weyrn enter. "Captain…"

Weyrn gestured him back to his seat. "Seri tells me that we need to discuss this situation."

Seri could almost see Lefet's hackles rise again and sighed. He was standing close behind Weyrn, but the other elf didn't seem to notice.

"What's the problem?" asked Weyrn, since Lefet didn't seem inclined to volunteer anything.

Lefet made an impatient noise and looked away, folding his arms. After a moment, he said, "I will not forgive Petir, no matter what."

Seri sighed again, looking around as Weyrn once again explained that that was not what they were asking. He was a little curious to see that they were alone in the room. He didn't think he'd been to a meeting with a thane where there was nobody else present.

"Lefet," said Weyrn, breaking into Seri's thoughts. "If you think you can prove Petir is the murderer, let me see your evidence."

Lefet stared at him for a moment, then stammered, "Who else could it possibly have been?"

Weyrn looked over his shoulder at Seri, raising an eyebrow. Seri shrugged and said, "No, I don't think that's much proof either."

Lefet folded his arms, scowling. Seri glanced at Weyrn, wondering at what point he should draw attention to the thane's lack of respect for his Captain. Weyrn didn't seem to notice his discomfort, though, and continued watching Lefet expectantly.

"Fine," Lefet muttered at last. "Fine, that's all I have."

"Why would he even have done it?"

"How should I know?" snapped Lefet.

Seri responded instinctively. "Watch your tone." He was only glad he kept his voice low. Weyrn glanced at him, then back at Lefet, who had the grace to look abashed.

"I'm sorry, Captain," he said softly, his eyes on the floor and his arms still folded. "That was out of line."

Weyrn nodded, but all he said was, "I see no reason you have to continue this toll."

"What about maintaining the ford?" asked Lefet.

Weyrn looked back at Seri. "Could you go and find Petir? I think we now need to have everyone here."

Seri nodded. "Shall I fetch the other Swordmasters?"

"Yes, if only as witnesses."

Seri left without looking to see how Lefet was reacting to this and went back to the room where the other two were waiting. When he arrived, Derdhel was pacing about the room while Alatani picked at a loose thread on her cuff, but they both looked up.

"Weyrn thinks we may be getting close to an agreement," said Seri.

Alatani sprang up. "That is good news! Do you know where Petir is?"

"I do," said Derdhel. "Shall I fetch him?"

Seri nodded and made way so Derdhel could leave. He and Alatani hurried back to the receiving room, but even before they arrived Seri could hear Lefet's raised voice.

"Of course he'd say that! He wants you to take his side!"

"Well then," said Weyrn, much more calmly, "tell me what you have done to improve the ford."

Alatani must have seen Seri shake his head. "Things haven't improved, then?" she asked with a smile.

"Weyrn shouldn't let him speak to him like that."

"He doesn't like to pull rank."

Seri knew that perfectly well, but he didn't have time to reply before they were walking into the room. Lefet glanced up – Seri noticed he looked very red in the face – and Weyrn looked round.

"Petir?" he asked.

"Derdhel's fetching him," replied Alatani.

Weyrn nodded. "We'll wait until he arrives, then."

Lefet was eyeing Seri and visibly trying to keep his temper, clenching and unclenching his hands on the stone ends of the arms of his chair. Seri frowned at him, but then turned back to Weyrn.

Weyrn was also frowning, though. "I want this agreed, Lefet," he said calmly. "I think we've established that you can't avenge Lendë's death on Petir without more evidence that he was actually responsible rather than just being the one to bring you the news. That just leaves your claim that they should contribute to maintaining the ford. I agree: they should. Which is why I want you two to discuss *what you have done*. Then we can come to an arrangement. But I want something in place from today."

Lefet's eyes slid to Seri again and Seri frowned, wondering what was so interesting about him. Perhaps it was just that he was the one who had challenged Lefet's bad manners earlier. There wasn't time to ask, though, as at that moment Derdhel arrived with Petir following closely behind him.

The two thanes glared at one another. Petir started rubbing his wrists while Lefet tensed again in his chair.

"I'll not forgive you," said Lefet.

"I didn't do anything wrong," snapped Petir.

Weyrn held up his hands. "I don't believe Petir murdered Lendë and have no reason to. I don't think it'll ever be proved, so that just leaves the toll. Lefet, *what* have you done to improve the ford?"

At length, Lefet said, "We put down new gravel: larger stones that would bear the weight of a cart better."

"When was that?" asked Petir. "We never had trouble getting carts across as long as they kept to the middle of the ford."

"Well, we maintained the edges." Lefet's eyes kept darting towards the Swordmasters.

"When? I've never seen any of your people out there."

"Obviously, you haven't looked," snapped Lefet.

Weyrn held his hand up. "Lefet, how much have you collected with the toll? Enough to pay you back for the work you've done?"

"But he hasn't –"

Seri glanced at Petir and he fell silent, chewing his lip.

Lefet looked uncomfortable, but under Weyrn's stare he nodded. "But in future?"

"We'll put in the work to maintain the ford if there's something wrong and you let us use it," said Petir.

Seri sighed a little in relief. If Weyrn could chase that... He caught himself. Weyrn was Captain for a reason.

Sure enough, Weyrn was nodding. "It sounds like, if you can agree on that, we can settle there."

The two thanes glared at one another for a moment. Lefet looked down first. "All right," he muttered.

"Before witnesses," said Weyrn, glancing at the others. "You heard the terms?"

As the most senior there apart from Weyrn, Seri said, "Lefet will stop charging the toll and will inform Petir when repairs to the ford are needed. Petir and his people will help with those repairs."

"Doing equal work," Weyrn added, looking at the two thanes. "If there are any problems, send to me."

They nodded, Petir looking considerably happier than Lefet, even if not completely satisfied.

Weyrn smiled. "Is there anything else either of you think should be drawn to my attention?"

After a moment, Lefet blurted, "What about the humans?"

There was a moment's silence, then Petir said, "You've heard about them too?"

Lefet ignored him. "We need some sort of support – I don't believe for a minute they're not a threat." He nodded at Petir. "Stone's Breath are all right on the Naith, but the rest of us?"

"What are they doing?" asked Weyrn.

"Just settling at the moment," said Petir, "Unless you know something I don't, Lefet?"

Lefet shook his head. "But I'm worried about it."

"We know there are human settlements developing east of Duamelti," said Weyrn.

"Perhaps you... perhaps if would be best if you did look into it," Petir said softly. "Though..."

"We will, and I do remember what you said about them last night," said Weyrn with a small smile. "Don't worry about that." He looked back and Seri caught his eye. "We'll discuss what to do in a moment. It could be one of us will go and see what they're doing on our way home." Seri nodded slightly and Weyrn turned back to the two thanes. "In the meantime, I expect you both to stick to that agreement. I'll come back if there's any trouble. Is that clear?"

They nodded and Petir hitched up his cloak on his shoulders. "I'll head back to the Naith to share the good news," he said, and smiled. "Thank you, Captain." Then he left, barely glancing at Lefet.

Lefet scowled. "One day I'll find something to prove it to you," he said.

"If you prove it to my satisfaction, I've given my word he'll hang," said Weyrn, but he shook his head a little. "I don't believe you will."

***

They left almost immediately after that, only going out of their way to catch up with Petir and say goodbye. Away from Lefet, he was far more talkative and thanked them profusely for their help. Weyrn parted from him with a smile and repetition of his promise to return if they were needed again.

Then, at last, they turned for home.

Seri noticed that Alatani in particular had a definite spring in her step now, but he had to admit that she'd handled herself well. There had been little for her to do in the end – Derdhel had done all the necessary tracking – but he gave her credit for never agitating to return home when that became obvious.

"Seri," said Weyrn, "Did I read you right? You're willing to go and see what these humans are doing?"

"I can guess where they are, I think," said Seri, "Since I assume they must be fairly near to the group that sent the messenger."

"Yes, that was what he wanted to tell Petir."

"In that case, they're not that close to any settled clans, but they'll be in the usual areas of some of the nomads and these things do change. I'd like to check."

Weyrn nodded. "Do you think you can go on your own?"

"Perhaps Derdhel could come, just in case, but I think I can manage." It would be harsh to demand Alatani, but nonetheless he added, "Though Alatani hasn't had much chance to show her skills."

Alatani shot him a glare. "That's true, but I wasn't called on."

Seri raised his hands. "I said you'd not had a chance, not that you hadn't taken one."

"Alatani, calm down," said Weyrn, putting a hand on her shoulder.

She sighed and looked away. "I could go," she said softly. "I admit I'd rather not."

Seri looked back at Weyrn, but Weyrn didn't meet his eye; he was looking at Derdhel, who was walking on Seri's other side.

"I'm happy to go," he said. "A delay getting back means nothing to me."

"And you've your wolves to look after," said Seri, unwilling to once again make Weyrn and Alatani feel that he was deliberately putting them in a difficult position. He didn't like to see them shirk their duties when they were needed, but he wasn't malicious.

Alatani took the offered feather-of-peace and nodded. "I hope nobody's decided to hunt them while I'm gone."

"They don't cause trouble?" asked Weyrn.

"Not unless trouble comes to them."

Weyrn nodded and said, "It's settled, then, if you don't mind, Derdhel?"

"Not at all."

"Don't do anything to offend them if you can help it – Petir's hoping to trade with them."

Seri nodded and Weyrn smiled. "Thank you both."

Weyrn waved goodbye to the two other Swordmasters shortly after that and watched until they'd vanished over the crest of a hill, then he and Alatani walked on. As they went, their hands met and clasped. Her touch was warm and he smiled, feeling himself relax.

"A couple of days until we get home," she said with a sigh.

He kissed her cheek. "But we are on the way."

"I'm glad Seri didn't decide to make a fuss."

He caught the edge of anger in her voice and winced. "I don't think he means to pick at us. He thinks he's doing the right thing."

"That's the worst kind of attack."

"I don't think it's fair to call it an attack."

"Then what would you call it?" she asked, turning suddenly to look at him.

He blinked. "You know that he's actually right in principle. We both took our oaths and we have our duties and" – she looked about to interrupt and he spoke quickly – "the fact that there's now a second duty doesn't make the first one go away."

She shook her head, folding her arms. "I just wonder sometimes…"

"Wonder what?" he asked, feeling like a hand had clenched his heart. There was a strange look in her eye as she looked at him.

"You always said you worried about leaving Seregei fatherless," she said bluntly. "But I don't think you've really thought about how many ways there are to do that."

Weyrn felt as if he'd been kicked. "You think I'm abandoning him?" he croaked.

She waved her hands, making odd sounds as she tried to find the word she wanted. Finally, she blurted, "Yes! Not because you have a *choice*, but still yes!"

It couldn't have hurt more if she'd hit him. Weyrn swallowed hard against the lump in his throat, looking at the ground. "I don't have a choice," he said, forcing out the words. "Neither of us do. I'm damned either way, so I just have to make the best of it."

"I know." He heard her voice catch and looked up. To his surprise, her eyes were full of tears. "I didn't think it would be this hard…"

He held out one hand, wiping his eyes with the other. "Nor did I. But…"

"That's the way of it," she finished, taking his hand with a wan smile. "Come on, we're wasting time."

They walked on, but the silence was strained as if it would snap at any moment.

"I still don't want to leave him fatherless," said Weyrn softly, at last.

Alatani nodded. "I know that." Suddenly, she laughed. "Remember what I said when you proposed?"

"That you'd once wanted a long and happy life, but then grew up and decided you preferred short and exciting, and now you wanted someone to share it with." He smiled, remembering the fierce smile on her face, his heart beating a little faster. They had both been so young and full of fire then…

"I think I put it more poetically," she said, squeezing his hand gently. "And I think I've changed my mind again: I want a long and happy life for three. But I'll not pay too high a price for that."

He looked at her. "What's a fair price?"

She sighed. "If I knew that, it would be far easier to pay. We bring safety to our people from everything we can fight against and that's not something I'll sacrifice, I do know that."

He put an arm around her shoulders and hugged her close.

She sighed. "I just want him to be safe and happy."

He kissed her cheek again. "That's what I want. As much as we can give him."

"Without breaking our own oaths?" she said with a bitter smile.

He nodded. "And he's safe. We all see to that."

"But happy?"

"As much as he can be. We can't always be with him, but one day he'll understand."

For a while longer they walked on in silence, then Alatani said, "Do you think he'll make a Swordmaster himself?"

"I don't know." Weyrn looked up at the sky. The clouds were lowering and he wondered absently if it would rain. "He can't while I'm alive, at any rate. I think that might be one of Bladedancer's laws: a father and son can't be Swordmasters together." After a moment, he added unhappily, "I suppose that would also apply to mother and son."

"It can't be one of his; Bladedancer thought Swordmasters should never marry."

He glanced at her. "Be fair: I don't think that was actually him. I have a feeling Etsu made it law, it just happened that Bladedancer and Aiona never married."

She leaned her head against his shoulder. "In any case, given that, I hope

Seregei finds another calling."

He kissed her hair. "And we'll do all we can to make sure he's happy in it."

She nodded. "I just wish there were more."

Neithan had sent Seregei and Lessai to follow one another's tracks through the forest and was sitting outside the Guardhouse, listening to the occasional shouts and shrieks as one caught up with the other. He suspected that they were chasing one another rather than actually trying to follow tracks, but it was keeping them occupied. He kept half an ear out while he worked on mending one of his winter boots; autumn was approaching and he wanted to be ready.

An especially loud shout made him look up. He recognised Seregei's voice, but then made out the words.

"Mummy! Daddy!"

Neithan got up, grinning, and went to meet Weyrn and the others.

To his surprise, it was just Weyrn and Alatani. Seregei was swinging on his father's hand while Lessai hovered a little way off. As Neithan approached, Weyrn passed Seregei over to Alatani and came to greet him.

"All's well here?" he asked with a smile.

Neithan nodded. "Nothing's happened. Things are still tense, but nothing's come of it, though these two" – he gestured to Seregei and Lessai and smiled a little – "have developed an interest in pretending to be little Swordmasters."

Weyrn and Alatani exchanged a look.

Neithan added, "Just playing, but we've been doing what we can to keep them occupied, especially as there's actually been little else to do. Where are Derdhel and Seri? How was your trip?"

Weyrn sighed as they started walking back towards the Guardhouse, Seregei trotting along beside his mother and telling her all about the game he and Lessai had been playing. Weyrn smiled for a moment at that, but then sobered as he said, "It was a mess. It turned out that there was a personal feud between the thanes and, though I think we managed to persuade them to set that aside, it wouldn't surprise me if there were more trouble from that area."

"I'm glad you got something worked out, though."

"Yes... but they mentioned that they were worried about a human settlement; it was about the one thing they were actually prepared to agree on, though even then one saw it as a straightforward threat and the other as a possible trading opportunity."

"Humans? Connected to the ones I met?"

"I think so. They seemed to be heading in the right direction, at least. I sent Seri and Derdhel to investigate."

Neithan smiled, looking back at Alatani and the two children. She raised an eyebrow at him and said, "We agreed it fair and square."

He raised his hands a little, grinning. "I never thought otherwise." Then he patted Weyrn on the shoulder and said, "It's good to see both of you."

Seri hugged himself as he watched Derdhel crouching over the verge of a dirt track. They were having trouble finding the humans that Petir had mentioned and the weather was starting to become threatening. Derdhel seemed not to notice the bite in the wind as it whistled over the bare hills, whipping Seri's shoulder-length hair around his face. Seri tried to ignore it, but he had to admit that he missed the sheltered forests in and around Duamelti. He would be glad to get home.

"Anything?" he asked, shivering as another gust blew his hair into his eyes.

Derdhel glanced up, brushing his own silvery hair out of his face. "Not here," he said.

"Is it worth carrying on along this road, or should we strike across country?"

"That I don't know." Derdhel got up. "You know where the settlements are, are there any particular empty places where they might have gone?"

Seri frowned, picturing a map in his head and trying to guess where they were by looking around at the shape of the hills. The sun was invisible behind the clouds, but he could still guess where it was.

"I think," he said slowly, "we can carry on along this road for a while, but then we should leave it and head north, out into the wild. It goes over the mountains to human realms to the south and if Petir was correct – and we're looking for the same humans as Neithan met – we needn't go anywhere near that far."

Derdhel nodded. "I'll keep looking for any signs of them," he said, "but if they didn't pass recently there may not be anything to see."

Seri nodded. "It'll probably be of more help later," he said, starting to walk. "If we can't find them in a couple of days, though, I think we should head back."

Derdhel fell in beside him. "I expect we will," he said. "I worry more about the group that messenger came from; it wouldn't do to meet them again without someone to help us."

Seri scowled. He liked to think he wasn't proud, but it had been humiliating how easily they had captured him before.

"It's in the past," said Derdhel implacably.

"I know, but I still don't like to think about it."

"Why?"

Seri shrugged. "It's not a pleasant memory. I agree we should avoid meeting them again; they didn't want to be disturbed."

Derdhel smiled, but just nodded and they walked on in silence.

***

It was some hours before Seri thought they needed to leave the road. They had passed a few side tracks, but he knew that they all led to settlements and they went past with only a glance at them. They didn't see another soul, elf or human, and very few animals or birds. Seri looked up at the clouds again with a shiver.

"It's not very late in the year," he mused. "Not even autumn yet. I'd expect there to be more birds, at least."

Derdhel shook his head. "I'd expect them to stay nearer the settlements, where they could be surer of finding food. The birds of prey will follow them, except for eagles, which I imagine would fly out of sight."

"You're not worried?" asked Seri. "No, wait: should either of us be worried? Honestly and given that I worry more than you do?"

Derdhel grinned a little, but just said, "No."

Seri nodded and looked around at their surroundings again, this time to get his bearings. "I think we should leave the road soon."

Derdhel nodded. "Here seems as good a place as any."

"It'll get dark soon in this weather and there won't be any stars, so we should also look for a place to camp."

"All right." Derdhel headed for the side of the road. "I wonder if the humans use this road at all? I'd expect there to be some sign of them."

"They might not. If Neithan's group are anything to go by, they're using roads closer to Duamelti. I suppose that means they're nothing to do with the humans over the mountains."

"Or they wish to be nothing to do with them."

"I suppose so." Seri followed Derdhel, narrowing his eyes as he looked at the rolling moor spread out in front of them. There was a faint plume of smoke from an elven settlement to his left – they had passed the road to that one some time before – but nothing else. "I don't like it."

Derdhel raised an eyebrow at him.

"Surely there should be more sign of life than this."

That just got a shrug and he sighed. It would be difficult to see smoke against the clouds, he told himself. Perhaps tomorrow they would have better luck. In the meantime, they should concentrate on finding a place to camp. That in itself would be difficult on this terrain; he suspected that a sheltered hollow behind some rocks was the best that they could hope for.

If the same thought had occurred to Derdhel, he gave no sign of it, but just started walking, watching the ground as he went.

"Let me know if you see anything."

"I will."

"Or if it's starting to get so dark that you'd miss a track we might need."

Derdhel smiled. "I will."

As they walked, the light was noticeably fading. Seri looked around more than ahead, trying to see any sign of a settlement or even a camp. Derdhel kept his eyes on the ground. It was an inhospitable country that made Seri shiver to look at it, even without the wind. All he could see was heather and rabbit-bitten grass. They had at least seen a few rabbits now that they were away from the road, which made their surroundings feel a lot less unnatural. There were also large gorse bushes and Seri suspected that one of those would have to do for a campsite.

At last, he looked up as he felt a drop of rain land on his cheek. "Derdhel, we should find somewhere to stop."

Derdhel sighed, but followed Seri over to one of the large gorse bushes. When Seri crouched down, he found that the bush was almost hollow underneath, just as some of the ones on the outer fringes of Duamelti were. They wouldn't be able to sit up in this makeshift shelter, but it would do and they took their packs off to crawl under it, both occasionally hissing and cursing as they found fallen needles.

Once Seri had found somewhere to lie down, though, it wasn't so prickly and he rolled himself up in his cloak with a sigh, wondering how difficult it would be to get his bedroll out. Outside, the rain was falling more heavily, but it seemed that the bush was thick enough to protect them from the worst. They would have no fire tonight, but he could live with that.

"You couldn't have carried on looking for tracks in this anyway," he said, gesturing.

Derdhel shook his head. "Yes, it is worth resting if there's nothing else to be done." He reached into his pack and took out some biscuit, chewing on it and looking up at the branches above his face.

"Should we set watches tonight, do you think?"

"I never saw any sign that anyone comes this way but rabbits."

"Nor did I." Seri frowned. "I hope Petir and his messenger haven't sent us after wild geese."

"If he has, we'll find out and be on our way."

"And if it's a trap?"

"What will be will be."

Seri shook his head. "Sometimes I wish I could look at the world the way you do, Derdhel."

Derdhel made an odd sound that was half sigh and half chuckle. "Likewise."

***

In the morning, it was still raining and Seri sighed. He had dragged out his bedroll, so he wasn't sleeping directly on the ground, but he was still chilled and there would be no fire this morning either. Still, he shook himself a little and glanced over at Derdhel.

The other elf was half propped up on one elbow with his back to Seri, staring at something.

"What is it?" breathed Seri.

"I can see something moving," said Derdhel, only a little below normal speaking volume. Evidently, whatever it was, it was some distance away.

"Any idea what it is?"

"Not from here. It's a fair size, though."

Seri rolled out of his blankets and began doing his best to roll them up. "Breakfast on the road, I think."

"I agree." Derdhel also packed up his own bedroll and swung his pack onto his back, brushing the twiggy debris out of his long hair and pulling it back into its customary ponytail as he waited for Seri to get ready. The rain didn't seem to trouble him.

Seri hurried through putting away his own bedroll, though he took a little more care to ensure that it was properly stowed and put his cloak on before taking the pack from under the bush. Even in that time, a few raindrops had hit and he could feel them strike through the cloth of his tunic and shirt. He sighed and started walking in the direction Derdhel indicated. He couldn't see anything, but trusted that the other elf was right and there was something there. Even if it were only an animal, it could be a sign of settlement.

The ground was rough and the overnight rain had made it boggy. Seri watched where he was putting his feet, worrying every time they went into a hollow that he'd find a mire at the bottom. Derdhel didn't seem concerned; he kept his eyes fixed on the spot where he'd seen movement.

Seri was startled as they crested the hill to find a small group of humans heading along the hollow in front of them. As they saw the humans, one of them looked up and called a warning to the others. All of them moved together defensively, eyeing the two elves.

Seri held up his hands to show he wasn't armed. "Good morning!" he called. "Where are you going?"

"Same to you," said one of the humans: the eldest, by the look of him, with fair hair and a full beard. His Elven was heavily accented, but Seri could understand him.

"Some of our people were worried about things going on in this area, so they asked us to investigate."

"Elves?" the human asked, frowning.

Seri nodded.

"We've not troubled elves."

"What are you doing?" Seri asked again. "There aren't any settlements in this direction that I know of."

"That's our business."

"It becomes ours when elves ask us to find out." Seri folded his arms.

He knew he wasn't supposed to provoke them, but this was suspicious. In any case, if this was their attitude then Petir's hopes were vain anyway.

The human scowled, hitching up the bag over his shoulder. Seri noticed that three of the humans were carrying coils of rope while the others carried tools, but from this distance he couldn't make out what exactly they were.

"We've got as much right being here as you," the human said at last. "We've not caused you any trouble, so leave us alone."

"Have you caused any of us any trouble?"

"Who are you?" the human demanded. "What makes you think you can ask us about what we're doing?"

"We're Swordmasters: guardians and leaders of the Mixed-blood elves."

"Yeah, well, when they need you, you can cause trouble for us. Until then, leave us alone." The human turned his back and waved the others on.

"Shall I stop them?" asked Derdhel.

Seri shook his head. "If they've not done anything, they've not done anything. I'd like to know where they're going, but…"

The human had evidently heard and understood what they were saying, for he swung round again. "Planning to follow us?"

"We want to make sure of what you're doing," Seri called back. "We don't mean you any harm."

"Well, nor do we, but we will if you don't leave us alone." The man waved a fist. "We know what to do with footpads, whatever fancy names they use!"

Seri gritted his teeth, keeping his temper with an effort. He glanced round as Derdhel laid a hand on his shoulder.

"Words mean nothing," the other elf whispered.

"We came all this way to get away from this kind of interference," the human said to his companions, though loud enough for Seri and Derdhel to hear and gesturing obviously to them. Then he went on without even looking at them again. A couple of the humans were clearly stifling laughter as they looked up at the elves, but others looked frightened and, as they followed their leader, they kept glancing back. Derdhel kept his hand on Seri's shoulder.

"It's all right," whispered Seri. "I'm not going to chase them."

Derdhel nodded, but didn't move until the humans were over the horizon.

CHAPTER SEVEN

Seregei was old enough that one of his teeth was loose and he wiggled it constantly. Sometimes it bled and he would have to stop, but he hoped if it wiggled enough it would come out like Lessai's teeth did. His mother had told him that when elflings were growing up their teeth fell out and were replaced with grown-up teeth and he very much wanted to be old enough for such a badge of honour as a gap.

He wiggled it with his tongue as he peered around the doorway from the corridor into the Guardhouse common room. His parents were sitting side-by-side on the window seat, talking in hushed voices to his uncles Seri and Maelli. He watched them curiously, wondering what was happening. Over the last few days he'd noticed his parents seemed worried about something. They barely paid attention to anything he wanted to show or tell them and he knew that meant there was something important going on. Usually, he'd run to Neithan instead, but Neithan was away.

He looked up as he caught Neithan's name among the whispers, but then his father suddenly caught sight of him and got up. The others fell silent instantly and turned to look at him.

"Seregei," his father said severely, "It's rude to eavesdrop."

"What's happened to Uncle Neithan?"

"He'll be fine," said Maelli, coming over. "Come on, let's go outside."

Seregei shook his head. "What's happened to him? Where is he?" he jerked his hand away when Maelli tried to take hold of it. "I don't want to go outside. It's cold."

"Seregei, go outside," said his father. Seregei looked appealingly at his mother, but she shook her head and gestured to him to go with Maelli. He folded his arms and stomped out alongside the grown-up elf.

As soon as they were outside, though, he asked again, "Where's Uncle Neithan? You were talking about him, weren't you?"

"You shouldn't have been listening," said Maelli, handing him his cloak.

"But I've been wondering for ages." Seregei half shut his eyes as he spoke; it wasn't entirely true, but he had wondered a couple of times what Neithan was doing. "Has something bad happened to him?" He opened his eyes wide again and looked up at Maelli as he asked, "Can I go rescue him?"

Maelli smiled wanly. "No, you're too young."

"No, I'm all grown up. See?" Seregei wiggled his loose tooth with his tongue, opening his mouth wide so Maelli could see.

Maelli's smile broadened a bit. "Very impressive, but you'll need to have lost them all and had all the new ones grow in and be quite a bit taller before you'll be old enough."

Seregei folded his arms and looked at the ground, pouting and scuffing his feet in the frosty grass. "S'not fair. Nobody tells me anything."

Maelli crouched down to his height. "Listen, Seregei, whining won't help anything. If you want to be treated like a grown-up, you need to act like one."

Seregei kicked the ground again. "But I want to," he said. "I want to go out and fight things and rescue people when they're in trouble. That's what you do."

"But it's not all we do." Maelli looked round. "Listen, it's really too cold to be standing out here."

"Daddy told me to come out here," said Seregei, still pouting. "I told him it was cold and he said I still had to."

"I know, but that's because you shouldn't have been listening to what we were saying." Maelli tapped Seregei's chin to make him look up. "Do you understand that?"

He looked very serious and Seregei nodded unwillingly.

"All right. Don't do it again, understand?"

Another nod, looking at the floor. "But... where *is* he?"

"He went to look for some humans. I'm sure he's fine." But as he spoke, Maelli's eyes strayed up towards the hills. Seregei frowned at him. He wasn't stupid and he knew that wasn't true.

Neithan choked as another kick caught him in the gut. The shock sent pain searing through his injured ribs and his vision faded for a moment. He couldn't even raise his head, let alone struggle against the bonds on his wrists and ankles.

But he could hear voices nearby and he struggled to understand what they were saying.

"But what if the others..."

"... scared? Kill him and... never find..."

Neithan could only make out snatches, but they were enough. He struggled to stay conscious despite the pain. Every breath tightened iron bands around his chest. He could taste blood in his raw throat.

A breath caught and he coughed despite himself, almost fainting at the pain. He just managed to stay awake, but then someone kicked him again and he finally dropped into unconsciousness.

***

When he woke, it was even harder to breathe. He was cold. The voices were an indistinct murmur above the rushing noise in his ears. He tried to moan and realised dully that there was something stuffed in his mouth. Perhaps that was why he couldn't breathe.

For some time he drifted in and out of consciousness. He didn't understand what they were saying; he wasn't even sure they were speaking in a language he knew, though they had before. He just tried to lie still and breathe steadily and shallowly though his nose.

He thought it was getting colder. Shivering hurt, but he couldn't stop.

After a while, he heard the crunch of feet approaching and made the effort to open his eyes. Even then, he couldn't see much. It was dark and his vision was blurred, but he could tell there was a figure looming over him. He hoped he wasn't about to be kicked again. He didn't think he could survive much more of that.

The realisation made him feel even colder.

The human just turned away, though, shouting something to the others. Neithan closed his eyes with a sigh and instantly regretted it; breathing out was just as painful as breathing in. He whimpered faintly into the gag and squeezed his eyes shut. He was more awake now and he concentrated on breathing steadily, trying to stay that way.

He tensed as he felt something hit him and whimpered again. More tiny blows fell and he wondered if someone was kicking stones at him. Then he heard the agitated voices of the humans and made out the word 'rain'.

"Shall we take him inside?"

"Leave him. They don't feel the cold."

There was a scraping and pattering of feet, then a door slammed. Neithan lay where he had been left, feeling the rain getting heavier and colder as it soaked through the ragged remains of his clothes.

He was going to die. There was no way out...

Something in him did rebel at that last thought. There was always a way out. No matter what, there had to be a way out of this. He screwed his eyes shut and tried to think past the pain and cold. He wanted to escape. That was the most immediate thing. He had... almost nothing. His hands were too numb to search for a sharp rock – though he knew he was lying on some – and he hadn't the strength to move about much. All he really had was solitude and rain. The thought almost made him chuckle, but then an idea struck him. The bonds on his wrists were leather. He remembered seeing them when he was captured. Leather stretched when it was wet. If he could just stretch the leather enough for some slack, he might be able to free his hands.

It was only a little more than nothing, but it would be better than just waiting to die, so he started to strain against the leather strips.

He'd never appreciated how much moving his arms meant moving his chest. It hurt more than breathing, than coughing, than trying to roll over. Tears ran openly down his face, mingling with the rain. He desperately wanted to stop trying, rest, maybe even sleep a while, but he couldn't. In this cold, sleep was death.

The pain was numbing slowly, though it flared again every time he tried. He was getting wetter, colder, with every passing moment. But he thought the leather was stretching. All he needed was an inch…

Another coughing fit left him teetering on the edge of consciousness. He hoped the taste of blood was from the rag in his mouth. He couldn't think of the alternative. Not now. He had to hope. Just a moment longer. He'd get his hands free and then think of the next step.

He thought he could move a little more now. He paused a moment, fighting the urge to gasp for breath. He felt smothered, unable to get the air he needed into his lungs. He'd almost drowned once. This was worse. His head swam and he shook it, trying to rouse himself. Sleep was death. He couldn't give up now. He kept telling himself that, repeating the words in his head as a distraction.

Finally, he managed to slide a loop over his right hand.

He sighed, rewarding himself with a brief rest. He couldn't lie still for long, though. He could no longer feel the cold rain falling on him, but he could hear it pattering on the shingly ground by his head. Sleep was death and he had to fight on.

It was easier now, though, and he gradually managed to ease his hands free. The feeling of the blood returning to his cramped muscles was like a thousand pins, but he ignored that. He'd been fighting with the pain in his chest so long that the fireblood was easy.

His head was swimming and it was hard to open his eyes. He realised dully that he wasn't shivering any more and welcomed the fact; even those little movements had hurt.

As soon as he could, he reached up to pull at the gag. Fortunately, it wasn't too tight and he managed to work it off his chin and spit out the rag stuffed in his mouth. Almost at once, he started to cough.

He knew he had fainted when he recovered consciousness and he counted himself lucky that he'd ever woken. Gradually, hesitantly, he pushed himself upright and tried to think of the next step: freeing his legs. He couldn't drag himself anywhere.

He remembered that he had been lying on sharp stones and groped about for one, his hand eventually closing on a broken flint. He could barely grip it and knew it must have lacerated his palm by the time he had picked it up, but he didn't care for that, or for the slashes on his legs that he left as he chopped at the leather strip at his ankles until he felt it give.

He'd never prayed before, but as the flint fell from his fingers he sent a heartfelt word of thanks to Valcae and the Lady equally. Now he had a chance.

But he needed to take the next step: getting away from his captors. For the first time, he wondered where they'd gone. When they'd dragged him into this clearing, he remembered glimpsing a building like a long, low hut. Presumably they'd gone in there to seek shelter. He couldn't see, but he thought it was on his left with the trees on his right. Hopefully those would shelter him a little from the rain, if he could only reach them. He'd not felt drops for a while, but when he listened he could make out a faint hissing. Snow, he realised. The first snow of winter. It was colder than he'd thought. He wasn't sure he could crawl, but that was the only way, so he had to at least try.

He could barely move. The cold had set into his muscles even without the weakness of hunger, bonds and injuries, but he had come so far that he couldn't bring himself to give up now. There were elves in this forest somewhere. If he could only reach them, surely they'd help him. It was a distant hope, but all he had and he pushed himself up on his hands and knees to try to take the first step.

He could feel tears in his eyes as the pain crept through him again, hot and shrill, like a fire. He concentrated on it, grappling with it as he moved, trying to picture it as a knot in a piece of string that he had to untangle. He was able to move now. He had that. He could use it. He could make it to the trees and then think of what to do next. If nothing else, he would be out of the snow.

Another coughing fit made his elbows buckle and he collapsed to the ground, landing in icy rainwater and gathering half-melted snow. The taste of blood was stronger and he spat. No time to think about that. He shoved himself back up and struggled on, concentrating on moving and controlling the pain.

He didn't know how far he'd come. There was earth under him now, no more stones, but he didn't know if he was under the trees. He suspected that if he stopped moving he would never start again, so he kept going. Kept the rhythm going: hand, hand, knee, knee, his mind wandering. He dreamed of home: a warm bed, friendly voices, hot soup, a healer's tending... He could almost feel it now, a contented warmth creeping through his body even as he crawled. He knew in the back of his mind that that was dangerous, knew that he had a long way to go before he was home, knew that he had to fight the instinct to find some warm corner and go to sleep, but it was so tempting...

A sudden shout startled him out of his dream. One elbow buckled. He collapsed again, all the pain and cold and exhaustion rushing back. For a moment he tried to stay conscious, but he couldn't fight any more.

With a last, despairing whimper, he fainted.

"Even Seregei's noticed something's wrong," said Alatani softly as she and Weyrn lay together in bed.

He sighed. He'd guessed that Neithan's disappearance was weighing on her mind too, but he had hoped he was the only one who was really worried. "He's very capable," he said softly, "But there's no denying it: he went on a one-week journey and tomorrow marks two. Something's happened."

She nodded, her hair tickling his nose. He sighed again and turned away, though he kept his arm around her. He needed to think. It wasn't a problem that could be left alone any longer.

"I'll speak to the others tomorrow," he said slowly. "We can send out a search party. Some of the clans might have seen something..."

"What about the humans? They were the ones he went to visit, after all."

"They're also the ones most likely to have attacked him."

"What about Esren's little group?" She drew away slightly to pull the blanket over them more warmly.

Weyrn couldn't help worrying that that was to be hoped for. His instincts told him that, whatever else, Esren's group would ensure that even a prisoner was protected from the winter chill. No matter what he tried to tell himself, he couldn't be so sure about the strange humans who had always seemed so needlessly hostile.

"Who will you take?" she asked softly, once the silence had stretched a while. He smiled, appreciating the fact that she never questioned that he would go himself.

"We'll need rangers: Derdhel for sure. I can track a little and so can Seri, and we'll need him anyway. Celes has been making a lot of progress on wilderness survival and Maelli's good all around."

"That leaves me," she said softly.

"Are you all right with that?"

She nodded. "I... do want to know what happened to him, but if someone's to be left behind I'm very happy for it to be me."

He kissed her hair. "It's not because I don't think you'd be useful."

"Oh, you don't need to reassure me," she said with a short laugh. "You made good points there and I do think you have everything you need. I can also go to Hurion, if you like? See if there's anything the Royal Guard can do?"

Weyrn wrinkled his nose.

"Consider it payback for when you found the three ambassadors," said Alatani seriously. "That's certainly what I'll say if he tries to take it as us begging for help."

"All right."

"I'll go as soon as you've all left," she said with false briskness, "Seregei will enjoy the trip into the city."

He smiled and kissed her again. "Thank you."

Neithan slowly revived to find himself lying on something soft, his head slightly raised. He could hear the crackling of a fire and smell smoke and something cooking, along with a confusion of other smells that he couldn't quite identify.

He must have stirred or made some small sound, for he heard footsteps approach and a voice said, "Hello?" in the human language.

Neithan tensed and instantly regretted it as a spasm went through his torso. He groaned.

"It's all right, you're safe here," the voice said.

Neithan wasn't sure whether to believe it, at least without seeing where he was. He didn't think he was bound, though it probably wouldn't have been necessary; his limbs felt as if they were made of lead.

"Can you hear me?"

He nodded, still trying to open his eyes. At last, his eyelids slid apart and he blinked up at the human, squinting as he tried to focus.

"Ah, that's better. How do you feel?" the human asked.

All Neithan could see was a vague blur, but there was only one figure and it didn't seem threatening. He took a breath to reply, but it caught in his throat and he began to cough. That brought the pain back. He couldn't stop, no matter how much it hurt. His mouth seemed full of blood. He was too weak to roll. He couldn't breathe... He looked helplessly up at the human, still coughing.

Fortunately, the human seemed to realise what he needed. He grabbed Neithan's shoulder and rolled him onto his side so the blood could drain from his mouth and, gradually, the fit eased. It had cost what little strength Neithan had, though, and once he could breathe again he fell still with a sigh. He didn't try to open his eyes again. Rest first.

"Are you still awake?" the human asked.

Neithan hardly dared try to speak, but he croaked, "Yes."

"Oh, good, you *can* talk. You had me worried. I'm Ilian. This is my home; I found you out in the forest. Can you tell me your name?"

The others had never bothered with details such as his name, but Neithan still hesitated to answer any question.

"Listen," said Ilian, "I'm not in league with whoever did this to you, so you needn't worry about that."

Neithan nodded. It could have been a lie, but he couldn't help thinking that, in any case, telling his name couldn't do too much damage. "Neithan," he whispered. "Neithan the... the Crafty."

"Well, it's good to meet you, Neithan." Ilian gently patted his shoulder. "You seem a lot better than you did."

"I... feel better." Warmer, certainly, and it was a safe warmth. He remembered with a shudder how he had been so cold he could no longer feel it.

"Good." Ilian patted his shoulder again. "You'll be safe here, don't worry about that."

"Thank you." Then Neithan started to cough again.

This time it was worse. Despite everything, he couldn't breathe. Iron bands tightened around his chest. He could feel tears in his eyes. His whole body convulsed with every cough...

The next thing he knew, it was over. He wondered if he'd fainted again. He felt even more tired.

"Neithan?" Ilian called, sounding unnerved.

Neithan nodded.

"Are... you all right?"

Neithan just sighed slowly. "I... no."

"Would you like something to eat?"

Neithan again noticed the savoury smell. He wasn't certain he could keep food down, but he had to admit he was hungry. His captors had fed him, but not much. "Please."

He lay quietly and gathered his strength as Ilian fetched him some food. He felt exhausted, but Ilian helped him to sit up, moving him slowly to hurt his ribs as little as possible, and set the edge of a cup to his lips. "There you go. It's broth."

Neithan was really only aware that it was hot and easy to swallow, though it stung the cuts on his lips. It warmed a path down to his stomach and he sighed as he felt that warmth spreading through him. Hope followed in its path: perhaps he could live to see his friends again.

"Thank you," he whispered again, once he'd finished.

"That's all right. Get some sleep." Ilian helped him lie down again and, within moments, he fell asleep.

When Weyrn went to the common room first thing the next morning, Seri was already there, sitting on the window seat and nursing a cup of tea.

"The kettle's probably still warm," he said softly, without looking round.

It wasn't, but Weyrn moved it over the fire. "How long have you been up?"

"I couldn't sleep."

Weyrn nodded. "You should have got your rest. Do you think you'll be able to join me on a search?"

At that, Seri looked round. "For Neithan?"

"Yes. It's been a week now." Weyrn sighed. "That's long..." – he trailed off as he noticed the view out of the window – "it snowed?"

Seri nodded absently. "It's melting fast, but yes."

"Spirits, I hope he's all right..." Weyrn shook his head, looking down at the fire. "Giving him a few days' grace... something might have come up. But a week is too long. Something's happened."

"I'm sure of it." Seri sniffed his tea as he got up. "So I'm going with you?"

"If you're fit."

"Who else?"

"All but Alatani, if they'll come." Weyrn looked sharply at Seri, waiting for any sort of comment about the fact that he was leaving Alatani.

Seri just smiled. "I'm sure they all will. Thank you."

Weyrn blinked. "Thank me? He's my friend too, you know."

"I know that, but..." Seri looked out of the window. "Still. I'll go and pack."

Weyrn nodded and went to look outside. The lowering clouds had the green tinge that promised more snow to come. Travel would be miserable in this slushy weather, but being lost or otherwise in trouble out there would be worse.

Next to arrive was Celes. "First snow," he said with a small smile.

"Yes. It's not sticking, though. Will you come and help search for Neithan?"

"When do we leave?" Celes sounded relieved.

"As soon as everyone's ready."

***

As Seri had predicted, everyone was willing to come and help search for Neithan, and they were ready to leave by mid-morning. Weyrn was crouched down, checking Seri's pack while Seri checked his, when Seregei came over.

"Daddy?" he said softly.

Weyrn looked up with a small smile. "Yes, Seregei?"

"Where are you going?"

"Well, you know yesterday you were asking where Neithan is?"

Seregei nodded. "Are you going to rescue him?"

Weyrn ruffled his hair and kissed his forehead. "I hope we won't need to. But if we do, then yes."

Neithan woke to the feeling that someone was leaning over him. It was a familiar feeling, one that made him cringe slightly.

"I think he's waking up."

The unfamiliar human voice made his heart sink and he gritted his teeth, waiting. Perhaps it had all been a dream, when he thought he'd escaped…

"Neithan, can you hear us?" That was Ilian's voice. "Neithan?"

Neithan wasn't sure what to make of this. He had been sure Ilian was trustworthy, but what if he was wrong?"

Consciousness was seeping back slowly, though, and he realised that he was still tucked in a warm bed and there was still a smell of food. He winced inwardly, but as the humans talked in low voices between themselves he went wearily back to his favoured method of solving problems: what did he want? What did he have? How could he use it?

It was difficult to think clearly, but he worked through the questions methodically. Most immediately, he wanted food. He also wanted certainty about where he was and what was happening. He had very little: just himself. He didn't even think he was strong enough to raise a hand – now that he was paying attention to his hands, they burned with pain – but there was one thing he could do: he opened his eyes.

"Neithan!" cried Ilian. "You *are* awake!"

Neithan nodded, feeling relieved, though his gaze drifted to the other vague figure worriedly.

"This is my brother," said Ilian.

"Arens," said the other man, raising a hand slightly. "Good to meet you."

Neithan nodded, not quite trusting himself to speak. He could feel his throat getting clogged again and it took effort to breathe past that.

"How's your breathing?" asked Arens, crouching beside the bed. "Ilian told me you were coughing blood."

Neithan glanced at the pillow under his head. There was a rag under his cheek, smeared and spattered with dried and drying blood. He nodded, an irrepressible cough sending a flash of pain through him.

Once he'd started, he couldn't stop.

As soon as Alatani had waved off the other Swordmasters she set out for the city to see what she could do to enlist Hurion's help. Seregei went with her, holding tight to her hand. She couldn't help noticing that he seemed unusually quiet; normally he'd have been trying to run off and investigate things or point out new sights as they went, but today he just walked, his eyes on his feet.

"Seregei?" she said at last. "What's the matter?"

"Is Uncle Neithan in trouble?" he asked quietly.

She winced to herself. "We don't know."

"Has Daddy gone to help him?"

"Yes, just like he told you this morning."

"Why aren't we going to help him?"

"Well... you're too young." She instantly added, "Don't show me your tooth, you're too young."

Seregei pouted, putting his finger in his mouth to wiggle his tooth anyway.

"And I have to stay and look after you and the Guardhouse."

He blinked. "But the Guardhouse is a building."

"It just means... I have to stay there in case someone needs a Swordmaster."

"But Uncle Neithan needs Swordmasters," he said, tears brimming in his eyes.

Alatani sighed and picked him up to cuddle him. He was getting heavy and she sighed as she nuzzled his soft hair. "I know," she said. "And they'll find him and bring him home, you'll see. Everyone but me has gone, after all." She started walking again, carrying him on her hip. He wrapped his arms around her neck. "Would you like to go play with Lessai while I visit the king?" she asked him.

He nodded.

"All right. I'll go see if Lessai's mother can babysit you for a bit."

"I'm not a baby," he protested sleepily.

She smiled and murmured, "You are to me."

***

She left him with Elar and Lessai and went straight to the palace, trying to work out what to say as she went. She had felt far more confident the night before.

Still, she hitched her shoulders as she walked into the courtyard in front of the palace, her head high. She had every right to be here and every right to ask for help in finding Neithan. As she'd hoped, the guards let her in at once, though not without some curious stares. Hurion's honour guard seemed a little more unsure.

"Where's Captain Weyrn?" he asked. "He's usually the one who comes if the Swordmasters have any business with Lord Hurion."

"He's busy at the moment," said Alatani. "That's actually what I came to speak to Lord Hurion about."

The other elf didn't move from in front of the door, though he still looked uncertain. "Will you tell me what it is? I can ask him if he'd be willing to speak to you."

Alatani frowned a little. "It's urgent and rather private." They could easily be overheard out here and she didn't want the news of Neithan's disappearance to become common gossip.

The guard looked at her for a moment longer, but then nodded and went in. Alatani had time to shift her weight and hope that she had said enough before he returned.

"I'm sorry, Swordmaster Alatani, but Lord Hurion is rather busy and without –"

Alatani hadn't wanted to do this, but she had no intention of simply being dismissed. "Remind him of how, a few years ago, Captain Weyrn and some others went to search for the Wood-elven ambassadors at his request, and say I want to speak to him."

The honour guard nodded and went into the study. Alatani folded her arms and fought the urge to tap her foot. She tried to tell herself that some caution was reasonable, but she was still offended.

Fortunately, it wasn't long before the guard was back. This time, he gestured her in, though he came in with her.

Hurion was standing by the fire, warming his hands, though when she came in he went to get her a drink. She accepted it with thanks and took a sip of the warm mead. The thought of the others – especially Neithan – stuck out in the cold made it taste sour.

"To what do I owe this pleasure?" asked Hurion, his expression guarded.

Alatani sighed. "I apologise for being blunt when it came to getting in to see you, but…"

He waved a hand. "I know I owe you a lot; I'm not offended to be reminded."

She nodded. "In this case, it's actually a similar problem: Swordmaster Neithan is overdue returning from a journey."

Hurion frowned. "It must be serious for you to have come to me. Why are you so worried?"

"It's been a week since he should have been home, and he was spying on the humans that have been gathering near the valley."

Hurion frowned. "Some of my own men have had trouble with them. Last time the scouts were driven off with stones."

Alatani felt like her heart had skipped a beat. "You never told us that!"

"I didn't think it made a difference to you."

"If we'd known you were also having problems and that they'd been so violent, he'd not have gone alone!"

"For that matter, you never told me you were having anything to do with them." Hurion took a sip of his mead, though Alatani noticed his hand was shaking slightly. "All right," he said, once he'd lowered the drink. "I owe you many favours, in any case. What is it you want of me?"

"Captain Weyrn and the other Swordmasters set out this morning to search for any sign of where he might be. As time passes, they may need more help, or they may need resources of some kind."

Hurion nodded. "So at the moment it's not really clear what I can do."

"No, but if we do need something…"

"Ask." He smiled. "I like Neithan, you needn't worry about that."

Alatani smiled. "Thank you. And… maybe in future it would be best if we discussed what to do about the humans."

He half turned away and took another sip of his mead. "Well, that's something I should probably speak to Weyrn about."

Alatani nodded a little. "That's probably true. I'll ask him to speak to you."

"Please do." He nodded a little, then made a small gesture of dismissal. "Please let me know if there's any more I can do."

Ilian had given Neithan some more food and watched as the elf drifted back into unconsciousness. As soon as he was sure Neithan could no longer hear him, he stepped away from the bed and looked over at Arens. "What are we going to do?"

Arens shook his head thoughtfully. "He can't stay. We only laid in enough food to see us through the winter and it won't feed three. He's in no condition to travel, though."

"I know." Ilian looked back at Neithan as the elf's breathing hitched for a moment and he coughed faintly in his sleep. A few more beads of frothy blood spattered the rag they'd laid under his head. "I knew things were bad the moment I saw him; I just couldn't bear to leave even an elf out there to die like that."

"I agree, but, even apart from anything else, much though I want to help him, I don't want him here if the people who did that come knocking. It can't be too long before they will."

"You think so?"

"I'm sure of it. In that state he can't have come far."

Ilian licked his lips nervously. "And what if they look further afield?" His thoughts went to their sister, living with her husband only a day's journey away. Neithan wouldn't have made it that far, but his attackers might look there.

Arens shook his head distractedly. "I don't know."

Another cough made Ilian look round, but Neithan still seemed to be asleep.

"I think the best thing to do is to work out where he comes from and see if we can get his family to come and fetch him," Arens continued, starting to pace up and down. "They can probably do more to treat him than I can anyway. I can set out almost at once." He laughed "I barely opened my pack after last night."

Ilian nodded. "Well, when he next wakes up, I can ask him."

Behind him, Neithan coughed again, and this time it turned into a coughing fit. Ilian winced in sympathy as he crouched down beside the elf and took his bandaged hand, wiping the sweat from his brow.

Finally it was over and Neithan groaned softly, curling up a little around his battered ribs. He opened his eyes after a moment, though, to blink hazily up at Ilian.

"Thanks," he whispered.

Ilian nodded. "We're going to try to get a message back to your family," he said. "Where are you from?"

Neithan's eyes cleared a little at that. "D—" – he coughed – "Duamelti. Look for the... the Swordmasters."

Ilian nodded, though that instruction left him none the wiser. "We'll find them."

Neithan smiled. "They'll be looking for me."

The Swordmasters searched for a full day without finding anything. Once or twice they stopped at small settlements where, to their relief, they heard reports of Neithan visiting. Nobody had seen him in the last week, but one elf told Weyrn that when Neithan had left them he had been intending to go directly home. He pointed out the road Neithan had taken back west: a different route to the one they had arrived by. Weyrn nodded and thanked him, then went to rejoin the others.

"We're on the right track, at least," he said, and repeated what the elf had said.

"Only a week," said Celes with a small sigh. "That's something."

"A week is still a long time," said Seri, a little sharply.

"I know, but shorter than two weeks."

"Come on," said Weyrn, cutting off the brewing argument. "Let's go and see what we can find."

He knew they couldn't keep going too long; night was beginning to fall and he wanted to get a camp set up before it was too dark. That thought made him shoot a nervous look at the sky, though. The clouds had been there all day, but he thought they were blowing off towards Duamelti.

"Maelli," he said softly, not wanting to disturb Derdhel from his search for tracks, "Do you think it'll snow tonight?"

Maelli looked up, frowning. "If... I don't know. I don't *think* so."

"There's another hour's light in any case," said Weyrn, guessing that Maelli didn't want to stop to camp yet.

Maelli smiled sidelong at him. "Honestly, I can't be sure." He licked his finger and held it up to test the wind. "It's hard to tell the direction of the wind under the trees, but..." He tilted his head to listen. "I think there's strength in it and the last time we could see how the clouds were moving..."

"Towards Duamelti," Weyrn finished.

Maelli nodded. "I think we'll be all right."

"We'll need to find somewhere fairly sheltered in any case," Celes interrupted.

"I know," said Weyrn, "But not immediately." Still, he also knew that they needed to keep watch and have somewhere fairly defensible. Though five together were less likely to be a target than one alone, if Neithan had been attacked they might also be in danger.

"Here!" Derdhel said suddenly, pointing.

Weyrn hurried up beside him, careful not to step on the ground he was inspecting. "What is it?"

"I know this bootprint. Neithan, for sure."

When he squinted, Weyrn could make out the nicks Neithan had cut in the sole of his boot on one side: part of an experiment that hadn't quite worked. He nodded. "Where was he going?"

Derdhel didn't answer aloud, just crept carefully along the side path he'd found: barely more than an animal trail. Weyrn gestured to Celes as the most light-footed to go with him. He himself returned to the others.

Maelli was looking around distractedly while Seri looked after Derdhel and Celes, chewing his lip. Weyrn didn't say anything, just patted him on the shoulder.

"I know he's probably fine, but he's my mentor," said Seri.

"And my trainee," said Weyrn, forcing a smile. "Believe me, I want to see him safe."

It wasn't long before Derdhel and Celes returned, looking grim.

"There's the remains of a camp," said Celes. "He'd set up a shelter. It's been knocked down, but we can see where it was."

"It was definitely him?" asked Weyrn. He could be creative, but Neithan's wilderness shelters didn't tend to be too distinctive.

"I'm pretty sure," said Derdhel. "In any case, we found more of his bootprints."

"How old was the camp?" asked Seri.

"Almost a week, but that wasn't all," said Celes. He sighed. "There were other prints."

"At least four or five and heavier than Neithan's," said Derdhel. "Humans, I'm sure."

"Any signs of a battle?" asked Weyrn, dreading the answer.

Celes nodded, but looked at Derdhel, who said, "There was a lot of confusion and the snow hasn't helped, but I would guess there was a fight. They left in a group, but if he was with them I couldn't tell."

"We'll follow them, then," said Weyrn. "I assume there was no sign he left in any other direction?"

"He could have taken to the trees, but I doubt it. I can look again."

Weyrn nodded. "Do that. In the meantime, Seri, look up and down the road and see if there's any sign of what's been happening along here. I'll be doing the same." He wasn't the best tracker, but he wasn't expecting there to be much. He was mostly wondering if there was anything to show that humans had been going up towards the village.

The path was beaten dirt, though, muddied by the previous night's snow, and he couldn't see anything but their own tracks. Presumably, Derdhel had only found Neithan's footprints because they were away from the road.

"Anything?" he asked, looking over at Seri.

Seri shook his head and sighed.

"Nothing there either," said Celes, coming back from the campsite. "Derdhel's just making sure."

Maelli pushed away from the tree he'd been leaning against, opening his eyes. "I was listening to make sure nobody was coming," he said, in answer to Weyrn's enquiring look. "There's nothing but forest sounds."

"All right. We'll follow the humans' trail." Weyrn loosened his sword in its sheath. "With luck, he'll be all right."

Neithan had just finished some more soup when he heard a knock on the door of the little house. Any hope that it was nothing to worry about vanished when he saw the fearful look that flashed across Ilian's face.

"Not Arens returning?" he whispered.

Ilian shook his head. "Try not to cough and keep hidden as much as you can."

He helped Neithan roll onto his side, facing away from the door, and pulled the blanket up almost over his head. Neithan lay as still as he could, his eyes closed, aware of his heart hammering in his chest. He wanted to trust Ilian, but there was no denying how easy it would be for the human to betray him. He couldn't even see what was happening, but he heard Ilian go to the door and open it, then low voices. He strained to hear what they were saying, but couldn't quite make it out.

He was also beginning to feel blood in his throat again.

He knew that coughing would draw attention to him. That was how Ilian had found him, after all. He struggled to keep breathing normally, to hold back the cough, while he listened to the voices murmuring. He hoped desperately that, whoever it was, they would leave soon.

But the door didn't shut and, at last, Neithan had to cough. It exploded out of him, sending fire through his chest as though his body were full of burning pine cones. He clamped a hand over his mouth to try to muffle the sound, but he couldn't stop. Pain and fear made tears well in his eyes. The voices were louder, but he couldn't hear the words over his own coughing.

He couldn't hold on to consciousness any longer.

***

When he woke, someone was bathing his forehead. Despite his own dazed state, he knew that he couldn't have been recaptured. He sighed and winced at the familiar pain.

"Neithan?"

He nodded. "What… happened?"

"I told them you were Arens and that you had bloody lung."

Neithan coughed on a laugh. "I *do*."

"No, it's… a disease. Is it true elves can't be ill?"

Neithan opened his eyes, blinking to clear his vision. "I… infections, but… not diseases." He remembered the city where he'd grown up. Humans had suffered from all sorts of illnesses, but elves never had.

Ilian sighed. "I'm jealous."

"Do… you think that's… why they hate us?"

"What?"

"The ones…" Neithan gestured weakly at himself. For the first time, he noticed that his hand was bandaged into a fist.

Ilian shook his head. "That I don't know, but… listen, don't take this the wrong way, but…"

Neithan shook his head. "Need… to know."

Ilian nodded. "All right. I think there are plenty of us who are jealous. I, uh…" He scratched his head. "Think about it: you never get ill, you live forever, you've been here forever… We, uh… some of us…" He apparently noticed Neithan's questioning look and sighed. "All right, jealous is a good word and… yes, I do mean 'us'. Listen, though, you're our guest. We're not going to do anything to you."

Neithan nodded, but couldn't speak; he was about to start coughing again and looked away.

In the morning, Celes woke Weyrn, having taken the last watch.

"Anything?" asked Weyrn as he sat up, shivering as the cold air cut through his shirt.

Celes shook his head. "It was quiet most of the night. Apparently Derdhel saw some lights and heard voices, but it was only for a moment."

Still, Weyrn looked over at Derdhel, who was also stirring. He'd apparently heard the conversation, for he looked up and nodded. "I couldn't understand what they were saying, but they seemed agitated. They headed further east."

"Do you think they might have Neithan?" asked Seri, sitting up in his bedroll and rubbing his eyes.

Weyrn frowned, looking in that direction. "Let's see if we can find any trace of them," he said. He glanced around. "Where's Maelli?"

"I woke him first," said Celes.

"So he could pray?" Weyrn frowned. "He probably shouldn't be alone."

"He said he'd not go far." Celes looked around.

At that moment there was a whistle from up in the trees. Weyrn looked to see Maelli perched in the branches of a bare oak, waving to them. Seeing that he'd got their attention, he pointed.

"Come on," said Weyrn at once, snatching up his sword. "Derdhel, Celes, stay here. Seri, you're with me." As he spoke, he gestured to Maelli to stay where he was.

Seri nodded, rolling out of bed and picking up his own sword.

The two Swordmasters hurried along the road, keeping to the edges and watching for any sign of a trap. Weyrn was sure Maelli would warn them, but he kept an eye on a patch of bushes by the road, glancing ahead as often as possible. He could feel his heart beating, a thrill going through his limbs at the anticipation of battle.

Then a lone human stepped around a corner up ahead.

Weyrn focussed on him, frowning. He had stopped at the sight of them and seemed unsure. He certainly didn't look like a threat. As they watched him, he waved and called what sounded like a greeting.

Weyrn frowned. "Seri, watch my back."

Seri nodded. "Be careful."

Weyrn sheathed his sword and went to meet the human.

It was difficult to see much about him; he was muffled in a hooded cloak and scarf, but he didn't look very strong. He was carrying a pack and evidently on some sort of journey. Weyrn couldn't see any weapons.

As he approached, the human pulled down the scarf wound over the lower half of his face and said, "Do you speak my language?"

"A little." Weyrn had learned it on the same trip as he'd met Neithan.

The man sighed in relief. "I'm looking for the road to Duamelti. Am I going the right way?"

"Yes, but… what takes you there?"

The human looked sidelong at him, then at Seri. "I, uh… I'm looking for some people called 'Swordmasters'."

Weyrn stared at him for a long moment, but then shook his head. "We're Swordmasters."

"Oh, good." He sighed. "We've, uh… met a friend of yours."

Weyrn's eyes narrowed as he wondered if this was a prelude to being told Neithan was a hostage. "What do you mean, 'met'?"

"Well, my brother found him out in the forest and we took him in. He told us he was from Duamelti and to look for the Swordmasters." The man pointed back the way he'd come. "I'm glad I found you so soon; he's in a bad way."

"Can you tell us his name?"

"Neithan."

Weyrn sighed slightly in relief; at least this meant Neithan was alive. "Where is he?" he asked, once he'd translated the conversation for Seri.

"Back at our house."

"And when you say he's in a bad way…?"

The man winced. "He's had his ribs kicked into his lungs, I think.

Whatever it is, he's coughing blood."

Weyrn's heart dropped and he once more translated for Seri. The other elf went pale. Weyrn swallowed hard and looked back at the human. "Will you take us there?"

"Of course."

Weyrn nodded and dropped back into Elven to whisper to Seri, "Tell the others to follow along behind, then rejoin us. Bring my pack. I don't want to advertise our numbers."

Seri nodded and hurried back the way they'd come. Weyrn turned back to the human. "All right, lead on. What's your name?"

"Arens. Yours?"

"Weyrn." Weyrn suppressed another shiver as he fell into step beside Arens, but then he set his thoughts on the road ahead.

Neithan was still drifting in and out of consciousness and Ilian was worried. He couldn't help worrying about the potential consequences if Arens brought these 'Swordmasters' and they found their friend already dead. He wondered if they'd blame him for the death.

"Neithan?" he called softly as the elf coughed, but there was no reaction. Ilian frowned; Neithan had seemed much stronger before, able to hold a proper conversation. Perhaps that had worn him out. "You all right, Neithan?" he asked, laying a hand on Neithan's brow. It felt cool and clammy, but still warmer than before. Still, the lingering chill made Ilian wipe his hand on his trousers, shuddering. At first, Neithan had been so cold that Ilian had wondered if he was already dead. He'd heard stories of ghosts in this forest...

Neithan stirred and moaned softly, muttering something in his own language without opening his eyes. It had been a while since he was last awake and Ilian wondered if he was hungry. Again, he stirred a little and coughed, a couple of drops of blood starring the rag under his cheek, but he didn't show any other sign of consciousness.

Ilian shook his head and went back outside to cut some more firewood and keep watch for anyone who might approach. He didn't think Arens would be back so soon, but he was worried in case the other men returned. They had asked immediately about Neithan, though not by name. He glanced back at the door with a wince as he heard Neithan coughing again. He'd not have given them back a dog if he'd found it in that state.

It felt strange: he'd often been jealous of elves, with their long lives and their immunities from the many things that plagued humans. He'd thought they didn't feel cold and that if they were hurt they would heal overnight, but... Now he'd seen an elf lying at his feet half frozen and heard him struggling to breathe for hours upon hours.

He spun round as he heard footsteps crunching behind him. His heart in his mouth, he hefted the axe and stepped in front of the door, but then sighed and relaxed as he recognised Arens. There were a couple of elves with him.

"That was quick."

"Neithan was right: they were looking for him." Arens glanced at the elves. "Weyrn, Seri, this is my brother, Ilian." He indicated each as he spoke.

Weyrn nodded a greeting to Ilian with a wan smile.

"Come in," said Ilian, gesturing to the door. "He's just inside."

Neithan looked dead.

That was the first thought that went through Weyrn's mind. He had never seen a living elf so pale and still. Even Neithan's soft features had grown pinched and thin; his face looked like a skull.

He felt Seri step a little round him, but the other elf didn't pass him. The movement broke his concentration, though, and he crossed the space to Neithan's side in a couple of steps. "Neithan?" he called softly, crouching beside the bed.

Nothing. Neithan didn't even twitch.

Weyrn looked over at the two humans. "Has he been this way the whole time?"

"Not the whole time," said Ilian, "But for the last several hours…"

"Weyrn," said Seri, who didn't understand the human language very well, "What's happening?"

"He's been like this for hours." Weyrn reached out, but remembered what Arens had said about Neithan's injuries and hesitated to touch him. "Seri, we're going to need help getting him back."

"I'll send someone."

"Thanks." Weyrn looked back at Neithan as Seri left.

"Where's he going?" asked Arens. "To tell the other elf what's happening?"

"Yes, and send him for help."

Neithan coughed and Weyrn looked back at him, taking his hand. It sounded like he was choking as his body jerked with the wet, hacking coughs, but Weyrn resisted the urge to slap him on the back; he didn't want to worsen his injuries. Still, he felt as if the bottom had fallen out of his stomach as he watched the blood frothing on Neithan's lips as he coughed it out of his lungs. Weyrn's hands were shaking as he tilted his friend's head slightly to help the blood run out of his mouth. Gradually, the fit eased and, to Weyrn's relief, Neithan's eyes fluttered open.

"Neithan?" Weyrn called softly. "Can you hear me?"

Neithan blinked and slowly focussed on Weyrn's face. At last, he whispered, "Weyrn?"

Weyrn grinned. "Yes, I'm here." He laid his hand on Neithan's head. "How are you?"

Neithan's eyes slid closed again. "Not good."

"Seri's gone to send someone for help. We'll soon have you home." Weyrn lowered his voice to ask, "These humans...?"

"They've been" – a faint cough – "kind to me."

Weyrn nodded and looked round at Ilian and Arens, who had been standing by the door and talking in hushed voices. Seeing him looking at them, though, they fell silent.

"How is he?" asked Ilian.

"He... not good." Weyrn sighed. "We need to get him home." He looked up again. "Thank you for looking after him."

Arens nodded, leaning back a little against the wall. "I'm glad I found you when I did. I was worried..."

Weyrn looked back at Neithan. He couldn't tell if the other elf was conscious. He was breathing, at least: a rasping, snoring sound that made it sound as if he would start coughing again at any moment. "Well, we'll soon get him home." He looked up. "Do you know who did this?"

Arens shook his head, but Ilian said, "There's a nomadic group moving about here. I think it was them."

"How do you know?" asked Arens.

"They came to the door."

"*What?*" Arens jerked forward. "What happened?"

Ilian held his hands up calmingly. "I didn't let them in and did my best to keep Neithan hidden completely."

"Did it work?" asked Arens. Weyrn read the answer in Ilian's pause. His eyes went back to Neithan as Arens said, "What happened?"

"He started coughing and I told them he was you."

Weyrn looked from short, slim Neithan with his relatively-long, pale hair to tall, dark Arens. "I'm surprised they believed that."

"I'd pulled a blanket up to hide him. All they could hear was the coughing." Ilian glanced at Arens. "I said you had the bloody lung."

Weyrn didn't ask what that was; he could guess well enough to be going on with "What if they come back?"

Ilian shrugged. "I don't know."

"Men who'd do something like that to a prisoner are *not* people to lie to," said Arens, gesturing at Neithan.

"Well, what else was I meant to do?" snapped Ilian, "Hand him over?"

Neithan whimpered faintly and Weyrn's head snapped round. "Neithan?"

Neithan's expression twitched and he whimpered again.

"It's all right, they'll not get you back. You're safe now."

Behind him, the brothers were still arguing in low voices, but he focussed on Neithan. The other elf was clearly struggling to breathe. He scrabbled helplessly at the pillow with a bandage-wrapped hand. Weyrn took and held it gently, murmuring soothingly until Neithan quietened again. He did smile briefly, though.

"What happened here?" Weyrn asked, gently running his fingertips over the bandages.

"Frostbite and wear, I think," said Arens. "His knees and feet are much the same way; he must have been crawling."

Weyrn nodded and once again gently stroked Neithan's hand. When he was sure Neithan was asleep again, he looked up at Arens and Ilian. "Are they likely to come back?"

"They might," said Arens.

"You're in danger because you protected a Swordmaster," said Weyrn slowly. This wasn't something that had been offered to humans before, but it was only right that he offer it now. "Come back to Duamelti with us and we'll protect you."

Arens was already shaking his head. "We'll work something out. Our place is here."

Weyrn nodded. "All right. But we won't forget. It… would have been easy for you to have left him to die or protect yourselves by betraying him…"

"I don't know what humans you've met in the past," said Arens, "But we're not the sort of men who'd do a thing like that."

Weyrn smiled. "That's good to know." He looked back as Neithan coughed in his sleep, but the other elf slept on once he'd cleared his throat. "Seri will organise help to get him home, but…"

"He can stay another couple of days." Arens winced. "The rest of you will have to fend for yourselves."

"Thank you." Weyrn sighed. "Though this is a good place and you've cared for him very well… I think he'd be more comfortable at home."

The other Swordmasters had been away for a couple of days and Alatani had to keep telling herself not to worry. It would take some time to comb the forest, after all, and then there was the possibility that they were having to track Neithan further afield or were having problems getting him back.

The question of why that might be was bothering her, though, no matter how she tried to hide it.

Seregei looked up from the sums she'd given him to work out and frowned. "Mummy?"

"Nothing, Seregei."

"You look upset."

"It'll be fine."

Seregei frowned. "That's what Uncle Maelli said about Uncle Neithan, and then the next day they all went to look for him."

Alatani shook her head, wondering how much was too much for Seregei to know. on the one hand, she didn't want to tell him what was happening, but she also didn't want him to guess for himself.

Fortunately, she was spared having to answer; at that moment a Valley-elven guard jogged up to the door and called, "Swordmaster Alatani!"

At once, she got up from her seat and went to meet him. "Here I am. What is it?"

"Swordmaster Celes has just arrived back. He's at the east gate."

Alatani blinked. "Alone?"

"Yes. He had a message, but I came to fetch you straight away."

"Thanks." Alatani glanced over her shoulder at Seregei. While she wanted to hurry straight down to the gate to meet Celes, she didn't want to leave her child alone. He would probably be fine, but she didn't want to take the risk. He looked up at her with wide eyes and she nodded slightly. "Want to ride pick-a-back, Seregei?"

He grinned and dropped his wax tablets as he scrambled up to climb onto the couch and then onto her back. He was heavy, but this was probably still the quickest way to bring him with her.

***

When she arrived, she was immediately directed to the gatehouse, where she found Celes sitting on a bench, leaning forward with his elbows on his knees, his head hanging.

"Celes?" she asked as she put Seregei down. "Are you all right?"

He looked up and grinned wanly, reaching out to ruffle Seregei's hair. "Yes... just tired. I ran half the way here."

"What news?"

Celes glanced at Seregei, who stared back and showed no sign of leaving. Then he cleared his throat and said, "We found him." As he spoke, he gestured across his chest.

Alatani's breath caught. That hand signal indicated a serious injury. "How far?"

"A couple of days on our way out. They'll take longer. I was sent to get Eleri and a cart."

"Why do you need Eleri?" asked Seregei.

Celes winced, looking appealingly at Alatani.

Alatani patted Seregei on the shoulder. "Run along, Seregei. We'll explain later." She caught the guard captain's eye and he smiled slightly.

"Come on, lad," he said. "I'm sure we can find something for you to do."

"Nothing dangerous," said Alatani severely. "I'll be through to fetch him in a moment."

He nodded and took Seregei through to the next room, though the boy kept looking back.

Alatani turned back to Celes. "What's happened?" she asked softly.

"He was captured and tortured by humans. He..." Celes took a deep breath and ran his hand through his hair. Alatani poured him a cup of water and he drank, spilling some as his hand shook.

"It's bad?" she asked.

"Very. I... Seri was almost in tears when he told us." Celes didn't look far off tears himself. "He just said we needed Eleri and a cart. Maelli took him off to talk to him. I ran."

Alatani nodded. "You've already sent for Eleri?"

"Yes. One of the guards went. I'll need to show them where we found him."

"Where was it? I... could go; you need rest." Alatani fought the urge to glance towards were Seregei was waiting.

Celes shook his head. "I know where the house is. He was taken in by other humans. They've been nursing him and it was one of them told us where he was."

Alatani nodded. "I suppose it will be quicker with someone who knows the way... are you fit enough?"

"I think so. I'm tired, though..."

She looked hard at him. His eyes were bloodshot and his breathing sounded slightly wrong: too deep with a rasp in the throat. His shoulders still drooped and he was holding the cup in limp fingers. He seemed to realise his own state, for he smiled wanly. "I can do it. I'll be riding on a cart, after all. I can rest."

"I'll ask Eleri when he gets here." This time she did glance towards the door as she heard a burst of high-pitched laughter from the next room.

Celes smiled. "I don't want to drag you away."

"If I have to go, I suppose I have to go." She sighed and shook her head. "You... didn't see Neithan yourself?"

"No, Weyrn wanted to keep the numbers small."

Again, Alatani nodded, then she went and fetched Seregei back to wait until Eleri arrived.

Weyrn had been considering starting home with Neithan straight away, but as he looked out at the flurries of snow around the house, he knew it would be too dangerous. They would have to stay a little longer.

Ilian and Arens were clearly also worried, but they told Weyrn that he could stay by Neithan's side if he didn't mind sleeping on the floor. He accepted, but slipped out for a little while to speak to the others. Derdhel, Maelli and Seri had built a small shelter by a fallen tree, only just big enough for four if they lay close together, but comfortable for three. He sighed a little in relief. They'd be safe there.

"How is he?" asked Seri as soon as he saw Weyrn.

"Still bad. I don't think we can risk moving him in this snow."

Seri nodded, his eyes straying back towards the house. "I... has he spoken much?"

"Very little. I think he's conserving his strength as much as he can."

Maelli joined them, looking a little pale. "Do you think he'll live until Celes gets back with Eleri?"

Weyrn wasn't sure. Neithan was weak and having problems breathing, but he didn't seem to be getting worse, which was a mercy. In Weyrn's experience, the battle with such serious injuries was for time. Elves were strong and he had seen recovery against incredible odds if the elf could only live long enough to heal.

Maelli and Seri had read his silence and looked at one another. Maelli gently laid a hand on Seri's shoulder and tilted his head a little to look into his friend's eyes.

Weyrn looked at the ground and let the silence continue a little longer. He couldn't shake the feeling that they were already mourning.

At that moment, Derdhel arrived. He'd been hunting; he was carrying a rabbit and smiled a welcome at Weyrn. "What's happening?" he asked.

Seri frowned at his easy tone and his smile faded.

"He's alive," said Weyrn. "I came to see how you three were."

"We're comfortable," said Derdhel, looking at the others. "Are you going to stay with Neithan?"

"Would you rather go to him?" Weyrn asked Seri.

"I can't speak to the humans," said Seri, shaking his head angrily. "They don't speak our language, do they?"

"No, not at all."

Seri shook his head. "Then if it's to be one or other of us, it had better be you."

Weyrn nodded. "Come and see him, at least for a while."

Seri smiled. "Thanks."

They walked back down together, leaving Derdhel and Maelli to put the finishing touches on the shelter. Seri still looked disconsolate, but Weyrn wasn't sure what to say to comfort him. As they went, though, he patted Seri on the shoulder in silence and the other elf forced a smile.

When they arrived, Weyrn explained to Ilian and Arens that Seri was only there to visit and the three drew away as best they could while Seri went and crouched beside Neithan's bed.

"How long do you think it'll be?" asked Arens hesitantly.

Weyrn shook his head. "I shouldn't think too long provided that the snow doesn't start deepening. I doubt it will."

Arens looked glad at that and Ilian hastened to add, "It's not that we want to throw you out, but…"

"I understand," Weyrn assured them. "It's dangerous to have him here, apart from anything else."

Ilian looked pained, but nodded.

"Do you know why they did this?"

"Well…" Ilian scratched his head. "I told him that some of us… are jealous of elves."

"Is that enough for this?" Weyrn gestured at Neithan.

"Well, not for us," said Arens dryly. "Otherwise he'd be dead."

Weyrn smiled despite himself. "I appreciate that. But for others…?"

"Perhaps."

Neithan coughed and groaned and Weyrn looked round. Seri was talking to him, though, and he seemed calm. Weyrn sighed.

Arens nodded to Weyrn and went over to join Seri and Neithan.

"He has some healing training," said Ilian in answer to Weyrn's enquiring look. "Not much, but a little."

Weyrn smiled. "I'm glad."

"Yes, he's done what he can, but there isn't much."

Weyrn glanced back over to Neithan. "Who are they, do you know?"

"They've not been here long. We don't know a lot about them, but we don't know much about anyone else living near here."

Weyrn nodded. "I just want to know *why*."

***

Celes and Eleri arrived a couple of days later, to Weyrn's relief. He'd shared the food he'd brought with the two humans, but he still felt that he was putting a strain on their hospitality. Finally, he and Neithan and the others could start on their way home.

"Did you have any trouble?" he asked Celes as he went out to meet the cart.

"No, Alatani had organised things with Hurion so we would get the help we needed. I gather she called in a favour."

Weyrn nodded. "Do you mind waiting out here?" he asked, already starting back towards the house with Eleri.

Celes shook his head and went to check on the horses.

Eleri didn't speak the human language, but when Weyrn introduced him he still bowed his head in greeting to Arens and Ilian. They willingly let him in and Weyrn stepped aside to let him hurry to Neithan's side.

Eleri's heart sank as he looked at Neithan's face and listened to his breathing. The situation was very bad. He could tell that without any further investigation. Still, before he could decide what to do he needed to know exactly what the injuries were; Celes hadn't been able to tell him much. He could see that Neithan's hands were injured, but from what Celes had said, he knew that there was much worse.

He could hear the murmur of voices behind him, but he didn't even try to understand the conversation between Weyrn and their hosts, instead looking at the mess of bruises and welts that was revealed as he carefully pulled the blanket away from Neithan's torso. He winced in sympathy as he identified the majority of bruises as the marks of kicks. Others were more diffused while a couple had folded patterns: blows from a cudgel over Neithan's clothes, he guessed. Others were small and sharp-edged, peppered with cuts and grazes. Eleri gritted his teeth. Stones.

Neithan stirred and moaned, coughed a couple of times and opened his eyes.

"Neithan, can you hear me?" asked Eleri, sitting back on his heels.

"E- Eleri?"

He nodded. "How do you feel?"

Neithan coughed and shook his head. "Eleri, tell me..." he whispered, "am I dying?"

Eleri hesitated, but made the decision after only a moment's thought. "You're still alive. That's already a good sign."

"Please tell me." Neithan sighed and winced. "Just me. No-one else. Am I dying?"

On the one hand, Eleri knew it was wrong to outright lie to a patient and he was not optimistic about Neithan's chances. On the other, he didn't want to tell Neithan that and destroy what hope might be keeping him alive. The question needed to be answered, though, and eventually he said, "I don't know. I don't think it's hopeless yet."

Neithan nodded and coughed. "I don't want to die."

Eleri patted his arm. "Keep that in your heart and you'll have a better chance. It's when you give up that you'll really start to go downhill."

Neithan nodded. "I'll keep trying."

"That's all I ask." Eleri looked over Neithan's body again. "Where does it hurt?"

"My chest. I... can't breathe."

"Can you tell me what happened?"

Neithan closed his eyes as tears started to well up.

Eleri gently took his hand. "If you don't want to, don't."

Neithan nodded, then went into a coughing fit. Eleri could hear the blockage in his throat and the shallow, gurgling breaths that made him sound like he was drowning. His heart sank still further. He was starting to seriously doubt that there was any hope.

He felt someone step up beside him and looked up at Weyrn, who was watching in horror as Neithan finally stopped coughing and fell still, exhausted.

"Neithan?" he called softly.

Neithan moaned and his eyelids fluttered, but he didn't open them.

"Is there anything you can do?" Weyrn asked Eleri. "Even if only for the pain?"

"I don't dare drug him in case he never wakes."

Neithan moaned again and curled up slightly, huddled around his ribs. Eleri frowned as he noticed a welt across the back of his neck, like a rope burn. He swallowed the question that came to his lips; Neithan wasn't ready to relive the experience by telling what had happened. Not yet.

Still, he had to do something and he very carefully touched Neithan's chest, murmuring comfortingly as he looked for the signs of injury. Neithan groaned, flinching a little, but gritted his teeth.

"Are you all right, Neithan?" asked Eleri softly.

"I know... know you'll help me." Neithan coughed faintly.

Eleri hissed through his teeth as he felt Neithan's flesh crinkle slightly under his touch. It made him want to snatch his hand away, but he locked his muscles, fighting the instinct to flinch from something so wrong. That, after all, was the sign of air inside Neithan's chest. Blood in the lung and air in the chest... Eleri winced. Still, there was something he could do.

"Eleri?" Neithan whispered.

"I can help, but it involves cutting your chest open."

Neithan nodded. "Will it make it easier... to breathe?"

"Yes." At least for a while.

Neithan nodded and Eleri smiled at him, then turned to Weyrn. "Weyrn?"

Weyrn had looked away, but when Eleri called his name he turned back to him. "What's happened?"

"I need to cut his chest open; there's air between the inside of his chest and his lungs and it's stopping him breathing properly."

"I'm choking on blood," whispered Neithan.

Eleri squeezed his hand. "But this will make it easier for you to breathe nonetheless."

"All right..."

Weyrn told the humans what was happening, then came over as Eleri took out a large piece of soft leather from his bag and started to lay it under Neithan's torso to protect the bed. There hopefully wouldn't be much blood, but that would be a fine way to repay the humans for their help.

Neithan whimpered as Eleri tried to slide the leather under him, but Weyrn gently slipped an arm under his shoulders and half lifted him, then stroked his hair while Eleri took out a knife.

One of the humans came over and spoke, but it wasn't until Eleri glanced up that he realised the man had been addressing him.

"His name's Arens. He wants to know if there's anything he can do to help," said Weyrn.

"Oh..." Eleri had the equipment he needed, but after a moment he held out the knife. "Could you run this through the fire, just to be sure?"

Weyrn translated that and Arens took the knife over to the fireplace while Eleri found a suitable small piece of leather to put over the wound and passed Weyrn a strap for Neithan to bite.

"Are you sure there's nothing to be done for the pain?" asked Weyrn.

Eleri nodded. "I'm sorry," he said, addressing them both.

Neithan hesitated before letting Weyrn slip the leather strap between his teeth, his eyes wide and dark with fear.

"It's all right," Weyrn murmured to him. "We don't mean you any harm."

Arens tapped Eleri on the shoulder and handed him the knife. Eleri nodded thanks and turned back to Neithan, once again gently laying a hand on his chest. Once again the skin seemed to crackle under his touch and he suppressed a wince. He heard Neithan make a strangled noise of pain, but did his best to ignore that, focussing on the correct placement of the knife.

Very slowly, he pressed down, keeping his movements as small as he could. Fortunately, Neithan stayed still, though his muscles were tense. Eleri gritted his teeth as he cut a little more.

Then there was a rush of air, filled with a mist of blood. Eleri gasped, fighting a moment's nausea as blood spattered on his hand and face and ran down Neithan's side. As if from a distance, he heard Arens yell something – he assumed a curse.

Neithan tried to take a breath and Eleri clamped his hand over the wound to stop air rushing back in.

"Any easier?" Weyrn asked.

"A… a little." Neithan breathed again. "Ack…" – he groaned – "Eleri, that hurts."

Indeed, Eleri knew he was probably pressing on a broken rib, but he kept his hand where it was. "Hold on a little longer," he said as he slipped the small piece of leather into place, holding it on three sides so that air could get out, but not in. He could bandage it just about well enough and that would have to do. "Help him sit up again, Weyrn. Arens, hand me a bandage." He'd laid them out ready, but he didn't have a hand free.

Weyrn translated the instruction as he helped Neithan sit up again. The movement made him tense and whimper, then he began to cough.

Eleri could hear the blood gurgling in his throat. A rill of it ran from under the leather patch against his side. Eleri pressed on it as hard as he dared as a few bubbles appeared along the free edge. That was a good sign as far as it went; his lung was still pierced, but the blood and air were escaping, not pooling.

Still, Neithan whimpered between the coughs. His hand went to Eleri's, scrabbling at it as best he could.

"Hurts…" he gasped. "Please…"

Eleri took the hand. "It's all right," he said. "It's all right, it'll help you breathe."

Neithan just whimpered, but at last he stopped coughing. For a moment Eleri thought he'd lost consciousness as his head lolled against Weyrn's arm, but then he moaned. Eleri nodded and took the bandage Arens held out in a shaking hand.

He was able to bandage the leather into place so that it was a little loose on one side, and he could remove the bandages if he had to, so it would do. Neithan was still breathing shallowly and unevenly, his eyes closed, but when Eleri touched his cheek his expression twitched a little in response.

"All right," Eleri said softly. "You should be able to breathe a little easier now." He sat back on his heels, wiping absently at the blood that had dried on his cheek, then looked up at Weyrn. "Let's get him home."

***

It was a difficult and delicate job to load Neithan into the back of the cart, but at last they laid him on a pallet and wrapped him in blankets; hopefully that would be enough to protect him from the jolts of the road. Eleri climbed in with him and left Celes to drive. The others would follow on foot.

"Eleri?" Neithan called softly.

"Here I am, it's all right."

"What's happening?"

"You're on the way home."

Neithan sighed in relief. "They... they were kind," he whispered. "I wondered... if all humans..."

Eleri stroked his brow and frowned at its clamminess. Still, he tried to keep his voice comforting as he said, "I doubt it. I expect there's just as much variety among humans as among elves."

Neithan chuckled. "I know, but... I wondered if only cruel ones came here." He coughed a few times. "They said I was planning to... steal away and eat their... children."

"What?"

Neithan nodded. "They kept telling other humans that. I don't... know why."

"When did they do that?"

Neithan sighed and for a moment Eleri thought he'd fainted, but then he whispered, "Dragged me through settlements... tied me up and... said things like... that."

Presumably, that was when he'd been stoned and where the rope burn on his neck came from. Eleri gritted his teeth.

"I don't understand," said Neithan faintly. Eleri took his hand, looking at the swollen, blistered fingers that poked out of the fresh bandages. Neithan's palms had been cut and grazed, worn bloody, and his knees were similarly ruined. There were also knife gashes on his legs. The marks of some other torture?

Regardless, he had cleaned them and bandaged the worst.

"Eleri?"

"Still here."

"It's so cold…"

It had snowed again on the way there and Eleri nodded, tucking the blankets around Neithan a little more warmly. "You'll be home soon."

"Actually home?"

"Well… I think the plan is to take you to the healing wing."

Neithan shook his head. "I want to go home."

There was probably little to be done wherever he went. The main thing now was to make sure he was comfortable. And if that meant staying in his own bed… "I'll tell Celes and we'll take you there."

"Thanks." Neithan sighed and relaxed. He wasn't quite asleep, though; he kept mumbling things about what he had been through. Most of the time Eleri couldn't make out what he was saying, but it seemed to make him feel better to bleed disjointed words into the silence. At last, he lost consciousness.

By the time they arrived at the gate, Weyrn shared Eleri's worry about Neithan's chances. The younger elf was sometimes lucid and could hold a conversation, but he was constantly short of breath, his face pale and pinched with pain. He thought that when it came down to it Eleri would change his mind about taking Neithan to the Guardhouse, but the healer was adamant.

"It's where he wants to go," he said quietly.

"But surely he can be better cared for in the healing wing? And there's no-one stopping him being taken there." The reference to Ninian's death had slipped out before he could stop it and Eleri looked sharply at him, but didn't comment.

"He'll be more comfortable in his own bed and…" Eleri bit his lip, looking back at the cart.

"And?" prompted Weyrn, his heart sinking.

"I… don't know how long he has left. I'm doing all I can, truly, but…"

Weyrn shook his head. "I know. Are his chances…" he couldn't finish the question.

Eleri shook his head. "They're not good. He's right: he's drowning in his own blood."

Weyrn felt a little sick. "He won't heal?"

"I'm not sure he has time." Eleri looked at the floor. "I'm sorry," he said softly, and sobbed on a laugh. "If we'd got to him sooner…"

Weyrn recognised the words and had to turn away. All he could say to

Eleri was "Do what you think best."

He kept his back turned until he heard Eleri sigh and walk away. Even then, it took a moment to control the tears that welled in his eyes. The gate guards were talking to Seri, fortunately, so he had a little time. He had to make it short, though, and he felt a moment's rueful envy for the fact that, even though that was Seri's mentor lying in that cart, the other elf could still manage to pull himself together. Weyrn himself felt as if he too were drowning.

"Weyrn!" He looked up thankfully as he heard Alatani's voice. She jogged down the road and took his hand as soon as she arrived. "How is he?"

"Eleri says… Eleri says he's dying." Once the words were out, Weyrn started to feel better. Winded, but no longer as if there was something crushing him.

Alatani's eyes widened and she squeezed his hand. "How long?"

"I'm not sure. Just… where's Seregei?"

"I guessed I'd not be down here long." Her eyes strayed back up the road. "He's still at the Guardhouse."

"Go back," he said, letting go of her hands. "And… make sure he's out of the way. I don't want him to see."

She nodded and fled. He took a deep breath and went back to join the others.

***

It was a rough road back to the Guardhouse but, fortunately, Neithan was unconscious throughout. Weyrn sat beside him with Eleri, in awkward silence.

Though the others were on foot, they had arrived first and Maelli and Seri were waiting with a stretcher. Alatani stood with them.

"Seregei's in his room," she said as they set about lifting Neithan out of the cart. It was a difficult business as they tried not to move him too much. Nonetheless, he whimpered, trying to push them away.

Weyrn just nodded thanks at Alatani and turned to Neithan, taking his friend's hand and murmuring soothingly.

"W-Weyrn?" Neithan's voice cracked and he began to cough, taking in shallow, hacking breaths between fits. His face was going red as he struggled and Weyrn helped Alatani prop him up a little to make it easier for him to breathe and spit out the blood.

"Eleri!" Weyrn shouted, but the healer was already there. "Help him!" He didn't know what Eleri could do, but surely there was *something*.

"Keep him propped up," said Eleri, supporting Neithan's head. "All right, Neithan, you're all right…"

And, finally, the coughing stopped. Neithan went limp, his breathing so shallow that for a moment Weyrn thought it had stopped.

"Get him out of the cold and keep him calm. It's worse if he gasps." Eleri wiped the blood from Neithan's lips.

"All right," said Seri, his voice shaking. "Let's get him inside."

They hurried through the common room to Neithan's room, down at the end of the corridor. Fortunately, as Alatani had said, Seregei's bedroom door was closed.

"Weyrn..." whispered Neithan, and gasped. "I can't breathe..."

"Help him sit up a little," said Eleri. "It'll make it easier on his ribs."

Neithan coughed, but it didn't turn into a fit. He just let out a small groan of pain and his head lolled to the side.

"He was stronger..." Weyrn said helplessly as they lifted Neithan onto his bed and drew the blankets over him.

Eleri nodded. "Rest will help. That coughing fit has worn him out."

Neithan moaned and nodded. Weyrn stroked his hair gently. "What can we do for him?"

"Keep the air warm and a little damp. Don't make him clear his throat any more than he already has to." Eleri frowned as he twitched the blanket aside to look at the bandages around Neithan's chest. "I need to check this – it could be I'll need to re-open his chest." He glanced round. "I'll need help to drain any pooled blood..."

"I'll take over," said Seri, putting a hand on Weyrn's shoulder. "Go to Alatani."

Weyrn looked round and saw the pallor of Seri's face and the miserable set of his mouth. He nodded. "Thank you. If he wakes, tell him where I am, and let me know if..."

"I will." Seri forced a smile. "He's strong. I..." His voice caught and Weyrn put a hand on his shoulder in response.

"Take care of him," he said, and left.

Alatani was waiting outside and for a long moment she and Weyrn looked at one another. Then she hugged him, burying her face in his shoulder, and he hugged her back.

"Thank you for getting things organised," he whispered. "It would have been impossible without the cart."

"Hurion sent his best wishes," she said absently. "Are you all right?"

At the question, tears began to well in his eyes, spilling from under his closed eyelids. "No."

Seregei wasn't sure what was happening. They tried to hide it, but he could tell that something was upsetting his parents and the others, and though he had been told that Uncle Neithan was home from his trip, he wasn't allowed to go and see him. All he knew was that Neithan was shut in his room and that Eleri spent a lot of time with him.

Seregei knew that Eleri's job was to look after people who were hurt, and he also knew that when people were hurt it was good for their friends to go and visit them, so he couldn't understand why his parents refused to let him go.

He knew when Neithan had arrived back, and it had started then. His mother had just suddenly arrived back from a trip down to the gate and had bundled him off to his room, telling him to stay there and keep the door shut even though he hadn't done anything naughty enough to deserve such a punishment. And then all she'd said was that Neithan was home and Seregei couldn't go and visit. That had been the day before yesterday.

Now, he was lying awake, wiggling his tooth between his fingers. It felt like a loose button and he was sure it was almost ready to come out. He wanted to show Neithan and didn't see why nobody would let him. Maybe they thought he'd do something silly that would hurt him more. Well, he knew better than that. He'd been careful when Lessai's arm was broken, hadn't he? And that was the worst hurt he'd ever seen anyone. Even Lessai, who was big enough to have lost three teeth already and have the big ones grow in, had cried. He wasn't a baby and he wasn't scared of anything, so that was all he could guess: that they thought he was too little to understand that Neithan was hurt.

Suddenly, to his shock, the tooth came free. He sat bolt upright and stared at the little white thing in his hand. It looked almost scary and he quickly put his tongue where it had been to find a gap and a tender spot where it had just come out.

He squeaked to himself, giggling into his hand as he looked at the tooth. It was out! His very first tooth!

He had to show someone.

His parents would probably scold him for being out of bed and he didn't want to wake any of his other uncles; he didn't know what they'd say. That left Neithan. He wanted to show Neithan anyway, and what would be the harm? He'd be careful, and Neithan was probably lonely. He'd like a visitor.

Decided, Seregei scrambled out of bed and pattered down the hall to Neithan's room. Turning the handle took some effort, but then the door swung open easily and silently.

His first impression was how damp it seemed in there, and how warm. It was like a hot summer, when the air tasted of steam. He wondered if that was good for injured people.

As he tiptoed in, he heard Neithan move in his bed and cough faintly. Then he asked, "Who's there?"

"It's me," whispered Seregei, going over to the bed.

"Seregei? You... you shouldn't be here."

There wasn't much light, but Seregei could see that Neithan was very pale. He kept his hand by his cheek as if to hide something on the pillow.

Seregei didn't wonder what, though. "I know, but Mummy and Daddy always say it's good to visit people when they're hurt. But then they said I couldn't come and see you. But I wanted to show you my tooth." He held it out.

"You... finally lost it?" Neithan reached out his other hand to take the tooth. He almost dropped it and Seregei caught it with a gasp; he didn't want to lose it. Neithan didn't try again; he just let his hand fall to the pillow and smiled wanly. "That's good."

"Do you think it means I'm grown up now?"

Neithan shook his head with a small sigh, wincing as though it hurt. "Not quite."

Seregei frowned. "Do I have to be taller?"

"Among other things." Neithan coughed, turning his face into the pillow. Seregei listened with a frown that turned to wide-eyed worry as the stifled coughing went on, seemingly forever.

"Uncle N-Neithan?"

"I'm... fine," said Neithan, his voice strained.

He didn't sound it and Seregei stated at him, wondering what to do. Fortunately, he eventually stopped coughing and fell still with a small, stifled whining noise. Seregei had never heard of coughing hurting, but that definitely sounded like hurt.

"Uncle Neithan?" he said again, his own voice tilting towards a whimper.

Neithan looked up and smiled that strained smile. "I'm fine... at least..." He sighed and winced again.

"Shall I... go get Eleri?"

"No, he'll be back soon anyway. You... should go back to bed." Neithan reached out and patted Seregei's hair, looking oddly at him for a moment. Seregei frowned, feeling like he was being treated as a baby. Neithan's behaviour was strange, though, and he didn't move away.

"What's wrong?" he asked softly, noticing for the first time as Neithan drew his hand back that it was wrapped in a bandage.

Neithan shook his head with a small sigh. "Just..." He hesitated. "Go to bed, Seregei. You're a good lad. Thanks for visiting me."

Seregei stepped away unwillingly. The sense of wrongness was so strong he could almost taste it, but he didn't know what to ask or what to do apart from go to bed, as Neithan had told him.

"I'll come visit tomorrow," he said uncertainly.

"Ask your parents first."

"All right... good night."

"Good night."

Three days after they had brought Neithan home, Weyrn was startled awake by the sound of knocking on the door. Beside him, Alatani stirred sleepily as he shook his head and went to answer, pulling a blanket around himself.

It was Eleri. He was pale, his eyes wide. Weyrn could tell at a glance that something was badly wrong. "Neithan?" he asked.

Eleri nodded. "Come quickly."

"Go and wake Seri," said Weyrn, hurrying back to grab some clothes. Alatani had evidently heard; she was already holding out trousers and a shirt and he pulled them on as fast as he could, leaving the shirt open as he hurried over to Neithan's room.

His friend was half sitting up, propped up on pillows, and Weyrn pulled over a chair to sit beside him. His breathing sounded bad, rasping and gurgling in his throat. Weyrn could see every muscle in his shoulders and neck straining as he struggled to breathe.

"Neithan?" asked Weyrn, taking his hand.

Neithan's eyes fluttered open. "Weyrn?"

"I'm here."

"Weyrn, I…" He coughed and gasped, tears springing in his eyes. "I'm scared…"

Weyrn took a deep breath and let it out again, pressing Neithan's hand. "It's going to be all right, Neithan."

"It's not…" Neithan was crying now, between gasps and pants for breath. "I don't want to die. What's going to happen?"

Weyrn pressed his hand again. He wanted to hug him, but didn't dare risk causing him more pain. "Just stay calm. You're wasting strength, worrying like this."

Indeed, what little colour had been in Neithan's face was gone. His lips were cyanotic, his skin cold and clammy to the touch. He was still straining for breath, but it was getting weaker. His eyelids were starting to droop.

"Neithan!"

"How is he?" came Seri's voice as the other elf hurried in. Weyrn didn't look round.

"Seri…" Neithan forced his eyes open for a moment, then they slid closed again. His lips moved as if he were trying to speak, but all that came out was a whimper. A spasm of pain and fear crossed his face. Weyrn could hear the others gathering at the door, whispering among themselves. Neithan didn't seem to notice, lost in his own struggle to keep breathing, even if only long enough to say goodbye.

He didn't manage it, though. His face went slack as he lost consciousness, though he kept gasping a little longer.

Weyrn's vision seemed to tunnel as he looked at his friend's face. It felt as if he couldn't breathe either. He remembered in a flash how he had met Neithan and taken him on as a guide and helper, realised that the bright young elf had potential to be a Swordmaster, brought him home and trained him. He remembered little gadgets Neithan had made and the times they had fought together. He remembered his own attempts to teach Neithan the flute, remembered how Neithan had loved stickball, remembered Neithan's laugh, his pride when Seri had taken his oath…

Then he heard Seri suddenly sob beside him and was brought crashing out of his memories. He focused on Neithan's face again. With a sick feeling, he realised that there was no longer any strain or tension to the muscles of his throat. The gurgling had stopped.

Neithan was dead.

Derdhel was standing outside the room when he saw Seri bury his face in his hands, sobbing. Maelli slipped past him and went to put an arm around Seri's shoulders. Alatani stayed in the doorway, looking at Weyrn as he sat motionless, staring at Neithan's face.

At last, though, she moved and went to join the little group beside Neithan's bed. The room was getting crowded and Derdhel stepped back, watching the obvious distress of his friends. He wanted to help. He didn't like seeing them so miserable, in such pain, but he didn't know what to do; he didn't understand their grief. He had seen how much Neithan had been suffering. He was free of that now. Why were other elves always so unhappy about that?

Still, Derdhel would miss him for the time they were parted, and he looked away with a sigh.

Then he saw Seregei staring around the door of his bedroom, wide-eyed.

"Uncle Derdhel?" he half-whispered, his voice trembling.

"Come on," said Derdhel, going to take Seregei's hand. "I'll tell you what's happened."

Seregei trotted along beside him, looking over his shoulder. "I heard people running around," he said softly. "What's happening?"

Derdhel picked him up and sat him on the window seat. "You know Neithan was hurt?"

Seregei nodded. "Did he get worse?"

"No. He died."

Seregei's eyes went even wider. "Wha-what?"

"He died. Do you… know what that means?" At Seregei's age, Derdhel had known, but he knew that Seregei was much more sheltered.

Indeed, the boy shook his head.

"It means he's not here any more. His body is, but that's not him. It's just where he used to live, like an empty house."

"Then… where's he gone?"

"Somewhere else. You don't need to worry; it's better than here."

"But…"

"After you die, you go somewhere where you can't be hurt and there's nothing to be scared of." Derdhel smiled and put a hand on Seregei's shoulder. "It's a great adventure to reach a land where it's always summer when you want it, with sweet rains at night to keep everything fresh, and winter, when it comes, always comes with snow and a warm hearth. Neithan's on his way there now, and you know he'll already be looking for ways to make his journey easier; that's what makes him happy. And when he gets there, he'll be able to spend the rest of forever making things and working on projects and waiting for the rest of us to join him."

Seregei blinked. "So… everyone dies?"

"Everyone dies eventually. Life is only a passing thing, like a swallow flying through a barn. But during the journey we make friends and change the world we passed through, and afterwards we can find those we love again."

Seregei slowly smiled. "But he's happy? He won't be coughing like that any more?"

"No. And he never will again. There's no reason to in the place we go after death."

"And he'll get to make things? And finish that thing he was mixing… the powder that burned?"

"Yes."

Seregei rubbed his eyes. "That doesn't seem so bad."

Derdhel smiled. "Indeed not. We miss him here, but it's important to remember that he's in a better place and that we'll be there too, one day. We just have to be patient and spend the time as best we can." He bent forward to kiss Seregei's brow.

"Derdhel?" Alatani's voice at the door sounded indignant and Derdhel looked up. She'd been crying, but at the moment she just looked angry. "What have you been telling him?"

Derdhel blinked. "The truth."

Seregei scrambled off the window seat and ran over. "He told me all about how Uncle Neithan's going to somewhere where he'll be happy and he won't cough any more."

The look Alatani shot Derdhel was almost savage, but she picked Seregei up and hugged him. Derdhel returned the glare.

"Where's Daddy?" asked Seregei.

"He's with Neithan."

"Uncle Derdhel said that Uncle Neithan was gone." Seregei snuggled against his mother's side.

"He… I suppose, but… We still pay our respects."

"But if he's not there…"

She put him down. "Go to your room, Seregei. We'll discuss this later."

"But… I haven't done anything wrong…"

"You shouldn't be up in the middle of the night."

"But you keep sending me to my room!" wailed Seregei. "Why do you keep sending me to my room?"

"Because I need to talk to Derdhel about grown-up things!" She crouched down. "One day you'll understand, but you're too *young*." Her voice broke on a sob.

Seregei had been building up to a tantrum, but at that he froze. "Mummy?"

"Just go to your room."

"But... why?"

She didn't answer, just hugged him. Derdhel sighed and slipped out of the building to breathe the free air. She'd understand when she was less upset. He still believed it had been right to tell Seregei the truth about what had happened.

He was startled to find that he wasn't alone. Eleri was wandering restlessly about at the edge of the grassy space around the Guardhouse.

"Eleri!" he called and the healer looked round but didn't come over. Derdhel went to meet him instead. "He's dead. What are you doing out here?"

Eleri chuckled, the sound breaking to a sob halfway. "I couldn't face Weyrn."

"Why? He doesn't blame you; why would he? It was Neithan's time, that's all, and he spent his life well."

Eleri shook his head. "Derdhel, I know you think like that, and I wish I could, but I can't. Frankly, I don't see how I could heal if I did."

"What do you mean?"

"You're so..." Eleri waved a hand vaguely, then said, "resigned." He turned and began to walk away, but Derdhel kept pace with him as he continued speaking. "How can you not mourn? Your friend is *dead*."

Derdhel felt like he was explaining to another child as he said, "And now he's free from his pain. Why should I mourn for –" He fell silent as Eleri suddenly twisted away. "Eleri?"

"I couldn't free him," said Eleri bitterly.

"That isn't what I'm saying." Derdhel laid a hand on Eleri's shoulder, holding on as the healer tried to pull away. "Eleri, listen to me. You did what you could. I'm sure Weyrn knows it and I certainly do. Why can't you face him?"

"You know about Ninian?"

"Of course." Derdhel had heard that story from Seri, soon after he had begun his training.

"Then you should know why I can't bear seeing Weyrn lose his trainee again after another long, lingering death after *another* healer failed to help him."

"I don't understand. This isn't the same thing."

"It's close enough." Again, Eleri tried to pull away from Derdhel's hand, but again he held on.

"You know, I don't think Weyrn blamed Santhi for Ninian's death; why would he blame you for Neithan's? What more could you have done?"

Eleri shook his head. "Probably nothing. But that doesn't make me feel better." He shook his head again. "Leave me alone, Derdhel. I just can't face Weyrn at the moment."

CHAPTER EIGHT

They buried Neithan in the woods behind the Guardhouse, digging the grave themselves. As Weyrn carried him out, the body seemed light in his arms, wrapped in a sheet. He remembered what Derdhel had told Seregei: that this wasn't Neithan. It was just an empty shell.

"Weyrn?" Alatani's voice jerked him back to reality and he sighed, looking again at the bundle in his arms before he lowered it as best he could into the grave.

"Goodbye, Neithan," he said softly. Seri crouched down and laid a hand on Neithan's chest as if to make sure his heart wasn't beating. Then he stood up and reached for a shovel.

Maelli shook his head briefly, then said, "He'll return to the earth, and he'll always be with us." He smiled as he looked up at the trees around them. "His body will nourish the trees and we'll hear his voice on the wind." He began digging as he continued to speak, matching the rhythm of his movements to the prayer.

Weyrn felt too heartsick to take comfort in the words. Similar things had been said over his mother, and over Ninian, and over the other Swordmasters that had come before him. He wondered fleetingly how often he'd have to hear them and for a moment he looked over at Alatani, who was hard at work with burying. She didn't look up, but Weyrn gazed at her in silence for a moment, wondering if this was why family members were not supposed to be Swordmasters together. He had loved Neithan like a brother and it felt like something was gone from him. He tried to believe what Maelli was saying about how Neithan wasn't truly parted from them, but he had to shake his head and be glad that Seregei wasn't here with questions that Weyrn didn't think he could answer.

As he dug, his thoughts drifted towards vengeance. He wondered who those men were who had murdered Neithan. He might not have died while still in their hands, but they had murdered him nonetheless. He'd been warned about hostile humans in the forests around Duamelti, and though not all the human settlers were dangerous – Ilian and Arens, for example – he had to take the warnings more seriously now.

He wished it hadn't taken the death of his dearest friend to show him that.

Hurion had sent condolences, which was more than the regent who had killed Ninian had sent. Perhaps there would be help there. Weyrn stabbed his shovel ferociously into the pile of earth as he wondered what to do. Scouts were in danger, but they needed information on numbers and movements.

Perhaps a larger group would be safer. By the tracks, Neithan had been ambushed at his camp by greater numbers. But there were so few of them…

Again, as he dug, his thoughts turned again to Hurion. Valley-elves might be at risk, after all. Perhaps Weyrn could persuade him to help.

It was worth a try.

***

At last, he patted down the earth and stood back, brushing his hair out of his face as a cold gust of wind blew by. Alatani slipped an arm around his waist and he returned the gesture, looking in silence at the sad little mound of earth. All the Swordmasters were silent now. Maelli's prayer was over. Seri's expression was distant. Even Derdhel said nothing.

Weyrn took a breath of the chill air and said, "Well… that's it."

Seri nodded briskly. "I'll plant a tree here, come spring." Maelli squeezed his shoulder.

"Let's get back," said Weyrn softly, though it was hard to tear his eyes away from Neithan's grave. "We need to decide what to do, but… not just now."

"I agree," said Alatani, hugging him slightly. "Give us all today."

He nodded. He felt drained and knew that he needed that time as much as the others.

They walked back to the Guardhouse in a silent group and parted to go to their rooms, though after a moment Maelli hurried after Seri.

Weyrn and Alatani sat down together on the bed in their room and he rested his head on her shoulder.

"I still need to decide what to do," he said softly.

"Don't think about it now."

"They *killed* him."

She squeezed his hand. "You need to rest and try not to worry about that now. You're not thinking clearly."

He closed his eyes and pinched the bridge of his nose. "I… can't just not think about that."

"I know, but at least try not to."

For a long moment they sat in silence. He tried to stop his thoughts whirling, but eventually he said, "I've been thinking of going to Hurion."

"Weyrn!" she shifted to look at him. "Stop it."

"I *can't*." He ran a hand through his hair. "I just can't."

"I'm sure you can if you put your mind to something else," she said firmly, getting up.

He shook his head. "Nothing comes to mind... When will Elar bring Seregei back?"

She smiled wanly. "Not until this evening."

He nodded. "That's good... not that I don't like having him around, but..."

"I don't know; his questions might help." She smiled again, though it looked forced.

Just then, there was a knock on the door and Alatani went to answer as Weyrn rubbed his eyes and hitched his shoulders. To his surprise, it was Eleri.

"I've missed the burial, haven't I?" he asked softly.

Weyrn nodded. "Where were you?"

"I'm sorry. I just couldn't face it."

"I'm not the one to apologise to," said Weyrn, trying to soften the words with a smile. Nonetheless, Eleri scowled.

"Seriously, Eleri," said Weyrn softly. "I don't blame you for what happened. You did what you could."

"I know that." Eleri rubbed his eyes. "I know you don't blame me and that it would be unreasonable if you did, but..." He smiled a little. "I will admit it takes a load off my chest to hear you say it."

Maelli and Seri sat together in Seri's room, Seri on the bed and Maelli on the chair. Seri couldn't think of anything to say and, fortunately, Maelli seemed inclined to respect that.

At last, though, Seri couldn't take the silence any more. "I knew it would happen someday, I just wasn't ready for the reality."

Maelli looked consideringly at him for a moment, then nodded. "I know what that's like."

Seri sighed heavily. "And Neithan of all people. He never had a problem he couldn't think his way out of."

"He made it to those humans that took him in."

"But too late."

"No; it meant he died in his own bed rather than somewhere out in the woods or still a prisoner. It doesn't change the fact that he died, but it's worth something."

Seri had to smile as he looked at Maelli's earnest expression. "You've been talking to Derdhel."

"No, but it's true. That's why Eleri brought him back here: better to die in his own bed."

"I suppose so." Seri sighed. "I'm just not used to the idea of Swordmasters being, well... mortal. When I was a child, they were like the Spirits themselves."

Maelli looked carefully at him. "Do you still think that?"

"Of course not!" Seri looked away. "Even before this I knew that wasn't true. I just wasn't prepared for the reality. Even when Captain Larian died, it was in battle far away. It didn't seem... so real. Not like Neithan breathing his last right in front of me." He shook his head, remembering with a flash of bitterness how Weyrn had barely seemed to notice at first.

Maelli took his hand, but didn't say anything.

"I'll be fine," lied Seri. "I just need to come to terms with it."

It was the day after Neithan's burial when Weyrn went to see Hurion. He was let through to the king's study without any trouble and Hurion got up from his desk at once.

"Weyrn, it's good to see you. I am sorry to hear about Neithan."

Weyrn nodded. "Thanks. And thank you for your help. At least we found him before it was entirely too late." He paused a moment before adding, "I would like your help with finding the people who did that to him, though."

Hurion looked consideringly at him for a moment, then went over to the fire and stirred it with the poker. "Swordmasters are generally held to be great warriors and scouts, aren't they?"

Weyrn didn't answer, not sure where this was going. He hoped Hurion had the manners not to turn Neithan's capture, torture and death into some gibe against the Swordmasters and their training.

Hurion apparently read his expression, for he raised his free hand slightly. "I was just thinking that if they managed to overpower a Swordmaster, I'm not sure how I feel about sending out my people."

"Then what would you rather do?" asked Weyrn. "Sit and wait for them to come to you?"

Hurion looked sharply at him and went back to stirring the embers. "I hope you're not calling me a coward, Weyrn."

"No." Not in as many words, anyway. "I was just commenting that you seem to be very short-sighted about this."

"What do you mean?"

"If there is a danger here, ignoring it won't make it go away."

"I know that. I just don't see how sending others out to be killed will help that."

Weyrn gritted his teeth. He told himself firmly that it probably wasn't intended as a jeer. Hurion had every right to be concerned about his own people, especially as he knew the danger, which Weyrn hadn't.

Hurion didn't seem to have noticed his silence. He just put the poker away and turned back to Weyrn. "So, what is it that you wanted to say?"

"As I said, I want help finding these people."

"Do you have any suggestions? Any knowledge of where to start?"

Weyrn sighed. "I know where we found Neithan. He wasn't able to tell us much, but we do have a location, and some friends in the area." He wondered uneasily how much more Ilian and Arens would be prepared to help, and how much risk they would be in if they did.

"Friends?"

"Neithan was taken in by some humans. They were the ones who kept him alive until we got there."

Hurion nodded thoughtfully. "So they aren't all bad, then."

"It seems not, though most of our experiences of them have... not been good."

"But, again, what do you want of me?"

"There... are very few of us. One alone was apparently an easy target." Weyrn stifled a wince; he didn't like to think of Neithan that way. "There may be safety in numbers."

Hurion looked consideringly at him for a long moment, then nodded. "You could be right. So you want the help of the Duamelti army?"

"You've often said that the Royal Guard are the Swordmasters' equals."

That got a small smile. "I see what you're doing."

"I'm trying to avenge my friend."

"And manipulating my pride to do it." Hurion grinned and stepped around his desk to put it between himself and Weyrn. He drummed his fingers on the surface for a moment while Weyrn restrained the urge to speak, fidget or both.

At last, though, he could bear it no longer. "Hurion, will you help? It's in your interest too, you know. Trouble outside the borders will spread."

"I know that." Hurion sighed. "I admit that it would be a good idea to spend more time talking to you about this sort of thing. I didn't realise there was such danger until Alatani pointed it out to me."

"Really?" Weyrn paused a moment before adding, "She never said."

Hurion shrugged. "The valley is my main concern, and when I look outside it I look to Silvren. I've never thought that there could be an enemy sneaking up on my own borders. We'd had differences with the humans, but not on this scale."

"Perhaps we should talk more often, then. It would be good for you to pay attention to things that affect the Mixed-bloods."

"But the Mixed-bloods outside my kingdom. Your rule – in theory – stretches all over the world, wherever there are elves, but mine doesn't. If you caught me meddling in their affairs, what would you say?"

Weyrn shook his head. "What's done is done. We need to think about what to do next."

Hurion nodded. "Your points are good." He stood up, clasping his hands behind his back. "I'll see about sending a group from the Royal Guard with you to scout beyond the borders. I want you to treat them well, though." There was an edge in his voice.

"We'll treat them as is fitting," said Weyrn carefully. "As allies, not as masters or servants."

Hurion nodded slowly. "Very well. I'll send their captain down to speak to you."

Weyrn sighed a little in relief. "Thank you. That's very helpful, and we'll speak again about what we find."

***

When Weyrn arrived back at the Guardhouse, he was greeted by Seregei running up to him and hugging him around the waist. He smiled and tousled the boy's hair absently.

"Daddy?" Seregei looked up. "What's going on?"

Weyrn winced and disentangled himself from Seregei to go inside. "Well… you know what happened to Neithan."

Seregei nodded gravely. "I went to see where he was buried."

"Well, some of us are going to go and find the people who killed him."

Seregei blinked. "But… why?"

"Well…" Weyrn didn't want to say it was revenge. While he knew in his heart that that was exactly why, he didn't want to encourage Seregei along that road. "It's because…"

"Because they killed Uncle Neithan?" Seregei took his hand, looking up at him with wide eyes as they went inside. Weyrn sighed, looking away. The blue was fading from Seregei's eyes to leave them mostly grey. It was another reminder that he wasn't a baby any more.

"Well, sort of." Weyrn helped Seregei scramble onto the window seat and sat down beside him, ignoring the slight chill from the window. "You… remember what we told you Swordmasters do?"

"Fight monsters." Seregei smiled. "And Uncle Neithan said you rescue people when they're in trouble." His smile faded. "But when you rescued Uncle Neithan he died anyway…"

Weyrn winced, closing his eyes to fight back his own tears. "Yes, that… that happens sometimes."

"Does it still count?" Seregei asked forlornly.

This wasn't how this conversation was supposed to have gone, but there was no help for it. "That really depends. Sometimes yes, sometimes no."

"What about this time?"

"It meant we got him home." Weyrn wondered if it would have been worth it to let Seregei go and visit and say goodbye. He doubted it. Had Seregei seen the state poor Neithan had been in, he probably would have been far more upset than he was. "But that's not what we're doing here." Hopefully they'd not find that these humans had any more prisoners.

"Killing monsters, then? Was it monsters that killed Uncle Neithan?"

Weyrn sighed. He didn't want to tell Seregei about monsters in elven shape so soon, but there wasn't really a choice other than outright lying, and that wasn't something he was willing to do. "After a manner of speaking, yes."

Seregei blinked. "But if they're monsters, then they're not people, are they?"

"They can be. Some people are monsters."

Seregei hugged his knees to his chest and rested his chin on them, frowning. "But... how can you tell? I thought monsters... they had big teeth and claws and red eyes. Do these people have those?"

"No. Sometimes you can't tell until you've seen how they act."

Seregei looked at Weyrn, still hugging his knees. Weyrn put an arm around his shoulders and hugged him.

"I know it's hard, but that's the way things are. Sometimes people can turn out to be monsters, but still be people at the same time."

Seregei buried his face in his knees. "But what if you meet someone and they turn out to be a monster?"

"Then you have to decide what to do."

"What have you been telling him?" asked a voice from the door. Weyrn looked up and smiled at Alatani.

"I was explaining why we have to go and find the people who killed Neithan."

"He said they were monsters and there are monsters who look like people and..." Seregei added in a muffled wail.

Alatani sighed and came over to give Seregei a hug. "Some monsters do look like people," she said softly. "But you can always tell by what they do. If someone hurts someone else just because it's fun, they're probably a monster. That's..." – her voice caught – "that's what these people did to Neithan."

Weyrn smoothed Seregei's hair. "You'll understand when you're older. It's something that needs experience."

"Everyone keeps saying that," muttered Seregei.

Celes had been out for a walk, hoping that fresh air would help him feel better. For the most part, it had actually worked; as he turned back towards the Guardhouse he had to admit that he felt more clear-headed and as if his heart was beating more strongly.

He took a deep breath, the chill air cutting at his mouth and throat, and for a moment he relished being alive. He knew nothing they could do would bring Neithan back and the thought gave him a moment's melancholy, but if they could prevent something like that from happening again, that was something.

As he walked down the road towards the Guardhouse, he was surprised to see Captain Ekelid of the Royal Guard coming the other way.

"Ekelid!" he called, and waved.

Ekelid quickened his step, but then waited by the turning to the Guardhouse. Celes realised that was his destination too.

"What brings you here?" he asked.

"Lord Hurion has asked me to lead a group from the Guard and help you," said Ekelid as they started down the path.

Celes blinked. "I knew Weyrn had gone to ask…"

"The king agreed to help."

Celes sighed in relief. "I'm glad," he said fervently. "There's a lot we can do, but it's still limited."

Ekelid just grinned and looked up as they left the trees. The Guardhouse was in front of them and Celes noticed Weyrn and Seregei sitting on the window seat, their backs to the window. Squinting a little, he could make out Alatani, speaking earnestly to Seregei. None of them seemed to notice Celes and Ekelid until they went in.

"Ekelid!" said Weyrn, getting up. Celes noticed that Seregei was curled up in a ball looking miserable, but he looked up, rubbing tears from his eyes, as he heard the strange name.

Ekelid glanced at Seregei, but then turned to Weyrn. "Lord Hurion sent me. He said you needed allies?"

"I did ask him for some help," said Weyrn with a sigh. "You know what's happened."

"Yes. My condolences."

"Is he going to help you hunt the monsters?" asked Seregei.

Ekelid glanced at him again, then looked back at Weyrn, looking worried.

"Come on, Seregei," said Alatani with a small sigh.

"I've already spoken to Ekelid a little," said Celes, "and you can fill me in later." He held out his hands to Seregei. "Come with me, Seregei."

Seregei frowned. "I want to know what's going on," he said stubbornly.

"I'm sure they'll explain it to us both later."

Seregei looked up at his parents. "Will you? Promise?"

They shot each other a fleeting look, then Alatani nodded slowly.

"All right, we will."

Seregei smiled, then jumped off the window seat and ran over to Celes.

"Let's go and find some chestnuts," said Celes, taking his hand and heading for the door again.

Almost as soon as they were outside, Seregei asked, "Uncle Celes, do you know how to tell if someone's actually a monster?"

Celes couldn't help staring. "What?"

"Daddy said that some monsters look like people and the monsters who hurt Uncle Neithan were like that. But how do you tell?"

Celes hesitated. He knew he couldn't always tell. Sometimes it took experience to know not to trust someone. Sometimes, though, he could tell straight away, just by something in a person's manner. He didn't know how to explain that to a child, though.

"Uncle Celes?"

"Well... sometimes I can't."

Seregei blinked. "But how do you know whether to kill them?"

"Well, if we all knew that, maybe there wouldn't be so many in the world. But you have to be careful; you can't attack someone just because you don't like them, and you *can't* always tell. So you have to wait and see what happens sometimes."

"But what if..." Seregei's lip wobbled. "Do you think Uncle Neithan didn't realise they were monsters?"

"Probably not," said Celes with a sigh. "But imagine if you thought someone was a monster and they weren't, and you attacked them?"

"Does that happen?"

Celes sighed. "All the time. We try to avoid it, but... all the time."

Weyrn waved Ekelid to a chair and went back to his perch on the window seat. Alatani sat beside him.

"How much do you know about what's happening?"

"Very little," said Ekelid as he sat.

"All right. Well... You know that Neithan was captured by humans."

Ekelid blinked. "Not that it was humans. You're sure about that?"

"Neithan was able to confirm it" – Weyrn sighed – "and we met others in the area who said they knew the group that did it."

Ekelid nodded. "Was Neithan able to tell you anything more about them?" he asked carefully.

"Very little." Weyrn sighed bitterly again as he remembered how difficult Neithan had found it to speak. Still, he had been able to tell them a little during his last days. "He said that they seemed to hold a grudge. Apparently –" He looked round as the door opened, but it was Seri.

"What have I missed?" he asked, glancing curiously at Ekelid.

Weyrn explained that Hurion had sent Ekelid as an ally. "Incidentally, Ekelid," he added, "How many will be with you?"

"Eleven and myself."

"That's almost... that is twice as many Royal Guardsmen as there are Swordmasters," said Seri carefully.

"All I know is that you needed some extra blades," said Ekelid with a small shrug.

Weyrn looked hard at Seri, but the other elf just sighed and sat down. "I interrupted. Go on."

"Where was I?" Weyrn asked.

"What Neithan said," said Alatani, squeezing his shoulder a little. "About the grudge."

Weyrn nodded. "They actually knew the title 'Swordmaster'."

"How? You've not had dealings with many humans in the past, have you?" asked Ekelid.

"Derdhel and I met some," said Seri. "It was only in passing, though."

"When was that?" asked Weyrn.

"After the Naith."

"And what happened?" asked Alatani. "If they have a grudge against Swordmasters..."

Seri frowned. "We didn't do anything to them. In fact, they were very rude to *us*."

"What did they say?" asked Weyrn. If there had already been hostility for some reason...

Seri shook his head. "I don't really remember. We introduced ourselves and they shouted at us to leave them alone and walked on. I don't know what had provoked them, but it wasn't us."

"So it sounds like they already had something against elves," said Ekelid thoughtfully.

"Not because of anything we did," said Seri, a slight edge in his voice.

"I don't think Ekelid's accusing you of anything," said Weyrn. "It is something to think about."

Seri sighed. "It doesn't change all that much, though," he said sadly.

"It could help us prevent this happening again," said Ekelid.

Seri frowned at him a moment, then asked, "Why are you involved in this, Ekelid? I'd have thought that Hurion would be happy to let this lie."

Weyrn fought the urge to bury his head in his hands as Ekelid's head went up, colour springing to his cheeks. "What are you suggesting, Swordmaster Seri?" he asked coldly.

"Seri," said Weyrn, "I asked Hurion for help finding Neithan's killers and he sent Ekelid and his men. We do need their help."

Seri sighed, but nodded.

"Anyway... Neithan said that they accused him of crimes against them."

Alatani turned to him with some surprise; Eleri had repeated this to Weyrn, but nobody else.

"Yes, he... said that they dragged him through several human settlements with a halter around his neck and accused him of attempting to kill and eat their children, among other things." Neithan had dwelt on that while talking to Weyrn as well, and Weyrn tried not to remember his expression. "He said there were others, but that one preyed on his mind." He rubbed his eyes and Alatani put an arm around his shoulders.

After an awkward pause, Ekelid asked, "Several settlements? Was he able to say how many and how large?"

Weyrn silently shook his head.

"That's something we should find out regardless. And their attitude towards the accusations?"

"He didn't say."

"Eleri mentioned to me that some of the marks on him would match thrown stones," said Seri quietly. "So it sounds like some of these humans believed it enough."

Ekelid winced. Weyrn shook his head a little, trying not to imagine what Neithan had been through.

Alatani broke the silence. "We know that there are a few humans such as the ones who helped him who have no quarrel with us, and others who were at least willing to be persuaded. How much more can we know without going out there to investigate ourselves?"

"That's all I know from Neithan," said Weyrn. "Arens and Ilian said that the humans they believed Neithan had escaped from were new to the area."

"They must have some influence, nonetheless."

"It's been some time since we first started hearing news from the clans that there was trouble with humans," said Seri.

Weyrn knew he didn't mean it as an accusation, but it struck home nonetheless. He should have done more. With a cold feeling, he wondered if Neithan was the first elf to be tortured like this. In a perverse way he hoped that it was simply that these humans had some strange hatred of Swordmasters in particular.

"Arens and Ilian?" said Ekelid, jerking Weyrn back to reality. "Those are the humans who helped Neithan?"

"Yes."

"How much more might they know if you approached them again?"

Weyrn shook his head. "They were already in danger for helping Neithan. I don't want to make them more of a target."

"You offered them sanctuary, didn't you?" asked Seri.

"Yes, and they refused."

"If they might know something that would help, can you in good conscience pass that by?" said Ekelid seriously. "I'm not suggesting they should come with us on a scouting mission of any sort, but visiting and asking if there's any more that they know..."

"There's the language problem, which means that Weyrn would have to go unless some of your men speak the human language." Alatani glanced at Ekelid, who shook his head even as he mumbled non-committally.

Weyrn scowled. Arens and Ilian had done so much for Neithan that he hesitated to ask for more, especially since there was every chance that this would put them in further danger. But then the thought reared its head again that Neithan might not be the first or the last. And the very thought of Neithan's death, the fear in his eyes as he took his final breaths, twisted something in him. "I'll think about it," he said. "I'll have decided by the time we get there."

"You do know where they were camped?" asked Ekelid.

"We know where Arens and Ilian were and Neithan couldn't have gone far." Weyrn sighed.

"We'll need rangers," said Seri. "And I assume you'll go, Weyrn."

Weyrn nodded. Alatani sighed deeply, rubbing her eyes. "I suppose that was a call to me too."

Seri looked hard at her and Weyrn shook his head at him. He didn't think he could face another argument about his and her duties. Fortunately, he took the hint and looked away.

Alatani, though, said, "Who would stay? Before I make a decision, I want to be sure someone will be here to look after Seregei. I assume Derdhel will go, as our best ranger."

"I do have rangers among my men," said Ekelid dryly. "I don't think you need worry as much as this."

Weyrn nodded, but said, "We may need a lot of help tracking. Seri, you know the settlements, so, as ever…"

"Gladly," said Seri.

"That leaves me and Celes." Alatani sighed, shaking her head. "Neithan was always so good with him…" She shook her head again and said briskly, "I trust Celes well enough."

"He's looking after him now," said Ekelid, gesturing towards the door.

"Yes, I know. And I know he likes children, it's just that I don't know how long he's had to care for one in the past." She sighed. "But I suppose I had best go, since there is…"

"Think about it," said Weyrn firmly. "Talk to Celes and don't make a decision immediately."

She smiled. "Thanks."

"What about Maelli?" asked Seri. "He's also a passable ranger, though his senses are better than his tracking."

Weyrn nodded. "And I think it would be hard to keep him away. A group as large as this, I imagine we'll be making full camps?" He looked to Ekelid for confirmation.

"We may want to break into smaller groups, but my men can all fend for themselves, even in winter. I picked them carefully."

"So we probably won't need someone especially gifted in wilderness survival. Of those two, then, I'd leave Celes."

"Agreed," said Seri.

"I'll speak to him when he returns," said Alatani, glancing over her shoulder out of the window. Weyrn took her hand and pressed it and she looked back round with a small sigh.

"So that's the full count," said Weyrn with a sigh of his own. He turned to Ekelid and said, "Me, Seri, Maelli, Derdhel and either Celes or Alatani." Reeling off the names still sounded wrong. They were out of order anyway, but he was conscious of a gap after his own name.

Ekelid nodded. "I've told you our numbers. When will you be ready to set out? I'll bring my men to meet you here."

"Tomorrow morning, first light."

Ekelid nodded and got up. "We'll be here."

Weyrn also got up. "And thank you. I do appreciate the help."

Ekelid smiled. "I look forward to travelling with you again, though I do wish it were under different circumstances." He nodded to each of them, adding a small bow from the waist as he faced Alatani. "Until tomorrow."

"Until tomorrow," said Weyrn.

As before, it took them a couple of days to get near Arens' and Ilian's house. Alatani looked around with some interest as she went. It had been too long since she'd last spent a lot of time in this area of the woods, no matter how little she regretted the reason. She sighed and ran a hand through her hair, hoping that Seregei was happy enough back with Celes at the Guardhouse. She thought a little wistfully of the warm fire in the common room as she drew her cloak around her shoulders. It was dry, but the wind was biting.

"Swordmaster Alatani?" asked one of the Royal Guardsmen who was walking beside her.

"I'm fine, just a little cold."

He smiled sympathetically and glanced up to Weyrn and Ekelid, who were leading the little group. "It's been a quiet journey."

"Yes, I think most people would hesitate to attack a group so large." Weyrn had told her that Neithan had been ambushed in his camp. If that was how they captured a lone elf, they weren't likely to attack a large group travelling in force.

"That's true. Do you know if we should expect any trouble?" he asked.

Alatani frowned. Of course, the worry of ambush still remained, and they could have grown in strength having given other humans a reason to hate the elves. "If we should, I expect it won't be an open attack." She fell silent as she heard a whistle from somewhere up ahead. She recognised Maelli's signal and laid a hand on the guardsman's arm to stop him. Weyrn and Ekelid had also stopped and were whispering between themselves. Alatani started to go up to them and then Weyrn turned and beckoned.

"Will you go and see what that was?" he whispered.

"Where will Derdhel be by now?" she whispered back.

"On the other side of the road."

She nodded and darted off in the direction from which the whistle had come, hoping that it was wise to send all the Swordmasters off. With three scouting and Seri talking to a settlement he knew, she thought Weyrn was uncomfortably exposed no matter how much she trusted Ekelid.

Maelli was waiting crouched beside a tree and she squatted down beside him as he laid a finger on his lips, pointing further between the trees with his other hand.

She could hear shouts in the distance and her eyes narrowed as she listened. She couldn't make out exactly what was going on and she glanced at Maelli quizzically. After a moment, he beckoned to her and started sneaking forward. She followed, moving slowly and smoothly beside him. The noise was becoming clearer: angry shouting. Men's voices, in a language she didn't understand. She could understand the tone, though, and sped up a little. Maelli matched her pace. When she glanced at him, his eyes were fixed up ahead.

Alatani could see the side of a small building through the trees. There was a group of people gathered in front of the building and she frowned; the shouting had reached a greater volume and she heard a woman scream. Instinctively, she reached for her sword.

Beside her, Maelli was doing the same. He gestured to her to go around the back of the building, to the other side of the crowd.

Even when she was around the house, in plain view, none of them seemed to notice. She could see a couple of men bending over a figure on the ground. The rest seemed to be watching, shouting encouragement and threats. She saw one throw a stone.

In a flash, she remembered Neithan's bruises. She wasn't sure if the cry of pain was in her imagination. She screamed in rage and charged.

Some of the humans spun to face her, then stumbled out of the way. She saw Maelli dashing out of the trees on the other side of the crowd from her. Several people screamed and a few turned to run. Alatani ignored them, intent on those at the front.

One man raised a club with a shout. She slashed at him and barged him aside, hardly noticing his yell of pain. She spotted Maelli again. He cut down another man as she moved to defend their victim, keeping between him and his attackers as best she could.

Most of the crowd had scattered into the trees. The few who remained looked uncertain whether to run or attack the two elves. One of them shouted something, but Alatani couldn't understand it.

"Maelli?" she said, glancing over her shoulder at him.

He shook his head as he joined her, facing the other side of the clearing where a few humans were still standing. "I don't know."

She nodded and turned back, on guard.

The remaining humans were readying weapons again. They weren't many, but she and Maelli were outnumbered. She wondered whether they should have gone back for Weyrn. With a cold feeling, she realised that she and Maelli had hurried off so quickly that no-one actually knew where they were.

She heard a moan from the ground behind her, but didn't dare look down. "How is he?" she asked Maelli.

"I can't tell."

At that moment, Alatani heard the door of the hut open and saw a movement out of the corner of her eye. She risked a glance and saw a woman slip out of it and pause. She wasn't a threat and Alatani looked back at the remains of the crowd.

The woman shouted something, her tone hesitant, but Alatani shook her head to indicate that she couldn't understand, without looking round. She hoped that the woman would stay back near the house.

Behind her, Maelli whistled loudly, having evidently decided that this wasn't something they could handle on their own. She sighed in relief, but then tensed again as she heard a shout from somewhere to her left, in the trees beyond the building. Luckily, she didn't look; one human raised a fist with a yell and charged. The others followed. She saw the flash of a knife in the leader's hand and stabbed. The leader staggered aside. She saw him fall and the others faltered.

Behind her, Maelli was having more trouble. She concentrated on keeping his back safe.

The leader of the charge groaned and stirred at her feet and she glanced at him. She sidestepped quickly as he went to slash at her leg.

Right then, there was another yell from beyond the building. Alatani's heart fell; it wasn't Weyrn or Ekelid, so not reinforcements. She planted her feet, raising her dagger as well as her sword. She didn't dare look round.

Some of the newcomers darted past her. They were humans, but they turned to defend her and Maelli. Still, she didn't let her guard down.

The original humans, however, turned and fled. The new humans relaxed visibly and one turned to Alatani and Maelli while another beckoned the woman forward; she had been hovering by the house this whole time. She dashed forward and knelt by the man Alatani and Maelli had rescued.

Unfortunately, the human leader addressed them in his own language.

"You have no idea what he's saying?" Alatani asked Maelli helplessly.

He shook his head and shrugged at the human.

The human scratched his head, but then looked round and called out to one of his men. They consulted for a moment.

"Do you think Weyrn heard the whistle?" Alatani asked Maelli.

"I hope so." He sheathed his sword and, after a moment's hesitation, she did the same.

The human that had just come over, though, turned to them and hesitantly said, "Hello?"

"You speak elven?" asked Alatani.

"A little. You come from where?"

"Duamelti," said Maelli. "We're Swordmasters."

The human translated that and there was some muttering. Alatani's palm itched and she repressed the urge to lay it on the hilt of her sword. Some of the looks they were getting were less than friendly.

Still, the human spoke again. "Why come you here?"

"We're looking for the people who killed a friend of ours," said Maelli.

Both humans looked at the man they had been protecting. The woman was mopping at a large cut on his cheek, but he was awake, Alatani was relieved to see.

Then they heard a shout from the side of the clearing and looked round as Weyrn arrived, the Royal Guard with him. Several of the humans grabbed weapons.

"He's with us," said Alatani quickly, turning to meet them.

"What happened?" asked Weyrn. "We heard Maelli whistle again and came as fast as we could."

"There was a mob attacking this house and stoning that human." Alatani pointed. "We intervened, and then these other humans came and drove off the mob. Beyond that, we're not really sure. That human speaks some elven, but we only just started talking."

Weyrn nodded and turned to the human leader, addressing him in his own language. The human grinned, looking relieved.

With a sigh, Alatani finally looked back at the two humans on the floor. The woman seemed intent on looking after the man, but she apparently sensed Alatani's gaze, for she shot her a look of intense dislike before going back to her task. At that, Alatani blinked and stepped back a little, hurt, but then shook her head and turned her attention back to Weyrn.

Weyrn greeted the humans with a nod and introduced himself and the others. "I gather your intervention was a timely one."

"So was theirs," said the human leader after a moment's surprised relief at Weyrn's command of his language. "Though I'm not sure why the woman wouldn't let Reig's wife go to him. Did she think she couldn't protect them both?"

Weyrn glanced at Alatani. "He wants to know why you wouldn't let the man's wife come over."

"That's what she was asking? She said something and I told her I didn't understand."

Weyrn nodded and turned back to the human. "A misunderstanding, I think," he said, and translated what Alatani had said.

The man huffed out a breath. "All right. I'm glad one of you understands us, anyway. My man told me that you're here looking for a murderer?"

"A group of murderers." Weyrn sighed and swallowed hard, then said, "Some humans around this area kidnapped a friend of ours and tortured him to death." Putting it baldly helped a little, but not much.

The human winced. "Gods, I'm sorry to hear that."

Weyrn nodded. "Do you know of anything we might do to find these people?"

The human frowned a moment. "Hang on and I'll see what I can find out. I think I might know the group you mean, though."

Weyrn nodded and stepped back a little to give him some privacy and translate the conversation to the others.

"They think they know them?" repeated Alatani.

"For all we know, the group you interrupted might have been allied with them," said Ekelid. Evidently they'd filled him in on what was happening.

Weyrn nodded. "I rather hope so."

"Captain!"

Weyrn turned back to the human leader, who gestured over his shoulder. "We think we know who those people are."

"Just a moment," said the woman. "This elf: his name was Neithan?"

Weyrn stared at her for a full minute, too astonished to do anything else. The other elves were looking curiously at him, having heard the familiar name.

"Yes, it was. How did you know that?"

She smiled bitterly. "I think you've met my brothers."

"Arens and Ilian?"

"Yes." She looked down at her husband. "I... think those bastards had already been there."

"What?" Weyrn quickly translated for the benefit of the other elves, then said to the woman, "What's happened?"

"I don't know, but our kinship is why they came here."

Weyrn's first instinct was to send someone to check on Arens and Ilian, but he was still the only one who could speak to them. The human leader, though, forestalled him and ordered two of his own men away.

"Of course," he said, "there's not much they can do against a mob, but they can see what's happened."

Weyrn nodded. "We offered them sanctuary with us, but they refused."

"Of course," said the woman. She didn't elaborate, just leaned down to murmur in her husband's ear.

"Should we help her get him inside?" asked Maelli.

"Judging by the looks she's been giving me, I think she'd refuse," said Alatani.

Nonetheless, Weyrn decided to make the offer. "Would he be more comfortable inside?"

"You're not coming in my house," said the woman firmly.

At that, the man opened his eyes and said, "Whatever… others have done, we… owe these ones a debt."

"If you don't want us to enter then we won't," said Weyrn.

The human commander nodded to him and ordered some of his own men to help the injured human inside. Weyrn, though, once again translated the conversation.

"What do you suppose he meant by that?" asked Ekelid.

Weyrn once again thought uncomfortably of what Neithan said his captors had told the humans they visited. If stories like that were going around and being taken as fact…

The human interrupted his thoughts. "We plan to follow some of the ones who were here and find the rabble-rousers. Care to join us?"

"Gladly, since it might point us the right way. But what about these two?" Weyrn nodded towards the house.

"My men will guard them as best they can. I know we've just seen that, no matter how brave" – he smiled at Maelli and Alatani – "two can't hold out long, but I actually doubt that mob will be back."

Weyrn nodded. "If you're sure. I certainly want to see about driving these people away."

"You and me both. They've been stirring up trouble for months."

Ekelid tapped Weyrn on the shoulder and he once again translated.

"How is he involved?" asked Ekelid. "There must be a reason he's interested in fighting these humans."

"Isn't it enough that he is?" asked Alatani.

"He makes a good point," said Maelli softly. "It could be a trap."

"Fire, drink and chance meeting are all very well," said Weyrn with a small smile.

"The enemy of my enemy," countered Alatani.

"Make sure he is an enemy first," said Ekelid.

Weyrn nodded and turned back to the human leader. "We'd be glad of help," he said, "But what brings you here? Who are you?"

"I didn't think you were going to ask," said the human dryly and Weyrn suppressed a wince. "We're a militia from one of the older settlements. My name's Taril."

Weyrn nodded. "Good to meet you. Your settlement is near here?"

"Not very, but we're trying to stop this lot" – he waved a hand expressively in the direction of the forest – "from stirring up trouble. Getting through the winter is hard enough without fighting the elves."

"That's what they're trying to do?"

"Yes." Taril glanced at the house. "And it works. You hear that elves have been caught attacking human children and..."

"That wasn't true," snapped Weyrn before he could stop himself. Taril looked startled and Weyrn sighed. "That... that was said about my friend, the one they killed. He said they dragged him through human towns with a halter round his neck and made false accusations against him. That one stuck in his mind."

"I'm not surprised. It's a foul thing to do." Taril raised his hands. "Not that I'm saying he was guilty."

Weyrn shook his head. "He wouldn't do such a thing. He loved children."

"But couldn't eat a whole one?"

"It isn't funny!" snarled Weyrn.

"All right, all right, I'm sorry." Taril sighed. "That was out of place. Truly, I'm sorry."

Weyrn nodded. "But you understand why we want to find the ones who did that to him."

Taril nodded, glancing behind Weyrn worriedly.

"Weyrn?" said Alatani and Weyrn glanced round. The elves were watching warily, several of them with their hands on their swords.

"He made a really tasteless joke about what the humans were saying about Neithan." There was no point in repeating it.

Maelli scowled and Alatani folded her arms, frowning. It was Ekelid who said, "Do you think he can be trusted?"

"Apparently they're trying to stop these humans stirring up trouble. They're from a settlement near here. It seems fair."

"Could we go and see if they actually are helping Arens and Ilian?" asked Maelli.

"It could be a way of checking," said Alatani thoughtfully.

Weyrn nodded and turned back to Taril. As he was about to speak, though, there was a startled shout from somewhere in the forest and a crash of someone falling against a bush. Humans and elves alike went on guard, laying hands on swords. Weyrn caught Alatani's eye and nodded and she slipped into the woods. Maelli went to the wall of the house and peered round it, ready to guard the door if he had to.

The last thing Weyrn had expected to hear was laughter, but he sighed in relief once he had got over the shock. Alatani stepped out of the trees again with Derdhel, who actually looked rather abashed.

"He and one of the human scouts tried to ambush one another," she called.

Weyrn shook his head slightly and beckoned them back over as he explained to Taril.

"That's the last of your group?" Taril asked, sounding rather uncertain.

"There's one with an elven settlement not far from here, but I'll send one of my people to get him. I think we're ready to leave, if you want to talk on the way?"

"My men can catch up," said Taril, nodding briskly. One of the men standing beside him went to convey the message and gather up his men. Weyrn turned back to Ekelid and the Swordmasters and told them that they were leaving.

"Taril, will they be in the same direction as the men who helped Neithan before? I'd like to reassure myself that those two are safe."

"That is where they seem to have made their camp. From here it'll be a little out of the way, but I'd actually like to be sure myself."

"In that case, we'll go that way."

Taril nodded and hitched his cloak closer round his shoulders. "Agreed. Let's go."

Weyrn turned to Derdhel and asked him to go and find Seri and tell him what they were doing, then catch up with them. Only then did he beckon to the others to follow Taril.

***

As they travelled, Weyrn did his best to make conversation with Taril, still trying to find the root of the quarrel between elves and humans in the area.

"I don't understand why I've not seen it coming," he said. "Surely some of my people would have told me if it were as obvious as you say."

Taril shrugged. "It's obvious to us, that doesn't mean you'd notice. As far as the elves are concerned, they're just driving off a few interlopers." He scowled. "As if we had any way to know what land is already claimed!"

Weyrn frowned, wishing that Seri was there. Still, he was sure that the clans made their land fairly clear, and said so. "Certainly it should be obvious that farmland is claimed."

"And when we clear forest?" Taril folded his arms. "I know you were here first, but… some of those families had little enough to begin with. They put their heart and soul into those little farms and then elves come along to drive them off."

Weyrn shook his head. "I'll investigate what happened."

Taril did relax a little at that. "I'd appreciate it." He forced a smile. "At least some good can come of all this, if elves and humans can stop quarrelling."

"Is that all it is? Quarrels over land?" Weyrn remembered the conversation with Ilian; he'd not mentioned any such thing.

"Well, in practical terms."

"And in other terms? I heard there was some jealousy…"

Taril actually laughed at that. "Jealousy? A race that free from age and death and blessed with beautiful women? Why should we be jealous?"

"We are not free from death," said Weyrn curtly.

"Admittedly, that is what brought you out here." Taril shrugged. "You can't deny it's harder to kill an elf, though."

Weyrn frowned. "I don't think so."

"And the bit about the beautiful women. That's definitely true." Taril nodded back towards Alatani, who was deep in halting conversation with his interpreter; she'd been trying to learn their language.

Weyrn gave him a slow look. "If you try anything... untoward with Alatani, there won't be enough left of you for me to kill. That's the only warning you're going to get."

Taril looked hard at him for a moment, then smiled and shrugged a little. "Fair enough. But my points still stand."

Weyrn was about to reply when he heard a challenge shouted by one of the Valley-elves. Even as he turned, though, Seri's voice replied.

"Ah, good," Weyrn muttered. He excused himself from Taril and went to meet Seri and Derdhel.

"Good to see you," he said as they stepped out from their side path. "No danger on the road, I hope?"

Seri shook his head. "Unfortunately, I didn't find out very much about the humans." He looked around the large group. "Derdhel told me that... you had some new allies."

Weyrn nodded. "They know more about the humans in the area than we do, so it seemed like a good idea to work with them."

Alatani had also come over and she said, "Have you heard anything about militias in the area?"

"Not really. The elves I spoke to mentioned problems with humans, but nothing specific. I gather they used to have a good relationship with them, though."

"Not any more?" asked Weyrn.

Seri shook his head, then looked over Weyrn's shoulder and frowned. Weyrn looked round to see Ekelid coming over.

The Valley-elf didn't seem to have noticed Seri's frown. He smiled as he nodded a greeting. "What news?"

"Very little," said Weyrn.

"What about here?" asked Seri.

Ekelid just shook his head. "Little." He smiled slightly, though, as he said, "It doesn't help that most members of these two groups have no way to speak to one another."

Seri just nodded. "There... is a large group here now," he said carefully, looking between Weyrn and Ekelid.

Weyrn wondered fleetingly whether Seri would actually prefer the possibly-untrustworthy humans to the Valley-elves. He put the thought aside. It didn't really matter anyway, at least until they could be sure one way or the other about the humans.

"Once we get to Arens' and Ilian's house, we can split up," he said. "I imagine we'll need to search for where Neithan was being held."

A little way off, Taril cleared his throat. Ekelid frowned, but Weyrn shook his head a little.

"We're just hearing the news and deciding what to do next," he told the human. "Then we can move on."

***

It was another day before they reached the house and Taril went forward to knock on the door. Weyrn tagged along behind him.

Arens opened the door slowly, peering around it with one eye at first. He seemed to recognise Taril, though; he opened the door fully with an audible sigh of relief.

"Your men have been here for a couple of days," he said. "Is everything all right with Teysa?"

"She and Rieg are fine."

Arens sighed again and called, "They're all right!" over his shoulder. Then he looked back and finally seemed to see Weyrn; he exclaimed in surprise.

"Weyrn and his men - and woman - helped us drive off the Wolf-heads."

"Is that what you call them?" Weyrn asked.

"Recently," said Taril.

"Thank you," said Ilian fervently, joining Arens at the door. "And Neithan, is he…" He trailed off as Weyrn shook his head. "Oh. I'm sorry."

"No need. I'm grateful for what you did; without you we'd probably never have seen him again."

Ilian nodded.

"We were wondering if you could help us find where they might have been holding him before he escaped."

Ilian scratched his head. "I can show you where I found him," he said. "But I'll not go closer than that."

Weyrn nodded. "I'd appreciate it."

"We've not seen much of them recently," said Arens. "Perhaps they all moved off further north."

"I'd be glad of it," said Taril.

"I'll just get my cloak," said Ilian. "Then I'll show you."

"Thanks." Weyrn looked round at the other elves, who had gathered a little way off. "Ekelid, could you have some of your men patrol around this area? Just see if you can make out any movements towards or away; apparently there hasn't been much sign of these humans recently, so they may have left."

Ekelid shot a worried look back in the direction of Duamelti, but nodded.

"Seri..." Weyrn looked around for his new second. When the other elf stepped forward, Weyrn continued, "You and Alatani stay here." He glanced at her. "I know you're not fluent yet, but it could help."

They both nodded.

"Derdhel, you come with me and Ilian." Weyrn couldn't help thinking that, even apart from Derdhel's skill as a ranger, it would help to have someone beside him who wouldn't be too distressed by the sight of the place where Neithan had been tortured.

Derdhel smiled a little and came over to join him. By this time Ilian had returned and the three set out into the forest.

"I'll never forget it," said Ilian with a shudder as they walked. "I wondered if he was a ghost, he was so cold."

Weyrn bit his lip, but didn't say anything.

"I don't know why they'd do it." Ilian shrugged, hitching his cloak further up his shoulders.

"I remember you said that many humans are jealous of us."

"Perhaps." Ilian sighed, shaking his head. "Taril's men told me they've been raising half the countryside against you."

"Against the elves?"

"Yes. And if they'd do something like that..." Ilian hitched his shoulders again. "Here we are," he said abruptly. "Just here, by the side of the road."

"Thanks," said Weyrn, looking at where Ilian was pointing: a bare patch of ground with nothing to differentiate it from its snowy, leaf-strewn surroundings. There wasn't even so much as a bloodstain. "The camp is just a little further along here?"

"I couldn't tell you the exact distance, but... he can't have come far. Not in his state."

Weyrn nodded. "Thanks. We'll meet you back at your house, if that's all right?"

"I'll see you there." And Ilian hurried off.

Weyrn watched him go for a moment, then turned back to Derdhel, who was already crouched by the bit of ground Ilian had pointed out.

"I assume this is where I should start?" he asked.

Weyrn nodded and swallowed hard, pushing aside the thought of how dreadful it must have been for Neithan that night, cold and lost and alone. "Yes, and heading along the road."

Derdhel looked up, frowning. "Are you all right?"

"No, but I have to be."

Derdhel looked hard at him for a moment longer, then nodded, turning back to his work. "We'll find them," he said simply. "And avenge him, if you think it will help."

Weyrn sighed. "It won't bring him back, but I'll not let them do this to anyone else."

Derdhel glanced up with a smile, then started slowly along the road, moving in a crouch. "I think I have them," he said softly. "It's difficult with the snow…"

"Do your best," said Weyrn, falling in behind him. "We know roughly where we're going, but I'd like to know if there's more than one camp."

They didn't speak again as they walked. Derdhel kept his eyes on the tracks while Weyrn looked around at the empty forest, concentrating on looking for signs of movement and life. There was nothing: no humans and no sign of the scouts he had asked Ekelid to send out.

He almost startled as Derdhel hissed.

"What?" he whispered.

"Up ahead. There's a clearing and I think I see a building."

"The tracks…?"

"Making right for it."

Weyrn loosened his sword in its sheath and crept forward. Beside him, Derdhel did the same.

The clearing in front of them was empty and there was no smoke rising from the rough wooden hut built at one side.

"Deserted," whispered Weyrn.

"They could be hiding in there." Derdhel nodded at the hut.

"In this weather? They'd need a fire."

Derdhel shrugged, but then nodded after a moment's thought. "Sitting still, they'd get colder. Shall I go and check?"

Weyrn nodded. "I'll keep watch."

Derdhel set off across the clearing, moving quickly, and Weyrn followed more slowly, a few paces behind, watching their surroundings and the hut.

Everything was still and silent and Weyrn felt a little ridiculous as Derdhel looked up from an inspection of the threshold and said, "I don't think anyone's gone in or out for the last few days."

Weyrn sighed in relief and nodded. "We'll check inside, then, and rejoin the others. Perhaps one of the scouts has found something."

***

They returned to Arens' and Ilian's house empty-handed, but found that the others had had more luck: a couple of Ekelid's scouts had found a trail where the humans had forded a river.

"I suppose that's where we'll go, then," said Weyrn with a smile. He translated for Taril, who nodded.

"We're with you a little longer, at least until we know where they're going."

"Thanks." Weyrn turned back to Arens and Ilian, who were standing nearby. "Thank you again. And if you do wish to come to Duamelti, you'll find a welcome with us."

Arens grinned. "Thank you. Next time we have furs to trade, perhaps."

Weyrn nodded. "Good luck, and I hope you have no more trouble."

"Likewise. I hope your search is successful."

The whole group travelled on until almost nightfall, then both the humans and the Valley-elves decided to stop. Seri watched in frustration as they set up their separate camps, Weyrn going from one group to the other and talking to their leaders. Acting as a translator, Seri thought bitterly. Swordmaster Captain, running between the Valley-elves and the humans and translating between them.

"Seri?" Maelli's voice broke him out of his thoughts and he realised that he'd just been staring blankly down into the camp. He shook his head with a sigh, repeating yet again that Weyrn surely knew what he was doing.

"Yes?" he said, finally turning to face Maelli, who was giving him an odd look.

"There's a settlement quite near here, isn't there?"

Seri nodded.

"Weyrn asked if you and I would go on ahead and check if they're all right and if they've seen anything of these humans."

At that, Seri smiled. It would be good to get away from here; he felt stifled and something about the three groups in opposition made the back of his neck prickle. "Did he suggest it?"

Maelli nodded and Seri smiled again with a small sigh, turning to look around for Weyrn again.

The other elf was apparently deep in conversation with Ekelid, but just then he glanced up and caught Seri's eye. Seri waved and gestured over towards the settlement. Weyrn nodded.

"All right," said Seri, turning back to Maelli. "Let's go."

Maelli blinked, but hitched up his pack on his shoulders and nodded. Together, they walked into the forest.

Seri knew they would probably have to camp before they reached the settlement, but he was determined to cover as much ground as possible. Maelli kept close behind him, walking in silence and leaving Seri alone with his thoughts. He did his best to concentrate on the weather and the rough path up ahead.

"It's going to snow," Maelli said suddenly.

Seri blinked and looked round. The other elf was looking steadily at him and he felt uncomfortable as he looked back up at the clouds. "Yes, but we've a little time yet. We'll start looking for a campsite, but keep moving."

Maelli nodded. Seri still felt as if he was staring at him, though, and eventually sighed and said, "You obviously have something to say to me."

"Likewise." Maelli scrambled over a rock as Seri waited for him to catch up. "What's going on? You were staring at Weyrn as if he'd burned your badge earlier."

Seri winced. "It was obvious?"

"To anyone with eyes." Maelli looked hard at Seri. "Seriously, Seri, what's going on?"

Seri shook his head. "I just... I don't like the fact that Weyrn asked those Irnianam to come. I don't believe we need them and I don't like to feel beholden to them, and with the addition of these humans... there's too much..." He shook his head. "I feel that Weyrn's failing to do his duty as a Swordmaster because he's too busy catering to everyone else."

"And what would his duty be in this situation?" asked Maelli.

"Well, what we're doing now would be a start: checking on the Mixed-bloods those humans might have attacked, working on finding where they are and what danger they might cause." He folded his arms. "I'm sure he thinks he knows what he's doing."

"If you were sure, you'd not be ranting about it," said Maelli.

Seri glared at him. "Nonetheless."

"Anyway, this goes back further than this trip. I haven't forgotten the look you shot in his direction after Neithan's death. Honestly, Seri, what is it?"

Seri frowned, looking away. As he did, he noticed the lowering clouds and paused to look a little more carefully. "It's going to start snowing soon."

Maelli's look turned knowing, but he looked up at the clouds and nodded. "With all this brush around, it shouldn't be difficult to build a shelter against a fallen tree," he said with a note of hope in his voice. After a glance around, he pointed out a large log. "That one will do. Unless you'd like to go a little further tonight?"

"Tired?" Seri asked.

Maelli sighed. "My patrol took a rough road back at the camp."

"Sorry, I didn't realise." Seri changed course to go over to the tree.

"I'm hardly in desperate straits just yet." Maelli smiled as he spoke, but he didn't hesitate to follow Seri.

As it happened, they hadn't stopped a moment too soon; even as they gathered brush to make a roof, Seri felt the first feather-touches of falling snow on his hands and cheeks. Maelli looked up.

"We've a little while before it gets very heavy."

"I know." Nonetheless, Seri hastily started leaning his bundles of brush against the fallen trunk. "I'd rather not sleep on gathered snow, though."

Even working quickly, it was almost dark and the snowfall was getting heavy before they had finished. Seri noticed as he lashed the roof into place that Maelli was flagging.

"Get inside and rest," he said. "I'll finish out here."

Maelli didn't argue, just ducked into the shelter. Seri tied the last knot and went round making sure all was secure. His thoughts went back to the rest of the party, but he knew they would be all right; if nothing else, they had had far more time to put shelters together and pitch tents. He sighed and crawled into the shelter to join Maelli.

There wasn't enough room to sit up straight, but they sat hunched against the tree to share some biscuit, staying close together for warmth.

"You never answered my question," said Maelli, so suddenly that his voice made Seri jump. "What's really behind this?"

Seri grimaced. "I just don't agree with Weyrn on... a lot of things, actually. I think he's too heavily involved with the Irnianam, I think he neglects his duties as Captain - and yes, I know he can't very well abandon his duties as a father, but..." He fell silent, unsure how to finish the sentence.

"But Swordmasters used to be celibate for a reason?" Maelli prompted gently.

"You agree?"

"No, but it seemed the logical thought."

Seri laughed a little. "I know it's a difficult balance," he said, rubbing his eyes. "And I don't know what I'd do in his place, but I think he's taking us in a dangerous direction."

"Have you told him that?"

"Of course not; he's my Captain. He's been chosen to lead and I shouldn't gainsay that."

"Tell him. Honestly, Seri, you should talk to him; it does neither of you any good for you to spend your time glaring at him when his back's turned."

"I don't - " Seri cut himself off and sighed. "All right," he said. "All right, when we get back I'll talk to him."

"Thank you."

As snow began to fall, Weyrn looked up in disgust. This would obscure any remaining tracks.

"I'm glad we stopped," said Taril, stepping up beside him. "We couldn't have travelled in this."

Weyrn licked his lips. "I've sent two scouts, but we need to have some idea of where those tracks are heading before they're blotted out." He looked around for Ekelid. Though Taril and his men might know the area better, he knew there were rangers among Ekelid's men.

"Towards the east," said Taril. "I had some of my men look a little way ahead before we stopped."

East. That was the vague direction of the settlement. Weyrn looked around again and this time saw Ekelid and called him over. It took only a moment to explain the situation.

Ekelid shot a worried look at the sky himself. "It's almost dark and my men don't know the ground," he said before Weyrn could even ask him to send scouts. "They'd have to stop again almost as soon as they set out. I'll instruct a couple of patrols to go at dawn tomorrow, though."

Weyrn sighed. "I suppose it's better than nothing."

Ekelid nodded. "A sight better. But I am pleased to see they're heading away from Duamelti, at least." He raised a hand. "Not that I'm saying I'll be glad if they prey on your people, Weyrn, but my duty lies with Duamelti."

Weyrn frowned. "So if it looks like they'll not trouble you again…"

"I'm sorry. Lord Hurion ordered me to help you, but only in as much as these humans are a threat to us." Ekelid hesitated, looking at Weyrn's expression. "Look, don't think I don't want to help you to your revenge, but…"

"It isn't just about revenge."

Ekelid looked consideringly at him for a moment, but then nodded. "You have people outside the valley to worry about. I understand that, but what do you plan to do? Spend the rest of your life hunting them across the world, anywhere where there might be elves?"

Weyrn sighed. He didn't know what his plan would be in that case; he knew he couldn't keep chasing them forever. "It depends where they go next," he said grudgingly. "As long as I think they're a threat, I think it's only right that I try to protect my people from them. I know you're confined to the protection of a border."

Ekelid nodded and patted him on the shoulder. "But think about it," he said softly. "As for me, I have my orders and my men to think of."

Weyrn nodded. "I understand."

Seri and Maelli reached the settlement after another couple of hours' travel the next morning. The first thing that Seri noticed was the tension in the air. As they approached, they could only see a couple of elves in the clear space between the houses. Both of them were hurrying from one building to another, not looking around as they went. Seri frowned. Although it was cold and that alone might drive elves indoors, he was sure there was something not right here.

They knocked on the door of the first house they came to and for a while there was no answer, though Seri could hear movement and whispering from inside. He frowned and knocked again, calling out a greeting.

This time, the door opened a little and the elf inside peered out.

"We're Swordmasters," said Seri, moving his cloak a little so the elf could see his badge. "I'm Seri the Teacher, this is Maelli the Faithful. Can we talk to you?"

The elf opened the door a little more, though he still looked worried. "Is this about the humans?"

Seri blinked. "Yes, it is. Have there been humans here?"

"Yes, last night."

Seri licked his lips, looking around again. Fortunately, there didn't seem to be any damage. "What's your name?" he asked.

"Neska."

"Can we come in and discuss what happened?"

Neska looked uncomfortable, but shook his head. "I'll come out." He opened the door just enough to slip through, wincing as the cold bit through his tunic. "It's upset everyone," he explained. "I don't want to bring in any strangers, even Swordmasters."

Seri frowned, but put that aside for the moment. "We'll try and keep this short and let you go back as soon as possible. Tell us about these humans."

"They came through last night and tried to get into a couple of the houses. Mine was one." He shot a nervous look back at the house. "We'd barred the door and were waiting in case they broke in, but it frightened my children terribly."

"Understandable," said Maelli softly.

"I don't know how many they were, but after a couple of hours they left." He shivered, though Seri wasn't sure if it was with cold or fear. "Are you chasing them?"

"Yes, we're trying to work out where they're going and prevent them from harming anyone." Seri nearly said 'anyone else', but he cut himself short, not wanting to discuss Neithan's death.

Neska's expression had lightened a little at that. "You'll make sure they don't come back here?"

"We'll do what we can."

"Thank you." He sighed, his breath misting, and hugged himself, shivering.

"Is there anything else you can tell us about them?" asked Seri. "We should let you go back inside."

Neska nodded. "I heard someone say they'd found tracks." He pointed to one of the side alleys between two houses. "A large group, and they weren't there yesterday."

Seri nodded as Maelli turned to look at the alleyway Neska had indicated. "Thank you. We'll look that way first."

"I'm glad to help," said Neska, shivering again.

"Go back inside and stay warm," said Seri. "Can we call on you if we need to know anything else?"

Neska nodded, then slipped back inside. Seri watched him go with a small frown, then led the way over to the alley.

Indeed, there was a profusion of footprints leading back out into the forest. Seri's frown deepened as he looked at them. "Can you read anything from these?" he asked Maelli as they crouched to look more closely.

Maelli shook his head. "It's such a mess I'm not sure even Derdhel could. A large group with heavy feet, which alone suggests humans."

"I agree." Seri got up. "Come on, let's go."

The tracks were pretty easy to follow through the forest, but Maelli was finding it difficult to concentrate. There were too many thoughts running through his head and he didn't have time to stop and put them in order, or even try to make them fall still for a little while. He hadn't prayed that morning, which he suspected didn't help.

"Maelli?" Seri's voice broke into his thoughts. "You're not paying attention." The older elf's tone was admonishing, but also concerned. "What's wrong?"

Maelli shook his head with a sigh. "I... didn't pray this morning."

Seri frowned, but sighed, looking around. "Make it quick. I'll keep watch."

Maelli nodded and leapt for the nearest low tree branch, pulling himself up with a scramble. He kept climbing until he was well above the forest floor, then settled down in a fork, leaning against the trunk. Though it was winter, he still fancied he could hear the life in the tree. He sighed, finally relaxing, finally letting the babble of thoughts fade from his mind as he listened to the quiet of the surrounding forest. Even in that, he thought he could hear the voices of the Spirits. He drew a deep breath, feeling the cold air cutting at his lungs, tasting the snow. He listened wistfully for Neithan's voice on the wind, though he couldn't hear it. He offered prayers for their companions, for the budding feud between Seri and Weyrn, for the elves of the little village they had just visited.

He couldn't stay up the tree as long as he wanted, though. With a last, whispered prayer to Valtaur, he took another deep breath and started to let the welter of thoughts and worries seep back.

But as he let his awareness range a moment longer, he heard voices. Angry, shouting voices, the rough tones evidently human.

He blinked and the world came back in a rush. He couldn't hear them any more, but he had no doubt that they had been real and began scrambling down to join Seri.

The other elf's first question died on his lips as soon as he saw Maelli. "What's wrong?" he asked.

"I heard voices." Maelli pointed.

Seri frowned, his shoulders tensing as he turned to look in the direction Maelli had indicated. "Do you know how far?"

"No."

"Right. We'll go carefully." Seri set off, Maelli tagging behind him, mentally giving thanks for the help.

They hadn't far to go before they could both hear the voices again. Maelli couldn't understand what they were saying and, judging by his expression, nor could Seri. That alone told them that these people were probably humans.

"What should we do?" whispered Maelli.

"We'll see what they're doing and how many there are, then decide."

Maelli nodded.

Then they crested a small ridge and Seri dropped flat. Maelli copied him before even looking down into the hollow in the side of the hill.

There was a camp with maybe half a dozen humans, gathered around a single campfire. They were talking between themselves, apparently arguing about something. Unable to understand the language, the two elves had to rely on tone and gesture, and neither was particularly helpful. A couple of the humans seemed to be pointing back towards the elven settlement – a fact that made Maelli's heart sink – but the others seemed to be overruling them. It was difficult to tell.

Then one of the humans who had been pointing back towards the settlement got up, shouted what sounded like a stream of invective at the remaining humans, and stormed off towards the road.

"Follow him," whispered Seri. Maelli nodded and began to crawl around the edge of the dell, ignoring the way the wet and cold of the snow struck through the knees of his trousers and chilled his hands.

The human was walking up and down, rubbing his arms and muttering. Maelli watched him as best he could from behind a tree, wondering if Seri was able to learn more from watching the others. At least this one didn't seem too inclined to head back towards the village. Maelli didn't like to think of them making another determined attempt to get into Neska's house.

Suddenly, he heard a crunching of approaching feet. The human turned and called out a greeting. Maelli did his best to edge around the tree so that neither human would see him standing there. He slowly pulled up his hood, hugged his cloak around himself, and closed his eyes to listen.

It didn't do much good, of course. Though he could hear the tones of their voices, he couldn't understand the words and swore to himself. Still, at least he could tell it was only two, and they didn't seem to be going anywhere.

Maelli suddenly heard another set of feet approaching. He froze, holding his breath, hoping that he was just about camouflaged enough.

He wasn't.

As soon as he heard the shout of alarm, he crouched and sprang into the branches overhead, grabbing the nearest one. His right hand slipped on the icy bark, but his left hand held and he managed to scramble up. The three humans gathered below, staring up at him. One shouted something excitedly. Another started yelling in the direction of the camp.

Maelli debated for a moment what to do. They hadn't drawn any weapons and he didn't want to make the first move. It could be that they'd leave him alone.

If they were the same ones as had killed Neithan, that wasn't likely, but he still didn't want to precipitate anything.

A few more humans ran up and they had a discussion amongst themselves, some pointing up at him, others back towards the settlement. He fought the urge to look around for Seri; he didn't want to let them know that he wasn't alone.

They seemed to be coming to a conclusion. One of them reached for a bow and Maelli gasped, then once again sprang upwards, aiming for a higher branch. He kept climbing, as fast as he could without slipping. It wouldn't get him out of range, but if he kept moving...

An arrow hit the tree near his leg and he gritted his teeth. A fall from this height risked breaking his neck whatever they had in mind for him. An image of Neithan's broken body flashed across his mind and he frowned as he kept climbing. That was not how he was going to die.

Seri had heard the shout of alarm and realised at once that Maelli had been seen. His first instinct was to run and help, but he forced himself to lie still while the humans at the camp ran to investigate. It wouldn't help his friend if he too were captured.

As soon as they were gone, though, he set off in the direction of the raised voices. He couldn't hear anything of Maelli. He didn't expect cries for help, but at least it didn't sound like they were hurting him.

Seri crept through the undergrowth, making his way by hearing to where the humans were gathered. They were around the base of a tree, looking up into the branches. One had nocked an arrow to his bow and was aiming.

Then Seri saw Maelli scrambling up the tree. He wasn't captured, but he was cornered.

Seri carefully strung his bow, trying not to catch the humans' eyes with his movements. He balked a little at shooting them from the bushes, but when he saw a couple more of them producing bows he knew he had to do something; it was only a matter of time before one of their arrows found its mark. Fortunately, it seemed that they were all watching Maelli. He looked up himself as the first human archer loosed an arrow, but it seemed he'd missed.

Six on one was poor odds, but Seri nonetheless nocked an arrow, knelt up, and aimed at the one who seemed to be giving the orders.

The man screamed and dropped to his knees as the arrow struck him in the shoulder. The others spun round as Seri nocked another arrow. One of them pointed him out with a yell. Another loosed at him, the arrow catching his cloak.

"Maelli, get down!" he shouted as he loosed his arrow. One of the bowmen dropped. There were others, though, fanning out into the forest, trying to get around him. He couldn't aim in all directions.

One of the other men let out a gurgling noise and clutched at his shoulder as his knees gave way. An arrow had apparently dropped out of the sky. Evidently Maelli had a stable perch from which to shoot.

Three left. Seri looked around as he nocked an arrow, but then a blow to his back sent him sprawling. His bow snapped under him and the nock end of his arrow gouged along his cheek, barely missing his eye. For a moment he lay still, instinctively feeling at the injury.

"Seri!" Maelli's shouted warning made him look up. He saw a flash of metal over him and rolled to the side. His pack stopped him. He whirled up the broken shaft of his bow and struck the human across the face.

Then he felt the cold touch of steel at the side of his neck. The human that now had him at knifepoint barked an order. Seri couldn't understand the words, but the meaning was obvious and he dropped what was left of his bow.

They dragged him to his knees and one grabbed a handful of his hair to pull his head back. The sword was still at his throat. Out of the corner of his eye he could see one of the humans shouting up to Maelli – a small figure high in his tree – and gesturing towards the ground.

Seri winced as the one holding his hair yanked it again, but his hands were still free and he still had his dagger. Very slowly, he started to bend his elbow, reaching for it.

The new leader was still shouting up at Maelli, who seemed to be hesitating. Seri wanted to tell him to stay where he was, but he wanted to have the knife in his hand before drawing attention to himself.

Just as his fingers brushed the knife hilt, though, one of the humans looked down. He let out a shout and grabbed Seri's arm, yelling to the others. Seri cried out as he was suddenly shoved forward, landing face-down in the snow. The human was still holding his arm and twisted it up behind his back. He could feel the strain in his shoulder and lay still, frightened that he would pull it out of its socket if he struggled.

Then the human wrenched it a little more.

Seri couldn't bite back the scream as he felt something crunch and pain seared through his shoulder.

Maelli had been debating what to do when he suddenly saw the humans slam Seri to the ground. A jolt of horror made him stiffen as he heard Seri scream, then he started to scramble down. He had hoped that staying where he was would be the best way to make them keep Seri alive, but if they meant to torture him... Maelli prayed that there would be a way to rescue him when he got there.

Seri's cries withered in his throat as he fainted. Maelli paused, fumbling for his bow. From here he could see that the knife wasn't against Seri's throat any more.

But he couldn't shoot all three at once and they were standing in line with Seri.

Then he saw movement out of the corner of his eye: a couple of figures making their way between the trees. He squinted, trying to see who they were. The humans didn't seem to have seen them.

He didn't want to draw attention to them if they were elves, but in that case he did want to make sure they knew he and Seri were in trouble.

A whistle would draw eyes to him. Before he could change his mind he stuck two fingers in his mouth and whistled an alarm.

As he'd expected, the humans immediately looked up at him, distracted even from the task of tying Seri's hands. Then one dropped, clutching at an arrow in his throat.

As Maelli began to scramble down from the tree, the lead human drew his sword again and brought it down towards Seri's neck. Maelli cried out, snatching an arrow and nocking it. There was barely any time to aim. He didn't know if the other elves had seen the danger. He drew and loosed.

He heard a cry of pain, but was too busy keeping his balance to look. His foot slipped on the snowy branch. He dropped his bow and only just caught the branch again as he fell.

The shock sent a jar through his shoulders and he winced, but held on. He heard another cry of pain from below him, but couldn't look beyond trying to scramble down. Without his bow, there was little he could do to intervene.

When he was on another branch, though, he saw the two elves just running up. Two humans lay dead. The third was trying to drag himself away, Maelli's arrow in his leg. Maelli sighed in relief.

He was close enough to the ground to drop and he jumped. The landing sent another shock through his back, but he rolled with it and hurried over to guard Seri just as the other elves ran up. They were Valley-elves of Ekelid's party, he finally realised.

"Swordmaster Maelli?" one said. "What happened?"

"We were tracking them from a settlement and they saw us," said Maelli quickly.

The other Valley-elf went over to the wounded human and drew his sword. At that, the man fell still, shaking as he looked up at the elf.

Maelli drew his boot-knife to cut the hastily-knotted rope around Seri's wrists. Even though his friend was wearing a heavy cloak and a pack, Maelli could still make out the angular form of his dislocated shoulder.

"We'll take care of those two," said the Valley-elf as there was a moan of pain from another human.

"Thank you," said Maelli. "What are your names?"

"I'm Tarfin, that's Otir." Tarfin smiled, then walked away.

Maelli began to unbuckle the strap of Seri's pack to pull it clear of his shoulder, but at that moment Seri groaned and stirred, starting to struggle as he felt Maelli's hands on his arm and back.

"It's all right, Seri. Lie still," said Maelli softly. "We're safe."

Seri gasped. "They... They pulled my arm out."

"Yes, so I see. I can reset it, though. Don't worry." Maelli didn't know much about healing, but he could set bones and bandage wounds, which was usually all that was needed.

"What... happened?"

"Some of Ekelid's scouts found us."

"We heard the sound of the battle," called Otir, who was kneeling over the first human Seri had shot.

"If I get the pack off, do you think you can roll over?" asked Maelli.

"I'd rather not try, but I'll manage if you brace my arm."

It was a delicate operation, but at last Seri was half sitting against his pack and Maelli looked carefully at his elbow.

"If you don't think you can do it, say so," said Seri softly.

"I think I can." Maelli took one of the straps from the pack and slipped it between Seri's teeth. "Ready?"

Seri nodded and Maelli took his hand, beginning to rotate his arm.

Suddenly, there was a cry from behind him and he startled. Seri stiffened and yelped around the strap between his teeth.

"Sorry," whispered Maelli, freezing.

Seri pulled the strap out of his mouth. "What are they doing back there?"

Maelli carefully released Seri's arm and looked round in time to see Otir bending over one of the humans. As he watched, the Valley-elf slammed a foot down on the human's chest.

"What -" Seri half startled up, then fell back with a hiss of pain.

"I'll find out." Maelli scrambled up and went over. "What are you doing?"

Both elves and both living humans looked round, looking startled.

"We hoped to question them," said Tarfin. "Do you think they really don't speak our language?"

Maelli looked down at the humans. One was looking between them, his expression blank. The other stared straight ahead with a scowl, but didn't look like he could make out what they were saying either.

"I don't think so. We'll have to find an interpreter; perhaps if we rejoin the others Weyrn can talk to them." He looked back at the humans, but there was still no sign of understanding. "In the meantime, I saw you tread on him" - he pointed to the human he had shot in the leg. "Don't do that. We won't sink to their level."

The Valley-elves shot another look at each other, then Otir nodded with a small sigh. "I apologise. It won't happen again."

Tarfin nodded and Maelli forced a smile, then went back over to Seri.

"All right?" asked Seri, shifting a little with a wince to cradle his arm more securely.

"I think so." Maelli took Seri's hand. "Ready for a second try?"

Seri winced in anticipated pain, but nodded and bit down on the strap again. Maelli took a deep breath and let it out to brace himself, then took Seri's hand, bent his elbow and began slowly to rotate his arm. Seri jerked and stiffened, making a muffled sound of pain. Maelli gritted his teeth and kept going, trying to ignore the increasingly desperate noises Seri was making as he tried to force the shoulder joint back into place.

It was a shock when he felt it suddenly clunk into its socket. He kept hold of Seri's arm for a moment, staring at his shoulder, but then Seri relaxed, his head falling back as he gasped for breath.

"All right?" Maelli asked him.

Seri groaned, pulling the strap out of his mouth "Y-yes. Spirits…" another whimper as he reached for his shoulder. "I still can't move it."

"I'll try to find something for a sling."

As he was carefully tying Seri's arm to his body with a length of rope, Tarfin came over. "We've bound the humans and gagged them," he said. "They're both wounded, but strong enough to travel. I've been thinking, though: the one you shot in the leg will be slow and it'll take a long time for us to rejoin the rest of our party with them. In the settlement you visited, might there be someone who speaks their language and could translate?"

"That's possible, actually," said Seri. "Many of the elves around here have learned human languages, since more humans started moving into the area."

"How far is it?" asked Tarfin.

"It took us about half an hour," said Maelli. It'll be slower with that human, but much quicker than trying to make it all the way back."

***

It was indeed a long, slow walk, but at last they made it back to the settlement. The villagers seemed to be getting over their fright from the night before, but there were still very few out of their houses. Those ones stopped in their tracks as the four elves and two humans stepped into the settlement.

Neska was among them and he stepped forward. "Swordmaster Seri?

Swordmaster Maelli? What...?"

"We went after the humans who attacked your village last night," said Seri, looking around a little as other elves began to gather. "Most of them are dead, but we took these two prisoner."

Maelli noticed that one of the humans was looking very uncomfortable, looking around at the elves with barely-disguised fear. The other remained impassive apart from a look of scorn at his companion.

"Is there anyone here who speaks their language? We hope to question them and find out if there are any more of them."

Neska nodded. "I do," he said. "I'd be willing to try."

Seri smiled. "Thank you. If there's somewhere out of the weather we could take them..."

Neska led the way to a barn half filled with bales of hay and straw. After being out in the forest for so long, it felt almost stuffy to Maelli, but he was glad to be inside. Judging by their expressions, the other elves were too and even the humans looked a little more comfortable.

"Right," said Seri, looking around. He pointed at a bale of straw on the ground at the edge of the pile. "Tarfin, have your human sit there. Otir, are you all right with the other one?"

Otir nodded as Tarfin led the human whom Maelli had shot in the leg over to the straw bale. He looked momentarily relieved to sit down, even as he looked worriedly up at Seri. Maelli stepped up on one side of Seri while Neska, shifting uneasily from one foot to the other, stood on Seri's other side.

"Ready?" Seri asked him.

He nodded and Tarfin removed the human's gag.

"Can you understand us?" Seri asked first. Neska promptly, if slowly, translated and the human nodded. Seri sighed a little, then asked, "Who are you?"

Maelli looked round as the other human made a muffled noise behind them. Otir seemed to have him under control, though.

The human they were questioning looked over at his companion and licked his lips, but then looked back at Seri. At last, he hung his head and answered, "We call ourselves the Wolf Pack."

So Taril's name for them hadn't been that much of a misnomer. Maelli stifled a smile.

Seri paused a moment, then said, "How many of you are there?"

"I'm not sure in total."

"And where are you going?"

"I don't know."

Seri sighed and glanced at Maelli, who shrugged a little. He didn't have a suggestion for that.

"Why did you come to this village last night? What were you doing?"

Neska's voice had a lot more passion as he translated that question and the human looked sidelong at him for a moment before answering. Neska scowled and asked again, taking a step forward. Seri put a hand on his shoulder.

"What did he say?"

"That he didn't know." Neska scowled. "How can he possibly not know?"

"He seemed to have some kind of authority," said Seri with a small frown, touching his neck where the man had held a knife to it.

Again, there was a scuffle and muffled noise from behind them and Maelli looked round. The other human was struggling in earnest and Maelli hurried over to help Otir with him.

The human pulled away as Maelli went to grab his shoulder and Maelli remembered that he'd been shot there. Instead, he grabbed his arm. Behind him, Neska was translating, "At least we didn't shoot anyone in the back."

Otir frowned, but before he could speak, Maelli said, "They did, actually." There had been an arrow lodged in Seri's pack, after all. "And when Seri shot this one" - he nodded at the one he and Otir were holding - "they were trying to shoot me out of a tree."

Otir nodded, looking mollified.

"I think he's the leader anyway," said Seri thoughtfully. "He was in charge before I shot him."

"Shall we question him instead?" asked Tarfin.

"In a moment." Seri addressed the human in front of him again. "We've heard stories of... how you treat elves."

The human pulled back against the straw at his back and didn't reply until Neska repeated the remark, his voice quiet.

The human finally said, "What of it?"

"Why are you trying to make out that elves..." Seri paused for a moment.

"Murder humans," suggested Maelli.

Seri nodded. "For a start," he said, and nodded to Neska, who translated the question.

"It's true," the human answered promptly. Still, he didn't look entirely convinced.

"You don't believe that," said Seri. "So why spread it around?"

"Just because I've never seen it doesn't mean it's not true," the man said stubbornly. "Everyone knows it." He looked around at them suspiciously. "You're going to kill me once you're done here, aren't you?" His voice broke a little as he asked the last question.

"Are we?" asked Neska after he'd translated. He looked like he wasn't sure what to make of the prospect.

Seri shifted on his feet and Maelli bit his lip. It would be a long explanation for those involved who didn't know about Neithan, and he didn't want to kill two humans simply for revenge, especially since they might not have had anything to do with it.

"We'll see," Seri said at last and Maelli let out a breath he'd not known he was holding. Then he looked back at the human. "Where are you going next? You must have some idea."

The human shifted uncomfortably, but Maelli missed his response; at that moment the one he was guarding made another spirited attempt to break free.

"Shall we try questioning this one?" asked Otir, nodding to him.

Seri glanced round. "Just a moment," he said, then turned back. "What's your place in the group?" he asked. "And his?"

"I'm just a warrior. He... he was our leader."

"It stands to reason that he would know more," said Otir.

Maelli glanced down at the human, who ignored him, eyes locked on his subordinate. As best Maelli could tell around the gag, he was scowling ferociously.

"All right," said Seri after a moment. "Gag this one and bring that one over."

The human continued to struggle as best he could, but then he pulled his wounded shoulder awkwardly and almost collapsed. Otir and Maelli practically had to carry him over to the straw bale after that.

Once there, though, he seemed to revive a little and glowered up at Seri. As soon as they had removed his gag, he spoke.

Neska's eyes widened as he listened, then he translated, "Whatever you do to me, we'll find you and you'll all die like dogs. Kill me and prove all our suspicions right." He looked up at Seri. "I... suppose that means my village as well."

Seri frowned and caught Maelli's eye. "We need to decide what to do, especially if they might be traced here."

"We're not necessarily going to kill them," said Maelli. "We can decide when we make that decision."

Seri smiled fleetingly at him, then looked back at the human. "You heard what we asked your companion?"

The human nodded curtly when Neska had translated for him.

"Where are you going?"

"That's none of your concern."

"Why do you make false accusations against elves?"

The human suddenly frowned, looking hard at Seri's shoulder. "I know that mark," he said slowly. As he translated, Neska's eyes also flicked to the Swordmaster badge on Seri's sleeve. After a moment, the human suddenly laughed. When he spoke again, still laughing, Neska didn't translate. As he listened, the colour drained from his face.

"Neska?" said Seri, frowning. "Are you all right?"

"Is... was that true?" asked Neska shakily. He looked like he was about to be sick.

"Is what true?" asked Seri.

"He said that... there was another elf with that badge. Another Swordmaster."

Maelli suddenly also felt a little sick. Seri's head had gone up and his hands twitched slightly as he said, "They have killed a Swordmaster. Is that what he said?"

Neska hesitated again. "That's not all."

Everyone froze, eyes on Neska, except the human. He seemed to realise how much distress he'd caused with whatever he had said, for he laughed again. The other human looked increasingly nervous.

After a moment, Neska took a deep breath and blurted, "He said that he personally beat that Swordmaster until he begged for mercy."

The human laughed again.

Seri moved too fast for Maelli to see. Before he knew what had happened, the human cried out in pain and half-fell against the straw at his back. Seri was raising his fist for another blow, eyes wild, face chalk-white.

"Seri!" Maelli lunged forward, shoving his friend back.

"Let go of me! You heard what he said!"

Maelli braced himself against Seri's chest, still shoving him towards the door, barely remembering to be careful of his injured shoulder. "You need... fresh air," he grunted.

He managed to half-drag Seri outside and shoved him to stand against a wall. Away from the human, Seri seemed to relax.

"Sorry," he whispered.

Maelli nodded.

"I hit him, didn't I?"

"With your fist. In the face. When he was bound."

Seri grimaced, tilting his head back against the wall. "Spirits, I'm sorry. I shouldn't have lost my temper like that, just..."

"I know." Maelli sighed. He'd barely had time for the human's words to sink in, but he mostly felt tired and disgusted.

"I wish I hadn't done it in front of the Valley-elves." Seri shook his head, gritting his teeth.

"Stay out here," said Maelli. "I'll go and see if there's anything else he'll say."

Seri looked for a moment as if he was about to protest, but then just nodded. "Thanks. Make my apologies, too."

"I will." Then Maelli took a deep breath to steel himself and went back in.

Weyrn felt like a cat in a box, staying with the rest of the main group as Derdhel and Alatani went on scouting runs on either side, checking every path they passed and everywhere people might be living. There were a surprisingly large number of little collections of humans, sometimes a single family living alone like Arens and Ilian, sometimes two or three houses clustered together. They were all within easy travel distance of one another, though.

Many of them shot the elves suspicious looks and eventually Weyrn had to admit that it was easier to find out what they had seen if the elves waited nearby for the humans to ask the questions.

There were a few rumours: people had seen the Wolf-heads pass through. A few had actually seen Neithan, but although Taril looked tempted to repeat details of what had happened, he shot Weyrn a look and skimmed over that.

At last, though, they stopped for the night. Again, Weyrn felt they had stopped too early and he, Derdhel and Alatani gathered at the edge of the camp. They travelled lightest and had very little to set up.

"Shall we look around again?" asked Alatani.

"I'd feel better if we heard something from Seri and Maelli, and some of Ekelid's scouts aren't back yet either." Weyrn frowned. He knew that the missing elves would be entirely capable of tracking this cavalcade, but there was an uncomfortable thought in the back of his mind that two alone might still be vulnerable.

"They'll be able to follow us," said Derdhel softly. "They'll be all right."

"It's if they - " Weyrn looked round as he heard a familiar voice call his name. Seri was just stepping out of the trees behind them and Weyrn heaved a sigh of relief as he hurried over to meet him, noting as he went that his arm was tied across his chest in a makeshift sling. There was also a nasty-looking laceration across his cheek.

As Weyrn approached, Maelli and two of Ekelid's men also arrived. With them were two human prisoners.

"Are you all right?" Weyrn asked Seri.

"Yes, it's fine."

Weyrn nodded and looked back at the others. "What happened?"

"We found they had been to the settlement, though they hadn't managed to get into the houses. Then Maelli and I tracked them from there."

"We heard the sound of battle and came to investigate," said one of the Valley-elves, glancing over Weyrn's shoulder and saluting as he spoke. Weyrn looked round to see Ekelid coming over. Taril was hot on his heels.

"We killed the others and captured these two," said Seri, gesturing. "We've questioned them about their intentions and what they've been doing..." He gritted his teeth for a moment, then said, "Perhaps you could ask Taril what the usual human punishment for murder is."

"Murder? I thought you said that…" Then Weyrn realised whose death Seri was referring to. "These two were involved?"

"That one was. And is very proud of it." Seri pointed to one of the humans, who regarded him coolly. "I thought we should let their own people punish them."

Weyrn agreed, as long as the punishment was death, as it would be among the elves for such a crime. Still, he turned to Taril and passed on the news.

Taril's expression went deadly serious. "The torture alone warrants hanging," he said curtly. "Are you finished with them?"

Weyrn passed that on to Seri, who nodded. Taril called over some of his men and they took the prisoners away.

"What happened to the rest of the group?" he asked. "And what were they doing?"

"They're heading eastwards over the mountains," said Seri, looking at Weyrn as he spoke.

Ekelid sighed and looked sidelong at Weyrn as he translated.

Taril smiled. "In that case, our work is done; they're far enough from our village. Did they suggest they'd come back?"

Weyrn winced, but asked Seri.

"I didn't think so," said Seri. "But surely we should follow them and find out for certain?"

"If you do, you'll be on your own," said Ekelid. "I've got my orders and it sounds like Taril won't follow you."

Weyrn nodded a little, looking again at Seri's obviously-injured arm. They were essentially down to four. Still, he translated for Taril, who smiled.

"Thank you," he said. "That's good to know. We'll be off in the morning." He smiled at Weyrn and Ekelid again. "Thank you for your help, and good luck." Then he turned and left.

Weyrn made a frustrated noise and turned back to the other elves. Ekelid looked sympathetic, but simply shook his head.

Alatani and Derdhel had been listening and Alatani said, "Can we go on alone? Just the five of us?"

Seri nodded, but Derdhel was frowning.

"It helps nothing for us to put ourselves in danger for no reason," he said.

"No reason?" echoed Seri.

Weyrn held up a hand to forestall the argument. "Ekelid, could you excuse us a moment?"

Ekelid nodded and left. Weyrn turned back to the other Swordmasters. "The reason I asked Hurion for reinforcements is that we need them," he said softly. "Especially with you injured, Seri…"

"It's fine," said Seri, gesturing dismissively. "It's just bruised."

Weyrn frowned at him. "If that were the case, you'd not still have it in a sling. Maelli?"

Maelli held his hands up. "We've had it like that since the injury, so I don't know."

Seri frowned. "I don't want to turn back because of this."

"We were few anyway, and vulnerable."

"We're Swordmasters. Do you really think we can't handle a simple scouting trip?"

"How did that happen, anyway?" Weyrn looked from Seri to Maelli.

It was Maelli that spoke. "We were ambushed as we spied on them," he said with a sigh.

Weyrn nodded. "And what's to say it wouldn't happen again?" He looked at Alatani and Derdhel. "What do you two say?"

"They won't trouble us from there," said Derdhel, looking towards the mountains with a frown.

Alatani was shifting uneasily from foot to foot. "If we need the help, we need it," she said softly.

Seri shot her a moment's scornful look and she glared back until he dropped his gaze.

"I think we need to go back for now," said Weyrn softly. "I'm sorry, Seri, but I don't think we have a choice."

Seri looked hard at him for a moment, but then nodded curtly and walked away.

***

As Weyrn arrived home, he felt tired. Seri was obviously still angry and Weyrn also doubted himself. Still, there was no choice for now. Once they'd had time to regroup and Seri's shoulder had healed, they could try again to see what was happening, but until then he had to put up with the decision he'd made.

As they arrived at the Guardhouse, Seregei came running to meet him, slipping on the snowy ground, and Weyrn caught him just before he fell.

"Daddy! Did you fight lots of monsters?"

"Seri and Maelli fought more," said Weyrn, pointing at Seri, who smiled a little half heartedly.

"Seri, what happened?" That was Celes, coming out of the Guardhouse after Seregei.

"A human dislocated my shoulder. Maelli set it, it's fine." Still, Seri awkwardly adjusted the rope sling holding his arm.

"We've got proper bandages if you want to replace that," said Weyrn.

"I know."

"Do you want me to fetch Eleri?" asked Celes.

"I'll be fine," said Seri. "I'd appreciate some help putting on a new sling, though. It's still painful."

He and Celes went inside and Maelli went with them with a small smile at Weyrn. Weyrn himself passed Seregei to Alatani and turned back to Ekelid, who had dismissed his men at the gate. "Would you like to come in?"

"I should go and report to Lord Hurion, but thank you. I expect he'll want to speak to you as well."

Weyrn nodded. "I'll go down at some point."

"I'll tell him that." Ekelid sighed, looking back towards the hills. "I hope that's the last we'll see of those humans."

Weyrn nodded again. "I'm... not all that confident, but hopefully it'll be a little while, at least." He would have rather seen where they had gone, even if he and the others hadn't been able to fight them. But with only four able to fight... He sighed.

Ekelid seemed to notice his discomfort. "Yes... well, I'll see you later."

"Thank you again. It would have been quite a different journey without you. Especially given what almost happened to Seri and Maelli."

Ekelid shivered. "Believe me, I'm glad Tarfin and Otir were within hearing. The humans spelled their own fate there, though. I'm told that what actually caught their attention was the fact that Seri cried out when they injured his arm."

Weyrn winced. "Nonetheless, thank you, and please thank them for their help."

"I will." Ekelid bowed a little to both Weyrn and Alatani, then left. Weyrn sighed as he took her hand and they went inside.

"Did you fight?" asked Seregei. "How many monsters did you kill?"

"I didn't actually kill any myself," said Alatani. "Nor did your father."

Seregei's face fell. "But Uncle Seri and Uncle Maelli did?"

"Yes."

He smiled. "And they won't hurt anyone now?"

Alatani kissed his hair. "No, they won't."

He nuzzled his face into her shoulder. "Good."

They listened as he told them everything that he'd been doing, then Alatani took him to his room for a nap. Weyrn hung up his cloak and looked round as he heard someone come into the common room. It was Maelli. He smiled a greeting, then went to warm his hands by the fire.

"Cold?" Weyrn asked him.

"Not really, but it's good to have proper warmth again." Maelli sighed.

"How's Seri?"

"He's fine. I think Eleri should look at his shoulder when he next visits, but it should be all right. We patched up his cheek, too."

Weyrn nodded. "I'll go and see him. Is he in his room?"

"Yes and... I think that would be a good idea."

Weyrn blinked. "What do you mean?"

Maelli shook his head. "Something's been bothering him. I really do think the two of you need to talk about it."

Weyrn frowned, looking down the corridor towards Seri's room. "All right. I'll go and talk to him now. At least..." He looked back at Maelli. "Are you all right? I know it was Seri who was nearly killed, but..."

Maelli smiled a little. "Really, I'm fine. I spent most of the fight up a tree, so the only thing that came close to hurting me was the jump."

"And...?" prompted Weyrn.

"My back and head hurt for a couple of days, but that's faded now."

"Good." Weyrn laid a hand on Maelli's shoulder. "I'm glad you're all right."

Maelli put his hand over Weyrn's and pressed it. "Go and talk to Seri," he said with a smile.

Weyrn squeezed his shoulder again, then headed down the corridor.

Seri's door was closed and Weyrn knocked, wondering if Seri might actually be asleep. The call of "Come in!" was prompt, though, and Weyrn pushed the door open.

Seri was standing by the window. He had apparently been looking out at the few flakes of snow falling outside, but he stepped away as Weyrn came in.

"I came to check on you," said Weyrn. He noticed that Seri's arm was now in a linen sling and, as Maelli had said, there was a pad of bandage stuck to his cheek.

Seri smiled a little as he went to sit on his bed and gestured Weyrn to the one chair. "I'm fine. I think both are healing well." His hand went to his cheek.

"I'm glad to hear it. Was there anything that would have helped the two of you?"

Seri looked at the floor with a small sigh. "I don't think so, not that you could have done. We got too close and they saw Maelli, pretty much by chance, I think."

Weyrn nodded. "I'm glad it wasn't worse."

"So am I," said Seri drily. "It was a close thing." He sighed. "I suppose you were right to have brought the Valley-elves. Certainly, I'm not sure how Maelli and I would have escaped without them."

Something in his tone, though, had caught Weyrn's attention. "You didn't think it was a good idea?"

Seri scowled at the floor. "No. I didn't." Then he sighed and shook his head. "But you're my Captain."

Weyrn frowned. "Seri... have I given you the impression that you don't have the right to criticise me?"

"No, not in as many words, but I know I really shouldn't give you as much criticism as I do." Seri scowled at the floor again. "As I say, you're my Captain. You're the one the Spirits have chosen to rule, even if..." He cut himself off there.

"Even if what? Even if you think I'm wrong?"

Seri nodded.

"What's brought this on all of a sudden? My bringing Ekelid and his men into the search for those humans?"

"That and..." Seri sighed, looking at the ceiling for a moment, but then his words came out in a rush. "There have been a lot of things you've done that I don't agree with. That's not wrong; we have different minds and won't think the same way. But there are times when I doubt why you're doing the things you do." He reached up to adjust the sling with a jerky, angry movement.

Weyrn stared at him, his mind immediately drawing a conclusion as to what this was about. Nonetheless, he did his best to dismiss it. Surely Seri had seen that Seregei wasn't causing trouble for them in doing their work.

But he also knew that he had his own doubts about the balance he was keeping.

The mixture of the two made his voice come out sharper than he'd intended as he said, "What decisions?"

Seri glanced at him. "I know you have to choose between being a Captain and being a father, and I know that's not easy."

"This *is* about Seregei!"

"Not directly; it's about how you handle yourself!" Seri took a deep breath, clenching the fist of his good hand. "And don't ask me what I'd do in your place. I don't know."

Weyrn bit back the curt response to that and did his best to actually think about what Seri was saying. Even apart from the fact that it would have been unfair, he couldn't quite bring himself to shout at someone so obviously injured. "All right," he said, as evenly as he could. "How long have you thought this about me?"

"Some time," said Seri flatly. "And... there's something else too." He looked down, his voice dropping in intensity.

"What?" asked Weyrn, his own voice almost a whisper.

"Neithan was your dearest friend."

"Yes." Weyrn swallowed hard, wondering with dread what this was building to. "Is this about those humans you captured?"

"No, no, not that. It was me that suggested giving them up to human justice. It's... when he died, I realised it the moment he drew his last breath." Seri's voice hitched. "I looked at you, looking to see what you were doing... you weren't paying attention." At that, his voice hardened again and his head shot up. "You *weren't paying attention*," he repeated, almost savagely.

Weyrn felt as if the wind had been knocked out of him. "You're holding it against me that… you have a grudge about the way…" He got up and paced to and fro across the room, fisting a hand in his hair. "You thought I didn't care about what was happening? Is that it?" He could feel tears starting in his eyes and a sensation like a hand squeezing his throat. "What did you think was going through my head, Seri?"

"I have no idea!" Seri's voice started to ring loud, but he stifled it, looking towards the door. "But… I just didn't know." He buried his face in his good hand. "And I…"

"Assumed the worst?" Weyrn still felt winded.

"I didn't know what to think. It hurt." Seri took a sobbing breath and let it out again. "I expect that kind of thing from Derdhel. He… I'm used to him not caring. Good and bad, it just bounces off, but you… Neithan loved you with all his heart. I thought you were just as fond of him and then…"

Weyrn wasn't sure whether to be more angry or upset. He kept walking up and down, doing his best to steady his breathing. He couldn't shout, even if he wanted to. And he couldn't leave, even if he wanted to. This had to be fixed. "Seri," he said, keeping his voice as steady as he could. "Do you want to know what I was thinking about?"

"Yes."

"I was remembering. All the good times we had…" Weyrn's own breath caught and he forced the words out. "You're right. Neithan was very dear to me. I was remembering his life." The sob came out in a bitter chuckle. "And at the end I was lost in that." He looked back at Seri directly. "Did you really think it was because I *didn't care that he was dying*? What, did you think I…" He couldn't manage any more.

"I… I just didn't know what to think." Seri shrugged helplessly and winced. "I couldn't imagine that you wouldn't be upset, but… I don't know what's going through your mind or what influences you any more. And then when you didn't want to keep chasing the ones who'd killed him…"

"You know damn well why that was."

Seri scowled, looking down at the sling. "Yes, I know it was my fault."

"I'm not assigning blame. It's a fact that we couldn't carry on hunting them when you were injured and we were losing our allies."

Seri nodded unwillingly.

"And once it's better weather for travel and you've healed, a few of us can go and at least see what's happening."

Seri did look up at that. "I'd like to take part. I know they went into predominantly human territory, but I don't like to just sweep them under the rug and forget until something else happens."

Weyrn couldn't help frowning. "That isn't what I intend to do."

"Good."

"Listen, Seri… something as deep as this…" Weyrn started pacing again. "How far back does… and how *deep* does this *go*? That you really think that's the kind of person I've become?"

Seri sighed and shook his head. "A long time. I couldn't pinpoint it."

The silence stretched as Weyrn stared at Seri, but at last he had to say something. "Why haven't you said anything before?"

Seri shook his head, finally looking at the floor. "Because… I know I've not exactly given this impression, but I do tend to believe you know what you're doing. Just…"

"You don't agree with how I do it?"

"No. I don't."

"But…" Weyrn sighed. "I'll not say you've never brought it up because you certainly have."

Seri actually smiled at that. "Sometimes rather tactlessly, I know," he said softly.

Weyrn smiled too and sat down. "Did I do something on those occasions to make you think you were doing the wrong thing?"

"No, not really, but" – he shook his head a little – "I meant it: you're my Captain. The Spirits chose you to lead, not me, and they must have done it for a reason." Seri sighed. "So I try not to, but…"

"Not to what? Disagree? The Spirits may have chosen me to lead, but they gave you your own mind and it sounds like it would have saved a lot of heartache if you'd said some of this to me before."

Seri shrugged. "Would it have made a difference? Haven't you already been doing your best?"

That question had barbs on it and Weyrn didn't reply for a long moment. There did need to be some sort of response, though, and he said softly, "Yes, I have. But it would be good to know when something I do has been completely misunderstood."

Seri chuckled softly, resting his head on his hand.

"Are you all right?"

"Yes… just tired."

"If you want to rest…"

"I'd rather get this sorted out as best we can."

Weyrn sighed. "Well… all right. Let's see if we can tell what the problem actually is before we try to solve it. You don't agree with things I've been doing."

Seri was still resting his head on his hand. "No. Like the Valley-elves, and… that's a bad example." He sighed. "But only in hindsight. I admit it seemed a better idea to bring them after they saved our lives." He chuckled.

Weyrn also smiled. "But you didn't agree before that."

"No. I don't like the precedent it sets, telling them we need their help."

Weyrn frowned. "It's for Hurion's benefit just as much as ours."

"But what if that's not how he sees it?"

"It's how it is. He owed us a favour, I didn't go and beg for help."

Seri blinked, looking up. "I didn't know that."

"Well, I did."

Seri looked down again. "All right," he said softly.

Weyrn sighed and went over to put a hand on Seri's shoulder. "We… It'll be all right."

Seri smiled wanly back. "I do hope so."

***

It was the morning after their arrival home before Weyrn went to visit Hurion. Fortunately, the king didn't seem too annoyed about the delay, though he didn't get up to greet Weyrn as he arrived. He looked up from the letter he was reading and smiled a greeting, but no more.

"Good morning, Hurion," said Weyrn, going over to the desk.

"Welcome home." Hurion gestured him to a chair. "I hear one of your people was injured?"

Weyrn nodded. "Seri. Did Ekelid tell you what happened?"

"Not in detail."

Weyrn nodded. "Seri and Maelli were almost captured and Seri was injured in the fight."

Hurion smiled. "Yes, that level of detail. If you don't want to tell me more, though…"

Weyrn shook his head. "I don't think so. It's not important at the moment." He leaned forward, his elbows on the desk. Hurion looked at them irritably, but didn't say anything. "Alatani mentioned that the Valley-elves have also been having trouble."

Hurion nodded. "But, in turn, Ekelid said you'd driven them off."

"Or, at least, they left on their own. By the same token, they might come back one day."

Hurion nodded. "Nonetheless, I'm glad they're gone for the time being. Do you think it's likely they'll return?"

"I don't know."

Hurion frowned. "You don't know?"

Weyrn frowned back. "We didn't have a choice but to turn back," he said. "It would have been helpful if Ekelid could have stayed with us."

Hurion nodded a little. "I didn't want to assign him a wild goose chase."

"I plan to send scouts over the hills after the humans," said Weyrn, ignoring Hurion's choice of words. "But not quite yet due to Seri's injury."

Hurion nodded. "Well, good luck," he said. "I for my part am glad to hear that they're moving away from the valley."

Weyrn scowled, but just nodded, bade Hurion farewell and left.

"Short-sighted," he muttered. "Let's just hope it doesn't come back to bite."

CHAPTER NINE

One snowy evening, a few years after Neithan's death, Weyrn and Alatani were sharing the couch and a blanket, the last ones awake.

"Did I tell you that that village has adopted the wolf as their emblem?" asked Alatani sleepily, snuggling closer against Weyrn.

He kissed her hair. "No..."

"They seemed to have warmed up to them."

"That's good." He kissed her again and this time she tilted her head up so that he kissed her lips instead. For a moment the kiss lingered, then she drew back with a small smile, her dark eyes shining. "It's chilly out here. What say we go to bed?"

He grinned and they kissed again.

Just as they were about to get up, though, there was a hammering on the door. Weyrn groaned, letting his head fall back against the back of the couch. "Spirits above, who's *that*?"

"I'll go and see." Alatani slipped out from under their blanket, letting Weyrn pull it around himself as he pushed himself upright, trying to refocus his thoughts. She opened the door with a gust of cold, snowy air and an elf ducked in, barely stopping to kick the snow off his boots.

Weyrn got up, picking up the dagger he'd laid on a side table. Alatani had also slipped into stance.

The elf pulled back his hood to show a familiar face. Alatani gasped, but Weyrn frowned, trying to place where he'd seen this person.

"Esren?" said a voice from the corridor leading down to the bedrooms. Weyrn looked round to see Maelli standing there. Now that he heard the name, though, he did recognise the elf.

Then Esren turned to look at him fully and Weyrn also gasped and recoiled.

The other elf's cheek was horribly scarred. It looked like someone had held a hot piece of metal to it: the skin was pale and waxy and had contracted to pull up the corner of his mouth in a permanent half smile. The other half of his mouth was turned down and his eyes were wide as he looked from one to the next of the three Swordmasters, though his eyes lingered on Weyrn. He no longer looked frightened, just sad.

"Captain Weyrn?" he said tentatively.

Weyrn shook his head a little. "Come in, Esren. Sit down and warm up."

"Th-thank you." Esren hurried over to the fire and held out his hands to the flames with a sigh, his shoulders sagging.

"I'll" - Maelli's words were interrupted with a sudden yawn - "I'll put the kettle on."

"Thank you," said Esren again. "I tried to arrive in daylight, but I got lost. I... I'm sorry." He shot Weyrn a nervous, fleeting look, looking for a moment like the frightened boy Weyrn remembered.

Maelli stepped around Esren to swing the kettle over the fire. Esren moved away and went to perch on the couch, his shoulders hunched.

Weyrn sat opposite him. "It's been a long time," he said softly.

"Thirteen years," said Esren. "I remember it well." His hand went to the scar. "My clan gave me this in punishment for helping you then."

Weyrn felt sick. He had thought at the time that it might not be a good idea to leave Esren behind. Still, he swallowed hard and said, "Then what brings you here now? Won't you be punished again?"

"This time I was sent." Esren sighed. "They said that since I was your friend anyway, I might as well come."

Weyrn wondered if it was more that Esren got all the tasks that nobody else wanted, but he didn't say so. "It must be serious for them to have sent to us."

Alatani laid a hand on Weyrn's shoulder. "Shall I wake the others?"

Weyrn hesitated a moment, but then nodded. She kissed the top of his head, then hurried off. Maelli finished making tea and handed a cup to Esren, who hugged it to his chest.

"Are you all right?" Weyrn asked.

"Yes, just... just cold."

Weyrn nodded and, with a small sigh, picked up the blanket and draped it around Esren's shoulders. "How long did it take you to get here?"

"I came as fast as I could." Esren rubbed his eyes. "I did... did get delayed once."

Weyrn glanced round as he heard footsteps and saw Alatani returning with Derdhel.

"Seri and Celes are coming," she said, going to the chair beside Weyrn.

"Seregei's still asleep?"

"Yes."

"Good." Weyrn nodded a greeting to Seri as he arrived, pulling a cloak around his shoulders. The other elf looked a little startled at the sight of Esren, but leaned against the wall by the door to listen.

"What delayed you?" Weyrn asked Esren, mostly to make conversation while they waited for Celes.

"Well... that's part of why I came. I wasn't the only one, you see; Stone's Breath sent someone too. He mentioned he'd been here before. His name was Surian?"

"Surian?" blurted Derdhel. "Yes, we have met him."

"What happened to him?" asked Seri.

Esren sighed. "There's a human group coming into the area. I think they've been here before, but they vanished for a few years."

Weyrn heard Celes come in, but didn't look round. He just kept listening to Esren, trying to hide the fact that his heart was sinking. Seri and Maelli had gone after those humans to see what they were doing. They had seemed to be settling in their new lands, but perhaps something had changed.

"They're back now, though. They've killed two of my clan and hemmed Surian's in, that's why he was coming to you for help. They... caught up with us, though."

"They're coming towards Duamelti?"

"Yes, and burning as they go, as best they can in this snow." Esren rubbed his eyes and took a sip of tea. "There were more of them than us. Far more."

"When? When they caught up to you and Surian?" Out of the corner of his eye, Weyrn saw Maelli glance over at Seri.

"Yes." Esren took another sip of tea. Weyrn noticed his hands were shaking slightly.

"Are you still cold?"

"No, much warmer now." Esren forced a smile. "Thank you." He looked back at the mug in his hands, his smile vanishing. "It's just..." He hitched his shoulders, took a deep breath, then looked back at Weyrn. "They came on us out of nowhere," he said brusquely. "We were on the edge of a... I suppose a ravine. The ground was all snow and ice and I slipped into the ravine and hit my head." His hand went to a lump on the side of his head and Weyrn frowned, making a mental note to have Eleri talk to him if he was going to be staying long. "I was stunned, and the next thing I remember night had fallen. I was still in the ravine and the humans – and Surian – were gone." He looked down, hunching his shoulders again.

Weyrn bit his lip. "Where was this?" he asked.

"It took me about two days. It'll take them longer, but not by much. I was dazed for some time..."

"Do you know what happened to Surian? Have you seen any trace of him since then?"

Esren winced, rubbing his eyes with the back of his hand. "I... thought I heard screams. I didn't go and investigate; I didn't want to be next." He shifted, looking away.

Weyrn looked round. Seri had gone a little pale and the others also looked uncomfortable. Only Derdhel kept his eyes focussed on Esren, frowning slightly.

"They're coming, though." Esren's eyelids were drooping and his speech had slowed. Now that he had delivered his message, his weariness was catching up.

"Celes," said Weyrn, "Will you find Esren a bed?"

Esren looked up and opened his mouth to speak, but then nodded. "Thank you."

Once Celes had taken Esren to a spare room, they gathered together again in the common room. Seri hovered near the corridor, keeping an eye on Esren's door out of the corner of his eye.

"We won't have much time," said Weyrn, breaking the silence. "If they're heading for Duamelti they're either intending to take out the largest elven settlement in the area or they are actually targeting us."

"They do have a grudge," said Seri bitterly.

Weyrn nodded. "We need to find out what's happening."

"He mentioned they were burning as they came." Maelli's eyes strayed towards the door. "At least some of us should go and see if it's true."

Weyrn nodded. "Seri, Maelli, go back to bed and set off in the morning to check just over the border."

They nodded and Maelli headed for his room. Seri hesitated a moment, but then followed. "Tell us in the morning what else you decide," he said over his shoulder.

"I will." Weyrn turned back to the others. "Celes, where did you put Esren?"

"In the empty room between me and Seri."

"Good, so one of you will be able to hear any noise." Still, Weyrn couldn't help wondering if they should set a watch tonight. He didn't know Esren, after all, and last time they'd met the younger elf he had been part of a hostile group. He balked from the idea of setting a watch in their own home, but it couldn't really be helped and he sighed. "Someone should stay awake."

He heard Alatani sigh as well, but didn't do anything to draw attention to her.

"I wasn't asleep anyway," said Derdhel. "I'll take first watch."

"Thank you." Weyrn glanced at Alatani. "I'd like to see Seri and Maelli off – they'll be leaving at first light – and then someone needs to tell Hurion what's happening as soon as he's likely to be up. I can take last watch."

Celes and Alatani looked at one another and Celes held up a hand.

"Knife, cloth, stone?"

"All right." She tucked her hair behind her ears and held up a fist. "One, two, three… Knife cuts cloth."

Celes looked ruefully at his own flat palm, but nodded. "I'll take second watch then."

"All right," said Weyrn, getting up. "We'll talk in more detail in the morning. For now, everyone to bed." He smiled a little at Derdhel, who nodded and went to sit down.

Weyrn and Alatani went to their room, undressed and got into bed in silence, curling up together in one another's arms.

"How long do you think we have?" she asked at last.

"Right now? Not long. Before the humans arrive? I don't know… it could be as little as a day."

She sighed and kissed his jaw. "I suppose you should go straight to sleep, if you have to get up to keep watch."

He kissed her back. "We might not have much time…"

"You think not?" she asked between kisses.

"I don't know. If there are many of them and they're coming for us…"

"Let's make the most of it."

***

Weyrn went to see Hurion as soon as he could in the morning, once he had said goodbye to Seri and Maelli. Hopefully, they wouldn't find anything amiss. For now, he had to concentrate on Hurion.

He was surprised when he was shown into a small dining room where the family was having breakfast. The queen and young Kerin stared at him in shock while Caleb's eyes narrowed. Hurion got up.

"I hear you've something very urgent for me, Weyrn."

Weyrn nodded. "A messenger arrived late last night. He says there's a large group of hostile humans heading for the valley."

Hurion blinked, freezing for a moment. Behind him, his family looked nervously at one another. "Hostile?"

"We think it may be the same group."

Hurion nodded slowly, taking a deep breath. "They're heading for the valley, you say? They intend to cross the border?"

"We're not entirely sure, but they apparently had some purpose and were travelling in a straight line, though the messenger said they were burning as they came. Seri and Maelli have gone to investigate further."

"When will they be here?"

"Potentially within the next couple of days."

"Did your messenger say anything about their numbers, beyond that there were many of them?"

"Mostly that, but he said he only saw outriders and too many of them to count." Weyrn thought of the saying that a fleeing man counts every foe twice, but he still thought it must be a formidable group.

Hurion nodded again and looked back at his family. "I'm sorry, I have to go and deal with this."

"Can I come, father?" asked Caleb, scrambling up.

Hurion smiled and nodded, beckoning Caleb to follow. Weyrn nodded to the queen and younger prince and fell into step beside Hurion.

"What are the other Swordmasters doing?" asked Hurion as they walked.

"Alatani's at the Guardhouse, keeping an eye on our guest and looking after Seregei. Celes and Derdhel are going around the borders on the inside."

"I'll send some of my own men to do the same and increase the border guard. What direction?"

"North-east."

Hurion nodded and glanced at Caleb. "Go and send for the guard captains."

"Yes, father." The boy hurried off.

Hurion turned back to Weyrn. "When will your people return?"

"I'm not sure. Derdhel and Celes later today, Maelli and Seri probably tomorrow."

Hurion nodded as he went into a meeting room off the main entrance hall. "Well," he said with a sudden smile, "They say there's nothing like an outside threat to bring people together. I don't believe a Swordmaster has ever been invited to a Valley-elven military meeting before, let alone... You'll brief my commanders for me, won't you? After all, you have the information on the threat."

Weyrn stared at him for a moment, but then nodded. "Of course."

***

It took very little time to explain the situation, and a couple of Valley-elven runners accompanied him back to the Guardhouse to wait for the scouts to come in.

Alatani was listening to a young Mixed-blood who sat on one of the couches cradling a mug of tea. He didn't seem to notice Weyrn coming in, but Alatani glanced up and nodded a greeting before looking back at their latest guest, who had paused his narration to take a drink. A glance around showed Esren hovering in the doorway to the corridor and Seregei perched on the window seat, hugging his knees and watching the newcomer wide-eyed.

"Has your mother said you can listen?" Weyrn asked, sitting beside him and waving the Valley-elves to the other couch.

Seregei nodded. "He says he was with a group that was travelling and some humans attacked him." He looked up, looking worried and upset. "He says he doesn't know what happened to the others."

Weyrn put an arm around his shoulders and turned to continue listening to Alatani and the Mixed-blood, who had now stopped talking and was staring at the floor, shaking his head helplessly.

"I came to you," he said softly. "Please… I don't know what to do now." His voice caught on the words.

"Can you point out on a map where they were and their direction?" asked Alatani.

"I think so? I know on the ground."

Seregei jumped up and went to fetch a map of Duamelti and its environs from a cupboard. Weyrn couldn't help a smile, but didn't say anything. Alatani carefully unrolled the map on a table in front of the elf and pointed out the main landmarks; judging by his frown, he was having trouble interpreting it for himself.

"In that case… They were about here," he said at last. "Very close to the hills."

Alatani's shoulders tensed and Weyrn craned his neck to look, but he couldn't see where the elf was pointing.

"That is close," said Alatani in measured tones. "And they were moving?"

"Not as fast as I ran, but yes. I didn't stop to see which way once I knew they weren't following close behind me."

Alatani looked up at Weyrn. "They're approaching the hills behind the Guardhouse: the wooded pass."

Far closer than they'd thought. Weyrn just cut off a swearword, remembering that Seregei was still hovering by the map cupboard. The boy was old enough to realise the import of his mother's words, though, and was looking between them, biting his lip. "Are we going to fight them?"

"*You* aren't," said Weyrn firmly. Seregei opened his mouth to argue, but then fell silent again. Weyrn turned back to Alatani. "I'll send for the scouts," he said. "We'll see what they're doing." He glanced at the runners, one of whom stood up. "They've gone around the border in both directions," said Weyrn. "You should both go. If you can't find them on the road or near it, start spreading word that elves who can't fight should move deeper into the valley and those that can should start gathering here, and pass word along to Seri, Maelli, Derdhel and Celes that they should return as well. If there's someone you can send without breaking that off, send word to Hurion too."

"Yes sir," said the runner who had risen to his feet. He glanced at the other and they quickly decided who would go which way, then they left.

"Eleri's already on his way," Alatani told him, looking round.

"We may need him," muttered Weyrn. "Once more people start arriving I'll see what our resources are and start preparing for a battle." He wiped his palms on his tunic. Open battle wasn't something the Swordmasters knew very well. At least he had the help of the Duamelti army on this one.

"What should I do?" asked Seregei.

Weyrn looked at him with a sigh as Alatani deliberately turned her attention back to the Mixed-blood visitor, who was starting to tremble again.

"For now, keep out of the way," he said, wondering if there was anything he would feel happy telling Seregei to do.

If these humans were coming for the Swordmasters... He shuddered before he could stop himself, remembering Seri's shoulder even without the thought of Neithan's shattered ribs. And then there was Seregei. What might they do to a child?

But Seregei was still waiting for a real answer. Was he old enough to run messages before the danger arrived?

"I'm brave," said Seregei in his still-high little voice. "And I can fight."

"All right," said Weyrn, ignoring the way Alatani turned to stare at him. "Go and run down to the city and get a message to Lord Hurion. You've been listening to everything that's going on?"

Seregei nodded, grinning broadly.

"All right, off you go."

Seregei dashed off and Weyrn watched him go with a sigh. "Come straight back!" he called after him.

Seri had been out in the hills for several hours without seeing anything until he finally crested a hill and was able to see out over the landscape above the trees. Then he froze as he saw a plume of smoke against the lowering clouds. It was lit from below by flickering flames. It only took a moment for him to get his bearings and realise that that had been a settlement. Only a cluster of a dozen houses, but he knew there had been Mixed-blood elves living there, even with a couple of human families. He swallowed hard, then turned on his heel and hurried back towards the valley, making his way along the border. There was a pass that he could use to get a better look and he knew there were a few other settlements close enough that he could pass through and warn them.

But when he reached the first one, they were already preparing to evacuate. The village leader left the cart he was loading and hurried forward to meet him.

"You already know?" asked Seri, clasping his hand.

"Yes, a messenger came though. A Valley-elf, but sent by Captain Weyrn."

Seri couldn't help a frown, but he hid it as quickly as he could.

"He said that Captain Weyrn was summoning all who could fight back to the Guardhouse, and that all the Swordmaster scouts should also return there."

Seri nodded, but his eyes strayed back up towards the hills. While Weyrn was gathering his forces and consulting with the Valley-elves, homes were burning. Someone needed to do something and it fell to him. "Are you going there yourself?"

"As soon as my people are on the road deeper into the valley."

"Let him know that the humans are burning villages out in the forest and that I'm going to do my best to warn and intercept. If Swordmaster Maelli comes here, send him after me."

The other elf blinked, but nodded. "I will, sir."

"Thank you." Seri looked around the village again, at the hurrying, frightened elves, loading what belongings they couldn't leave into barrows, carts and packs, marshalling children, doing what they could to secure what had been left behind. He sighed. "Good luck. I hope none of this is necessary."

The elf smiled and clasped his hand again. "It's just in case. I'm sure that with you to lead us we can turn these humans back at the hilltops." Still, his face was pale and his smile strained. "Bladedancer's ghost still watches the borders."

Seri nodded, wished him luck again and left.

He cut as straight a line as he could towards the pass, going uphill almost on his hands as the slope became steeper. Thankfully, there was no ice under the trees. He thought he had enough distance in between him and them that he didn't have to worry about noise, but he was still aware of the crunching and cracking of leaves and sticks under his feet, the occasional rustling slide as he dislodged a fallen branch or stone and it slid down the hill. He didn't look over his shoulder or slow down; he didn't dare.

At last, though, the slope flattened out as he began to approach the path that led through the pass. He paused a moment to catch his breath and frowned, staring between the trees, but he couldn't see anything on the path and breathed a small sigh of relief. Not too late.

Still, he was rapidly realising that it hadn't been wise to come up here alone. He had asked for Maelli to be sent after him, but that relied on that village leader either encountering him or passing the message on another way and Seri couldn't help the fleeting worry that Weyrn would countermand it.

He dismissed the suspicion as unfair. Weyrn had given him no reason to think he might be abandoned. With that thought, he hitched his cloak up on his shoulders and started more carefully down the hill.

Weyrn listened in horror as one of the elves who had just arrived at the Guardhouse told him about the approaching humans.

"And Swordmaster Seri's gone to intercept them? Alone?" he echoed, just to be sure he'd heard correctly.

The elf nodded. "He said to let you know and to send Swordmaster Maelli after him."

Weyrn frowned and looked around. He would do better than that. He would have to, if they were really that close.

He was about to start picking out some warriors to follow him up towards the pass when he heard hoofbeats on the path from the road. He turned in time to see a steaming horse trot out from between the trees, ridden by a Valley-elf. Weyrn went forward to meet him.

"Captain," said the elf as he dismounted. He sketched a bow in Weyrn's direction, then said, "Lord Hurion is gathering his forces in readiness to support you. Advance parties should begin arriving soon. Do we have any better idea of the size of the attacking force?"

"Not really," Weyrn admitted. "Scouts are still coming in. They're closer than we thought, though. I'm about to lead a force to meet them."

The messenger nodded. "I'll take that back," he said and began to mount again. "Oh," he added as he swung into the saddle. "Your son is back at the palace. Lord Hurion thought it would be safer for him to stay away from the battle."

Weyrn felt a flash of irritation, but then looked away; he had to admit that that was reasonable. He just didn't appreciate having his decision overridden.

Still, Seregei would be safer down there and he looked up again. "Thanks," he said.

"Will you be here when I return?" asked the messenger.

"Probably not." Weyrn thought uneasily of Seri out on his own. "There will be a Swordmaster here, though."

The messenger nodded, then turned and rode off. Weyrn turned away and met Alatani's eye for a moment.

"I need you to stay here," he said softly.

She nodded, though didn't look any happier than he was. "I'm sure he'll be fine." She smiled a little. "And we'll see him soon."

"Seregei or Seri?" Weyrn asked, forcing a small smile.

"Both."

Weyrn nodded, though her words had given voice to the worry that he'd forced to the back of his mind. He once again tried to put it aside.

It was inescapable that something could happen. He and Alatani had already discussed who would care for Seregei should they both be killed, and he knew that Maelli had had a premonition about the coming battle and had written down his final wishes, just in case. Still, there was no time for worry now. He just looked around at the gathered elves, squeezed Alatani's hand for a moment and turned away; he couldn't give her a proper farewell in front of them. He already worried that he'd showed his fear too clearly.

Still, he couldn't help a look back as he and a handful of others started off towards the road. She waved at him and he waved back, calling, "Get the others ready and send runners if there's anything I need to know!"

"I will!" she called back.

Seri realised as soon as he had gone down the hill a way and saw the human force that he was out of his depth. The group heading up the road consisted of about a dozen and he could see flashes of movement beyond them, though the bare trees, indicating that they weren't alone. Too much for one elf. He needed help. He needed to run back to the Guardhouse. He needed to warn them…

For a moment he felt a flash of rebellious pride as he thought again of their new alliance, but he crushed it. Weyrn knew what he was doing. If they needed that extra strength now, they needed it and such qualms would get people killed. He needed to fight another day.

Decided, he pulled his hood up to hide his gold-blond hair, then turned and started back up the hill, going as quickly and quietly as he could. It wasn't easy, off the road; now he had to avoid the litter of leaves and branches on the ground rather than running straight over them as he had before. He was aware that the humans were actually catching up as they walked along the road with no apparent caution at all.

That fact made him pause. If he could teach them caution, they would slow down. The elves would have that much more time to prepare.

He had his bow and, as he crept along, he took it and strung it. He'd need a good place to shoot from and he chose a rocky outcrop overlooking the path. It would hopefully take a little while for them to look for him up there and he darted round the far side to scramble up, slinging his bow on his quiver. Then he just had to wait for them to come into sight.

Indeed, from here he could see that they weren't watching the woods. He noticed one carrying a torch and saw red for a moment, reaching for an arrow as that one turned and said something to one of his companions with a laugh. For a moment he aimed at that human, but then thought of flame and dead leaves. They weren't soaked enough for safety. Instead, he sighted on the one who was laughing at the comment.

The human dropped with a cry, an arrow standing in his chest. At once, the others froze, looking around, talking wildly as they looked for the archer. Seri dropped on one knee and ducked out of sight.

The talking and shouting continued and he peered over the edge to look down at them. They were now milling around, some fighting to be in the middle of the group, others looking around for him. A leader was trying to instil some kind of order. None of them looked up.

Seri couldn't use his longbow without standing, so he got up and loosed another arrow at the leader. If he could stop any order…

His shot had been too hasty. As he dropped back down out of sight, he could see that he had only winged the man. Still, he could hear him yelling in pain and peered out again to see what was happening.

The man was clutching at his arm. The other humans crowded around him. They weren't keeping watch beyond nervous glances over their shoulders. Seri decided it was time to go. He carefully crept down the rock and started on his way back up the hill. He'd probably bought himself enough time.

Snow was beginning to fall and he sped up as much as he could. Under the trees it might not stick enough to show tracks but he didn't want to take the risk.

Then he saw movement up ahead. He glanced back at the humans, who were finally beginning to advance again, though much more warily. Then he looked up and narrowed his eyes, trying to make out who was approaching.

To his relief, he made out that they were elves, Weyrn in the lead. They were advancing cautiously and he hurried up to meet them as quietly as he could manage.

"Weyrn!" he called, keeping his voice to a whisper.

Weyrn looked round and waved a greeting, gesturing to the others to stop as he went over to greet Seri.

"You're all right?" he asked.

"Outnumbered; there's a large force approaching up the hill."

Weyrn nodded and gestured the others to hide as best they could. He and Seri ducked behind a holly bush.

"What are you doing?" Weyrn whispered. "We were hardly ready; I'm still gathering help."

Seri scowled, but looked away. Weyrn put a hand on his shoulder and shook it gently.

"Seri, I gathered a few to come and help you, but only a few. I warn you of that now. What are we facing?"

With a sinking feeling, Seri once more glanced at the group Weyrn had brought. They were still outnumbered, but he nodded. "There are a dozen or so in the lead. I killed one and wounded another, but there are more behind them. They were coming quickly and without much caution, but they started keeping better watch after I shot at them."

Weyrn nodded and gestured to his men again. They started stringing bows. Seri pulled another arrow from his quiver.

"Seri, before this starts… If Alatani and I should both die we want Seregei raised in the Guardhouse."

Seri blinked. "What?"

Weyrn put a hand on his shoulder again. "Promise me."

Seri swallowed hard, but nodded. "Of course. And I'll do my best to raise him well."

Weyrn smiled. "Thank you."

Weyrn looked away from Seri and took a deep breath, then nocked an arrow to his own bow, waiting. He could see the approaching humans through the leaves of the bush. They were coming slowly. Watching. Talking softly amongst themselves. He took another deep breath and let it out again, wondering if it was too late to move some of his men – led by Seri, perhaps – further down the road. He suspected it was; the humans were keeping watch now.

Another deep breath, then he stood with a shout and loosed the first arrow.

Mayhem broke loose at once. His elves were shooting at the humans, keeping hidden as best they could. Some humans turned to run. Others fell, screaming in pain. The leader Seri had wounded fell dead, clutching at a second arrow in his throat.

But there were others behind them. Weyrn could see them fanning out, advancing as fast as they could. Some of them had bows.

"Archers!" shouted Weyrn even as one of the humans yelled something in his own language.

But as the elves turned to meet the new threat, the survivors from the original group were rallying. Bolstered by their reinforcements, they drew swords and dashed forward, spreading out to attack as many elves as they could. Weyrn dropped his bow against the bush and drew his sword. A ring of metal behind him was Seri doing the same. He glanced round, but Seri wasn't looking at him and after a moment he lunged forward and Weyrn lost sight of him.

He heard someone running up to the bush on heavy feet and dodged round it himself. A human stopped short, slipping on the increasingly-snowy ground, and Weyrn struck him down before he could raise his sword. Another shout in the human language made him look up and he saw several humans coming towards him, swords at the ready.

He parried a blow, twisting as he glimpsed another man slipping behind him. A flash of pain as a sword bit his leg. He gasped, barely dodging a stab.

"Seri!" he shouted, seeing the other elf a little way off. Seri didn't seem to hear.

Weyrn parried another stab, twisting his blade to wound his opponent. The man stumbled back, but one of the others stepped in to take his place. Weyrn barely pulled away in time to avoid a blow aimed at his arm.

He glimpsed a rock out of the corner of his eye and turned to put his back to it. At least they couldn't surround him now. But there were still two unwounded and he only had one sword. They split and attacked him from each side.

"Seri!" he shouted again as he dodged and stabbed up. Still nothing. The other elves were occupied too. They were still outnumbered.

He was tiring, his arm aching as he kept having to twist back and forth. He had taken more wounds to his side and legs. He could feel the blood running down.

But then one of his parries went through his opponent's defences. The man gasped and fell. Weyrn hissed in relief and pulled his blade free.

He felt a blow on his back. It drove the wind from his lungs. The strength left his arm and he dropped his sword, trying to draw breath.

Then the pain hit. His knees buckled and he dropped to the ground, his sight fading. He couldn't breathe...

He had never said his goodbyes.

At least Alatani would live.

But Seregei was going to grow up without a father.

Seri had heard Weyrn shouting his name, but he didn't look round at first, occupied with his own fight.

When he did, he cried out, his vision seeming to tunnel as he saw a human pulling a sword out of Weyrn's back. Weyrn dropped to the ground and didn't move.

Seri started to run as the human raised his sword again to deliver a final blow. He bowled another human out of his way, yelling at the one standing over Weyrn. He looked up, but then Seri was on him, stabbing him to the hilt. He pulled free and stood over Weyrn, determined that if he were still alive nobody would have the chance to deliver a coup de grace.

They seemed to be dispersing, though, and Seri looked around, counting heads as quickly as he could. Apart from Weyrn, one elf and six humans lay unmoving on the snowy ground. One of the other elves was already checking the second casualty and Seri crouched down to check on Weyrn.

He could tell almost at once that it was too late. Weyrn's silvery eyes were wide and blank and his cheek already seemed cool to the touch, but Seri searched at his throat for a pulse anyway, biting his lip to try to keep the tears back. Nothing. He was dead.

For a moment Seri crouched beside him, his head bowed, struggling with a lingering feeling of guilt. If he hadn't been so proud as to run off on his own... if he had obeyed Weyrn's orders and returned with news of what he'd seen... He knew such thoughts weren't helpful, but he couldn't stop them. His hand shaking, he reached out to close Weyrn's eyes.

"Captain Seri?" one of the other elves had correctly divined the meaning of his stillness and silence.

Seri shook his head a little to rouse himself and got up. "Yes," he said aloud, more to himself than the other elf. "Captain Weyrn is dead."

There was a moment's shocked silence, then Seri shook his head again and looked up. The humans had moved on, having cut through what resistance the elves had managed to raise. He guessed that most of the group had actually gone around the battle.

That meant that they were now heading for Duamelti, which was likely still unprepared.

"We need to go after them," he said, looking round again. "Who's the fastest runner?" One elf raised his hand and Seri nodded at him. "Go on ahead and warn those at the Guardhouse." The elf nodded and darted off. Seri looked around at the others. "We'll follow." He took a deep breath and said, "Leave the dead. We'll come back for them."

That got a couple of shocked gasps. One elf looked worriedly past Seri at Weyrn, but he just said again, "Leave the dead," and started up the hill after their advance messenger.

Alatani continued to organise the elven militias as they arrived. They were flooding in from all directions in dribs and drabs, but she managed to group them together and send them off to patrol and guard the borders. Eleri had also come up with a group of Valley-elves and had taken shelter in the cellar of the Guardhouse with medical supplies.

At least the elves Seri had sent had given them some idea of the direction the humans were coming from.

"Swordmaster Alatani!" a voice called from behind her and she looked round to see a Valley-elf dismounting from his horse. He saluted quickly. "Is Captain Weyrn here?"

She shook her head. "He led a small party up over the border. We got a message that the humans were coming from that direction and drawing close. He's not sent word back yet."

The Valley-elf nodded. "I'm leading a group of thirty light horse. My men are waiting on the road. I suppose you're the most senior here?"

Alatani nodded, racking her brain for somewhere that cavalry would be useful.

The Valley-elf apparently guessed the problem, for he added, "We can also fight on foot."

Alatani nodded. "You know what the slopes up there are like," she explained.

"I can find a way to block their path further up the hill," he said. "We'll need to go by road, but we can move fast."

She nodded. "That seems the best idea. If we can stop them getting into the valley, I'll be glad."

"Me too," he said, looking up at the hills. "Are those your orders, then? My lord has told us that we're to follow you in this."

She nodded. "Do that. I'm sending groups out on foot in all directions along the border, just in case they try to flank us, and to defend villages."

"Alatani!" another voice called and she glanced round to wave a greeting to Maelli as he ran up. The Valley-elf, meanwhile, saluted them both and left.

"What's happening?" asked Maelli. "I met a group of refugees who told me that Seri had said I should follow him over the border as soon as I could."

Alatani winced. "He sent a message back here saying that they're closing faster than we thought."

"Swordmasters!" a voice called and an elf pushed forward. "Look!"

They both turned to look up and Alatani swallowed hard, her heart sinking, as she saw torches glimmering on the hilltop. She was suddenly very aware of the many eyes on her.

"You've been giving instructions so far," said Maelli softly in her ear. "You know the situation better than I do."

She nodded. "Are there any signs that they might be crossing anywhere else?" she asked quickly.

He shook his head. "Not that I saw."

"And the villages on those hillsides have been evacuated?"

"Yes." There were other confirming nods from around the group, a few elves shooting nervous, unhappy looks back towards their abandoned homes.

"Right." Alatani looked up at the torches again. They were a surreal sight, flickering among the desultory flurries of snow. She sighed and watched her breath mist, then turned to the other elves, splitting them into groups by pointing. As she did that, she said, "If you meet a group of humans, try to get around them and funnel them inwards, towards us here. If they're able to spread out they'll do much more damage, but if they're grouped we can use cavalry. Shoot if you can. Once you're around them, harry them from the sides and rear if you can without being flanked yourselves."

As soon as she had divided them up, she began pointing out where they should go so that they could flank the approaching torches. The groups left as soon as they had their orders. She was just working out where to send the last group, still looking up at the hill, when she heard someone arrive behind her and glanced round to see another Valley-elf.

"I'll talk to him," said Maelli.

"Thanks." Alatani looked up again, but then suddenly saw a curl of smoke rising from the trees. She gasped. It was much lower down the slope than she'd expected. Much closer to the Guardhouse. The trees had hidden them from view.

"Stay here," she said. "They're coming here. Maelli!" she turned.

"I see it," said Maelli, then added to the Valley-elf. "We'll need you here."

It didn't take them long to all get organised: Valley-elves and Mixed-bloods spread in mingled clumps through the trees around the Guardhouse,

Alatani and Maelli together with a handful of brave volunteers in the middle of the clearing. Alatani's best idea was to draw them out so that the elves in the forest could ambush them. She took a deep breath and let it out again, grateful that Seregei was safely back in the city.

She could glimpse the torches twinkling between the trees and took another breath. Maelli glanced at her and she nodded to him, though she couldn't help wondering where in all of this the other Swordmasters were.

Then, with a shout, the humans poured into the clear space around the Guardhouse. Alatani screamed back in challenge, drawing her sword. None of them was going to so much as touch her home.

Beside her, Maelli locked swords with a human. They seemed to be ignoring her and she swung round to guard Maelli's back, cutting down one who tried to stab him. That seemed to draw their attention.

As she dodged a blow, she heard Maelli kill the one he'd been fighting. She parried, slipping her sword past her opponent's guard, and he fell. They were being beaten back, though.

"Valley-elves?" panted Maelli, catching a blow aimed at Alatani's head. She didn't have time to answer before there was a sudden, human, cry of alarm from one side.

"To the Swordmasters!" yelled a voice. "Lord Hurion to the Swordmasters!"

"There they are," said Alatani with a grin, stopping another blow aimed at her chest. At the same time she side-stepped and the attacking human ran onto the point of her sword.

But then the blade jammed. She ducked down as she tried to pull it free, shouting to Maelli. He glanced round and stepped to defend her.

She felt like there was a target on her back as she pulled on the hilt of her sword. Sweat made her palms slippery.

A crash of blade on blade was horribly close, but finally the sword slid free. She swung it up in a single movement, narrowly missing Maelli but deflecting a blow aimed at his face.

There were more shouts from the other side of the clearing as more elves attacked, but Alatani couldn't see what was happening over there through the confusion of moving bodies, flashing blades and blood. She saw some humans moving round towards the front door, though, and gritted her teeth. Not on her watch. Even though Eleri was safely hidden in the cellar, she was not letting them near her home. She broke free with a shout of "Front door!" to Maelli and dashed towards them.

Her determination was increased as she saw one of them raise a torch towards the eaves at the side of the Guardhouse.

She caught up with them in a few strides and cut that one down before he'd even realised she was there.

They turned and two went for her at once. She barely parried one blow, dodging just enough to reduce a second to a shallow gash across her shoulder blade.

"Alatani!" Maelli shouted behind her as she twisted again. Out of the corner of her eye, she saw him run over and attack one of the humans while she parried a blow from a second. This time, though, she couldn't disengage. The blades locked. His sword was shorter. If she stepped back, he could swing before she could.

He realised his advantage at the same time and shouted to one of the others, who dashed in with a dagger, aimed for Alatani's side. Maelli killed that one. Alatani glanced up again.

Too late. The human took a step back. Alatani stumbled as he disengaged. His sword flashed down and deep into her thigh.

She screamed as her leg buckled. She barely saw Maelli kill that human. Only realised in a daze that he was the last, that the other defenders were beating back the ones that were left, back into the trees, up the hill. She clutched at her leg. Her sight was dimming. She could feel blood pumping between her fingers. No matter how hard she tried, it wouldn't stop.

Maelli just glanced around long enough to make sure everything was under control before he dropped on his knees beside Alatani. Bright-red blood was spurting from under her hands, soaking her trousers and the grass underneath her. She was shaking.

"Get Eleri!" he shouted as he heard someone approach. "He's inside!"

"Maelli," whispered Alatani.

"It's all right, you're going to be fine," he said, stroking her hair.

"I'm not…" She sobbed softly. "Listen, I didn't write anything… tell Weyrn…" Her voice broke and he stroked her hair again, trying to soothe her.

"I'll tell him," he promised.

"I barely got to be a mother," she said faintly. "And I never said goodbye… I never told him I loved him one last time… Oh, Spirits… Look after him? Look after…"

"We'll help Weyrn look after Seregei."

She didn't seem to hear. She was still bleeding, but she'd lost consciousness.

Maelli swallowed hard, but looked round again. No sign of Eleri, but the battle was dying down, moving off towards the hills again.

"Maelli!" a voice called. Celes. Better late than never.

"I'm waiting for Eleri," Maelli said quickly as he saw the younger elf running towards him as best he could across the bloody, body-strewn clearing. "Help drive them off!"

Celes nodded and swerved towards the battle that was still raging in the forest. Maelli looked back at Alatani. Still bleeding. Her heart was still beating. But the pulses of blood were weaker now. He swallowed again. Where was Eleri?

Then it suddenly struck him. Of course, he was hidden in the cellar. Where no intruder would find him. It was the traditional place for a Swordmaster healer to go...

And now he would be too late. Even as Maelli knelt there, trying to stop the bleeding, it faltered and stopped on its own. He knew that Alatani's heart had stopped driving it out of the gash in her thigh. She was dead.

For a moment he was still, silently commending her spirit to the air and the earth and the trees. She was one of many dead today, but he knew that he would never be as smitten by those deaths as he was by hers.

There was no time to mourn, though. He got up with a sigh, looking down at his blood-covered hands, just in time for Eleri to dash around the corner of the building.

Eleri understood at once what had happened. His shoulders slumped. "Too late," he muttered.

"Not for everyone," said Maelli, trying to put as much force as he could behind the words. "There are others here who need your help." Work was better than idleness at a moment like this. He did his best to wipe his hands on the snowy grass, but it was no good. In the end, he took a moment to compose Alatani's body, then took his sword and went to join those who were still fighting. After all, their home wasn't safe yet.

He had hardly gone any distance before an exhausted-looking elf came trotting up. He looked at Maelli, panting, and his eyes lit up as he saw the badge on his sleeve.

"S-Swordmaster," he gasped. "I've a message... from Captain Seri."

"From..." Maelli felt like he'd been kicked as the full import of the title hit him. "Captain Weyrn is dead?"

The elf nodded. "The other part... you know... I had to... go around them." He reeled and Maelli caught him, helping him to lean on a tree.

"Yes, there's been battle here too. I'm on my way to help continue it."

The elf nodded. "Captain Seri and... the others are... coming."

"All right. I'll meet them. Go to the Guardhouse and rest."

The elf nodded, rubbing his eyes with the back of one hand, and set off down the hill at a stumble.

Maelli couldn't move for a moment. He just stood alone in the forest, barely even noticing the distant sound of battle or the chill of the wind or the sticky feeling of the blood on his hands and sleeves. Weyrn and Alatani, both dead in one sweep. He'd not seen anything of Derdhel since they had set out to scout. For all he knew, he too had fallen.

For the first time in his adult life, Maelli felt lost.

Night was falling by the time Seri thought the battle was over. It might not be quite safe for any of the elves to return to their homes – not until warriors had been back to check if any humans were hiding in the villages – but the fighting had stopped. They'd hunted the humans for hours across the hills, but they'd never penetrated deeper into the valley than the Guardhouse.

And now Seri could finally rest.

He didn't know where the others were or how many of them were still alive. His messenger hadn't returned with word from the Guardhouse and the fleeting bits of news he'd heard from elves who had fought there had been confused.

They all agreed on one thing, though: at least one Swordmaster was dead there too.

He thought with a pang of Maelli as he finally let himself slump onto a rock, barely noticing the wet cold of the snow as he sat on it. He knew there were more constructive things he could do, especially if he was worried about his friends, but he felt drained, exhausted to the marrow.

He took a breath and let it out again, holding back the tears with an effort of will. He knew they were more from exhaustion than grief. Even though he knew that there were at least two Swordmasters dead, he still felt numb, not quite accepting that. Some part of his mind still expected that when he got back to the Guardhouse Weyrn would be there and they could argue about the role of the Valley-elves or... something normal.

But Weyrn was dead. And whatever else that meant, it meant that Seri was now Swordmaster Captain. He couldn't sit and indulge his shock and grief any more than Weyrn should have indulged the fact that he was a husband and father as well as a Swordmaster. He had to get up and do something.

He took another deep breath and sighed, letting his hands drop into his lap as he braced himself to stand. There was a lot to do, after all. The immediate battle was over, but that didn't mean there wasn't still danger. And he did need to establish contact with the others, speak to the Valley-elves that had helped them, make sure of what had happened to the humans and start dealing with the dead on both sides.

Including sending someone to collect Weyrn's body.

He swallowed. He couldn't keep sitting here, but when he tried to stand his knees felt like they would buckle.

"Captain?" a voice asked from behind him and he got up, turning. As he did so, he stumbled and fell.

The other elf caught him. "Are you all right? Are you hurt?"

"No, no." Seri found his feet, cursing himself. "Just tired." He looked up and gritted his teeth in shame; the elf who had caught him was Ekelid.

"I heard about Captain Weyrn. I'm sorry."

Seri nodded, looking away for a moment. "Excuse me, I need to make arrangements to have his body brought back. Him and another who died with him."

"I can do that, if you need to rest."

Seri looked sharply at him, but there was no mockery in his expression. That was something, at least. "No. It's my duty."

Ekelid nodded. "I'm already seeing to my men, and when we find Mixed-bloods dead we've laid them out too. I assume you have your own customs, though."

Seri nodded. "I need to contact their clans and make sure they're properly taken care of. If you could keep doing that, though…" He paused. He didn't want to have to ask this, but the alternative was to leave his own people's dead lying while the Valley-elves were cared for. "I would… appreciate it."

Ekelid nodded. "I hope you'll do the same for any Valley-elves you find."

"We will." Seri swallowed again, concentrating on the next task. He knew there were others already going about finding and laying out the dead and taking the wounded to healers. "Have you heard any news of the other Swordmasters?"

Ekelid nodded. "Some of my men fought at the Guardhouse. Swordmaster Alatani died there and Swordmaster Maelli came to join the battle as it moved back up the hill."

Seri sighed, looking at the floor. Suddenly he heard Weyrn's words about Seregei as clearly as if the other elf were standing beside him. It fell to him to raise their son now.

And that meant that his first duty was to tell him that his parents were dead.

Later. Later. For now he had to deal with the immediate aftermath of the battle. Seregei was safe for the time being. He could wait where he was a little longer.

Again, Seri felt a wave of exhaustion wash over him. For a moment he wondered how it was that Ekelid could look so tireless; hadn't he fought? He crushed the thought as best he could; it wasn't fair.

"Seri?" said Ekelid.

Seri shook his head again. "I'm sorry. I'm all right. Just…"

"You're sure you're not hurt?"

"I'm fine. I need something to do. Have we really driven them all away, or are there any pockets still holding out?"

"You're not going to fight in this state."

"I need something to do." Seri looked away.

Ekelid laid a hand on his shoulder. "I will not let you fight when you can barely stand."

"You won't *let* me?" Seri whirled to face him, almost nose to nose.

Ekelid stood his ground. "I know you're Captain now and that makes you the equal of my king, but I will not let you harm yourself and put others in danger again because you think you need to prove yourself somehow."

Seri blinked. "What?"

"Isn't that why you went forward alone in the first place? I did hear that much about why a sortie went out before our forces were prepared."

The guilt that Seri had managed to suppress came rushing back. It was true that he'd gone forward alone and put himself in danger. It was true that Weyrn had come to rescue him, before they were ready.

Still, he couldn't let Ekelid see that his words had bitten so deep. He shook his head again. He wasn't cutting a very fine figure as Captain.

The thought shook him a little and he sighed deeply. "I'm sorry," he said. "It's been a long day and a difficult one. I… didn't mean to shout at you."

Ekelid paused before answering, but then said, "I understand. Would you like to go back to the Guardhouse and see the situation there?"

"I should finish things here, but thank you."

At that, Ekelid nodded and left. Seri sighed again and closed his eyes, trying to pull himself together. He had to make sure all was well here, then he would go back.

And see how many of his friends were still alive.

***

It was fully dark by the time Seri arrived back at the Guardhouse, but he could see a light in the common room. He opened the door and went in with a sigh, glad to be able to shut out the night.

"Seri!" He looked up to see Maelli just starting out of his chair. Derdhel was crouching by the fire, warming one hand while the other poked out of a sling, wrapped in bandage.

"You two are all right," sighed Seri, going to meet Maelli. He hugged him quickly, then turned to Derdhel. "What happened to your hand?"

"Nothing much: a cut to my arm and then I wrenched the wrist trying to spare it. It'll heal." Derdhel got up. Though his words had been dismissive, he looked ashen and tired. Maelli looked worse and Seri hugged him again.

"Are you all right?" he asked softly.

"Yes." Maelli rested his forehead on Seri's shoulder. "Weyrn and Alatani, though…"

"I know. Where's Seregei?"

"Still down at the palace. The queen said she'd find him a room for the night, and longer if we needed him to stay there."

"And… Celes?" Seri almost dreaded to ask the question.

"He's fine. He's just making sure that those without homes for the night are sheltered."

Seri winced; he should have been doing that job. Normally, he would have been doing that job. Still, he was glad to hear that Celes was also alive and safe. "Where are... where are Weyrn and Alatani?"

Maelli glared Derdhel into silence before the other elf could speak, then said, "They're laid out in the cellar. We can bury them tomorrow." He looked towards the window, his eyes wide and shoulders hunched.

"Maelli?"

"I'm all right. I just... I don't really know what to do." He laughed awkwardly.

Seri shook his head a little, stepping back. "The same as we've always done, I suppose."

"I never thought..." Maelli went over to the window. "I never thought something like this could happen."

"That we'd be attacked on our own ground?"

"Yes, and with such consequences."

"We lived out the day," said Derdhel quietly. "No, don't try to remind me that some didn't; I'm aware of that. But we lived and so did many others. It's no use thinking of what could have been or should have been or we wished had been."

Maelli sighed and Seri kept watching him. "I know, but that doesn't mean I can take it in stride."

Derdhel frowned. "Don't think I don't see the price we had to pay, but it is paid and we cannot take it back. And would you give the lives they saved to have them?"

"Of course not," said Seri. Who knew how many might have been killed were it not for Weyrn delaying the attack and Alatani putting herself in danger to lure the humans into their arms?

Maelli, however, hadn't spoken. He stood and stared out of the window for a while in silence, then suddenly said, "Alatani's last words were of Seregei and they're still echoing in my mind."

Seri blinked. "You were with her?"

"Yes. I stayed at the Guardhouse despite you asking me to join you. I was with her when she fought and died." Maelli looked at his hands. "I think I still have her blood around my nails. I couldn't get my hands clean."

Seri went over to him and took his hands. "Maelli, look at me."

Maelli looked up and forced a smile. "She was stopping one of them from setting light to the Guardhouse. Until then, we fought side-by-side and defended one another."

As if the voice was echoing in the room, Seri heard Weyrn shouting his name. He should have looked round. He could have done something.

He should have followed orders in the first place and reported back with what he had found.

With that thought, the tears finally came.

Seregei had spent the night with Kerin and his family and now sat at the breakfast table with them, swinging his legs and wondering if the battle was over outside. He assumed so from the fact that he and Kerin had been allowed to come out of the corner where they and a few guards had hidden. Seregei had been given a small sword so that he could help defend Kerin and he still wore it proudly.

Beside him, Kerin was eating his breakfast in silence, one eye on his parents and elder brother, who were talking softly together. They looked worried and Seregei frowned as he watched them. Perhaps the battle wasn't over. He patted the hilt of his sword. Well, he was ready. They'd called him a brave little Swordmaster yesterday, and if evil humans came today he intended to fight just like his parents and uncles.

That thought did raise the question of where his parents were, though, and he fell still, his eyes straying to the door.

"Seregei?" Kerin's mother said and he looked round. "Are you all right?"

"When will my parents come and get me?" he asked.

Kerin's parents exchanged an alarmed look, but didn't answer. Instead, Caleb said, "I hear you took care of Kerin yesterday, Seregei."

Seregei grinned, the energy rushing back, and he waved his fork as he said, "The guards said I could help them guard him! I waited by the door with my sword and if any humans had tried to get in I would have killed them all! Like this!" He stabbed his fork into a piece of bacon.

Kerin giggled and Caleb looked quellingly at them both. "It isn't funny," he said. "It's very serious."

Seregei blinked at him and glanced at Kerin, who had stopped eating and was staring at Caleb. Apparently he hadn't ever heard that tone either.

"Caleb," said his father warningly.

"Good elves died yesterday to protect all of us," Caleb continued. "So don't you two sit here and laugh about it!"

"Caleb, that's enough!" snapped his father, bringing a hand down on the table with a bang. Seregei jumped, dropping his fork, and Kerin squeaked. Caleb ducked his head.

"Sorry, Father."

His father nodded and looked back at Seregei and Kerin. "Sorry, you two. Go on with your breakfast."

Seregei picked up his dropped fork and nibbled the bacon, wondering afresh why everyone seemed so worried. What Caleb had said continued to niggle at him. Lots of people had died, like Neithan.

"Did we lose the battle?" he asked, finally.

Caleb's mother shook her head, smiling. "No, no. They'd have come here if we had, after all, and then we couldn't all sit and enjoy our breakfast."

"You might have had to fight them for me," said Kerin with a small smile.

Seregei grinned. "And I would have done!" He waved his fork again. Caleb frowned, but Seregei ignored him.

"Yes, yes," said Caleb's mother with a little laugh. "You're a very brave young man, Seregei. Now eat your breakfast."

Still grinning, he took a bite of bread and went back to happily thinking of how he could have fought just like his parents did and been brave just like all the Swordmasters were.

His thoughts were interrupted, though, as he heard a familiar name. He looked up to see that a guard had come in.

"Swordmasters Seri and Celes are here to pick up Seregei, and Swordmaster Seri wishes to speak to you."

Caleb's father winced, but nodded. "Could you ask them to wait until we've finished?" he asked.

Seregei, however, was already scrambling up, despite the question in the back of his head about why his parents hadn't come to get him. Perhaps they were busy, he thought wistfully.

"Seregei!" Caleb's father called. "Come and finish your breakfast."

Seregei ignored him. "Are they just outside?" he asked the guard, who shot a look back towards the grown-ups. Then he said, "Yes. If you've finished, come on."

Seregei nodded. "Thank you for having me," he said, looking back at the four Valley-elves.

"A pleasure," said Caleb's mother. Kerin waved and Seregei waved back, then he darted out into the corridor.

Sure enough, Celes and Seri were waiting a little further down and Seregei ran to meet them, talking as he went.

"Celes! Seri! I helped guard Kerin and look, I've got a sword! And everyone said how brave I was..." He ran up to them and bounced up and down on the balls of his feet.

Celes crouched down to his height, smiling in a slightly funny way. Seri was talking to the guard, but Seregei ignored them.

"I'm sure you were very brave," said Celes. "And I'm glad to see you safe and sound."

Seregei smiled, but something in Celes' tone didn't seem quite right. "What's happening?" he asked, his smile fading as he spoke. "Everyone's saying that we won the battle, but they seem sad about it."

"Well, we did win, but there was a cost." Celes looked up. "Will you wait here, Seri? I'll walk him home."

Seri nodded. He looked rather annoyed, but he forced a smile as he looked down at Seregei. "I'll see you soon," he said. "This shouldn't be a very long meeting."

Celes got up and took Seregei's hand, then led him back out of the palace and onto the road home. Seregei looked around appreciatively at the drifted snow on either side of the road, thinking of building a snow fort and persuading Lessai into a snowball fight. Perhaps Kerin would want to join in too and they could get some other children together to form teams. Caleb wasn't invited.

He looked up at Celes, though. The older elf was looking ahead, chewing his lip as he walked.

"Celes? What's wrong?"

Celes sighed, closing his eyes. "Let's take the longer route back home. There's something I need to tell you."

Celes looked down at Seregei again as they turned onto the side path. The boy was staring up at him, eyes wide with confusion. Celes had had to break the news of deaths before, but never to tell a child – one he was fond of, especially – of the deaths of both his parents in one fell swoop.

Still, it had to be done, and he was the one left who was closest to Seregei, no matter how much he wished Maelli was here instead of him.

"Of course," he said lamely, "You know there was a battle yesterday. A big one."

Seregei nodded, his hand going to the hilt of the little sword that the royal family had given him. He didn't speak, though.

"Well... you know what happens in battles?"

"People fight," said Seregei uncertainly. "And I bet Swordmasters fight much more than everyone else because they're fighting against monsters." He looked up at Celes again with a hopeful smile.

Celes nodded, forcing a smile in response. "Well, sometimes when people fight they end up... being killed."

Seregei blinked. "Caleb said a lot of people had died."

Celes nodded, feeling torn between gratitude to Caleb for preparing Seregei a little for this and annoyance that he'd overstepped the mark. "Yes, they did. And... Seregei, I don't know how to put this other than bluntly, but... your parents were among them."

Seregei stopped and Celes stopped with him, looking down worriedly. Seregei didn't show any sign of tears, though; he just stared up at Celes as if waiting for a punchline.

"Weyrn and Alatani are dead," Celes said again. "Your parents, they're... that's why they didn't come to get you."

Seregei continued to stare at him. "But..." he said at last, "but they're Swordmasters. Surely they can fight better than anyone else?"

Celes sighed, looking ahead. "Neithan was a Swordmaster too."

"Yes, but the humans didn't let him fight properly." Now Seregei's lip was beginning to wobble. "Didn't Mummy and Daddy get a proper chance to fight them either?"

Celes sighed, closing his eyes as he momentarily saw the scenes again: Maelli kneeling over Alatani's body and, later, Weyrn being carried home on a litter. "No, they fought. They were both very brave, but... such things happen."

"But they were Swordmasters!" wailed Seregei, yanking on Celes' hand. "They were the best fighters!"

"But there were lots of humans and... sometimes that's enough to beat even the best fighter."

Seregei was staring at him again, tears spilling from his eyes. "But..."

"I'm so sorry, Seregei," said Celes, swallowing hard against the lump in his own throat. "But it's true. They were very brave and they fought very well, but... they're dead."

Seregei stared at him a moment longer, then finally broke down into tears, rubbing his eyes with his fists and sitting down in the snow. Celes crouched beside him, put his arms around him and sighed, working to hold back his own tears. Now was not the time.

Weyrn and Alatani's burial was a couple of days after they had died. The four remaining Swordmasters carried them out one at a time on litters to the burial ground, to the graves they had dug beside the sapling growing over Neithan's body. Seregei tagged along beside Seri, looking more bewildered than upset.

Finally, they arrived and Seri helped Celes to lift Weyrn into his grave. Then he stood back and looked down at the shrouded body, chewing his lip to try to keep the tears back. He ignored the looks that the others shot him until Maelli stepped forward and put a hand on his shoulder.

"I'm all right," he said, shaking his head, and turned to help with Alatani. He noticed with a lump in his throat that a strand of ash-blonde hair was poking out of a fold in the shroud, and he quickly tucked it in.

"Derdhel?" said Seregei in a small voice. "That's not really Mummy, is it?"

"No," said Derdhel, stepping back from the grave. "No, it's just where she used to live."

"But we do this because we love them," said Maelli, putting a hand on Seregei's shoulder. "They'll always be with us, though, even if we can't see them."

Seregei sniffled and leaned on Maelli. "But I want to see them. They're not here if I can't see them."

Maelli hugged him a little. "Yes they are. It's as if we were all in the dark; we'd all still be there."

Seregei sniffed again, his eyes locked on the two bodies. "But I want them back."

"One day," said Derdhel, ruffling his hair before he reached one-handed for a shovel. "One day we'll all see them again."

Seri took his own shovel and did his best to think of nothing as he shovelled earth into the graves. He even ignored Maelli's prayers, letting the words wash over him without really hearing them. He wished he'd had more of a chance to say goodbye to Weyrn; he felt as if the last few years had been full of nothing but arguments between them, and now Weyrn was dead. He wished they'd parted as closer friends.

Still, Weyrn's last command had been that Seri should do a good job of raising Seregei, and Seri looked around for the boy. He had to smile a little as he saw that Seregei had a small shovel and was also shovelling earth into his mother's grave, smearing dirt across his face every time he tried to wipe away tears. He was taking it bravely and for a fleeting moment Seri imagined what Seregei would be when he grew up. Raised in the Guardhouse, it was natural that he would follow in his parents' footsteps and take the Oath himself.

Still, that was a long way in the future and he went back to his work.

They had just finished and stepped back to look down at the graves, Celes taking Seregei's hand, when Maelli looked round and a frown crossed his face. Seri followed his gaze and his heart sank as he saw Alatani's parents approaching.

"Are we too late?" her father asked, looking from one Swordmaster to the next.

"I'm sorry," said Seri, but Alatani's father spoke again before he could continue.

"No, no, it's all right. We did tell Maelli that we didn't want to be here." He looked past them at the graves. "Which... which is hers?"

Seri pointed to the further of the two graves. They'd made sure to lay Weyrn beside Neithan.

Alatani's mother let out a little sob, burying her face in her hands. Seri's heart went out to her and he looked away with a sigh.

"I am sorry," he said again. "We would have delayed..."

"Honestly, Captain, we only made the decision to come at the last minute," said her father.

Seri looked up again as Alatani's mother went to crouch beside her grave, staring at it blankly as if seeing something in the distance. Her father, meanwhile, had torn his eyes away and was looking at Seregei. The boy looked back, though he still kept reaching up to wipe away tears.

"You look too much like your father," the older elf mused. "But I can see Alatani in you too."

Seregei did smile at that, but Alatani's father had already looked away and he drew a deep breath before looking up at Seri again.

"Thank you for caring for him, Captain, but I think it would be best if we took him home with us."

"What?" demanded Maelli, his voice ringing loud.

Seri was also shocked and it took a moment for him to find his voice; the suggestion came out of nowhere and he guessed from Maelli's reaction that it hadn't been mooted to him when he broke the news of Alatani's death.

Her father, though, was frowning as he looked between them.

"He's our grandchild and we should raise him. After all, we're his only living relatives now." His voice shook, but he took a deep breath and squared his shoulders.

"Weyrn's last words to me were that he wanted us to raise Seregei," said Seri.

Alatani's father scowled at Weyrn's name. "And Alatani? He's her child, after all." He took a step towards Seregei, who threw his arms around Celes' waist with a squeak. "Come on, Seregei."

"I don't want to!" wailed Seregei, clinging harder to Celes.

Maelli stepped forward a little. "Is it really fitting to argue about what to do with their child when we're all but standing on their graves?"

"I don't want to go with them!" said Seregei.

"It's all right," said Derdhel, crouching down and putting an arm around him. "Let's go home."

Nonetheless, Alatani's father reached out to take Seregei. "Let me carry him."

"No," said Derdhel, shifting back.

"I'm his grandfather and you won't let me near him? What do you think I'm going to do?"

Seri sighed. That was a fair point, at least. Still, Seregei seemed perfectly aware of the situation and was now holding on around Derdhel's neck.

"I want to go home," he whimpered.

"Walk with your grandfather, Seregei," said Seri with a sigh. "We'll talk more when we get there."

Derdhel let Seregei go and the boy took the hand Alatani's father extended to him, but he didn't look happy and kicked the ground as he walked.

Celes, meanwhile, had gone over to Alatani's mother, who had spent the whole exchange looking down at Alatani's grave. When he touched her shoulder, though, she pulled away, looking round at him with a scowl that was almost a snarl.

"This is your fault," she snapped. "If it weren't for Weyrn and the rest of you, Alatani would still be alive! What were you thinking, letting her get into such danger? Where were you? And now you think you can raise her child?"

Celes stared at her in shock, his words of comfort dying on his lips. Though he was nowhere near her, Maelli reeled back as if she'd hit him and Seri instantly took a step forward to steady him.

"Not your fault," he whispered in his friend's ear. Maelli didn't reply.

Seregei, though, had pulled away from his grandfather and was yelling, "Don't say things like that to Uncle Celes! Mummy and Daddy were brave Swordmasters and they were fighting monsters to help people!"

"Seregei, don't be rude," said his grandfather sharply, taking his hand. "If you're to live with us, you'll have to learn some manners."

"No!" Seregei pulled away again.

Maelli, though, seemed to have got over the shock of the accusation, for he took a deep breath and said, "I think you're overestimating my control over Alatani."

"You said you were with her when she died, and you're the more senior Swordmaster. Weren't you in command?"

Maelli looked sadly back at the graves. "No," he said simply.

"Then what were you doing? What were any of you doing? Standing aside while our daughter was killed and then you think she would have wanted you to take her child from her family?"

"When was the last time you visited him?" asked Celes softly, suddenly.

"What?"

"We've already had more of a hand in raising him than you have."

"In any case..." Maelli's eyes had been on the graves, but as he spoke his gaze drifted up to the trees and he suddenly smiled. "We don't have to guess what they would have wanted. We know. They told us, after all." His expression turned wistful. "Alatani told me as she was dying that she wanted us to raise Seregei. She asked me to care for him, just as Weyrn asked the same of Seri."

Alatani's father looked pained again at Weyrn's name and Seri felt a flash of annoyance. He was prepared to give allowance to a grieving parent. He wasn't a monster, after all, but that was beginning to wear on him.

"Why do you keep doing that?" he asked.

"What?"

"Reacting to our Captain's name – your *daughter's husband's name* – as if it were a bad smell?"

Alatani's father looked at him hard for a moment, but then said, "As Swordmaster Captain, I acknowledge that Weyrn was my lord. As a warrior I appreciate that he died fighting to defend me. But he took my daughter, led her like a lamb to slaughter, put her in constant danger of her life and then abandoned her when she needed him the most!" As he spoke, his voice rose to a shout.

"And what else was he to do?" Seri's voice rose to match his. He barely noticed Seregei startle away from the sudden shouting, running back to

Celes. "Abandon his duty?"

"So you even admit that he held her second in his heart," snapped Alatani's mother.

"This is not an argument to have over their graves!" said Maelli, making as if to step between them.

"I want to go home!" wailed Seregei.

"Is this really how you plan to raise him?" asked Celes. "Tell him every slander you can think of about his father until -"

"Slander?" Alatani's father jabbed a finger at Seri. "Didn't you hear him, Swordmaster? Weyrn's duty wasn't with Alatani. It was never with Alatani!"

Seri remembered bitterly how often he'd quarrelled with Weyrn because he'd thought that he was putting the husband before the Captain.

"Don't speak of what you don't understand," he said softly, his voice cutting through the rising argument. "You never lived alongside them and watched them make that balance every day." He swallowed hard. "I'm not sure I ever saw the half of it."

There was a moment's silence, then Alatani's father stepped back, shaking his head, his eyes on the ground.

"Be that as it may," he said softly, "You can't change the fact that if it weren't for his neglect our daughter would still be alive. You can't grudge us that."

"We can protest your raising Weyrn's child by telling him every day that his father was neglectful, and Alatani's child by telling him that his mother was helpless, though."

"She wasn't," said Seregei resentfully. "She was a Swordmaster."

Maelli smiled at him, then looked up again. "She was a strong warrior and died in battle, defending her home and her people. She would never have wanted to be wrapped in wool and safely packed away. It was her choice to be a Swordmaster, after all." He laid a hand on his heart. "I trained her. It was I that spoke to her before she took her oath, told her of the difficulties and dangers of our life and what it might one day cost her. She understood. And you cannot say that she joined us for love of Weyrn -"

"It would be a cruel thing to say of her," muttered Celes.

"- because it was only after that that they began to love one another." Maelli paused to take a breath, and when he spoke again it was almost a shout. "Now can we *please* refrain from standing by their graves when the earth has barely fallen from our shovels and arguing over their *child* as if he were *goods* to be *divided?*"

Seri nodded and gestured to the path back to the Guardhouse. "If we're to settle this now, let's go home and talk about it there."

As soon as they arrived home, Celes took Seregei back to his room, ostensibly to help him put away his cloak and wipe the worst of the dirt off his face and hands. In fact, he just didn't want Seregei to have to listen to that any more.

"Uncle Celes?" the boy said, "Will I really have to leave? I don't want to."

Celes forced a smile and shook his head. "Of course not. We want you to stay here and we'll do our best to keep you here."

Seregei nodded firmly, picking up his soft cloth rabbit from where it lay beside his bed. "They can't make me go anywhere," he said. "This is where Swordmasters live, and I'm a Swordmaster, aren't I?" He looked up at Celes.

Celes sighed, patting his head. "Not yet."

He decided to take his time before taking Seregei back to the common room, just glad that he couldn't hear raised voices. It seemed that the discussion was going a little more calmly than it had at the burial ground.

"Did Mummy and Daddy really say I should stay here?" asked Seregei, cuddling his rabbit.

"Yes, that's what Seri and Maelli say."

"And Swordmasters don't lie, do they?"

"No."

"Why not tell Grandma and Grandpa that, then? Then they'll know I should stay here."

"Well, they think that your parents were wrong."

Seregei set his jaw, though the effect was somewhat spoiled by the fact that he was still clutching his rabbit. "Mummy and Daddy aren't wrong about anything, and I want to stay here."

Celes smiled and patted his hair again. "We'll do all we can to make that happen."

Back in the common room, Seri was glad that at least the recriminations had stopped. He didn't think he could hold his tongue if he saw that look on Maelli's face once more.

Alatani's father had sat down on the couch while her mother paced restlessly up and down the common room.

"Even aside from anything else," said her father, his voice flat with the effort of keeping it steady, "What sort of place is this to raise a child?"

That was a fair criticism, especially as it was a concern Seri had himself.

"He should be with his family, in a place where he'll be safe, not... not here."

Seri frowned, glancing around at Maelli and Derdhel. Maelli was sitting forward, his elbows on his knees, scowling. Derdhel was leaning against the wall.

It was Derdhel that spoke first, though. "This is where his parents wanted him to grow up," he said calmly. "And it's where they would have raised him, so why not continue where they began?"

Alatani's mother stopped pacing to glare at him. "Because they were wrong," she said. "I don't know whose idea it, was, though I have an idea…"

"Where else were they to raise him?" asked Maelli. "This was their home."

"She should have come home," her father said softly. "She was home for a while and she should have stayed."

"She wasn't happy there," said Derdhel. "She much preferred it here."

Alatani's mother shot him a look of intense dislike, but then looked at the floor. "She was a silly girl," she said softly.

"Not all the blame should fall on her," said her father. "What about Weyrn?"

"What about him?" asked Maelli. "He was our Captain and his place was here. Alatani was one of us and this was her home and we were her friends." He took a deep breath, then said, "I trained her, as I said. I knew her best other than Weyrn. She loved it here and she loved her work and she told me as she died that she wanted us to raise Seregei. She wanted him to stay here." He sat back. "That should be the end of it, surely?"

"It always has been," said Seri. "The last wishes of a dying elf are binding, at least in every custom I've seen in Duamelti. Perhaps the Irnianam need writing, but we are not Irnianam, neither were Weyrn and Alatani, and neither are you."

"Surely, common sense should dictate that he comes with us."

"He's always been raised by warriors," said Seri, swallowing down the doubts he'd had since being told that Alatani was pregnant. He sighed and rubbed his eyes. "Let me think."

"Captain Seri, are you seriously -" started Alatani's father.

"I need to think, which means I need silence," said Seri firmly, and closed his eyes, putting his head in his hands.

He had always worried about Seregei being a distraction. He had always thought Weyrn was having trouble walking the line. Oddly, Alatani had seemed to fare better, but she wasn't Captain. Weyrn had been and now Seri was and he was seriously considering taking on the task of raising Seregei.

But he would have the others to help him. There would always have to be someone safely at the Guardhouse anyway; adding the task of caring for Seregei wouldn't add that much.

Even as he thought about it, he remembered Weyrn's face: it had been drawn with worry, the scar on his cheek vivid, his voice soft and quick. Seri wondered if he'd had some premonition of his death. He sighed. He couldn't deny it. Not without a good reason and… he didn't think he had one. They could spread the work and the distraction. They could keep Seregei safe as he grew.

He sighed again and prayed he was doing the right thing as he opened his eyes.

"Of course, unlike Alatani and Weyrn, Seregei won't be going into battle," he said. "It was the last wish of both of his parents that he remain with us. We know him well and we knew them." He sighed. "I'm sorry. I know you want to take him home with you, but I can't let you." He pushed himself upright. "We will care for him. Never in his childhood will he face danger unless the whole valley faces it. I give you my word on that."

Alatani's father looked like his back had given way. "That's your final decision, Swordmaster?" he asked.

"Yes."

The older elf stood up, looking down at him coldly. "You've taken our daughter and now you're taking our grandson."

Seri also got up. "Alatani came of her own will," he said, equally coldly. "And we will not prevent you from visiting, but he will live here."

"Very well," the elf said, his voice breaking as he spoke. Then, without another word, he took Alatani's mother's hand and headed for the door.

She turned on the threshold to add, "If he dies, I hope you spend the rest of time knowing you killed a child when you could have sent him to safety."

Seri swallowed again, but nodded.

Once they were gone, he turned back to the others, who were staring at him.

"Did I do the right thing?" he asked, sudden worry sending a chill up his spine.

Maelli smiled. "I think so."

"Is it over?" asked Celes, coming into the common room, leading Seregei by the hand.

"Yes," said Seri. He smiled at Seregei, hoping that none of his misgivings showed on his face. "Welcome home."

"I can stay?" asked Seregei, his face lighting up.

Seri nodded and laughed as Seregei ran to him for a hug. "Yes, you can stay."

***

Seri was sure that Hurion had kept him waiting on purpose, but he pushed that thought aside as he was shown into the king's study.

"Captain Seri," said Hurion, turning from the window. His small smile faded almost at once as he gestured to a chair by his desk. "Please, sit," he said quietly.

Seri nodded and sat down, watching carefully as Hurion also sat.

"Weyrn was Captain for a long time."

Seri sighed, nodding. "He was a Swordmaster for as long as I can remember."

"So where do we go from here?" Hurion linked his fingers together and rested his chin on his fists. "Since we both know how important it is that we act as partners."

Seri smiled a little, glad that Hurion was aware that their relationship was indeed a partnership. "Personally," he said slowly, "I'm happy to continue with things as they are." Not too close.

Hurion nodded. "As am I."

"Just so long as you never do anything to oppress us."

Hurion responded with a long, slow look, but then nodded. "I wasn't aware that I'd done anything that could be construed that way."

Seri had to admit that he hadn't, but that didn't allay his fears. "I know that Weyrn made an effort to bring our two peoples together."

"Do you intend to continue that?"

"I don't want to become beholden to you."

Hurion smiled slightly, but his smile quickly faded. "For this latest battle? I was defending my home just as you were defending yours." He gestured vaguely. "Seregei told you about how we hid him and Kerin, I assume? I wouldn't have done that if I didn't think we were threatened just as you were." He leaned across the desk. "We did the same with Caleb. That isn't a step I took lightly."

Seri nodded, raising a hand to placate Hurion. "I understand that."

Hurion sat back, looking mollified. "I'm not going to claim anything back from you for the help I gave. And I hope you'll show me the same courtesy."

Seri nodded, looking away. "I will admit that the men you sent were invaluable." He sighed. "It was good to have a trained army alongside us."

"I'm glad." Hurion looked at the ceiling for a moment, drumming his fingertips against his chin. "I'd be glad to work together in such matters," he said, looking down. "Would you?"

Seri looked away, out of the window. It commanded a fine view of the snow-scattered valley and he lost himself in the sight for a moment, thinking of the people living there, the people who had just died defending it. He didn't want to become too close to the Valley-elves, but if there were another attack like that... They *would* need help.

He nodded.

"But," he added, snapping back to reality, "We are partners. Equal partners."

Hurion nodded. "Of course. I'm suggesting that we work more closely, not that I become your lord." He leaned across the desk, resting his chin on his fists again. "An exchange of information and help when either of us needs it, with no talk of fealty or debt. I don't especially enjoy having my favours called in either."

Seri frowned. "Would you have helped us without that?"

Hurion shrugged. "Who can say? But now I've seen that we can be stronger together."

Seri sighed. "So have I. Very well, then, perhaps we will try to help one another more often." Perhaps with more help and more people they would have had better warning. Perhaps then fewer elves would have died. With that thought, he sighed again and reached out a hand.

Hurion took it, smiling. "Care for a drink? I think a toast is in order."

"Thank you." Seri remained seated as Hurion poured two cups of mead and handed him one.

"To friendship," the Valley-elf said, raising his glass.

Seri sighed. "To safety for our people," he replied, raising his own.

Printed in Great Britain
by Amazon